Ragny rose from her prayers. She had no father now but God, and she had no mother at all. She was the rightful Queen of Spain. God would sustain her, if she served His cause. She would do what God willed of her.

"Princess, we must hurry," Seffrid whispered.

She opened the bundle of clothes, and put them on: coarse leggins, a hooded jerkin and belt, boots, a knife and hat. The harsh cloth hid the shape of her body. She left her gown lying where she had dropped it and stepped from the cave out into the sunlight.

"Now you must cut off my hair." She knelt down with her back to Seffrid. "Cut it off as short as you can. I must seem a man—no one must even look twice to see."

"But Princess!"

"Do not call me Princess," she said. "No one must ever hear you call me that again."

"What should I call you, then?"

She looked into the vast hazy distance, so out of reach, where anything seemed possible.

"I shall be Roderick. Call me Roderick."

BOOKS BY CECELIA HOLLAND

The Angel and the Sword
Lily Nevada
An Ordinary Woman
Railroad Schemes
Valley of the Kings
Jerusalem
Pacific Street
The Bear Flag
The Lords of Vaumartin
Pillar of the Sky
The Belt of Gold
The Sea Beggars
Home Ground
City of God
Two Ravens
Floating Worlds
Great Maria
The Death of Attila
The Earl
Antichrist
Until the Sun Falls
The Kings in Winter
Rakossy
The Firedrake

FOR CHILDREN

The King's Road
Ghost on the Steppe

THE
ANGEL
AND THE
SWORD

CECELIA HOLLAND

A TOM DOHERTY ASSOCIATES BOOK
NEW YORK

THE ANGEL AND THE SWORD

Copyright © 2000 by Cecelia Holland

This book is printed on acid-free paper.

Book design by Lisa Pifher

A Forge Book
Published by Tom Doherty Associates, LLC
175 Fifth Avenue
New York, NY 10010

www.tor.com

Forge® is a registered trademark of Tom Doherty Associates, LLC.

Library of Congress Cataloging-in-Publication Data

Holland, Cecelia.
    The angel and the sword / Cecelia Holland.
       p. cm.
    "A Tom Doherty Associates book."
    ISBN 0-312-86890-1 (hc)
    ISBN 0-312-86889-8 (pbk)
    1. Women soldiers—Fiction. 2. Princesses—Fiction. 3. Knights and knighthood—Fiction. 4. France—History—Charles II, 840–877—Fiction. I. Title.
    PS3558.O348 A8 2000
    813'.54—dc21
                                      00-030668

First Hardcover Edition: December 2000
First Trade Paperback Edition: November 2001

Printed in the United States of America

0 9 8 7 6 5 4 3 2 1

For Carolyn and Noel—

with love

THE
ANGEL
AND THE
SWORD

1

QUEEN INGUNN HAD MADE a mistake, and paid for it all her life, but now, with her life gone, she saw a way to make amends.

"My daughter!" She gathered her failing strength to call out into the room. "Where is Ragny? Where is my daughter?"

The heavy wooden bed made a case around her, a frame for her dying. Out beyond its edge, the room stirred to her voice, the men turning. Markold, her husband, came forward a few steps, his boots heavy on the rushy floor.

"She's wicked and uncaring, my Queen. She's gone off somewhere, not caring." His black eyes shone. Queen Ingunn saw how eagerly his gaze probed at her, summing up her weaknesses, her sighs, her pallor, and her trembling, seeing how close she was to death.

She knew he was lying abut Ragny. He had no power of truth. Certainly he had sent the girl away, to keep her and her mother apart, at this arch-moment. Even now, as Markold pored over her for every sign of her dying, he hung back, unwilling to come close to her. Markold, gross clod of human earth that he was, knew nonetheless the powers that attended her now, with the door of Heaven opening, and the whirl of force drawing her toward it.

Afraid, the fool. She shut her eyes, hoarding the last of her strength. Markold was her sin. Young and wild, she had chosen him for his body, his courage, and his strength, married him and made him King, careless of his soul, and in his soul he had failed her. He was dross and worse, wicked, and heartless.

He ruled only through her, his wife, the last vessel left of Roderick's sacred blood, the holiest blood in Christendom, now shunted off into this last little hill-fort, this last corner of the realm. Roderick's kingdom died with her. Markold could not be King, and he knew that, yet somehow he thought to make a profit from her dying. She intended to confound his coarse ambitions. At the end, the very end, she would set right what she had put wrong, so long ago, a heedless, lusty, willful girl.

Dying, she opened the way for her daughter, for Ragny to find a better King. To make up for the old Queen's sin, and set the House of Roderick on its true course again, the reconquest of the kingdom from the infidel, and the triumph of Christ. Ingunn had failed in her part in that great destiny, but now she would make it right, through Ragny.

She shut her eyes. She would not die yet. Markold could wait awhile longer. He had refused to send for a priest, at first, saying she was not so ill, and then of course could find no priest who would come anywhere near this tower, or Markold, even for the sake of the true Queen.

She cared nothing for the priest, but she had to see Ragny.

The eternal door stood open before her; she was face-to-face with death, and yet alive. While she held back, the tidal light grew stronger, insistent, almost audible now with its insistence, tingling in all her weary limbs. On its swelling strength, through that door, she meant to call forth a guardian for her daughter, a power that had been old before Jesus was born. The longer she held back, the stronger, the surer, that power.

Only, she could not hold back much more. "Ragny!" she cried out, again. "Where is my daughter?"

Markold came up again, keeping a little distance, peering at her with the cold lust of his endless appetite for death; he wrung his hands together. "I told you, my Queen, she has gone off somewhere, I cannot find her."

She gritted her teeth. Death was dragging her away. Ragny had to come. She said, desperate, a lie. "Get her here, Markold, or I will take you with me. I will not die, before you die, Markold—"

He backed swiftly away from the bed. Gross and earthbound, clod of human dirt, he feared stupid, unreal things. He said, "I will send Seffrid, my Queen."

She lay back; she had used too much of herself, threatening him. She could feel death taking hold of all her limbs, gathering her forward, inch by inch, toward the door. She had to have Ragny there, and she had to save her strength. She shut her eyes, patient.

Markold came away from the bed; by the door, Seffrid, who had heard his name spoken, straightened up, his arms falling to his sides. He could see that the Queen was not dead yet, however she looked, her eyes glazed and sunken, her skin grey; but not dead. He wondered, coldly, what Markold had given her. And why the King hadn't simply strangled her in the bedclothes.

Markold was King; Seffrid, his sergeant, did the King's will. That was all that mattered. Markold nodded to him.

"Go find the Princess Ragny, and bring her back here." He said this in a loud ringing voice that even the corpse on the bed could hear. The King's broad, pockmarked face glittered with sweat; they had been waiting for hours, and it looked like work to Markold.

He went with Seffrid to the chamber door, and there he murmured, "Don't look for her very hard, Seffrid." He clapped Seffrid on the shoulder, and winked at him.

Seffrid went out onto the landing. He had no liking for this, keeping the girl away from her dying mother. He had no say in it, either. It had occurred to Seffrid long before that he was prey to weak emotions, and so he had given everything like that over to Markold, who was strong, and who made Seffrid strong. It didn't matter what he thought, he had to do as he was ordered. He went down the tower stairs and across the wooden baille, which was Markold's hall, and in the courtyard sent one of the loitering grooms off for his horse.

It had rained hard the night before, but now the squat grey tower loomed up against a hard blue sky, the sun glaring bright off the puddles in the courtyard. A chicken somewhere was cackling. The smell of burnt grease hung in the air. The groom brought the horse splashing up through the mud.

On the wall by the gate, the guard was sitting down, eating something, a jug in his lap. As Seffrid mounted up, the guard called, "Does she live still?"

Seffrid rode to the gate. "She lives." He did not know how; she should be dead, the poor creature.

He throttled down that softness. Markold knew what he was doing.

The guard signed himself, surreptitiously, glancing over his shoulder. "God keep our lady Ingunn." He pulled the gate open, and loosed Seffrid on the world.

Markold's Tower stood on the height of a pass; to the north the road dropped off down into a mountain valley, and on the south curled away on down toward the Spanish plains. Seffrid reined in on the road, wondering where not to look for the Princess Ragny. The sun beat strongly on him, and the wind was light and warm, but westward the horizon was turning dark. Seffrid had not been born here—he was a Frank, had come down that northern road one day, to Markold's Tower—but he had learned the smell of a storm coming, and he was catching a whiff of that now.

He knew Ragny, too, strange and wild, and guessed she might have gone on north, to hunt. So he turned south, along the road down to the little cluster of stone huts at the foot of the pass.

Once this had been a village—when he came, most of these huts still had people living in them, but Markold had driven them all out, not even bothering to kill them, but simply taking away everything they had. And so now only one or two families still lived here, shepherds, who held their flocks out in the hills, and gave Markold sheep whenever he asked for them. They had nothing, only their sheep, their huts made of round white stones off the hillside. They were gone now, the place empty as a graveyard, but as he rode in, suddenly Ragny galloped down the slope toward him, her red cloak billowing out behind her, and her long pale hair streaming. She rode up before him and reined her grey horse down.

"Seffrid," she said, "how does my mother?" And Seffrid realized that she had been waiting, had known, somehow, that her mother would reach out for her, and had been watching the castle gate and waiting.

He bowed to her, deep, as befit the holiest blood in Spain. "Princess, she sends for you."

"Then I will go," she said. "Attend me." She put her heels to her pony and galloped away up the road; Seffrid wheeled his horse to follow her.

He thought it was a pity she had been born a woman; in her, Markold would have met his match. He knew she slept on the stone floor of her bedchamber, leaving the soft silky bed for her maids. Ate only bread and meat, while Markold and his friends glutted on pastries and sweets brought in the back door from the Moors. Yet she was not meek and mild. She rode out to the hunt with the men, even in the snows of winter, tracking down the wolves and bears that preyed on the herds; Seffrid had seen her shoot her bow and would not have wanted it aimed at him. He spurred his horse, trying to keep up with her.

At the gate, he caught her at last, while the guard struggled to lift the bar. The wind was rising steadily and now dark boulders of cloud were rolling up across the western sky. The Princess lifted her face into the scouring wind; her cheeks were blazing.

"I fear this storm to come," she said. "The sun will not shine on the death of my mother the Queen."

Seffrid said, "It is the time of year for storms." He thought uneasily there was no reason to see signs in everything. To see God's work in everything. Yet she was of holy blood. Uneasily he shook off thinking of it. The gate opened. They crossed the muddy courtyard, leading their horses.

She said, "Where is my father the King?"

Seffrid handed his reins off to a groom. "He sits by the bedside of the Queen."

The Princess Ragny drew her hand across her breast in the sign of the cross. "God keep my mother," she said. She wrapped her long cloak around her.

Seffrid said nothing. On the walls above them, the banners were Markold the Grim's. The men lounging around the courtyard in the warmth of the last sun were Markold's men. Seffrid was Markold's man. She was fair and she was true, this girl, but she was only a girl.

Nonetheless, she did not wait for him, she had reached the door into the tower before he could catch up with her, and the guard was opening it. Seffrid followed her into the wooden baille and up the narrow stone staircase to the tower, up to the room where her mother lay.

The air here was thick with the reek of death. Seffrid, coming in, flattened himself against the wall by the door, loathe to breathe this air. He wondered again what Markold had done to his wife.

The two waiting women were huddled by the window, saying prayers. There was a guard on either side of the door. The Princess went straight across the room, over the trampled rushes, to the bed with its swags of drapery embroidered with the arms of King Roderick, where Queen Ingunn lay like a rotting corpse.

"Mother, I am here."

Seffrid, by the wall, heard only the murmur of the Queen's voice, answering. His hair stood on end. The Queen spoke as if from the grave. He remembered all the whispering about her, that she was part water fairy, that she spoke with demons. How could she still be alive? Seffrid looked up, toward the foot of the bed, where Markold stood.

The King was frowning, his red mouth twisted in the thick black mat of his beard. His thick hands were fisted before him. His great burly shoulders were heaved forward, as if he were shoving at something mountainously heavy. Seffrid saw how his gaze shifted, from his wife, to his daughter, to his wife again, his eyes unblinking, fire-hot.

Then the girl was turning, her voice ringing clear. "Seffrid, come, you must be witness."

"I," Seffrid said, astonished.

Markold slouched forward. "What is it?" His voice was raw. "What would you have witnessed? She raves, the Queen. She says nothing to witness!"

"No," Ragny said. "Seffrid, come here."

Seffrid looked at Markold, whose face struggled. Finally he shrugged his great bear shoulders. "Do it," he said. One eyelid fluttered, a conspiracy, a warning. The King drew back a little, his eyes glaring.

Seffrid went up beside the bed. The Queen had been beautiful, only days before. Now on the broad silken platform she lay ruined. Her face was hollow as a nutshell. Her eyes seemed huge. She lifted one hand like a twig from a dead tree.

"Hear me. Hear this." She gasped for breath. Seffrid gave a little shake of his head. She would die with the thing unspoken. But the Queen gathered herself. "Before God," she said, in a breathy whisper. "He must not be King. My daughter alone. She alone is of the line of Roderick."

That name drew a cough from her, and the cough drew up a little rivulet of blood, that trickled down her chin. Ragny reached out and caught her mother's hand.

"Mother, I am ready."

"You alone are Queen," Ingunn said. "But you will have one to help you. I have sent for him." Her voice gasped away. Ragny gripped her hand and bowed her head; her lips moved. Seffrid thought, She is dead, and started up.

Then the Queen's eyes opened again. Her voice rasped out again.

"Go to the cave of songs."

"Mother—"

"Do as I bid you. You will find someone at the cave of songs. Go—remember—"

Over the Princess's shoulder, Seffrid saw the old woman's eyes shine with a sudden desperation, as if she could not say enough, and her free hand rose off the bed toward her daughter. "You—" The blood dribbled from her lips. Her eyes glowed with a terrible revelation. No more words came from her; she died as they watched; her eyes dulled, and her hands sagged down toward her breast.

Seffrid heard a choked sob from the girl before him. He drew back, his head bowed. He knew not what he had witnessed. They lived in a dream, these people, the dream of their lost kingdom, of witchy powers and signs and portents and prayers. But Ingunn had been his Queen for ten years, and to his amazement, now, his chest clogged, his eyes burned, he wanted to go away by himself and mourn. Instead he was between them suddenly, the girl before him, tall and thin and hard, and the King behind.

Ragny said, "What did you do to her, Markold?" She was looking over Seffrid's shoulder. Seffrid did not move; he felt the King behind him as if he gave off heat.

Markold said, "I did nothing."

"You are nothing," she said. "You are King no more here, Markold."

Markold growled at her. "I am King until someone throws me down, girl. Do you think you can do that?"

"I need not throw you down," she said, her voice hard and bright as a knife blade. Seffrid, amazed, saw that Markold did not frighten her. She said, "God throws you down. You were King because of my mother. Now my mother is dead, and you are King no more. I alone am the heir to Roderick. The kingdom is mine to rule, mine to bestow."

Markold shouldered past Seffrid, knocking the sergeant back a few steps, and went up before his daughter; he stood so close they brushed together, and yet she yielded nothing. Seffrid moved gratefully back out of the way.

"You want to be Queen?" Markold said. He reached out and took a fistful of her hair. "I shall make you Queen, girl."

"Let go of me," she said between her teeth.

Instead he twisted her long hair around his hand, and pulled her head back. He said, "I shall marry you, blood of Roderick. That makes me King once more, does it not?"

Seffrid twitched. This he had not expected. He saw the girl's eyes widen, dark with pain and sudden fear. She said, "You cannot. That is gravest sin."

"I shall marry you," Markold said again, "and breed on you a son. That's all I need. What your bitch mother would not give me." He bent over her, his lips open, to kiss her.

The girl twisted in his grip; her hand flashed between them. Markold let out a yowl. The girl leapt back, her dagger in her hand, and the King reeled away, his hand to his cheek, and the dark blood welling between his fingers.

Seffrid leapt forward; he got the girl by the wrist and swung her around and wrapped his free arm around her from behind. Markold swung toward her. His face bulged, dark, his eyes gleaming.

Ragny said, "Let go of me! I order it!" She wrenched at Seffrid's grip on her wrist; her strength startled him; he needed all his muscle to hold on to her. Markold wheeled around and struck her down to the ground with a single blow of his fist.

Seffrid cried, "My lord, my lord—" He stooped to gather her up. To his amazement, she was not broken, nor even cowed, but was rising up again, the dagger still in her grasp, and her eyes like agates. He called, "Ho! To me!" and the guards broke out of their fascination and jumped to help him, and so doing got between the girl and Markold. Seffrid tore the dagger from her grasp.

"Take her to the high tower room!" Markold shouted. "Lock her in! I'll marry her tomorrow! And then—" His ripped face broke into a smile. "Then we'll see how you can please your father, daughter."

In Seffrid's grip the girl was suddenly still, cold, unresisting. She said, "God is my true Father." Her voice rang, implacable, steely. Markold sneered at her. He stalked out, slamming the door behind him.

Seffrid backed up, letting her go. The two guards were fumbling and numbling around her, and he sent them off with a word. The girl gave him a single, unreadable look, and went to the bed where her mother lay.

"Come," Seffrid said. "You heard the King."

"He is not the King." The girl signed herself, and made the sign also over her mother. She reached out to stroke her mother's face. "He must not do this, Seffrid. God has sworn that we shall have our kingdom back, we of the House of Roderick. But only Roderick's House. If we fail, Spain is lost forever to the infidel."

Her voice was steady as stone. Yet Seffrid, looking sharply at her, saw the tears on her cheeks.

He said, "God's in Heaven, girl. Here, Markold is the King. Come along."

"He is not the King!" She spun around toward him, her cheeks slimed with tears. "She made a mistake, my mother. She knew it, all her life—she gave the kingdom to the wrong man. But it is mine now." She gripped her hands in front of her, twisting and twisting them, and wept. "You heard her say it."

Seffrid smothered down a sudden leap of anger. What did she think he could do? "I am Markold's man. I heard nothing."

"You heard her!"

"I heard nothing," he said, again, angry at her for this.

She turned her face away. Her voice sank. "I heard her. I know. God knows. But if he does this—this he says he will do to me—" Now suddenly she slumped down to the floor like a child, and sobbed.

Seffrid grunted, his anger gone at once. The two waiting women were watching from by the window. He pointed at the body on the bed. "Tend to your mistress." Stooping, he gathered up the Princess from the floor, looping his arms under her long legs and around her shoulders, and carried her out of the room, and up the twisted narrow stairs to the little top room of the tower, and set her down there, in the middle of the room.

There was a narrow window, too narrow, he thought, for anyone to fit through, even her. Anyway, the window gave out on a drop of nearly thirty feet to the courtyard. He watched the girl grope her way blindly to the little cot and sit down and cry into her hands.

"Markold is the King," he said to her. "Maybe you have the blood, but he is a man, and strong, and will have what he wants.

You can't escape this. My advice to you is to accept it. Then at least you can be Queen, as your mother was. It's an evil thing, but it's an evil world, girl." He felt a little hollow, like a gourd, rattling these words around. He said, "I'm sorry about your mother." Turning, he went out and shut the door, and locked it.

Ragny wept; she felt a great wound in her, something torn out of her body, out of her heart, and lay down on the little cot and called for her mother, over and over, without hope of an answer. Her mother was safe now, at last, from the blows of Markold's fist, the burdens of Markold's appetite. Her head pounded where he had hit her.

Tomorrow he would attack her again. She knew what he intended, he had tried to do it before. Then her mother had gone between them in a blazing rage, and he had recoiled from it, from some threat coiled secret in her voice. She laid her fingers against the bruise on her head. This time her mother would not be there; she would be alone.

She thought, I will die first. And knew that it was true: Roderick's blood in her would not suffer such a defilement.

Not alone. Her mother had said someone would come to help her. Ragny had not understood her, could not exactly remember the words, just a promise, maybe the empty promise of a dying, despairing woman. Go to the cave of songs. The cave was a long way away, half a day's journey, and she was locked up here.

Locked in her body, in the woman's body that gave Markold power over her. That she could amend. She tasted metal in her mouth. But she would not let Markold touch her.

She would not merely sit and wait. God's will was not always obvious. She crept off the bed and stood in the center of the room, spread her arms out, and said the name of God, of Jesus and the Holy Spirit.

Her arms trembled with the effort of holding them outright. She shut her eyes. Go to the cave of songs. What had her mother said? There will come one to help you. She went to the window, so narrow she could just fit her arm through, but no more. She stretched her arm out through it. The cold wind lashed at her hand, and raindrops struck her fingers like little stones. Go to the cave of songs. She set about looking for a way to do that.

Markold's face was ripped from ear to chin; she had narrowly missed killing him. The white bandage on it looked like a kind of mask. He sat slumped in his high seat, washed by the orange light of the fire in the hearth; the storm was still rising, and the wind shook the whole baille. Two of the house slaves brought in another load of wood for the fire. Markold's men were coming in to sit down at the table and be fed.

Seffrid went up before the high seat, and bowed to his King, and turned to take his place at the table. Two house slaves were turning meat on the spit over the fire; another brought around a basket of bread. The wind blew suddenly strong and gusted up a billow of ashes from the hearth into the room, embers floating into the dark deeps of the room like errant stars. Seffrid sat with his arms close around him. So far from the fire, he was cold. He reached for the warm bread; the slaves were bringing up the meat to the table, and he stood to hack a piece off the nearest roast.

The men around him let him go first, because he was Markold's chief man. He laid his slice of bread down on the table and dumped the dripping chunk of meat on top of it, and licked his knife clean.

"Take none of this feast to the Princess," Markold shouted. "Let her starve, for dealing with her father so."

Seffrid, like them all, let out a practiced yell of assent. This was like Mass, where you said what the Lord expected to hear. He stuffed roast mutton into his mouth, and reached for a cup of wine.

"The Queen is dead," Markold shouted, behind him. He had eaten already, first of them all, in the kingly way, and now drank and proclaimed himself, as usual. "Long live the King! The Queen is dead!"

They shouted, all together, their mouths stuffed with meat. The King fell still for a moment. Seffrid sat back, full.

"Seffrid!"

He jumped. Markold's voice had an unsteady edge that chilled him. He stood, and turned to face him. "My lord, what will you?"

"What I will, you know well enough!" Markold put his hand up to the bandage. "I am King here! King!"

All along the table, the gorging men bounced up, recognizing the elevation, the holiest part of the ceremony; they stirred sharply like rousing wolves, and out of their throats came a single howl.

"King Markold! King!"

Seffrid said, "King Markold." He wondered where this led; he had seen Markold in this dirty mood before and it went nowhere good.

Markold's beard split in a grin. He was looking steadily across at Seffrid, and as the clamor settled, he said, "Then let's have her down here, to swear to that."

Seffrid blinked at him. "My Lord?"

"Go get her!"

"As you will, my lord," Seffrid bowed again; if Markold imagined him to hesitate, he could end upon the wrong side of this entirely. He hoped the Princess had taken his advice into his heart. He started toward the door.

"Seffrid!"

"My lord!" He wheeled around.

"Don't you think you'll need some help?" Markold's fingers stroked the bandage.

Seffrid licked his lips; what was the right answer? Was there a right answer? He glanced toward the row of men, all poised, knowing Markold, for some violent command.

"You. You." He pointed to the nearest.

Markold smiled at him. "See you do her no harm." He lounged back in the high seat, the amber firelight all across him, the whites of his eyes showing. The two men followed Seffrid to the stairs and up out of the hall.

"He's wild," one of them muttered, when they had gone up through the hole in the ceiling, to the next floor. The other hissed.

"Shut up!"

Seffrid, lighting a lamp from the torch on the wall, knew they throttled themselves for his sake. Markold's sergeant, Markold's right hand: they feared him almost as much as the King. He squared his shoulders, trying to be that big. They passed the bed-chamber where the Queen had died, and went up the narrow stair. The wind's buffets shook the tower; Seffrid thought he felt it sway under him, the stones shifting, every bracing timber straining, and put one hand on the wall. The flame in his hand wavered and flut-tered and once, on the way up the stairs, guttered almost out. He stopped then, and let it climb back up its stem.

They went up to the little room at the top, and Seffrid handed the lamp to one of the men. He took down the key from beside the door and unlocked it. Before he opened it, he banged his fist on it.

"Princess, we are coming in." It occurred to him that might be the last such warning she would ever have. He pushed the door open.

She was gone. The room was empty. He knew at once, from some quality of the air; looking around was only to confirm it. He stood in the middle of the room and gaped. The man with the lamp held it up high, scattering its wind-whipped light. They could see into every corner. She was not there. Seffrid, in a rising panic, threw the blanket aside and pulled the tick off the bed. He went to the window and thrust his arm out; surely nothing could have gone out the window, and the raging storm outside was already chilling his hand to the bone. He drew his arm back, and then, out the window, saw something black and serpentine writhing through the murky rain.

"Hunh." He backed up, looking now at the lamp again, and saw how the flame flattened down in the wind that came, not so much from the window as from above, and he looked up at the rafter and saw the dust and cobwebs wiped away where she had climbed up there.

"Devil take me," he said. He grabbed the lamp from the guard and put it down and said, "Help me up there. Come!"

They made a step of their clapsed hands, and boosted him up to the rafter; he swung himself onto it, and groped along through the webby gloom to the edge, where the roof came down and met the wall. There, along the edge, the wall was rotten, had broken away, leaving enough room for a thin little girl to slip through.

The rain gusted in as he got close, wet his face. Feeling along the rafter, his hand touched a hard wet knot of cloth, and he traced the twisted length of the cloth by touch to the hole in the wall and out. She had made a rope of something. Her cloak. She must have torn it into strips.

He thought of climbing down a rope of cloth, with the wind howling and the rain like ice. "She's mad." He thought he would have preferred Markold, on the whole. On the whole, though, he would rather have crawled down the rope than faced Markold with the news. The hole wasn't big enough to let him through. He dropped down to the floor, took the lamp from the guard, and went tramping down the stair to tell Markold his daughter had escaped.

2

MARKOLD'S EYES BULGED, RED-RIMMED, furious. "She can't have. You're lying."

"My King, I swear to you, she went out a hole in the roof."

Markold's stare grew hotter. "You brought her back here, too. It was you the Queen summoned to witness." He showed his teeth, like a wolf, his face dark with suspicion. "She always favored you."

"My lord, as I have always been faithful to you, I've done only what you ordered. She probably fell, Sire. We should go find her—"

Now suddenly Markold was moving, heaving himself out of his seat. Seffrid turned and led him across the hall to the door. This thought had come on him suddenly as he went down the stairs: the girl fallen, lying shattered in the mud of the courtyard with the rain beating on her. He went out the door still two strides ahead of Markold, into the blast of the wind, and the streaming rain.

Around behind the baille, twenty feet above the ground, the rope made of Ragny's cloak was curling and uncurling through the wild air, its end still fast inside the tower. The courtyard below it was a lake of mud. There was no sign of the girl. Markold splashed up to Seffrid's side; one of the slaves hurried after, carrying a torch. There weren't even any footprints. Markold swore, and kicking out with one foot, drove a squirt of mud up into the air.

"The bitch! I'll make her weep for this—" He tramped off, staring up into the dark driving rain, where the rope snaked wildly. Seffrid calculated that the rope ended well above the ground. She had dropped a good way. The rain was dripping down his face and beard and he began to shiver with the cold; the wind tore at him.

Markold stamped back toward him. "Where has she gone?"

"My lord, I—"

"You know, don't you? You're in this, Seffrid, up to your goddamned teeth! The Queen always favored you—"

"I swear I—"

"Find her! Bring her back!"

"What?" Seffrid said, his teeth chattering.

"Find her, and bring her back, Seffrid!" Markold thrust his face down nose to nose with Seffrid's, eye to eye, his breath horrible. "Or I will see to you even before I see to her, Seffrid."

Seffrid took a step back. The slave stood nearby, and the torch light fell on Markold's face like a wash of blood. The flame gleamed in Markold's eyes. Seffrid said, "Yes, my lord." He turned and went back toward the tower, for his sword and his cloak.

"Be back by midday, Seffrid!" Markold's voice bellowed through the rain.

"Yes, Sire."

He took his sword, found a heavy cloak. When he went to the door Markold was sitting again in his high seat, a stoop of wine in his hand. His gaze fell on Seffrid like a blow. The fire roared high, crackling around the singed meat. Seffrid pulled his cloak around him and went out into the storm.

*   *   *

He knew, at least, where to go first; he had heard the Queen. The
cave of songs was well over a league distant, by a narrow difficult
path over the shoulder of the mountain, without so much as a
shepherd's hut on the way. But Seffrid was on horseback, and she
could not have gotten too much of a start on him: he imagined he
would come on the girl about half the way there, maybe sooner.

He hoped he need go no nearer than that to the cave of songs.
A country all sideways, that was, tipped up and down, and uneasy,
full of rumbles and echoes, where the ground shifted, rocks gave
way underfoot, the wind raked off anything loose. Outside the gate,
he forced his mount out across the treeless hillside, into the slanting
icy rain; the wind rushed into his face, pressing him back. He
hunched himself down into his cloak as much as he could, the hood
close around his face. His toes were already numb with the cold.

He expected to come on her on the broad grassy hillside, the
mountain's steep flank, where the southern sky went down below
the trail, and the wind poured off the heights like a torrent.
Through the last hours of the night he crossed the mountain and
did not find her. The storm bundled by, full of voices, and screams
and laughter; there were lights on the mountaintop, dancing like
fireflies, and he began to wish he kept more company with God, so
that he would have someone to call out to. The rain slackened.
Through the flying wrack of the clouds, stars shone. He was riding
toward the east, and now he saw the first daylight blooming along
the horizon, but he had not found Ragny, and he was coming to
the cave of songs.

He reined in; dawn was near, and he cared not to try that pas-
sage in the dark. The rain had stopped, although the wind still
whipped and whirled around him. Before him the mountainside
reared up into a steep cliff, its foot buried in tumbled grey boul-

ders. The spreading dawn light showed him nothing, no sign of the girl.

He had until midday, or Markold would hunt him down with her. He knew how Markold dealt with people who had failed him; Seffrid himself had helped prop a certain victim up before the hearth so that his dying eyes could watch his own guts frying in the fire.

He stepped off his horse; he picked his way up the stony talus below the cave, which opened just a little crack in the rocks halfway up the cliff. The rocks turned and slid under his feet and he stumbled and fell once. The wind gusted around him. It tore at him, as if trying to pull him off the cliff, and then abruptly hushed, and he heard, somewhere above him, a gust of a deep and thunderous music.

He froze. The ground under him seemed to tremble. It was the wind. High up there, keening on the rock, booming through the caves, just the wind. The long notes died. He could hear nothing now. He had imagined it. He thought of Markold, who might already be hunting him down, and on all fours scurried up the steep cliff to the seam in the rock that opened into the cave.

The crevice was so narrow he had to turn sideways to get in, scrape his chest and back against the walls. For a moment, wedged inside the wall of rock, he was afraid: he felt himself caught there, the rock slowly crushing inward against him, like the mountain closing its jaws. But then he slid through into the larger chamber beyond.

Another opening, high above, let in some fingers of the sun. The vast space spread jaggedly out before him, the high open chamber streaming with dusty sunlight, the walls riven and pleated like curtains. The sunlight did not reach down to the floor of the cave; Seffrid stood in deep twilight, cold and damp, a lake of night air. As he stood there blinking something fell from the ceiling, trailing its echoes.

The cave had no floor, only a layer of broken rubble, heaped up against spines and spires of limestone rising from below, and slippery with the droppings of bats and birds. He went in a few steps, wary, the cold dank air in his lungs, groping his way over shifting crunching rock. A thin high tower of stone loomed up through the gloom. The cave stank of dung and damp and rotten limestone. He straightened, peering through the dim space ahead of him, looking for Ragny.

Abruptly with a wash of terror he became aware of another presence, very close, a tremendous being, towering over him, huge and awful. He let out a shriek; then a blow struck him, and he fell, senseless.

He woke. He was still alive, he realized, to his surprise. The Princess Ragny was sitting on a rock nearby, watching him. There was no one else in the cave.

"Well, Seffrid," she said, "what happened to you?"

He sat up, dazed, looking around. "Something hit me." He put one hand to his head, feeling for a lump, but found nothing. "I swear, something hit me." He wondered how long he had been out. Not long, maybe. Moments.

She was staring fixedly at him. She wore only a long dark gown, considerably bedraggled; her wild hair hung around her shoulders like tangled dandelion fluff. She said, "I have been waiting here half the night, Seffrid, praying and watching. There has been no one else here. Nothing has happened. My mother said someone would come, to help me, but nobody has come except you."

He got to his feet, looking around. "There was no one else here? There was nothing here?" He peered off into the reaches of the cave. Maybe he had spooked at shadows. Something had fallen from the roof and hit him. That was all. He put his hand to his head again.

"No one but you and me. I can't think you were what my mother intended."

"Maybe," he said, leaping at this. "After all, she asked me to witness. Maybe she knew I could fetch you back home again."

"I'm not going home," she said.

"Princess, you have no choice. Markold will track you down if you don't go back. You must go back, and make the best of it—women have a way of managing—"

He stopped. She was not listening. She was walking off across the cave toward the little crack of the entrance, now blazing with sunlight like the passageway to Heaven. He followed her. He would have to carry her off by force, he saw; he began to calculate how to capture her without hurting her—he would have to surprise her.

She said, "My mother intended something. But I cannot wait for wishes, Seffrid. I have to get away, before my father does his will with me, and ruins everything forever." She turned toward him, facing him just as he was about to jump on her. "You're not what my mother meant to send me, but you'll do. Did you bring me a horse?"

He could not surprise her with her facing him, with her level grey eyes on him. His back tingled. He swallowed. He should jump on her anyway, but he could not bring himself to it. Watching him, she grew amused; above her steady gaze her mouth kinked into the beginning of a smile. She said, "You don't think you are still Markold's man, do you, Seffrid?"

He said, hoarsely, "He'll kill us both."

"No, he won't. We'll get away. I'll find a knight who will be true King, who will come back with me to take my birthright. You shall have your rewards."

This seemed so simple. Seffrid rubbed his palms on his thighs. His mouth was dry. He thought of Markold's eyes, bulging with rage and hate, and Markold's fist, and Markold's cruel devisings. He realized how he hated Markold, and how he liked this wild girl.

He had already made up his mind, somehow. Or she had.

He said, "Where do you think of going, my Princess?"

"To Spain, perhaps," she said. "Or north, to Francia."

That steadied him. He began to see a way through this, where he could profit from it, and not risk too much. "I am from Francia, you know. I can lead you there." A sneaking thought nudged evilly at his mind: from Francia, perhaps, he could even deal with Markold for her, make himself rich at a safe distance. He bowed his head to her, lest she see the double-thinking in his face. "I am your man, Princess."

"Good," she said. "Go now, there is a village only a little away; you must find us horses unknown to him and his men. And bring me man's clothes. I shall not escape like this."

Seffrid bowed again, master of this now. "As you wish, Princess." He went to the mouth of the cave, relieved to be outside, in the sun, and climbed quickly down to his horse.

She had no father now but God, and she had no mother at all.

She wept awhile, for her mother's sake, although Ingunn was surely happy now in Heaven; she wept for herself, motherless and forlorn. Seffrid did not come back.

She supposed he could be going to Markold, to give her back to Markold. When she thought that, a sudden rush of memory swept over her, of an olden time, of Markold, not wicked and angry, but kind, and vastly strong, holding her on his knee, and feeding her bits of apple. She shut her eyes, aching. She could go back there, take up that work, to find that Markold again: maybe that was what God wanted of her.

Without willing it entirely, she was standing up, stretching out her arms in the attitude of prayer, facing the sun. The strong light warmed her and gave her heart. She was the rightful Queen of Spain. God would sustain her, if she served His cause. She would do what God willed of her.

She thought, as she often did, of Jesus, faced with His enormous task, going to His Father, and saying, "Please don't make me do this." And God saying, "My Son, there is no one else."

She stretched herself into the cross that had been His task; she shut her eyes. She would not go back to Markold.

Presently, as she had known he would, Seffrid came back, with a big grey horse and a mule, some bread and cheese, and clothes for her. She devoured all the bread and cheese before she even thought that he might want some. He didn't seem to care; he only said, "Princess, we must hurry."

"Do not call me Princess," she said. "I am Queen now, for one thing. But no one must ever hear you call me anything like that, anyway, so you must forego it. He will be looking for us all over the mountains. Wait here." She took the bundle of clothes back into the cave, and put them on: coarse leggings, a hooded jerkin and a belt, boots, even a knife and a big floppy hat. The harsh cloth hid the shape of her body; she was skinny enough anyway. She left her gown lying where she had dropped it and went back out to the sunlight, where Seffrid stood, looking steadily west.

Watching for Markold. She said, "Now you must cut off my hair."

"Princess," he said.

"Do as I tell you," she said, and knelt down with her back to him. "Cut it off as short as you can. I must seem a man—no one must even look twice to see."

He laid uncertain hands on her hair; she felt the short sawings of the knife through it, and saw the first handful as he threw it down. She raised her eyes, looking east and south, the country spreading out before her in rolls of hillsides, and in the southern distance, a haze. "We should go to Spain," she said. "There is my kingdom."

The hands in her hair gave her a painful jerk. "Princess! I'm sorry—I meant not to hurt you—no, Princess, Spain has no friends for you—"

"Do not call me Princess," she said.

"What should I call you, then?" He hacked away another clump.

"I shall be . . ." She looked into the vast hazy distance, so out of reach, where anything seemed possible. "I shall be Roderick. Call me Roderick."

"Very well," he said, hewing at her hair.

Presently he stepped back, done. She put her hand up, and felt the stubble of her hair above her ears. "Ah, Seffrid, I hope you are better with your knife at other work."

"I'm sorry," he said, humbly.

She said, "Never mind. You think we should go to Francia, then." She suspected this wish of his, that some hidden purpose underlay it, but she thought he was right in his argument: in Spain she would find a thousand enemies. In Francia, at least, she would start even and unknown. As for Seffrid, she was going to trust him, and hope that made him trustworthy: she had no other choice, and so far, it was working. "Well, then," she said, "let's go."

They went to their mounts. He had put his saddle on the mule for her, she saw, and for himself had only a blanket. As she was scrambling up onto the back of the mule, it pricked its ears suddenly, and the big grey horse jerked up its head from the grass; then, distantly, she and Seffrid both heard the low bray of a hunting horn.

"He's after us," Seffrid said. "Damn him, he said midday." He bounded onto the grey horse's back, and they rode at a hard trot up over the mountain.

*   *   *

There were many roads for Markold to watch, and anyway, they could avoid the roads, mostly, but there was only one pass over the mountains to the north, and there, Seffrid knew, Markold himself would come, as quickly as he could. Their only hope was to get there ahead of him.

They went along a crease in the hills, a higher, rougher, swifter way than the pale road they saw sometimes twining throughout the valley below them. They heard the hunting horn once more, from farther down the mountain. After the rain, the day was wild and clear. Ragny—Roderick, he remembered, Roderick—kept to a swift pace, following sheep paths on the slopes above the road, stopping now and then to let the mule blow and to look around them.

The second time she did this, he said, "Roderick, you must not stop so that someone looking up will see you against the sky; they'll catch us right away."

She faced him, her eyes wide, and nodded. "Oh. You're right." Swiftly she took them on, down over the ridge to its northern flank. She turned to him again.

"You must tell me how to be a man, Seffrid. It must be more than merely the clothes."

Seffrid laughed. "You have been among men all your life . . . Roderick."

"Yes, but never as one of them," she said. "You must tell me what men speak of, when they are together—you must speak to me that way." Without her hair, her face seemed thinner; the wind chafed her skin ruddy. He could not see her as anything but a girl. She was looking him over, he saw, and as she did, she drew herself into another shape; she squared up her shoulders and shifted her weight, held her head higher, chin out, looked him fiercely in the eyes.

He cast about for something to say, and blurted out, "A man serves his lord. That's what a man is." He turned again, remem-

bering with a sudden tug the call of that hunting horn; a man without a master, he thought, was no better than an outlaw. Suddenly
he felt naked to the blast of the wind, and hunched his shoulders.

She said, "Then serve me." She was sitting her saddle with one
hand fisted on her hip; he had never seen her do this before. The
cant of her head also was different. Their gazes met, he looked into
her pale eyes, and saw no woman-softness there. Then suddenly
she was saying, "Let's go," and they were sweeping off across the
mountainside again.

They came to a river, bounding down through the rocks, and
followed it upstream, looking for a place to cross. Roderick drove
the mule on steeply up, and Seffrid followed, across boulders
where the moss grew like fairy beds, and trees no bigger than his
arm sprouted from crevices above the foaming stream. They came
out on a ridge, wind-blasted, covered with a low trembling mat of
brush and vines, and followed that to the stream's edge.

Here it seemed they might cross, the water bursting out of a
narrow gorge above and then splaying wide across the meadow;
the sun glinted on it. As they came down to the ford, Seffrid saw
someone rise from the shelter of a little crooked tree, and come
forward: a woman, he saw, startled, a young woman, wrapped in a
long cloak.

"Nobles," she cried, in a hoarse voice, "I crave your pardon, I
ask you only a favor, and shall repay"—she looked up at Seffrid
and her eyes were hot—"as even a poor woman might."

Seffrid heated at what he heard in her voice. He reined in,
keen, one hand on his thigh, and the other holding the grey horse
short. Roderick on the mule drew up on his far side. His eyes eager on the girl, Seffrid began working out in his mind how to get
rid of Roderick. "What can we favor you with, lady?"

"Only—" She lifted her arms, lifting the long cloak with them,
her eyes burning. "Carry me over the stream on your horse."

"That I'll do," Seffrid said, and reached down toward her, to lift her up behind him, thinking he could send Roderick off, and then, behind him, Roderick cried out.

"In Jesus' name, who are you?"

The woman was reaching up toward Seffrid's arms; their hands almost touching, he looked down into her blazing hot eyes, that suddenly went white as wrath. Her lips drew back from her teeth, and she roared at him. Seffrid screamed, recoiling, and his horse reared; the woman dropped down on all fours, and was a wolf, and wheeled and raced into the forest.

"Goddamn me!" Seffrid cried, shaking. "Goddamn me!"

The grey horse was scooting back and forth, its eyes rolling. Seffrid could barely keep his seat, and Roderick flung an arm around him, to steady him. Her face was pale, he saw, her eyes hollow.

"How did you know?" he screamed at her.

"She was a hag," Roderick said. She faced him, eyes sharp, and said as if certain: "A wretched old crone. Such as a woman could not pass by without helping."

"No," Seffrid said, amazed. "A young woman, beautiful, in a long cloak." He jerked his gaze around after the wolf.

Roderick gave a shake of her head. "So it seemed you saw her. Let's get out of here."

They went across the ford, and found there a path winding across the ledge toward the pass. Long after they had left the river behind them, Seffrid's heart was still pounding hard. He could not free his mind from the image of her long teeth, her blazing white-hot eyes. He blurted, suddenly, "You saved me."

Riding beside him, Roderick crossed herself, and said, "Jesus saved us."

Seffrid licked his lips. "What do you make of her? A demon, a fairy—"

"Some haunt of the place, very like." Roderick faced him; the wind and cold ruddied her cheeks. "You know how the peasants talk, here, that the high mountains are full of ghosts. Or, they say, there are those who can change their shape."

Then suddenly she looked away. "There is the road," she said, and hurried on a little ahead of him.

He went after her; it popped abruptly into his mind that she had also changed her shape.

His skin crawled. He saw again the long white teeth of the wolf-woman, her eyes like lamps from hell. Maybe Roderick also. How would he know? His mind scurried like a mouse over and over this, while he rode tamely along behind her toward the long brown highway roping over the barren slope. Where was she taking him? She had crossed herself. Called on Jesus. The Devil could quote Scripture, they said. How would he know? The impulse welled up in him to draw his sword, and slay her, to put it all to rest.

He shrank back from that thought; the wolf-woman had sickened his mind, somehow, shone evil through his eyes into his heart.

They reached the road, climbing up through the windy slope toward the saddle of the pass. Roderick said nothing to him. Above them now the black mountains blocked off the sky, their jagged tops crowned with snow. The wind blew harsh down off the mountaintops, raising the tears in his eyes, and he shivered inside his jerkin.

He saw the burning white eyes, the hands reaching for him. He heard, again, Roderick's voice ringing out. At the memory his heart leapt. She had saved him from the clutch of those hands; he owed his life and more to her. That was enough to know, he thought. He owed his life to her; he could go along beside her, at least for a while. Until she was safely away from Markold.

When she was safe, he could take his own path again. He drew in a deep breath as if he had not breathed for moments, and went easily after her up the rising slope.

The road angled across the raw ledgy rock face and rose steeply into the pass. Where the last hard climb began, Roderick drew rein again beside him, pulled up the hood of her jerkin around her face, and set the broad-brimmed hat over it and pulled the brim down. "Are you ready?" She turned toward him, her voice taut. "Are you with me?"

Their eyes met; he saw the faint frown between her brows, and knew she wondered at him. He looked up at the pass, ashamed. He realized that she meant they might have to force their way through, and he put his hand to his sword.

"You have no weapon," he said, suddenly.

"No: I must find one," she said. "But there's no time now. We have to hurry, Seffrid."

He pulled off his sword belt, and handed it and the scabbard and sword across to her. "Take this. I'll find something."

She gripped the scabbard; her eyes blazed. "Seffrid," she said, "you are a true knight." She slung the belt over her shoulder, and they hastened on. Seffrid rode a stride behind her.

Suddenly he felt that he was not last of them. Someone else rode along with them. His back tingled. For a moment he dared not look over his shoulder, but when he did, he saw no one. He hunched up his shoulders. And now he had only his belt knife, in case anything happened. Grimly he pushed on after Roderick, up into the steep of the pass.

The pass angled narrowly between two peaks; some scraggly trees grew there, and there was a large cistern for water, and a trough. Hard by the path some proud lord had built a tower once, with a stone foot, and wooden walls; the wood had rotted away mostly, but the round of stone gave some shelter to travelers. A string of mules was tethered around it, and some horses, and several men lounged around in the sun along the path.

Seffrid hung back. As Markold's man, he was known all over these mountains. But Roderick rode straight toward the trough, and swung down from her mule, swept off her hat in a grand gesture, and bent over the trough to drink, all unconcerned. Seffrid followed.

"Hey, strangers!" Someone hailed them from the little knot of men around the way into the ruined fort. "Where do you come from? Have you brought any wine?"

Seffrid turned; but, to his amazement, Roderick answered before he did, in a loud, rough, jesting voice.

"What, is that your toll here?" She stepped back, putting the hat on, shaking the water from her hands. "We come from Toledo—lost our horses in the storm, and must do with what we could find, as you see. Did you come down from Francia? How is the road north?"

"No, no, local men are we." One of them stood, stretching. "Have you seen any other travelers? Especially any women, we are to stop all women." He paced toward them, looking them keenly over.

"None: the storm was fierce." Roderick swung up onto the mule's back. Seffrid, taut as bow twine, nudged his horse forward. But Roderick reined in, not avoiding the man walking toward them, calling out to him. "What do you seek?"

"A runaway Princess!" His teeth flashed white in a laugh, and the men back by the stone tower let up a chorus of hoots and yells. Their leader, facing Roderick, added, "Some little King down under the mountain has sent word—his daughter's flown, we're to hold all women here until he comes."

"No wonder you want the wine," Roderick said. "We saw nothing, coming from Toledo, of any women, but then, as I said, the storm was fierce." She eased her mule into a trot, going slowly past the watchman, slowly on by the stone tower and the cluster of other men. She eased her mule into a trot, going slowly past the watchman, slowly on by the stone tower and the cluster of other men. Seffrid followed her. Looking back, he saw the man who had come to question them walking back toward his fellows. Seffrid went on after Roderick, across the steeply angled trail, circled a shoulder of rock, and climbed steadily through a narrow ravine, where a little stream ran down, running north now, into Francia.

"How could he get word there so quickly?" she asked, presently, as they rode side by side through the rocks.

"A King's words are faster than horses," Seffrid said.

"So it's said." Roderick nodded. "Yet that must be the margin of his reach—'some little King under the mountain.'" She laughed, harsh, not the silky laughter of a woman. "I thought once he ruled the whole world."

Seffrid said nothing; he imagined Markold's reach to stretch a little farther than that. He felt again, suddenly, as if there were three of them on the road, and his back pricked up. He turned and looked all around them. There was nothing, only, on the raw cliff above them, tufts of wild grass waving madly in the wind, and a couple of wooly goats running swiftly away out of sight.

He thought his eyes were tricking him. He thought there was something they were refusing to see. He hunched his shoulders, feeling naked.

The trail began to drop away under them, so that his horse leaned back and slid stiff-legged with each step on the hard rock. Just below the pass they met a train of donkeys, going south, and from these people begged a couple of stale loaves and a bit of cheese. The road went on down through a gorge between walls of black rock seamed with white like stone blood. The stream grew steadily, until by evening time it was a river, crashing and spraying up over the black boulders, with another leaping stream bouncing down from the height to join it.

Here, with the sun going down, and the western sky streaming with flags of red cloud, they came out at the top of a slope running down to a mountain valley full of oaks, just coming newly into their leaves, so that the whole valley before them spread out like a soft green fleece. On the side of the road was a shrine made of rock. Roderick drew rein, and dismounted. "Let us thank God for our deliverance," she said, and went into the shrine. Seffrid noticed, though, that she did not take the sword off her hip.

He stayed in his saddle, and stretched his gaze as far as possible into the gathering darkness of the night. The wind buffeted him, noisy and rapid around him; the whole forest churned and tumbled, and in the dim light he saw birds wheeling in the stormy sky. Suddenly all around him he felt the spirits of the air, crowding and jostling him and shouting into his ears. The whole world was full of invisible powers. He stumbled through it like a blind man, knowing only what he could touch.

A moment later, on the mountain's shoulder, a wolf howled.

He leapt down from his horse. Whatever Roderick was, he belonged to her now; he had chosen, so be it; that was his cause and his duty. He had only to do his duty. He went swiftly into the little shrine.

3

RODERICK STIRRED BEFORE DAWN, and rose, and went out of the little rock hut of the shrine into the dark belly of the night. The cold bit. There was no more food, she knew, and only water to drink. She prayed awhile, sitting on a rock, facing east, and watching for the first light of the sun.

She made a prayer to her mother, and the memory and longing overwhelmed her, so that she had to get up and walk around and kick at stones and weep. When she turned, with the grief blunted, she saw the pale shining of light along the horizon, and took that for a sign that her mother heard her, or God heard her, or someone heard her, somewhere. Her spirits rose. She went back to the rock and sat down and prayed again, happier.

In the forest around them, birds began to call out and flutter around and shrill long streamers of song into the brightening air, as if they too were glad that after the long night, morning had come.

Seffrid came blinking and stamping out of the shrine. He gave off a stink of bad temper. She looked him over, her man, proven now. He was not big, but knit together tight and strong, with bandy legs and a deep chest. His clothes were rumpled around him and his curly black beard was sprinkled with bits of dead leaves. He stretched himself out like a cat, arms and legs and back, scrubbed at his face with one hand, and went down the slope to fetch his horse.

The grey horse and the mule had wandered far down the hillside, looking for grass. When Seffrid led the grey back up toward the shrine, the mule came trailing after, and Roderick got the bridle and looped that around its neck to hold it while she tended to it.

"God's death, I'm hungry," Seffrid said.

"I wish we had a bow. Do you know where we are? Are there people living anywhere near?"

"I don't know." He flung the blanket onto the grey horse's back. "I don't think even God comes here. What a miserable place."

She mounted the mule. A pang of guilt pierced her; she was his lord, after all, she should provide for him. She crossed herself. Maybe God would send them something, Who was Lord of them both. Her belly growled.

"Well, let's go, then, and find something to eat," she said, and started off down the road. She turned to him with a sudden urgency. "And you must teach me the use of the sword—I will give myself away, I cannot even draw it properly."

That pleased him. He rode the grey purposefully over beside her. As they went on down the road into the forest, he showed her how to draw the sword without getting hung up in the scabbard, and how to hew with the edge and beat with the flat. She saw he was proud of his skill with this work. He talked reverently about fighting, how you watched the other man's hands as well as his eyes, to see where he was going, and always parried with the edge of the sword, which could bite the other blade, or club, or spear, whatever you were attacking.

"Attack the weapon," he said. "Not the man. If you have a shield—which is a good idea, by the way, a good lord always makes sure you have good equipment. And a helmet. If you have a shield, keep it close up on your off hand. Fighting, you move forward behind your sword, but you move backward behind the shield."

"Was Markold a good lord?"

"Markold took care of his men. He always kept us well armed, there was lots to eat, wine, good horses for us. Sometimes women."

He bit off, at that, his gaze wavering, looking embarrassed. They rode on in a little silence. Around them the great oaks grew far apart, the ground under them thick with dead leaves and fallen branches and acorn shells. She opened her ears to the sounds of the forest, the wind in the leaves, and the creaking of the branches, the calls of birds and the squirrels. If she had had her bow, she could have shot something to eat. Seffrid, beside her, twisted around to look behind them.

"What's the matter?" she said; she had seen that he did this often now. "What are you looking for?"

"I keep thinking someone is following us," he said, and straightened forward again, a little red around the ears.

She studied him a moment, seeing not Seffrid, but a man. Trying to be a man made her think about him differently. His dark eyes turned down a little at the corners. The skin of his cheeks was pocky.

She said, "Is that all, then? To being a good lord?"

"A good lord doesn't get you killed," Seffrid said. She could see he was struggling against the urge to turn and look around again. She wondered if the wolf-woman haunted him. "He only picks fights you can win."

"There must be more," she said. "This seems so mean and low."

Seffrid said, "Right now, nothing seems low about having something to eat."

She gave a sort of growl of assent, and faced forward. They were traveling through the deep forest; the sunlight came down where the road cut through, but on either side the trees closed in, gloomy with shadows, their massive warty boles like squatting monsters. Her spine prickled up. She felt the trees' attention on her, a grave and gigantic awareness. She shut her eyes. The air itself felt like fingers twitching at her.

She wished herself away from here. She wished she could slip her skin, expand outward, turning into forest, into wind, stretching toward God. For a moment, drawn from herself like a thread, she seemed all but gone.

She opened her eyes again. Came back into herself. She had to watch out now, not only for herself but for Seffrid, her man. She glanced at him again, pleased at his company. But her stomach hurt with earthly hunger. She clicked to the mule, hurrying on, looking for something to eat.

They crossed a river, and stopped to drink, and went on down through the oak wood. The forest grew more open, the trees bigger, their twisted squat trunks, bulging with galls, solid above the knobbed toes of their roots, and their vast crowns spread over all, so Roderick and Seffrid went along through a deep dappled shade even on the road. The air was thick with the dank smell of the earth. By a small stream mushrooms grew, and Seffrid, his belly grumbling, looked at them longingly, but Roderick said, "No—they could kill you," and he knew she was right. He looked for crawfish in the stream but found none, nor frogs nor fish nor snakes. It was the bad season of the year; in March all creatures starved.

Near midafternoon they came out of the wood onto a meadow, and their path ran into a bigger road. In the drying mud were the crumbling ridges of fresh new wagon tracks, and Seffrid swore a long delighted oath.

"These folk are just ahead. Maybe they have something to eat."

He reined the grey horse around, and with Roderick at his heels went at a gallop on down the road. The wagon that had made these tracks could not be too far on. If these people refused him food, by God's death, he thought, spurring his horse on, he would take it by force. The trees thinned out quickly and they came out onto a meadowland, sloping away down toward the northern horizon. The road crossed it like a brown ribbon through the new green grass, running down to meet the river in the middle distance.

There, where the road crossed the river, people were fighting.

Seffrid reined in, hard, throwing out one arm to stop Roderick. At the ford, a crowd of men, some on foot and some mounted, were swarming around a big open wagon; he could hear shouts and screaming, and saw arms rising and falling, clubbing downward. "Bandits," he said. "Somebody else got to them first."

Roderick said, "We have to help them."

"Roderick! There are too many—" He reached out and grabbed her arm.

She gave him a swift, unfocused look. "They need help." Throwing off his hand, she dragged the sword out of the scabbard.

"No!" Seffrid shouted. "Roderick, no!" Like an arrow from a bow, Roderick launched herself forward, down the slope, into the fight.

"Roderick!" The grey horse half reared. Seffrid reined down hard; that was death, down there, a score of bandits at least, and he had no sword, not even a club. He took breath to scream at her again, and then, suddenly, from behind him, something passed him, going after her, brushing against Seffrid so hard it knocked him almost to the ground.

All his hair on end, he scrambled back into his saddle, looking down the slope. Roderick was charging headlong into the battle, but she was not alone. After her, only half-visible, like a crumpling of the air too fast and too dazzling bright for the eye, something else charged with her, stooping like a great hawk across the plain.

Seffrid let out a yell and plunged after them. He needed no weapon. Down by the ford, the bandits were screeching in terror, wheeling to flee, throwing down their clubs and swords and scattering in all directions. Only two were left to meet Roderick as she plowed into their midst, but Roderick, with blows of her sword, laid one flat and sent the other reeling away. Seffrid, ten strides behind, saw the rest of them splashing and bounding through the river, scrambling up the far side, racing off across the plain.

There was no one left to fight. Seffrid drew rein, panting, next to one of the wagons; a wild exhilaration filled him; he felt that light around him like a magic cloak. Roderick swung toward him, the sword in her hand.

"I tried to do it properly," she said. Her face was white as candle wax. "But I missed with the edge."

Seffrid burst out laughing. The blaze of light was gone. Everything seemed to shrink down to ordinary. Before him, on foot, stood a tall fair man with a sword in his hand and blood all over his face, who was saying, in a dazed voice, "God sent you, God be thanked, they were too many for me." Three bodies lay twisted and broken in the grass around them. A tonsured man in a long dirty grey robe bent over the farthest of them, rose at once and went to kneel by the next.

"Where did the rest of you go?" The dazed man pulled off his helmet, looking around, wide-eyed. His leather hauberk, sewn with links of chain, proved him a nobleman, or at least a noble's knight.

"We are only two," said Roderick, who had managed clumsily to get the sword back into the scabbard; Seffrid saw he needed to teach her more of the weapon. "God be thanked we came in time."

"Only two," the knight repeated. He put his hand to his head, which was still bleeding. "I saw a score of you, I thought."

Out from under the wagon crawled another monk, peering cautiously all around. "God have mercy on us." He stood up, signing himself.

"You are hurt, Leovild." The first monk, tall and brawny like a ploughman, came over toward them, putting his hand on the wounded knight. "I beg you, sit down and let me see if I can do anything for your wound. Brother Deodatus, get over here and help."

The knight Leovild said, "Wulfran." He twisted, looking toward the bodies on the grass. "Pepin!"

The monk slid his arm around the knight's shoulders. "They are God's men now."

"Pepin!" Leovild staggered off toward the dead men in the grass.

The monk crossed himself. Somber, he faced Seffrid and Roderick, a big, keen-eyed man of middle years in a heavy grey robe; his dark hair grew all around the shiny dome of his head like a fringe. "Thank you for what you did, most heartily. I am John the Irishman, master of the King's chapel school, and, by your happy agency, still in the active voice." He held out a big bony hand. There were dark splotches all over his fingers.

"I am Roderick de Pelajo," Roderick said, "a knight of Spain." She clasped the monk's leprous hand, and then waved at Seffrid. "This is my man Seffrid."

John looked from one to the other. "God's peace on you both. And now I must ask you, who have already saved us once, to save us again—please, stay with us, and camp with us tonight. We are so few now, the thieves will fall on us at once if you leave us." He gestured toward the wagon. "We have food and wine aplenty."

"Well, Devil take me," Seffrid said.

Roderick said, "You do us a rescue, also, Brother John—we

are starving men, we lost all our goods coming over the mountains, as you see. We shall make our camp with you gladly."

"Thank you," John said. "Now, with your pardon, I go, and tend to these other men." He swung around, which brought him almost nose to nose with his fellow monk, who was standing there staring in horror at the bodies on the ground.

"Deodatus," John said, between his teeth. "I need your help."

"Ah," said the monk Deodatus, shorter by a head, and thin. "I can do nothing. I shall pray." He crossed himself.

"No," John said, harsh-voiced. "You will take these knights, who saved your hide also, and see that they eat. Mind me!" He shoved the monk hard and went by him, toward the wounded knight now kneeling in the grass beside a dead man.

The monk Deodatus staggered back, almost falling. He glared darkly after John. "Irish pig." He said it under his breath. Turning, he swept a look over Roderick and Seffrid. "The food is in the wagon. Mind you do not disturb the books." With one hand he sent them off, grand as any lord, and Seffrid led Roderick toward the wagon.

Leovild sat slumped on a rock, his arms on his knees; his head throbbed all over, not just where John was pressing on it. Leovild said, "You were right, I should not have hired those men."

John scrubbed a little harder at the side of his head. "Traveling is always dangerous." He wrung out the wet rag in a bucket of the river water. "Leovild, make no penance for it. You fought like a tiger. If it hadn't been for you, they'd have overrun us right away, and no interesting young Spanish lordling could have saved us."

Leovild looked up to meet the monk's eyes. "What do you make of them?"

John shrugged. "Interesting." He touched his fingertips to the sore place on Leovild's skull. "That looks worse than it is."

"Good that I'm behind it, then, because it feels pretty bad."
Leovild turned his gaze away. "Pretty bad for Wulfran. And poor
Pepin, he was only a boy."

Off by the wagons, the interesting young Spanish lordling
was sitting stuffing bread and cheese into his mouth. His rough-
looking man-at-arms sat next to him like a brother. Leovild struggled to remember what he had seen, when the bandits hacking at
him suddenly wheeled around and began to scream and scatter. He
had thought there were more than just two.

His head began to pound again. Bitterly he wished he had
done better, or been better, and prevented this. He felt a dull despair tugging at him. Pepin. He had liked Pepin, maybe overmuch,
a skinny, cheery boy, with a thought about everything. Leovild felt
the world closing over him like the lid of a coffin.

John said, "We will have to bury these dead men, and make
camp now as well." He washed his mottled hands off in the
bucket.

Leovild nodded. "We'll stay here. Night is coming anyway."
He brushed his hair back, stood, pulled his jerkin sleeves down,
and looked around, trying to get himself in order. "We have extra
horses now. I shall offer new mounts and weapons to these Spanish men, for their service to Paris."

"Good," John said. "Go get a good sup of the wine." He
clapped Leovild on the shoulder. John had thoughts, too, most of
them incomprehensible even in Frankish. Leovild got up and went
across the camp to the newcomers.

Of the two men Roderick had struck down, one had escaped; she
helped them bury the other one, with Pepin and Wulfran, the
Frankish dead. They dug the holes and rolled the bodies in, and
the big Irish monk said some holy words. Her arms ached from
the shoveling; she was tired.

She thought of that other work, and what it had led to, this dead body in the hole at her feet: man's work. It was not so hard, to be a man, after all. The monks, the Frankish knight, were all taking her as one without question. She only had to stand as Markold had, with her head back and her chin out, and walk as Markold had, that slow and heavy step, as if the world could move before he had to move. Look on evil and death, as he had, with a stony eye, and kill when necessary. Even the Frankish tongue was not so different from her mother language, some strange words, an accent like a frill on the words.

She wiped her face on her sleeve. They were covering up her dead man now. She looked on him. She was not a whole man yet. Against her will, she thought he had been a child once, some mother's darling, now dead, dead, dead, and she turned away before they saw her cry, and went down toward the river.

A moment later, the knight Leovild was calling her. "My lord Roderick."

She manned herself again; she faced him, as he walked across the muddy grass toward her. He was tall, with fair hair down over his forehead and his ears, younger than Seffrid. When he smiled he seemed younger still. He said, "Once again, sir, my thanks. We owe you more than our lives."

"What else could we have done?" she said; all this gratitude seemed excessive. "I have my honor. What more than your lives?"

"That in the wagon, what we are taking to the King, in Paris. There we must still go, myself and these two men of God—"

She laughed. The knight suddenly smiled at her, his blue eyes glinting. "Well. One man of God and one monk." His voice eased, as if they had passed together over some boundary, and were friends now. "I want to ask another favor of you and your man there, that you will accompany us to Paris. I can offer you horses and arms, food and lodging, and in the end, words of thanks from the mouth of King Charles himself."

She had been expecting this. Having saved them once, she had to keep on saving them. She liked them, and she had to go somewhere; perhaps at the court of this great King she would find her knight. "The King of Francia," she said. "I shall not refuse the chance to meet him. You may count on me and Seffrid."

"Thank you," he said. "Now if you will help me, we can go herd in the horses, and you can choose of them."

"We've had nothing but trouble since we left Barcelona," the knight Leovild said. "The roads are very bad, to begin with, and one of the drovers got sick, and then two other men ran away." He poked at the fire; they were all sitting around it in a ring, passing a wooden cup of wine from hand to hand. "Just yesterday I hired new ones, although John mistrusted them—wisely, I should have heeded him. When we got to the ford, the bandits were hidden among the rocks. The new men turned on us, they were all over us in a moment." He held the wine out to Seffrid.

"Coward," Seffrid said. "They ran like rabbits when we came at them from behind like that." He drank of the strong dark wine. Everything had somehow turned out very well. His belly was full of meat and bread and now he would have a blanket to sleep under, and tomorrow a better horse, with a good saddle, and better arms. "My young lord is a great knight, for all his green years."

From the three around him came a little chorus of agreement. The Irish monk John said, "He should be careful, nonetheless—where has he gone?"

"Probably off to pray. He is very godly." Seffrid gave the wine on to the rat-faced monk Deodatus, who seemed to enjoy it more than anybody.

"Praise him for that," John said.

"He comes," Leovild said, and moved over, to give Roderick a space by the fire.

Roderick came up among them. She had taken on a way of carrying herself, high-headed, with a sort of loose, arrogant swagger, that Seffrid knew he had seen before but could not place. Slender as a river reed, she sank down on Seffrid's right hand, between him and Leovild.

"God be with all here," she said, and from the others came a murmur of reply.

"The roads are dangerous," Seffrid said. "You said something of being on the King's business? I'm surprised he gave you no more escort than this, especially for treasure."

"We have nothing thieves would want," Leovild said. He jabbed hard at the fire. "We have nothing to steal, it was folly to attack us."

"John brought them down on us," Deodatus said suddenly. His eyes gleamed with sudden brimming malice. "At that inn, the other night, saying what a trove we carried." He sneered at the Irish monk. "They thought you meant real wealth, and not just some rotten dusty books."

The big monk growled at him. But his face sagged. He turned toward Leovild and said, "Probably he is right. Something brought them down on us."

"Bah," said Leovild. "It's done now. I made a mistake, definitely, you maybe. Who cares? God will sort it all out soon enough."

Roderick was listening to this; now she said, "What's this of *weights?*"

Deoadatus gave a great jeer of a laugh. John rubbed his hands on his heavy filthy robe. "Not weights—the word is much the same—but books." His face looked sad in the firelight. "You don't know of books?" he said.

"Fortunate innocence!" Deodatus said. "Filthy, pagan books, already they have nearly got us killed, or worse."

"The Greeks are Christian men like you and me," John said, in a rising temper. "These books came to us through the care and sacrifice of a lot of devout and learned people, including the Emperor himself in Constantinople. They are not—"

"Full of heresy and falsity and sin!" Deodatus was drunk; his red face redder for the firelight, he shook his finger at John. "If you loved God as you love those filthy books—"

John surged up onto his feet, roaring at him, first in Frankish and then suddenly in a volley of Latin; his bony black-spotted hands fisted. Deodatus, shouting retorts, scrambled backwards, trying to get out of the big monk's way. At something he said, John screeched, and sprang at him, grabbed him up like a rag, and shook him.

"Silence, you mouther of idiocies—until you can tell your cujus from your quibus—" He flung Deodatus down by the fire. "Get you out of my sight." He stamped away, out of the firelight, and Seffrid heard him around behind the wagon.

Leovild said, "He's wild for his books, is John."

Deodatus settled himself by the fire again. "I hate him," he said, quietly. Seffrid handed him the wine cup.

Roderick said, "The King of France wants these Greek books? What use are books to a King?" She had pushed off her hat, and her close-cropped head rose out of the collar of her jerkin like a dandelion. She lifted the cup to drink.

Leovild said, "The King loves books." Clearly Leovild's opinion of the books was closer to Deodatus' than John's. Seffrid yawned. The cup came to him, and he drank and passed it on; he was sleepy, and began to think of finding somewhere soft to roll out his new blanket. But it was good to sit in company, and share a cup. John had come back, looking ashamed; he had something in his hand.

"Young Roderick," he said. "This is a book."

"Ah, throw it in the fire," Deodatus muttered, slurring the words; he was halfway lying down, his eyes bleary.

John ignored him. Leovild moved, so that the big monk could sit next to Roderick and show her the object in his hand. Seffrid got the wine cup back from Deodatus; it was empty, and he went around the fire to the cask.

Out beyond the little circle of the fire the night lay dark and breathy with the wind. The river chuckled and moaned over its bed of stones. Seffrid drank half a cup of the wine, standing there; he wondered if the robbers were out in the dark somewhere watching. He would talk to Leovild about standing guard.

He looked back at the fire. The big monk had opened the scroll in his hands. Seffrid had seen books before, sheets of thin stuff rolled around sticks until they took the rolled shape and could not be easily flattened out, and on them marks. Words were only shadows of things, it seemed to Seffrid; marks intended to be taken for words seemed to him shadows of shadows. But the monk there spread the scroll open on his knees, pointing to it as if it were a map to Heaven. Roderick looked up, from the book to the face of the monk, her eyes wide, intent, reading, not the book, but the man.

Seffrid set his teeth together; he felt the stir of jealousy, like bile rising in his throat. What did she, courting this monk? The feeling shocked him, and he turned his back on them. He did not care about her, or should not; no good would come of it.

He felt suddenly that he had come to a crimp in this, an opening through which he could slip away utterly. He could leave her for this monk to deal with. She was going to get him into trouble; she already had. He should escape, get back to his real business, find a master to fight for, to feed and keep him. He stood there, drinking, not moving, knowing he was going nowhere.

The memory of the robbers slipped into his mind, and he gave a half-drunk weary satisfied laugh, remembering his and Roderick's charge down the hill. That had been a great work. Out there in the dark, he knew, the robbers were still running. He would not be one of them, running away. He would follow Roderick. To see again what he had seen, stooping down onto robbers like a blast of sacred fire, to wrap himself in that light again, he would follow Roderick forever. He dipped the cup into the cask, filled it to the brim, and took it back to her, like an offering.

4

THEY WENT ON IN THE MORNING, Roderick on her new black horse leading the way, and the Irish monk John with a quarterstaff to lean on walking alongside her. Seffrid drove the wagon, and Leovild went along beside him, and the other monk, Deodatus, walked along behind them all.

The black horse was lively; Roderick sported with it up and down along the road, learning its ways. Once it bucked her off, and all the men hooted at her. It had a good quick foot, and a sudden burst of speed that she loved. All over it was black as char, no white anywhere, except that its left eye had white all around it, like a human eye.

She sent it in a long hard gallop back down the road the way they had come; it tried again to buck her off, but she knew now what to expect and kept her seat and brought it firmly to a stamping, head-tossing halt. Leaning down, she slapped its arched black neck, pleased, and turned to ride after the others.

The forest had fallen behind them. The little train traveled away ahead of her across a rolling hilly grassland, with only thin stands of trees rising in the creases. Galloping the black horse up toward the train agin, Roderick saw that Deodatus had climbed into the back of the wagon and was riding along, hunched down to stay out of sight of the other men, his hands tucked into the sleeves of his robe. When he saw her coming, he tried to hide in among the baggage.

A man would drag him out, she thought, and make him walk, like John. But she rode by him without showing that she saw him, and told no one; if he was lazy, she thought, it hurt only him, and she felt a little sorry for him.

In the middle of the day the sky darkened and rain began to pour down, and they drove the wagon up onto the high side of the road and crawled underneath to wait the storm out. A clap of thunder boomed out like great barrels rolling across a wooden sky. Roderick lay on her stomach under the middle of the wagon, braced up on her elbows, with Seffrid on her left and Leovild on her right, and the two monks beyond them. The rain dripped in a rippled sheet down off the edge of the wagon, inches from her nose.

"You could get down some of the wine," Deodatus said, to Leovild.

Leovild said, briefly, "Later. It's almost gone. We have to save it."

Deodatus groaned. Swiveled his head to glare at John. "This is because of your stupid books." John gave him a brief, unfocused look, and abruptly crawled out of the wagon into the streaming rain.

"Idiot," Deodatus said, his teeth clenched. His eyes were red-rimmed.

"Ah, hold your tongue," Leovild said. "You useless drunken fool."

Deodatus snarled at him. John's legs in his sodden dripping robe walked around to the side of the wagon near Roderick; above her head she could hear him doing something with the baggage.

Making sure the rain wouldn't harm his books.

"Just a little of the wine," Deodatus said, in a voice like a honeyed wire. Leovild struck harder at him, saying nothing.

"This can go on forever," Roderick said, watching the rain. The thunder crashed again and for an instant the whole world blanched. The air smelled sharp. Her ears rang. The close quarters under the wagon already felt like a trap, Leovild against her side from shoulder and hip, knocking into her every time he moved to snap at Deodatus.

Seffrid said, "No, no rain falls this heavy for very long."

"It's John's fault," Deodatus began, and Leovild rammed an elbow into him. John was creeping in again under the wagon on Deodatus' far side. He gave off a heavy stink of wet wool.

Leovild turned to her suddenly. "Where were you going, Roderick, when you came on us at the ford? Are you not on some journey on your own, that we are turning you from?"

She jerked her head up, jolted. Foolishly she had not foreseen that she would have to answer this. But this was different from pretending with Seffrid; this was lying. In a flash she saw it was already too well begun, the lie, too far along to be dismissed.

"If you wish not to tell us—" John said, beyond Leovild. She realized they were all watching her, waiting, and she had to say something.

She kept it as near truth as possible. "I am going nowhere, only away from my home. My father and I had a quarrel, such that I could not remain." Reaching out her hand, she poked at the water sheeting off the corner of the wagon bed, pushing through it to the open air.

Deodatus said sharply, "A father's will is God's will."

She gave him a sharp look. "You know this matter not."

Leovild was smiling at her. "Was the girl yours, or his?"

"No, no," she said, startled. She drew her hand back under her, wondering that he had caught hold of so much of it, even in such a twisted way. "It was not about a girl. It was my father I could not abide." Then, feeling herself blush under Leovild's steady, smiling, too-knowing gaze, she twisted the lie a little more. "Well, it was about a girl, somewhat. He wanted me to marry against my will."

"Oh. That follows." Leovild looked past her. "You were his father's man first?"

"I was ever Roderick's man," Seffrid said. "But I did some service for the old King."

Roderick twisted to face Leovild completely, angry at the accusation in the question. "You think he deserted his lord. But Seffrid is honorable. He did what was honorable, helping me escape. It is my kingdom, not my father's. My crown. I shall go back, one day, when I have learned how to overcome him, and Seffrid shall go back, and serve me there, with all the honor due him."

She bit her lips shut, and turned away abruptly; she knew she had said too much.

Leovild said, "I meant nothing against Seffrid. A father makes a hard enemy."

Roderick stared away through the falling rain. It was mostly truth. She knew that the first lie tainted all. She should tell them who she really was, at once, no matter what they said or did to her for it. She shrank from that. They would hate her. The memory flashed into her mind of the wolf-woman, in the mountains. Roderick was a shape-shifter too. When men came on such creatures, they killed them.

She shut her eyes, belly-sick. The wolf-woman at least was one thing or the other, but Roderick was trapped in the middle, neither man nor woman, something monstrous in between.

Seffrid nudged her hard suddenly. She grunted, turned toward him, and saw him watching her, worried. He smiled stiffly. "Leovild's spoken to you three times now. Are you asleep?" His voice had an undertone of warning.

She turned to Leovild, who was watching her pensively. He had clear blue eyes like a spring sky, she saw. She said, "I beg your pardon, sir, I was dreaming."

"I only asked if you loved another," Leovild said, with a quick smile. "I think you do, but not a girl."

With a heat of shame, she lowered her head; somehow he took all this on the high side; he clapped her mildly on the shoulder. "I asked too much, and too close to the bone, young Roderick. I promise I will not do it again."

She mumbled something, seeing the lie stretching out before her all the way to Paris, and weary of it already.

The sun came back, soon enough, and they went on, slopping through the mud. The wind blew raw; that evening again they made a camp in the open. The meat was going bad, but they had nothing else to eat, and only a sip of wine and then water to drink. In such close company, Roderick could not easily get off by herself very much, but she had practiced, and had found if she pulled her jerkin up, and stood in a certain way and made water as hard as she could, she could piss standing up like a man. The first time she did this, turning modestly away from the others, Seffrid's eyes jumped out of his head, white as eggs.

In the gloomy margin of the night she went off a little to pray. Stretching her arms out, she faced into the east, toward Calvary. She begged God to forgive her for lying, and to keep her in His mercy; if she lost God's help, she knew, she would go down at once, like a deer when the wolves caught her.

She knew God would not tolerate a lie for long.

The high grass around her stirred with the rising night wind. Broad dark banners of the clouds lay across the last edge of pale sky. The world seemed huge around her, and she all alone in it. She thought of her mother with a great rush of longing and grief. She was far away from where she should be, and going farther every day. She wished she had not promised to go with these men to

Paris. That seemed now the doing of a stranger, the Roderick she was pretending to be, into whom she was disappearing, and whom they all liked so much.

She liked him also, that Roderick. She liked being him, making him up from the inside; she liked what he could do, that Ragny could not have done. But he wasn't who she was meant to be.

She had no choice. For the while, she had to be Roderick. The best way of it was to live that lie nobly. She knew what was most manly in those men she had seen: she would let that guide her.

Maybe, in Paris, she would find people who would help her against her father. Maybe there she would find her knight.

Then as she was turning around to go back, Deodatus came up to her, bowing and bobbing with his hands together.

"Young Roderick, let me give you instruction—" He placed his two hands palms together. "This is how to pray. As you pray, that was improper, not to say heretical, standing with arms out so. Pray with your hands together, as you would put your hands together between the hands of your liege lord, commending yourself into his service."

She stepped back away from him. He smelled of wine. She had, "I have always prayed as I do."

"It is wrong, even perhaps as I said sinful. God will not hear you."

A wild surge of rage boiled up through her; her hands clenched; she almost struck him. "My mother taught me to pray so." Spinning around, she stalked away toward the fire, tears hot in her eyes. The monk stayed away from her after that.

They went on again the next day across a broad lowland just sprouting with grass. Clouds like a flock of airy beasts roamed over the sky. Roderick went at the lead again, with John striding along beside her, his head by her horse's head. The road was bad and they had to stop and haul the wagons through gullies where the track had washed out, cut grass and brush to cast under the wheels so they would grip in the mud. Halfway through the day one of the wheels broke and they stopped and fixed it and at the same time ate their supper of rotten meat and water.

When they went on, John began talking. Striding along beside her, as she rode, he talked easily and quickly, like someone weaving on an old work, in a pattern he knew well, and loved.

It was church speech, lofty and invisible. He said that God was everywhere, which seemed to her excellent, that evil was the absence of God, an emptiness. Yet he said that Nothing was God also, which confused her. He made much of certain words, separating them into pieces, and then putting them back together again, as if the words were little boxes.

He said, "Reason is God's greatest gift to us, and we must use it to come to Him. Not to think is a sin as much as not to love. Look at the world around us! What a mysterious thing, how wonderful, and yet you can see that there is order, an order accessible to reason—"

Suddenly Deodatus, walking along just behind them, began to bawl at him. "How dare you poison his sweet and tender innocence with your sins, John! Tell him rather that the world is a test, a horrible corrupt place full of evil, where God tries us, to see if we are worthy of Heaven!"

John wheeled, walking sideways, and shouted back, "You are a frightened little man, Deodatus, hiding under your dogmas."

Deodatus stormed forward. His thin face was dark with rage. "Only God can save us, John, as surely even you know. Only faith in God our Father in Heaven. Your reason is a trap, truly and finally, a false virtue, a lure of the Devil who preys on men, even now with wicked cunning preying on your weakness of pride, and someday all you construct so reasonably thereof will give way and drop you into hell." He said the last word with vehemence. He wheeled toward Roderick, his eyes burning. "Right thoughts, young knight. Right thoughts are all!"

John swung around to the far side of Roderick's horse, and yelled up to her. "Why give us this wonderful mystery of a world, then, why give us this faculty of reason, unless He means us to use the one to find Him everywhere in the other?"

Roderick from her saddle looked from him to Deodatus, as they roared; she had to keep from smiling; this word trickery seemed so serious to them, but when Deodatus seized her leg, shouting, "This world is hell, not perfect, not wonderful, he is a liar, the fool," she thrust him off.

"Do not lay hold of me."

"Ah." He slid backward, fawning. "You must pardon me, young knight, I seek only to save your immortal soul, God helping me."

"Thank you," she said. "I shall pray for you." On her other side, John turned forward, and walked heavily along for a while, saying nothing, his head down. Roderick rode along in silence. She thought Deodatus was probably right, the world seeming more of a test than a wonder; but she liked John.

They came to a marshy stream, where some geese were swimming, off in the distance on the water, and she saw the chance to get away a little. She took a bow of Leovild's she had seen in the wagon, and while the rest of the company went on, she tied the horse to a willow clump, and stalked along the brushy shore.

The day was turning mild, with the sun right overhead. The birds came ashore, one by one, to graze on the meadow on the back of the stream. She moved in, slowly, carefully, sitting for long times on the mudbank, with the warmth of the sun on her, and the smell of new grass sweet in the air.

She had never really understood before the pleasure of being by herself. She felt the warmth and kindness of the day around her like great wings folded over her. Everything around her was alive. Birds clattered and brawled in the air overhead, and tiny black tadpoles swarmed along the shallow edge of the stream. Out in the middle of the clear water, a row of faint ripples curled over and over in the same place. At last she shot one of the geese and took it back to the others, and they roasted it that night in the fire and ate it, the best meat they had eaten in days.

Early in the morning, Leovild, riding first, saw that they were coming to the Roman road. Broad and flat and straight as the edge of a sword, the highway ran up out of the south along the plain, the grey stones hairy with green sprouting through the cracks, the ditches half-full of scummy water and boisterous with frogs. When they turned north onto it, Leovild felt easier, as if he had come into his own country. They were still a long way from home, but this road led straight to Paris, and along the way there would be inns for the night, and good food, in the King's name.

Still his heavy mood clung to him: he thought he had done ill, losing his friends to an ambush, and all for some crates of books.

Roderick got down from his saddle to see the road closer, to touch the great stones, and pace the width of it. The young man was endlessly poking and probing into things, as if he were new-born to the world. Leovild rode by him as he mounted his horse again. "Have you not seen such a thing as this before? It is Roman work."

"Where I came from," Roderick said, swinging into his saddle, "we put stones into upright things like walls, but then in my country nothing lies as flat as everything seems to here. How far does it go?" He twisted to look back along the road, and then peered forward again, into the distance.

"Across al Francia. Tomorrow or the next day, we'll come to Tours," Leovild said. "That's a very holy place; blessed Martin is buried there, who tore his cloak for the beggar. The road crosses the river there, the great river, the Loire."

"Is your King master of Tours?"

"He is master of all this country," Leovild said sharply, wanting Roderick's admiration. "All Francia belongs to him, as surely as the sun rises. Someday he will be Emperor, and then all Christian men must bow."

Roderick smiled at him. "I meant no slight. I know the King of Francia is mighty. I am ignorant only of where we are." The black horse was pushing at the bit, wanting to run; Roderick mastered him without paying much attention, his clear grey eyes on Leovild. Seffrid had come up on the far side of him. "You said it was Roman work," Roderick said, apologetically.

"This was all Rome once," Leovild said; he wished he had not jumped to take offense. Turning his horse, he rode along the road, and the rest followed, Roderick stirrup to stirrup with him. Leovild said, "And it will be Rome again, when King Charles is Emperor."

Seffrid leaned forward to see around Roderick to Leovild. "Tours lies ahead of us, I think."

"Some day or two on," Leovild said. "You are a Frank by blood?"

"Of Aquitaine," Seffrid said. "Tours have I never seen, nor Paris."

"Great cities both," Leovild said, "with many churches and holy relics, and the tomb of Saint Martin in the one, and the court of King Charles in the other."

"The King must keep a very rich and lavish court," Roderick said. "With many warriors, and much treasure."

"He keeps the greatest court in Christendom."

"These books, though. What use will he make of them? Why has he sent half across the world to get them?"

Leovild looked ahead of them, where John was walking along with his long swaying step; the monk seemed lost in thought. "They are John's books, really; he alone can read them."

"And the King finds this good?"

"The King's interest shines in all directions," Leovild said. "As for what is good in John, I think you must have seen that already for yourself."

"I have," Roderick said, with a nod. "I think I want to meet King Charles, more and more."

Twice that day the road went through fields freshly turned up for the planting. In one a plow behind eight yokes of oxen went along like a great jointed worm, folding the dark earth over in long even pleats; along the upper edge of the newest furrow the moist earth gleamed like silver. Clouds of little blue butterflies rose above the plowed ground, as if the earth breathed them up through its opened seams.

They came on other travelers, local people, going to and from the city ahead of them. Leovild watched them sharply, looking for thieves. John spoke to everybody, asking questions, listening to the answers even of lowborn people. He carried a woman's baby for a while, making faces at it and letting it pull at his fingers. Several people asked him for a blessing, which he gave with great delight. Leovild kept a watch on him, thinking it was John's loose tongue that had gotten them ambushed.

That seemed mean-minded, to him, to think that: it was his own fault, he was the captain.

Ahead, now, there was a haze of smoke in the sky, like a smudge; the rest of that day and most of the next, they went toward it, as it hung above the city crouched in the river's elbow. The road was full of people, some going in, many going out from the city, with loaded carts and baggage mules.

They came to a little stream, just south of the city, where there was a ford, and a toll, and they paid no toll, because they were the King's men on the King's business; John had a paper with a seal, saying so.

But the man at the gate into Tours only shrugged at the paper and the seal. John argued with him for a long time, and Leovild at last went up and tried to convince the toll taker, but the man only said, over and over, "The Bishop takes his due of everybody, sirs, the Bishop takes his due of everybody," smiling all the while. Finally Leovild paid the toll, which was not so much, anyway, since they were bringing in nothing valuable.

Roderick was staring at the gate and the city wall, built of massive stones, grey as the stones of the road. A little way down the wall from the gate, there had once been a watchtower, which had fallen, and a small tree grew up from the tumbled rock. A row of little ragged boys sat along the upper course of the wall shouting insults at the people below. The gate was deep and broad and the stone arch over the road was carved, although most of the figure was too worn away to recognize.

"This also is Roman work?" Roderick asked. They were going into the city, the riders two by two through the gate, and then the wagon and the monks. Seffrid came just after them.

Leovild said, "The wall here, and the great church also. You see that, beyond." He waved ahead of them, where the wooden steeple of the church rose up over everything. The church itself below the steeple was of ancient stones, being what was left of an old pagan temple, saved for God by the holy Bishops. The lesser buildings of the city huddled around the flanks like wind drift around a great rock. "Outside the walls, over there, is the tomb of the blessed Saint Martin himself. He does many miracles there, they say."

Roderick twisted in his saddle, looking back toward the gate, where a train of carts and people stood waiting to get out. "Where are all these people going?"

Leovild followed his gaze. The people waiting at the gate were loaded down with bags, and carrying their children. A chicken rode in a basket on a woman's shoulder, its head poking through the slats. Leovild grunted.

"Are they going to somewhere, or just away?" Roderick asked.

"An interesting question," Leovild said. "Come, we'll put up at the inn here, and have bread for dinner." He reined around, looking for John.

The big monk led them away to the inn, and got them a room to themselves. The inn seemed almost empty, although Tours was a market town. Leovild fought down a surge of disquiet. It was spring. Maybe all these people were going out to plow and plant. He and the other men unhitched the mules from the wagons, tethered their horses to rings in the wall behind the inn, rubbed them down and fed them hay. Then with Seffrid and Roderick, Leovild went out to look around.

They walked along the whole street, from the gate to the river. The city was quiet in the late afternoon sun. On the porch of the great church some folk were selling nuts and eggs, and from two big ovens just beyond came the aroma of bread baking. Three women in white coifs waited by the ovens, chattering away.

Seffrid hooted at them, whistling between his fingers, and the women tossed their heads and turned their backs. Seffrid said, "Ah, God be thanked for pretty women."

Leovild laughed; but he saw how Roderick's cheek blazed. He thought, The boy's a virgin. This amused him. Roderick's innocence became him as much as his courage and his strong arm. Leovild felt a sudden rush of affection toward him. Beneath the sunburn and the dirt his cheek was smooth as an angel's, that looked on the face of God. He clapped the boy on the shoulder. "Keep your innocence as long as you can, Roderick the Beardless."

Roderick muttered something; Seffrid gave a roar of laughter. "Oh, aye, he is a maiden knight." He jostled Roderick with his elbow. Roderick tossed his head back, taking the jibe like a spurred horse, and gave Seffrid a dark look. The man fell still, but chuckling. Leovild saw an old joke between them, more joke on Seffrid's side; he envied Seffrid, suddenly, his old joke with Roderick.

They went along past the sagging fronts of houses made of bits of stone and plastered wood. Between two houses was a midden heap where a sow with her little pigs was routing in the muck. They passed a house whose thatch was falling in, and another with no thatch at all, and the stones falling from the wall.

On the higher bank of the river, another of the ancient roads came in from the east, and one also from the west, all making one at the bridge across to the far side. Leovild and his friends went out onto the bridge, and sat on the edge of it and dropped stones into the water.

Roderick was on Leovild's right side. The young man said, "This was a much bigger place, once, it seems. What was that, over there?"

Leovild looked where he was pointing. Along the bank of the river, just east of the bridge, was a stretch of open ground, full of tumbled rocks, where the remnant of an old wall stood, and the weeds grew up over everything. Leovild rubbed his hand over his mouth. He felt all his forebodings gather like a boulder in his stomach, and he twisted around suddenly and stared away down the river.

"What are you looking for?" Seffrid said.

Leovild straightened again, and flicked another rock into the stream. "That—there—" He jabbed his finger at the broken wall on the bank, where the green vines all but buried the fallen, blackened rubble. "That was the monastery of Saint Martin. The Northmen burnt it, a couple of years ago. I am beginning to understand. That's why the city is so empty, because it is spring, and these people believe that the Northmen will come."

"Up the river," Seffrid said.

Roderick said, "Who are these—you called them Northmen?"

"You have not seem them in your country? Oh, but you said you lived in the mountains. They are like water rats, they follow the rivers with their boats. They come from the sea, and from the North, hence we call them so, and they call themselves Northers, even, or some of them. Otherwise they call themselves Vikings. In the summer, not every year, but often, they row up the rivers; when they see a village or a city, they leap out, grab everything they can, and run for their ships again." He looked away, his mind churning with everything that he was not saying.

"Are the city walls of no use, then?" Roderick asked.

"Not without men to fight behind them—they strike and go before we can bring swords against them." Leovild shook his head slightly. "In truth, when we face them sword against sword, the work is very even, they are great fighters."

He watched the water flow hollow around the pier of the bridge. The day before, he had boasted to Roderick that King Charles would one day be Emperor. Between them, the city toll taker and the Northmen had made a nothing of him and his King. His mood followed the smooth green water of the river plunging down around the stones of the pier.

Roderick turned to look west. The wind lifted the edges of his ragged pale hair. "I would see that sight, the boats coming up the river, and the warriors."

"God help you if you do," Leovild burst out. He pushed away from the side of the bridge. "Let's go back to the inn. At least we'll drink deep to each other, eat bread, and sleep soft tonight."

Roderick went into the old church, which grew up from the earth in massy rocks, sprouting green moss and grass between the stones. The side of the building was caving in and was braced with poles and piles of loose stones. In the porch where earlier there had been people selling things, now there was only one last old woman, perched on a stool, draped in shawls, her basket of nuts at her feet, gossiping with some of the town wives in their spotless white coifs. One of the wives was pregnant, and the old woman leaned forward and laid her hand on the great mound of her belly.

Roderick watched them keenly as she passed, trying to see them now not as another of them but as a man. Something twisted in her, a cold jerk of alarm; she tore her gaze away from them, blushing again.

Through the wide dark doorway she went on into the church. It reminded her of the cave of songs, except that no light shone down from the heights; the great space was all dark, except for straight ahead of her, where some candles burned, and above them, floating down into the light, hung the figure of Christ on the cross.

She went toward that, like a lost child toward the fires of home, and reached the altar and stood with arms outstretched and prayed to God for the strength to do what was right. The great comfort of God's attention fell over her. She felt easier, and only then saw that Irish John knelt at the altar beside her, saying his own prayers.

He said them Deodatus' way, with hands together and head bowed; she pushed off the feeling that such was a servile way to deal with God. If John used it, the practice must be good. She drew her mind back to her own prayers and shut her eyes and thought about her mother and asked God to forgive her for lying.

Her arms grew heavy, and she lowered them and took a step backward, away from the altar. John had risen and was standing nearby, waiting for her. They went together slowly back through the church. The vast close darkness all around them was full of twitterings and whisperings and shufflings, the old demons and spirits and gods, banished from the light of Christ. She glanced at John, beside her.

"What are these Northmen, that Leovild had told me of? Are they pagan men?"

"The Northmen," said the monk. He stopped. Roderick could just see his shape in the dark, more distinct on the side toward the altar and its candles. "They worship horses, and thunder, they have no knowledge of that which is real."

"Have you ever seen them?"

John said, "Oh, yes, they are everywhere. I wonder you have not. The Vikings are everywhere, not just in Francia."

"Then they were in Ireland also?"

"They came to Ireland first." John shifted his weight, in the dark, his feet scraping on the stone floor, and she could feel the temper rise in him, an old rage of grief. "Ireland was then the richest and most full of knowledge of all the Christian lands, where there were great monasteries, the wealth of books and learning. This was in my grandfather's time. I remember still how he spoke of it—they thought, when the first longships appeared, that these were trading ships, with goods to sell. They went down to the beach to meet them, like giving their necks to the knife."

"They should have fought," Roderick said. "Did they not fight?"

"They are fighting still, which is the greatest evil of it. As I said, before the Vikings came, there were great monasteries in Ireland, and such learning in Latin and Greek as astonished the whole world, with many ancient books copied out, and commentaries also. And there were many Kings, but they all bowed to the abbots, and there was peace for a scholar in Ireland. But when the Northmen came they burned the monasteries and carried off the monks into slavery. And the abbots ordered the books hidden, and a lot of the books also were sent over the water, to Francia and Italia, to be preserved, and the monasteries were abandoned. No one copied books anymore, or even learned how to read and write, but everybody went off to fight for and against the Kings of Ireland and for and against the Northmen."

"Better than to die," she said.

"Very like." He nodded to her, grimly. "Yet when men fall to

making war they show a customary want of wit about it, doing it
very ill, and they take it everywhere, like a man who treads in shit,
and then walks all through the house. You may ask my good King
Charles about that, when you meet him."

Roderick watched the solid shape of him, in the gloom, his
voice like music around the bitter, fiery words. "How did you
come here, then?"

"To find more books, and also a little peace such as a scholar
needs to do his work. But the Northmen are here also."

"Leovild said they only come in summer."

John's voice grated. "Leovild is unwilling to see the truth. At
first it was only in the summer. Now they have built winter camps
on the mouths of the rivers here. They are not leaving, save to go
back to their homelands and find more warriors to bring against
us, so that there are ever more of them."

"Are they God's work?"

"Ah," he said. "A new Deodatus."

Roderick said nothing, rebuked. She turned to look back at
the little golden glow of light where Jesus hung, suffering for the
sins of everybody. She said, "Did Jesus bleed for them, too?"

He seemed larger, somehow, as if he were drawing himself up.
"Yes. Surely he did. Surely that is the message of God. The Vikings
are God's work, also. But how to see them so is past my understanding." His voice was smoother now, the music of his accent
like water rippling, and Roderick could imagine that he smiled, in
the dark. He said, then, "What do you think of it, my Roderick?"

"I have not seen them," she said. "I am your child in this, I
thank you for your teachings, and will not presume to match my
wit with yours."

The monk gave a grunt of laughter. "In some things, I think,
your wit is father-wise to mine." He moved, walking slowly toward
the darkened doorway, and they went together toward the way out
of the church. "See, now, the night has fallen, outside, and we

must find our way to the fire, and some supper. This comes daily to all men, the Northmen surely among them; so also must God come."

As they were going out, some other people were creeping in the wide stone doorway, an old man in rags, and some children; Roderick guessed the church was their shelter at night. She stopped, on the threshold, and looked back, at the tremendous darkness, and the little glow of the flame. Everything she did not know weighed on her. The world was far wider than she had thought. She followed John away to the inn.

5

IN THE NEXT DAWN they crossed over the bridge and went along the road north, over the low rolling hills there striped with stands of trees, and down into the Beauce, with its broad wheatlands like lakes of green around the islands of the villages. There, on the third day from Tours, they came on more fleeing people.

These were struggling down the road from the north, bent, brown people, most on foot, among them a few carts, all carrying children, goats, bundles, greybeards and crones, a steadily growing stream. John spoke to the first few, who did not stop in their trudging southward even to answer him. When he turned and beckoned the rest of the company off to the side of the road, his looks gave away his words before he spoke them.

"The Northmen are at Paris," he said. "These people think a hundred ships at least."

Leovild grimaced. He pulled off his hat and swiped his hand through his hair. Another scraggling band of people made their way up the road toward them, three men, two women, a trickle of little children. Leovild turned his gaze north. He thought they would reach Paris late that day, maybe early in the next day. Roderick was watching him steadily; Leovild realized everybody was waiting for him, their captain, to say something.

He said, "John, do you want to go elsewhere—take your books out of danger?"

The monk lifted his head. His mouth twisted; Leovild could read the brief struggle in his mind. Deodatus was quicker to his conclusion. "Yes." He stepped forward, one hand on Leovild's reins, as if to lead him. "We could easily enough go to Orléans—"

Beyond him, John spoke, harsh. "We will go to Paris, with God's help and blessing. I have books there, also, and a King, who took me in when I was homeless, and whom I shall not abandon. Young Roderick. Here the choice is clearly yours. You delivered us from danger, and now we have brought you into more, and if you wish to go on your own way, we would rejoice always in the knowing of you."

Deodatus' face twisted, and he wheeled around. "You're mad. Why should we rush into danger willy-nilly?" He stamped off away from them all, furious.

Roderick said, in his grave voice, "I have not yet even seen an enemy, Brother John; you think ill of me if you believe I will run away from rumors. You have made me curious about Paris, and now about the Northmen, and I will go with you to see them." He glanced over his shoulder at Seffrid, sitting on the wagon seat with the reins in his hands, a smile half buried in his beard. "Seffrid and I."

John said, "I knew you would not flinch from this. For whatever becomes of you because of us, I pray, forgive us now, but I thank God for your company and your help. Leovild, we must push on hard. This man just now has said there are more ships coming up the river."

Deodatus wheeled. "Every day more Vikings at Paris, and still you are going there—"

John faced him. "You also, Deodatus."

The smaller monk braced himself, like a donkey at the end of a lead line. "I will not."

"Well, then, do as it pleases you." John's voice thinned, quivering with some unspoken threat. "Only, go naked, because you will find those clothes more a burden than a help, I promise you."

The little monk swallowed, his eyes glassy; his hands went to the breast of his cassock, where the cross hung. He stood there a moment, his eyes on the ground, alone in the middle of them. John gave him only another moment's attention, and then turned and started off again down the road, where now another weary line of people trudged by, barefooted, with all their lives bundled on their backs.

Leovild reined his horse around by Seffrid, who was driving the mules. "Are these brutes fit for a hard march?"

"Set us to it," Seffrid said.

"Let's go." Leovild drew his horse back. Seffrid prodded the mules up into a jiggling trot, the others closing in around the wagon, and John trotting easily along beside with his staff. After a few moments, Deodatus caught up with them, a little red in the face, and jumped up and rode along on the back of the wagon, and so they all went on down the road to Paris.

Around midafternoon a thin drizzle began to fall. The sky before them was very dark. Deodatus, riding along in the tail of the wagon, pulled the hood of his cassock around his face and drew his feet up under him, and ached for a stoop of wine. The jostling of the wagon woke up a thousand hurts in his bones; his teeth rattled; he felt now also the slow swell of his bowels, which soon would require him to get down and go off and relieve himself, and then have to run hard to catch up, because they would not wait for him.

He should have left them. Gone to Orléans. John had given

him permission, in a way, or said something Deodatus could have called permission, wherever he had the chance to argue his case— there were those of rank who held John in low regard, who would hear tales against him—

Through the grey mists he saw fields, and ahead, the long low line of the country, the broad open lands featureless in the foggy air, the stretch of forest only a dark blur. He wondered where they were. That was the real reason not to go off by himself; he had no idea where Orléans was from here.

He thought of a certain great one who held John in suspicion. When they reached Paris, Northmen or no, he would write to the Archbishop at Reims and tell him of John's sins. He warmed himself over the fire of that revenge.

Though here too were thorns and nettles. The letter would be hard; he had to be sure every word was rightly declined and conjugated. The Archbishop pounced like a cat on errors in the Latin.

Up ahead, Leovild gave a shout. They were stopping to rest the mules. Deodatus leapt down off the wagon and went swiftly away, across the ditch, into the fallow field beyond, and squatted and emptied his bowels. Back on the road his companions were standing close together, talking. His companions. He clenched his teeth over that; he was nothing of their kind; he shared with them the bread of the flesh but not the spirit. They held him in no regard, and he hated them all.

They were all liars, anyway, he knew, all sinners. No matter how much they pretended to be godly men, they were fallen, the more fallen because they made pretensions to godliness, the more sinners because they claimed to hate sin. Deodatus loved sins, especially the sins of other men, which he hoarded away in his memory like a treasure.

He watched the straight back of the young Spanish knight, who was listening with head cocked to something John had said; whatever Roderick said in answer made them all smile, and Leovild flung one arm around the young man's shoulders. Deodatus rose, pulling his garments around him, and went toward the wagons again. But he dared not join them; even when he stood among them, he was not one of them, as if they traveled in a little crystal sphere, and he outside in the rain. He stopped by the tail of the wagon.

"Deodatus," Roderick said, and turned and held out the wine-skin toward him.

He mumbled something, eager. Splashed up the road and took the skin, glad to have it, although he wished he did not have to take a favor from this man.

This Spanish Roderick he hated most of all, perhaps even more than John, his old enemy. Not merely that the boy openly favored John, and had driven him, Deodatus, away, but something else, there was something else, there was something wrong about him. Whenever Deodatus got too near him, he felt a slow rough heat in his skin, like a warning, sometimes strong as nausea. Something wrong. Something sinful.

He drank of the wine, a good long pull, looked to see if any-one was watching, and drank again, deep, although there was matter in it, from being jounced around. The other men were talking again, heads together, shutting him out. He drank several long swallows, heating his belly, his blood; his mind eased a little. For a moment he felt good, and warm, and one of them.

In a moment they were going on, the mules quickly moving out to a brisk trot; he ran along awhile, letting all the others get ahead of him, and then when none was watching, scrambled up onto the wagon beside the wine cask. Bundled in his cassock, warmer, a little drunk, he felt better. Soon he would be in Paris, in his own cell, with dry clothes, and warm feet. Then let John bellow his outrageous ideas and swing his big fists, and laugh. Deodatus would keep his nominatives and accusatives straight, he would avoid ablatives altogether, and properly and grammatically the Archbishop would know all. He drowsed.

A yell woke him with a start. The wagon shifted under him; he slid a little backward into the wagon bed, up against the hard edge of a box of books, and knew they were stopping. He leapt down out of the wagon and looked forward.

They had come up over the crest of a low rise, under a sky dark with heavy clouds, and the rain slapping in their faces. Across the western seam of the world, between the flat stretch of the cloud and the land's edge, the sky ran streaks of dull red. Much closer, to the east, the river curved around up from the south in its long loop through the rainy countryside, its surface brighter than the new green fields on either side. Greyed over in the rain, the trees along the river made a wooly line of darker grey-green. Farther over, to the east, a familiar knobby tree-cloaked hill rose, crowned with its monastery. They were almost to Paris.

Yet the monk's heart sank. Up from the lowlands along the river, long clouds of smoke were rolling. Down there half a dozen places burned.

But not Paris. Beyond the smoke, where the road leapt the river on its piers of stone, the city stood, sailing on the bosom of the water. The rain blurred the dark mass of the cathedral of Our Lady, at the east side of the island, and the palace to the west of it, but Deodatus knew them from old memory; he took a step forward, longing, toward that shelter. Then he saw what Leovild was pointing at, down there.

In the river west of the island, faint in the rain, like a cluster of reeds, were the masts of ships. They crowded the water all the way from the lower shore of the city's island, past the wharfs at the great monastery of Saint-Germain, on the south bank, at the foot of one of the long flat plumes of smoke, and on down to the curve in the river.

"They've burnt Saint-Germain," Deodatus said.

"And Saint Vincent and Holy Cross," John said, pointing toward the other smokes.

"There are so many of them," Leovild said, in a flat voice.

"Yet not a hundred ships," John said. "Not near to that." He leaned on his staff, staring down the road, the brim of his hood pulled far forward against the rain. "Likely, as they said, there are more to come. We must get across the bridge into the city. Let us go on quickly, and see what the Northmen will do."

Roderick said, "I mark the bridge—we shall have some trouble there, I think."

"Yes." Leovild's voice was taut. "Seffrid, can you get up a gallop here?"

"Depend on it," Seffrid said.

"Good, then we are agreed—we have to run for it." Leovild looked around at each of them. "John and Deodatus, you must ride in the wagon, behind Seffrid. Roderick, take the right side. Let us go as fast as we can make this wagon roll, but watch the bridge, it's always slippery, and there's no wall."

Deodatus was scrambling up the side of the wagon, in among the sealed caskets of books. On his knees, he peered up over the seat, past Seffrid, and looked down the road as if down a chute, down the flat stone channel of the old Roman bridge, to the rainy mass of the cathedral. Roderick reined his black horse up on the right side of the wagon, and Leovild on his bay rode on the other.

Roderick had put on his helmet; his face was white as death, behind the nosepiece, and Deodatus saw with a quick jolt of delight that the young knight was afraid. At a sharp word from Leovild they all started forward.

The wagon gathered speed, its wheels screaming in their axles, bouncing along so that Deodatus had to clutch the flat backless wagon seat with both hands. He leaned sideways to see around Seffrid, who was driving. Standing up, the reins in one hand, the whip in the other, Seffrid shouted and lashed out at the mules and they flattened down into the harness and the wagon wheels whined and skipped along the ground. Deodatus sobbed in his throat. The road flashed by them; the wagon skidded and slewed to one side and he wrapped his arm around the seat to hold on.

On either side were old fields, treeless and misty in the rain. They whipped through a low-hanging cloud of smoke that filled his nostrils with stench. Ahead of them, the road led straight down to the river and across to Paris, but it was no longer empty. Up from the riverbank a pack of screeching men was rushing onto the road, closing it off. Behind the first few came more, and more, shaggy men, with swords and clubs and axes. Their yowling stood Deodatus' hair on end and turned his guts to ice. He ducked down into the wagon and covered his head with his arms.

The wagon was hurtling along, jouncing and rattling, the high whine of the axles like the wood singing. If they broke down—if they crashed—he saw them all spilled out at the feet of the Vikings.

Through the crook of his arms he saw Leovild's bay horse galloping along by the front wheel of the wagon; now suddenly Leovild slowed, hacking down with his sword. Into the space at the wagon's side where he had been leapt a huge man with a wild yellow beard. He climbed up into the wagon bed and heaved up a great club, and brought it down at Deodatus, huddling on his knees.

The club swung down, but from behind Deodatus a sword flashed upward to meet it. Roderick leapt in between the monk and the falling club, and his sword struck deep into the club, caught it out of the Northman's hands, and flung it out and away. The Northman howled, grabbing for a knife in his belt, and Roderick lunged straight at him, sword first, and thrust him back over the side of the wagon; the Viking kicked up his heels and was gone.

Where he disappeared came another man scrambling up, and Roderick met him with heavy strokes of his sword, and knocked him away, and yet there came another. Deodatus crawled in under the seat and prayed as fast as he could make words.

Screams pierced his devotions. They were trampling back and forth almost on top of him. "Jesus! Get them!"

"Leovild—behind you—" Metal clashed together; someone grunted.

"Watch there—oh—" The whole wagon suddenly shook violently to one side, the feet pounded back and forth on the wagon bed, and somebody screamed. Deodatus shut his eyes tight, praying.

The wagon was hurtling along, the wood under him shuddering, and the thudding of the mules' hoofs in his ears. Abruptly the wagon jerked, careened around, tipping up on two wheels, and then crashed down with a thump that bounced Deodatus up off the wooden floor and cracked his head painfully on the iron bracket of the seat.

A foot brushed his knee. He felt the harsh heat of Roderick like a rash on his skin. Suddenly a terrible exaltation filled him, as if the life in him doubled. He surged up, his fists clenched, to fight beside the others. Scooting out from under the seat, he got up onto his knees, and looked, his eyes popping, backward across the swaying wagon bed.

The wagon was flying down the road, almost onto the bridge now, but on either side a mob of men ran along next to them, clung to the sideboards, heaved themselves up over the tailgate. In the middle of the wagon, Leovild and Roderick, back to back, their swords gripped in both hands, fought to keep the sides clear. Astride his boxes of books John stood poking with his staff at a man climbing up over the back of the wagon. In front, Seffrid, braced on widespread feet, lashed at the horses and the swarming mob with his whip. Deodatus looked wildly around for a weapon, to join them, to do battle beside them.

Leovild wheeled toward him. "Deodatus! Stay down!" There was a Northman running alongside the wagon; as he reached out to grasp the wooden side, Leovild wheeled, and the sword in his hand hacked down across the Northman's arm, and the blood sprayed up in a wave of drops.

Deodatus' belly rolled. The lust for battle left him like a gas. Not his work, this, not for him. He crept down under the wagon seat and folded his arms over his head. The heat made him itch all over. Tears came to his eyes. The wagon bed under him was bouncing up and down and banging his back against the seat above him. Through the screams and roaring he heard the thready whine of the wheels on stone, and knew they were on the bridge. He cried out to God, Who had abandoned him. Something horrible and heavy fell on him, pinning him down. He knew he was about to die, they were killing him; they had saved the books, not him. Then suddenly the wagon was slowing, the noise faded, and the wagon stopped.

The heavy weight still pinned him; he groaned. Surely he was dying, all his good works for nothing, all his prayers. The weight lifted up and heaved off, and John reached down and pulled him to his feet by the front of his cassock.

"No worse for it, Brother?"

Deodatus was shaking violently from head to foot. He looked into the Irishman's broad, unfrightened face, turned, and cast his gaze around them. There was a dead man sprawled in the floor of the wagon; that was what had fallen on him. Roderick was walking heavily away, head bowed, got to the end of the wagon, and jumped off. Deodatus lifted his eyes. The bridge was just behind them. They had crossed the bridge. The wagon stood on the edge of the great irregular common before Our Lady Church, and a crowd of people was rushing toward them across it. His own people, calling in Frankish, cheering their escape. His stomach heaved. They were safe, and he was home again. He staggered down off the wagon and blundered away through the cheering, excited crowd, to vomit in the street.

* * *

Leovild said, "Sire, young Roderick here fought like three men. Save for him and his man Seffrid, we would have died far from Paris. I commend them to you very much, if it please you."

"I'm very pleased." The King got up from his chair, and came across the room toward them; he reached out one hand to John, as to a bond friend, and the big monk took it, but the King's gaze stayed steadily on Roderick. "You are welcome here, sire, although you have come at a perilous hour. Let us hope you see more of Paris than war and Vikings."

Roderick bowed from the waist. She was exhausted, her mind knotted, and all these people around her, all this attention, wore on her like a buffeting. The King disappointed her. She had expected a god of majesty, but this was only another man, if a little smoother than usual, hairless as a monk, with a round belly under his fine coat. She said, "Sire, God saved us, not me. I am grateful for your welcome."

"No, no," the King said. "I am in your debt, for bringing John back, and his new books. You are my guest, Roderick, for as long as you stay. Make yourself free of my palace, you and your man there, and dine at my table." His mouth twitched into an unamused smile. "Let us hope our other guests prove only a momentary trouble."

"Thank you, Sire." She bowed again, longing to go, to get off by herself, and let her mind rest from being Roderick. She felt Roderick like an iron case around her. "Grant me leave, sire, to go and pray—God deserves all thanks for what you are so kindly praising me for."

"You have my leave," the King said. "John, see that they are properly put up here."

John was watching her keenly. He nodded. "Come find me, Roderick, when you are ready. You need only ask; everyone knows where I am."

The King said, "You may go, young Roderick, and my gratitude and blessing on you."

She backed away, with another bow, and with Seffrid went out
through a long dank hall hung with shields and weapons. The heat
of the blazing fire in the hearth barely reached into the room. The
heavy tables for the evening meal were still set up in the center of
the hall, the leftover bread gathered into a big basket at one end,
and at the other the servants were gathered, eating up the remains
of a roast. Roderick found the way out as they had come in,
through the front door.

The drizzle had turned to rain and the night lay on the city like
a lid of stone. Outside the palace, on the broad pavement between
it and the cathedral, a dozen little fires burned, people huddled
around them; she guessed these to be country people, fleeing from
the Northmen. The church beyond loomed in the dark like a
mountain. It would be full of people, also. She stopped.

Seffrid said, "I'm hungry. And I want a stoop of wine."

"The King will provide it." She turned, knowing he did not
care about God much, and did not need to pray. "Go, do as you
will; it is a small place, as the Irishman said, we will find each other."

Seffrid clapped his arm around her shoulders. In a low voice,
his eyes glinting, he said, "Well done, Roderick. All of it." And
walked away across the pavement.

Roderick turned her back on the cathedral. She had to be by
herself, the need like a pressure under her skull. Across the pavement, beyond the speckling of fires, were more buildings, houses
probably, but along the northern wall of the palace, she saw a little
path, and she went that way, past some pear trees, and a low stone
wall. Halfway down the outside of the old wooden hall she found
a little chapel, with a carved rood screen, and a single candle on the
altar, and nobody there.

She went gladly in. Above the altar, a cross hung on the wall;
she fixed her eyes on it.

She knew that God Himself had saved her. God had preserved her in the battle to the bridge, helped her fight like that, warded off swords and blows, brought her through alive. She could remember nothing but the wrench and wild swing, the screaming and staggering of it, a savage rolling red-shot eye, a spurt of blood, the crunch of bone under her sword. A dazed upwelling gratitude filled her, not that she had done such work, but that God watched over her.

She remembered what the monk Deodatus had said, about how to pray. That seemed right to her now. She knelt down on one knee and put her palms together, as if she were putting her hands between the hands of her Lord, and shut her eyes and thought, To God. To God only. Only God.

The weight of exhaustion slipped away from her; she felt at once lighter, warmer, safe. She felt God all around her, her true Father. Now her heart swelled, sore and weary, into a burst of weeping. My Father, she thought. My real Father Who loves me. She leaned on the altar, bowed down over her hands pressed together, her eyes squeezed shut, and yielded herself utterly.

The King said, "He seems only a peeled twig of a boy." He dropped into his chair again. Behind him was his little yellow-headed page; he lifted his hand, and the boy brought him a cup of wine.

John said, "What Leovild said is true. He fights like the finest knight in your service. Like Leovild himself." John touched his fingers to the table in front of him. They had opened the sealed caskets and brought out the books. The light of the bunched candles glowed on the soft crumbling edges of the scrolls. They would fall to pieces, he knew, as he opened them. He would have to transcribe them scrap by scrap. The work seemed like love to him, the warm welcome hearth-place of his mind. "It was a long trip," he said. "In faith, I would not have gone for less than these."

"My friend," the King said, "may these works take you on longer ones. I am to my supper, late. Will you sup with me?"

"I will, if it please you. First I should settle young Roderick."

"He is welcome also." The King rose. The page came up with his cloak.

"I cannot promise that," John said. "He seemed so spent. But soon you must sit down with him, and talk. He will please your soul, I vouch for that."

"Perhaps tomorrow, then. Early. I shall summon Leovild also, and some others; we must discuss what to do about the North-men."

John said, "Even now, they have not gone above the bridge. They cannot get their ships past the bridges, and they never go far from their ships."

"I think it's too late to build bridges," the King said. "Go; I will see you later." He went off toward the hall, with the page on his heels. Some of his other men waited for him by the door.

John put the scrolls back into the casket, left it on the table, and went out. His body ached, his back, his shin where a North-man's club had glanced off, and his wrists and shoulders from swinging his staff; his head hurt suddenly. He was tired. He went down through a side door, to go to his cell in the cloister just beyond the palace's back wall.

He stood on the threshold, the palace at his back. The rain had stopped, mostly. Through the pear orchard the west wind came, smelling of the river, the air softer than before the rain fell. The sun would shine in the morning. The city felt close around him. The stillness of the place bothered him. Now that he was home, he longed suddenly and perversely for the road he had just left, the wild country, the sounds of birds, the sleeping on the ground and drinking from streams, but especially the steady hard walking, such as he had done as a boy. Then he had walked all over Ireland from monastery to monastery, looking for books to read, and the broad sky like the face of God watching him. Inside these walls, confined like a tamed bird, he would sit more than he would walk. Against the pleasures of his study lay the grim work of the King and his endless wars. He thought of the Northmen in the river: he had brought his books into a perilous place.

Now, above him, through the branches of the pear trees, he could see stars shining. He had work to do here, which would last beyond the Vikings; he would be happy enough.

As he went along the path through the orchard, he came to the little chapel there, the King's church. He went to the door and looked in, and saw Roderick, by the altar, slumped forward over his praying hands.

John stood there a long moment, studying him, savoring the boy's sweetness and youth and innocence, and after a while, slowly, it came to him that he was looking at a woman.

This understanding slid quietly into its place in his mind; he knew it was true even before he thought it. Startled, he looked at her sharply, with new eyes, and as he did so he began to see, around her, a flush of yellow light.

His breath stopped in his throat. He froze where he stood, afraid to move. The light grew and deepened, all around her, and he saw that it formed a great being, man-shaped, but vast, bigger even than the chapel, kneeling over her with arms around her, protecting her.

Then the creature's head began to turn, slowly, to face John. The monk shivered, watching that great head turn; his limbs tingling, he came back to himself, and at the last moment, just before it would have looked full into his face, he turned his gaze away, to avoid meeting its eyes. He seemed to feel its gaze pass over him like a warm wind. When he looked back, an instant later, the flush of light was gone. Only Roderick was there, huddled asleep at the foot of the altar. But in the air, for only a moment, hung the trace of an ineffable, unworldly scent.

He crossed himself. He knew he had been warned. Quietly he went back out into the night, and stood there a moment. For the moment he could not think about this: too large for his mind. He went on to the cloister and his cell, to wait until she came to him.

6

JOHN WALKED ON TO the old monastery on the other side of
the pear orchard from the palace, which stood near where it
was said that Saint Denis had prayed, just before the Romans
took him and cut his head off. At this moment nearly every im-
portant churchman in Paris was gone off to Rome, to try to win
the Imperial Crown for King Charles, and so the dormitory was
nearly empty. He found a cell with a good mattress, put away his
cloak and staff, and went out to the pump in the yard to wash his
hands and face.

He watched his hands busily scrubbing themselves under the
rush of cold water, and dread flooded in on him. He thought about
what he had seen, back at the chapel. It was real, he was almost sure
of that, lacking substance but having essence, like sunlight, like the
wind. Therefore it came from God, and was good. He was almost
sure of that. His heart hammered. As he was shaking his hands dry,
he saw Roderick coming toward him across the pear orchard.

Even now, knowing, he found it hard to see her as a woman;
she walked like a man, slender and upright with her head high, a

little arrogance in her stride, her arms swinging loose. He crossed himself, unnerved: it was a lie, she was false, surely.

Yet her eyes were direct and honest. She came up to him, smiling, and face-to-face with her, he took heart. He liked her. Even now, knowing so much, still he liked her, maybe more.

She said, "John, I am here, and very tired—show me where we are to sleep."

He scrambled gratefully into the scaffolding of everyday talk. "I will, at once." He put down the pump handle and hung the bucket up and started off. "Are you not hungry?"

"That too." She strode along beside him; they went along the length of the cloister, to a cell near the end, which the monastery usually kept for guests of the King. It was empty, and cold, but there were two straw ticks on the floor, and a table. She looked around it briefly and nodded.

"Thank you." She smiled at him again. She looked exhausted, her eyelids drooping, even her smile heavy. "Now the food."

He laughed. "This way." He led her off back straight through the pear orchard, toward the palace again. He saw now the narrowness of her wrist, her long slender fingers, and wondered how she held a sword. He wondered why she disguised herself. The memory of their talk under the wagon leapt into his mind—the father, the forced marriage. He understood much better now.

He liked her. He trusted her. He would not worry any more about the other thing.

He said, "You may sup with the King and me, if you wish. The King himself suggested it."

She gave him a quick, alarmed look. "Should I do that?"

John laughed. "No, no, if you must rest, you have earned it, twice over. The King will see you another time. There will be many such times."

She sighed. "That's good," she said, and went into the hall ahead of him.

There the stewards had brought out bread and cheese for the hall servants. At the long tables men and women scrambled for the best of it. John took her to the head of the table, under the eyes of the stewards, and made her known to them; then her man Seffrid was coming toward them.

John stepped back, looking Seffrid up and down; now it struck him odd such a rough, rude man traveled with her. Seffrid treated her like a man, knocked companionably into her, looked her in the eye, made a rough joke. Yet certainly he knew. John watched her break a loaf of bread in her long sunburned hands.

"My lord—Brother John—"

He turned; it was the King's page, young Odo, who was a hostage for somebody: a well-born boy. "Yes," John said.

The boy said, "My lord the King will see you at table, sir, if you will come."

"I will," John said, and followed the page.

Odo led him outside again, and around to the far end of the hall, to the gynaeceum, the women's quarters, which had a separate entrance from the rest of the hall. The King's table was very near the door. When John came up to it, he found Deodatus already there, and knew why the King had not waited for him to come on his own.

The sight of Deodatus at once set John's teeth on edge. The other monk sat hunched like a toad over the table on the King's left hand. He kept his back to the women in the deeper part of the room. John went up and sat opposite him, on the King's other hand from him.

The meat was already on the table, with a good loaf, and some cheese. In a long-spouted ewer there was wine, and the page came up and poured John's cup full.

Beside him, Charles said, "Have you settled your young knight?"

"Yes—he is in the hall, now, eating." The King had spoken in Latin and so John answered him.

Deodatus said, "Roderick, you mean."

His voice grated on John's ears. He gave Deodatus a sharp, hard look. The other monk lifted his head, his eyes glittering.

"Have you told the King, by the by, how you nearly lost us all our lives, John?" Deodatus turned to the King. "John is always falling in with evil strangers—like this Roderick."

John tore a chunk from the loaf. In his mind he saw her in the chapel, with the angel all around her. "That same evil stranger saved your neck, you scaremonger."

The King seemingly paid no attention to this. He was cutting little bits off the joint of meat before him. John knew he listened keenly to it all. He heated a little at the King. Charles always heard best around corners; nothing ever satisfied him that came at him straight on. Deodatus reached for the wine cup before him. John did not see him eat.

"My neck would not have been in peril, as I say, save for your loose mouth."

"I think more than your neck is in peril," John said. "You should thank God that you are here alive, you sot."

The King grunted. "Not much to separate a sot from a Scot, surely, anyway?" He chuckled, and pushed the meat away. All Romans called the Irish Scots.

"The table is between us," John said, glaring at Deodatus. "Luckily for him."

The other monk drank again. "Rather the wine of the grape, don't you think, than the wine of false teachings."

The King said, "Leave off, will you, I am weary of it." He wagged his finger at John. "I need you to deal with the villagers, and all these other people who have come in for refuge."

"Where are they?"

"Many are in the church. And the village is crowded with them."

"Is there bread for them?"

"Go to the palace ovens and arrange it."

Deodatus was watching them with eyes shifting from one to the other, and now he said, "Sire, I have no place here, I should go."

John and the King turned toward him, surprised. "Then go," said the King.

"No—" Deodatus put his cup down. "I mean, I could leave Paris."

John leaned his forearms on the table. "What place do you have if not here? You are a monk of Saint Denis. We will need help tending sick and wounded—"

Deodatus was blinking rapidly at him, and now turned to the King again, his hands moving. "No, no, I am no good here. I will go and find help!" The last came out in a little rush, almost triumphant. "Send me to Orléans. Or Rome!"

"Anywhere there are no Northmen," John said. He sat back, one hand on the table.

"You're mad," said the King. "We need everyone here, as John says. Also there is no way out. You came in today; was that easy? So much harder to get out."

Deodatus' eyes widened, sleek with fear. "You mean we are trapped here."

John sat back. The monk swallowed, his eyes drifting toward the wine cup. At that moment, behind them, in the deep of the room, there was a little burst of women's laughter, and Deodatus jerked his head up, taken by another triumphant idea.

"The Queen is here, and the Princess Alpiada—I could get them to safety."

The King's face settled, and his eyes half closed. John said, "There is no way out, Deodatus."

"You could give me some soldiers!" Deodatus suddenly beat

his hands on the tabletop. He shot a furious look at John and then turned to the King, wheedling. "The Queen, Sire! Poor little Alpiada! Do you want them to be here when the Northmen take the city?"

John bit his lips together. Words simmered on his lips, and he fought them, knowing his sin, his anger, knowing also it would do no good to speak. The King twisted, trying to get out of Deodatus' way, and the monk went at him like a fox on a hare.

"The Northmen will seize us all to ransom, or worse, or worse, and the women, oh, how sorrowful that will be, Sire—"

John gripped the edge of the tabletop. The King was turned almost entirely away, and Deodatus leaned toward him like a serpent striking, like a crow, harrying him. "Sire, I can get them out—just to Sainte-Geneviève—They'll never take Sainte-Geneviève."

John said, "Deodatus, no more!"

The monk wheeled on him, snarling. "You stay out of this!"

The King said, "No more, Deodatus. There is no way out."

"A boat—at night—"

"No more!"

Deodatus subsided. His eyes glittered. He said, in a meek voice, "I think only of the Queen, and poor little Alpiada."

John clenched his fist. That, he knew, was untrue, and in a flash he saw that for Deodatus there was no truth, not God's truth, not the small everyday truths that got most men through their lives. All he saw was what he wanted. Looking out into the whole wide world, he saw nothing but himself.

He opened his fist. His anger dribbled away. He gave the King a look of sympathy. Deodatus was muttering again; he would not leave this alone, he would wait until John had left to start it up again. John wanted to leave. He was tired to his bones. He wiped his hand across his face, waiting for a moment when he could ask the King's permission to go. Deodatus turned to him, saying something.

John looked at him, surprised; he had not heard the words, and now, looking into Deodatus' face, he made no answer.

Deodatus said, "Well?"

John said nothing. He saw no reason to answer Deodatus, who was not really there. He turned to the King and said, "May I go, Sire?"

The King lifted his hand, not speaking. His face was seemed and pouchy. John got up and went to the door. Deodatus spoke after him, but John said nothing, and went out into the darkness and walked back to his cell.

The King sent Deodatus away as soon as he could. The women were already gone to bed. The page Odo came up toward the table, and Charles nodded to him.

"Go to bed, boy. Take the rest of the bread."

"Thank you, Sire." The boy took the loaf and went off. King Charles got himself off his chair; his bones creaked, and he felt stiff as if he already lay dead in his grave.

He took the candle, and went out to the hall, to the ladder that climbed into the loft of his palace, and went up.

From the round window there he looked out. The rain had finally stopped. What he could see of the little city around his palace was quiet and dark. Out there, out beyond the end of the island, the fires of the Northmen spangled the shores of the Seine all the way up to the bend in the river.

Charles leaned his elbows on the window's edge, and wondered how it had all come to this.

His grandfather, for whom he was named, had been the greatest man who ever lived, King and Emperor, warrior and philosopher, savior of Christendom, smiter of the heathen, purifier of the Faith, before whom even the Pope came humbly as a suppliant.

That great Charles had ruled from the Danewirk to Barcelona, from the Atlantic to the Danube, the Tiber to the North Sea.

Now it was all gone, what had seemed so mighty, so immovable and sure. This little, later Charles was negotiating now with Rome, moving one step closer to the Imperial Diadem—now that Lothar was gone, his half brother, last of his half brothers, who had been Emperor; only Lothar's weakling young son stood between him and it—but the crown was an empty circle; dreams filled it, and ghosts, and horrible memories.

He felt a practiced surge of rage against Lothar, who had destroyed everything. Leaning on the window, but seeing nothing now except what moved inside his mind, Charles struggled to keep up that saving wall of rage, until it gave way to worse, to a sickening, sliding, bottomless guilt.

He did not deserve the guilt; he had not asked to be born.

He had gotten one ability of his grandfather's: he could see the thing long and wide, a single, whole piece. He knew, looking back, that the ruin of the empire was his father's doing, as much as his brother Lothar's.

His father was Louis, whom men had called the Pious, although there were a lot of other names that fit as well. When he came to the Imperial Crown, on great Charles' death, the realm had been whole, still one, and still vast, all the world, save a few, unimportant places along the edges. On his accession the new Emperor, not then Charles' father, was already Lothar's father, in fact, had three sons, and he made an ordinance to divide the empire among them, neatly partitioned, but still one, unified under the Emperor, overseeing all.

Of the three sons, Lothar, the eldest, was to be co-Emperor with his father. The second son, Pippin, ruled Aquitaine and the South. The youngest, another Louis, took Bavaria and the territories around it. They would rule everything together, under the sin-

gle Imperial Crown. This was all written down and mapped out
and sealed and sworn to, to be for all time: the Order of the Empire. For all time.

People died, though. People died. Looking out at the Northmen's fires, King Charles realized he was clenching his fist, and
opened his fingers. An open hand caught more than a closed one.
He ran his palm over his face. All that great empire shrunk down
now to a single city, and that besieged.

The Order of the Empire began to come apart almost at once.
The Emperor's nephew, Bernard of Italy, had been excluded, and
maybe, offended, he plotted against the Emperor, or maybe he
didn't. In any case he was accused of treason. When the Emperor
marched against him with a huge army, the whole fyrd of the
realm, Bernard saw he could do nothing, and even before the Emperor crossed the Alps, he gave himself up without a fight to his
uncle's mercies.

Maybe that was when it began, Charles thought now: maybe,
when the Emperor's mercy was to order his nephew blinded, and
the work was done so violently that Bernard died. Maybe that was
when God abandoned the House of Charlemagne.

The Emperor regretted what he had done, almost at once.
Made hard penance for it. But penance, by its nature, changed
nothing.

Then Charles himself was born.

At the death of his first wife, mother of Lothar and Pippin and
Louis, the Emperor had been inconsolable. Folk said he wept until his eyes were sore, and would not see his friends or even go out
to the hunt, or hear petitions or judge his people. So his courtiers
went about and found him a beautiful young woman, Judith, to be
his wife. The Emperor loved this new wife even more than the first,
and she made him happy, made the world sweet for him again. He
loved the son she bore him, who was Charles, more than he loved

his older, fractious, rebellious sons. More than the peace of his realm. He tore up the old Order, and made a new one, giving the baby Charles a fat share of his three half brothers' lands.

Little Charles had not known, at first, the cost of this. He had known that he was a prince, that everyone petted and played with him, that his father the Emperor was God's warrior on earth, and everything was perfect.

He remembered one day as he sat with his nurse under the medlar trees some men burst in, caught him and the nurse up, and carried them swiftly away. He remembered sitting on a cold bench between two warriors, and realizing, from what they were saying, that they hated his mother.

That same day, he was rescued, but now for the first time in his life he understood that there was no solid ground beneath his feet. Looking back, he saw everything before that moment as a sweet quiet summer day, and everything afterward as winter.

Yet it had not been winter at the Lugenfeld, but spring, a pretty spring of budding trees and birds and the purling of the river there. He had been ten years old then. He had still then said his prayers at night at his mother's knee, and she told him, that night, that the next day there would be a battle, that his father, rightful Emperor, would strike these rebels, and because his father was the Emperor, God would see that he prevailed.

Charles remembered waking up in the morning and hearing from his weeping nurse that his father's whole army had deserted in the night, crept away from their fires and across the field to the camp of his rebellious brothers, and God had done nothing to stop it.

He remembered shivering, not from cold, as he watched his father lurch around the tent like a drunken man, cursing Lothar and sobbing and praying and clutching Charles' mother to him, and then catching Charles himself to him, holding him so tight it hurt; the little Charles had known from this that they were all close to death, the eyes put out, the knife at the throat or between the shoulder blades, the fall of the axe.

Then his father had taken him by the hand, and his mother by the hand, and together they crossed over the field, the last of all those who had crossed over, into Lothar's camp, and there were seized, and for a long time he saw neither his mother nor his father again.

He heard of the Emperor's terrible humiliation at Soissons. He knew his mother was in prison. Lothar ruled in Francia. The Emperor, held captive like a dog at Aachen, saw Bishops and Counts who had knelt before him to swear him sacred oaths walk by without a glance his way, to kneel before Lothar.

Charles knew now, grown as he was, himself a King now, why the fyrd had deserted his father at the Field of Lies. He understood how to them the dismemberment of the realm was worse even than rebellion. That was on the surface of his thoughts, like a reflected color. What he knew beneath that, like rock, was that no oath was sacred, and no man was loyal.

They had not stayed loyal to Lothar, either. The other brothers, Louis and Pippin, rose against him as they had against their father, freed the Emperor, and set him back on the throne. With many loud cries of forgiveness and remorse and regret and all sobbing and hanging on each other's shoulders and swearing to be true forevermore. The Emperor brought his wife lovingly forth from the convent where she had been immured, and sent for Charles from his prison in Trier, and they all pretended to be happy together.

The Emperor made another division of the realm, giving Charles all the best of it; the brothers rose up again. The Northmen had begun raiding on the coasts nearly every summer, but the Emperor paid scant heed, bending all his spirit and strength to putting down his wicked sons. In the middle of a march against

Louis in Germany, the Emperor sickened and died, with his last words sending the regalia of the empire to Lothar. Charles, barely a man at seventeen, came into his inheritance. Almost at once, Lothar attacked him.

He knew what to do, took it as if from his catechism, like a rite. He made cause with his half brother Louis, and together they met Lothar at the field of Fontenoy, on another soft June morning. This time, unlike most of the other times, there really was a battle, and men died, by the hundreds, the best of the Frankish warriors, more than half the kingdom's fyrd, in a single, terrible day.

At the end of it, Lothar had fled, and Charles and his brother Louis held Fontenoy, and all its blood and bodies and plunder, and so they said that they won that battle, that God had chosen them and their cause. But walking on the field afterward, watching the women wail and pick over the bodies of the slain warriors, Charles knew he was as bad as any of them, and that none of them could ask for much from God.

He fixed his purpose on keeping his kingdom together, and on bleeding as little as possible in the process. With his brothers, at Verdun, he made one last division of the empire. This one had stood now for nearly twenty years. None of them had any strength to overthrow it, and each had his other enemies, worse enemies even than brothers. Louis, in the East, had the Slavs and Magyars, Lothar in the South had the Moors. Charles, in the West, had the Northmen.

When the Vikings came again, and he had no army fit to take the field against them, he discovered another measure that worked very well. He bought them off with seven thousand pounds of silver. When they came back, he gave them more silver to go away again. This time they went only as far away as the mouth of the river, where they built a permanent camp, and there lived. Every spring they went out to raid and burn and carry off the people.

Charles could not call his loyal men to fight against them, because he had no loyal men. His splendid elder son was dead, and in the South the Basques and the Northmen and his cousins were dismembering his inheritance of Aquitaine like rats and mice creeping into an abandoned house. His younger son was dull, and weak, and sick, and could not even get a whole word out of his mouth sometimes. The dynasty of great Charles was pinching off like a vine nipped between the fingernails.

Everybody knew it. Anjou was rebelling against the King; Brittany had always been his enemy. Even the lesser lords ignored his orders now. The father of his page Odo had given him the boy as a hostage, and then betrayed Charles anyway. Charles had already put the son to his service as a page, and found him good, manly and quiet, one who did remain loyal, but it was the way of his kingdom to ignore its King.

The Bishops stood by him, preaching obedience to him, and leading prayers for him, but their kingdom was made of words, and he could not pay the Northmen with words, and he could not defeat them in battle with words.

John would have argued this, John whose wild Irish heart knew no master save God, and for whom words were the broad and glorious way to God. Charles wished he had John's heart. His was twisted, broken, bitter, a rotten heart, that knew no truth.

He laid his hands on the windowsill beside his guttering candle. The Northmen's fires were a kind of truth, he supposed, one he had to deal with. What Deodatus had said about his wife and daughter weighed on him. He had to do something.

They had appeared only a few days before, a few ships at a time, until the river was packed with them, and he saw them making a game of running from bank to bank across the moored ships. Their camp spread out along the south edge of the river as far as the next bend. They had not attacked yet, save to harry such as John and his books, and to drive the peasants in from the fields and burn the monastery down at Saint-Germain. They would parley first, to see if they could get what they wanted without trouble. When Charles gave them nothing, then they would attack.

He had some warriors, seasoned, solid men, like Leovild, not many, but honest men, the last faithful men in Francia. He had a supply of corn and water. What he had none of was hope. He knew a single wave of the Northmen could crush Paris into nothing, and drown his phantom kingdom in the Seine. He had to keep on going, but he saw no purpose in it: it seemed to him that he was doomed.

The candle winked, fluttered, and went out. He stood in the darkness. The cold wind touched him, blowing in across the river's swampy northern bank, heavy with the smell of rot. He should have sent his wife away, he thought, and his daughter, and their women. He could do that still, perhaps, as Deodatus said, put them in a boat and scoot them off upstream, except that he knew his wife would refuse to go. It was too late, anyway. He should have built more bridges, as John had said. He should have not been born. He turned away from the window, and with dragging feet went down the ladder.

7

RODERICK WOKE IN THE DARK, hearing cocks crow. She rolled onto her back on the straw tick. Across the little room, Seffrid snored on, his head on his folded arm. She had left the door and the little window in the opposite wall both wide open, because the room had smelled like mice, and now the first uncertain light was coming in. She could hear someone moving outside in the yard, heard the screech of the pump handle. A white cat ran suddenly in through the door and bounded to the windowsill and disappeared. Roderick rose up, found her cloak and hat, and went on outside.

The dark still hung over the island, but the dawn was coming, a thinning of the darkness, so that she could make out the shapes of buildings, and the line of the wall. The courtyard was empty. From the chapel on the other side of the pear orchard came the sound of several raised voices, the words blurred. She found clear water standing in the stone basin under the pump, and washed her hands and face. Gradually the day brightened around her. A bird

began to trill, somewhere toward the river. She spread her arms
out in the cross and made her morning prayers.

After, she went off down between the monastery and the pear
orchard, going down toward the downstream end of the island, and
came to a great earthworks, a high grassy bank all studded with
river stones. She climbed up the steep inside wall and from the top
looked out over the shelving western tip of the city's island.

The outer wall of the earthworks plunged down to the verge
of a stony beach shelving away to the water. Where the two streams
of the river joined again, at the point of the island, there was a
steady rolling curl of a wave. Above the rushing water the night
mists drifted like thin smoke; she could not see the Northmen's
camp through these vapors.

She walked along the top of the earthworks, which ran along
the whole end of the island, a wall of packed dirt much wider at the
bottom than at the top, with grass growing over it in patches. As
she went by the edge of the pear orchard, just before the King's
hall, she saw her black horse, still saddled and bridled, nibbling at
some shoots of grass beneath the trees.

She cried out, pleased; she had thought the horse was lost. She
slid down the earthworks and went to it. She remembered leaping
from the saddle onto the wagon, as they thundered out onto the
bridge, when she saw the Viking rear up over Deodatus with his
club. The horse must have come over the bridge in the calm of the
night. It rubbed its head against her arm, snuffling; she thought it
liked the way she smelled. Its human eye watched her, but with a
horse interest; it licked the salt from her hands, and went back to
cropping the grass.

She stripped off its saddle and the bridle and dumped them by
the foot of the wall. The saddle had left a sweat-slicked mark all
over its back and she took a handful of dry grass and scrubbed it,
and then rubbed the horse down all over.

Finding the horse again raised her spirits. At least now she could travel on.

She knew what she was looking for was not here. King Charles disappointed her. She had imagined a great and glorious Emperor, wise and strong, who would understand who she was, and know how to help her. Instead there was only this bald, uncertain man and his terrible enemies. The horse moved slowly along the little grassy patch, ripping up the grass in big mouthfuls, and she followed it, picking its mane straight, wondering what she should do next.

The sun had risen. The horse grazed along the foot of the earthwork; now she could hear men talking, up ahead of her, and she went on a little way and saw some of the Franks standing there where the great grassy wall came down.

Among them was Leovild. Her heart leapt. Among the other men, the center of them, he looked bigger.

He saw her, too, suddenly, and flung up an arm, and came toward her, smiling. He walked with a loose supple grace, a man on his own ground. She felt herself begin to smile, to see him come.

She flushed from head to toe. She could not meet his eyes suddenly; she turned, jerking her hand at her black horse. "See who followed me over the bridge."

Leovild let out a mild, wicked oath, his gaze going to the horse. "Well, well. He must have run for his life, back there." He put one fist on his hip. "He looks no worse for it. He lost his harness."

"I took it off him. It's over there." She waved back along the earthwork, her eyes meeting his for an instant. She was still warm, as if his look burned her; she went over to the earthworks, and stared out across the great cool emptiness of the river.

"Tell me how the Northmen fight."

He came up beside her. All along the river, the mists were drifting up and vanishing into the air; the clear day was opening around them, and they could see the Northmen now, a dark lumpy swarm on the southern bank, two long bowshots down the stream. Their ships packed the width of the river. Leovild leaned his forearms on the top of the earthworks.

"As they fought yesterday, with clubs and axes and swords. As much as they want loot, they want to be better than everybody else, and so they fight each on his own, you know, not listening much to orders, just trying to outdo one another, but they are strong, big men, they fight hard.

"I can hardly remember yesterday," she said. Being close to him made her feel much better. Being here was not so bad if he were here. She thought of what men would speak about, to weave this talk between them on and on. "This is a great wall, here. I cannot think they will try to storm over it, will they?"

"No—let me show you what they do—what they did the last time." He turned, and with her beside him, went on down past the end of the earthworks, past the other men. Roderick followed him up along the southern shore of the island, with the long wooden hall she recognized as Charles' palace on her left hand, toward the bridge.

The sun was coming out bright and strong, glinting on the rushing water of the river. This flank of the island dropped sharply off in a bluff, steep down to the water; near the bridge there was a landing for a boat, and a path up the bluff to the top, onto the broad flat ground before the church. Leovild said, "This is where they will strike. To take the bridge."

"Ah," she said. "Will they bring the boats up?"

"Who knows?"

She looked down the river toward the Northmen; if she were their King, she would sent up some of the boats packed with men, and try to seize the bridge from this angle here. Holding the bridge, she saw at once, they would control the whole island.

Leovild said, "Come meet my friends."

She walked back with him down toward the beginning of the

earthworks, where the men he had been talking to remained, lounging around, talking and passing a jar of drink. She gathered herself. Here were more people to lie to. Leovild was saying her name, and other names, and she nodded and murmured.

"You came across the bridge last night," said one, a young one, probably her own age, whose name she had already forgotten. "That was well fought. I saw you coming from the tower, I thought you were done, I did, but you beat those devils, you did, black and blue."

She looked up, startled, to see all their eyes on her. Smiling, bright with admiration. Something in her swelled and opened in that shining love. She straightened, pleased. Leovild wrapped his arm around her shoulders and shook her. "In a fight, he is seven men, I tell you."

She said, "God keeps me." Leovild's arm slid away, but the warmth of the embrace clung to her.

She shivered. She dared not believe in this, this friendship, this admiration. Leovild would not be so warm if he knew the truth. None of them would look so on her if they knew the truth. Still now they watched her with eager eyes. Wanting to turn the talk away from her, she nodded toward the distant bank of the river. "Have you seen anything stirring, over there?"

A man with a grizzled beard jerked his gaze that way. "Damn them," he said.

Gratefully she saw they all now fastened their attention on the Northmen. The young man swore under his breath. Leovild said, "They are drinking men, they crawl late out of their blankets, I think." After a moment, the old man passed the jar around again. Their calm irritated her. She thought with so many armed enemies so close they should have been bent toward some action.

She said, "I should pen up my horse, Leovild; will you show me where?"

"I will," Leovild said. "Louis, Hugh, mark you keep a good

watch, and come get me if anything does happen." He started along beside Roderick. "Nothing will happen before they parley."

She said nothing. She saw that to him somehow it was all up to the Northmen. They went on around the King's hall and through the pear orchard, and found the horse dozing hipshot near the little chapel. She collected the saddle and bridle and they took the horse across the orchard and past the cloister, where at the edge of a cluster of huts there was a pen already full of horses. She hung the saddle on the fence, and the bridle on the wall.

Leovild said, "Come back and stand watch with me. We'll have some bread, and more beer."

She started up, wanting to stay in his company, but then she thought of the other men. "I should find Seffrid," she said.

"When you find Seffrid, join us." Leovild lifted his hand; he was moving off, lean and lithe. "Until then." He turned and walked away across the orchard, and she let her breath go, as if she had not breathed until now, as if she had no room inside her for the air.

She shut her eyes. She remembered thinking she would leave here, travel on, seek her destiny. In a few words, an embrace, Leovild had drawn her in.

No, not even Leovild, not wholly. It was Roderick who kept her here. Roderick who had brought her here. God keeps me, she had told the men. Now it seemed to her God kept her prisoner inside Roderick. The horse had come up behind her, and nuzzled her arm, and then lipped her sleeve. She hung her arm around its neck, wondering how she could find her way out of this.

Seffrid got up, yawning; Roderick was nowhere. He went across the pear orchard to look for her around the hall, where most of the house servants were clustered by the fire eating their morning bread, but saw her not, and gave up. He had other business, anyway, and he went to the table, got himself a good loaf of the bread and a pot of beer, drank the beer and ate the loaf, stuck another loaf inside his shirt, and wen on out of the hall.

The day was bright and clear. He walked across the broad open common between the King's hall with its little tower and the squat lump of the church. All along the front of the church, and on the porch, were people in clumps like nests. Beyond that were the huts and sheds and shops of the city, all jammed together as if they had to prop each other up. Seffrid wandered along the front of the church, among the people huddled there, and quickly found a girl who for the sake of the second loaf would go with him into the church and in the back, in the dark, let him do as he wished with her.

The front of the church was full of people also, murmurous with their prayers; he kept his back to them. The girl made no sound, only leaned against the wall, her head turned to one side, so that he could not kiss her. His slid his hands under her heavy skirts and filled his palms with her buttocks, and fit himself into her like a man coming home.

Afterward, he pulled his hose together and his jerkin down, and gave her the loaf. She went immediately out of the church and he followed her. He felt good now, full, complete. The girl went on ahead of him, ignoring him, back across the porch and down to the hollow of the wall, where she had left her baby with another woman.

Seffrid stood on the porch looking down at her. She was much younger than he had thought at first. He remembered the young swell of her body under his hands. She sat the baby down on her knees, and tore bits of bread from the loaf he had given her and fed it. The baby gobbled the bread up, opening its mouth wide for more.

Seffrid straightened, scanning the porch and the open ground; there were people hurrying all around, going here and there, and into the King's hall on the far side. He looked for Roderick but did not see her. He thought he should go back to the hall. His gaze fell again to the girl, feeding her child. She wore no coif, her hair was matted flat, but he saw how she fed the child, patiently, every scrap of the bread, and he knew he would want her again. He stepped down from the porch, into the hollow of the wall, and sat on his heels beside her.

"I can bring you more bread."

Her face flushed under the dirt. The baby's chin was covered with crumbs and she scraped them carefully off with her finger and wiped them into its mouth. She said, "I will be here. Or in the village. I am living in the village, this is only my cousin here." Her voice shook a little. "My name is Erma."

She gave him a quick, unhappy glance. He wondered if he had hurt her. He said, "Where is your man?"

Her face swiveled away again. "I have no man." She took hold of the baby's hands.

"Is he dead, then? Where's your family?"

"No. Not dead—" She flushed again, and he saw she was near to crying. "My family has nothing. We are all poor, we have nothing." She brushed at her face with the back of her hand. "Now the Northmen even have our land." Tears rolled down her cheeks.

"Hnnnnh," he said. He realized she had gotten the baby on her own. No wonder her family would not feed it. He could guess at what had happened, the girl young and hot and foolish, the quick pleasure in the ditch, the long shame. "Do you live here, then? In Paris?"

She gave a little shake of her head. "Over in the Marais. But when the Northmen came—everybody was coming here. I came." She faced him again, steadier. "I had a garden. And a goat. I didn't—" Her head jerked toward the church. Deep lines marked the corners of her mouth. "Before. I didn't do that, before." She looked away, not at the baby, out over the open ground. The baby pulled on her hands. It had no more hair than a monk. Tears spilled down over the rims of its mother's eyes and rolled down her cheeks.

Seffrid said, uneasily, "I can't see it's much wrong, and I gave you the bread." He decided she was lying. She went with men by custom; she had this baby on her knees to prove it. Maybe he would not come back. He stood up, restless, looking around for Roderick, or anyone he knew. "Well," he said, "it was merry enough, girl," and went away, cutting across the great flat common toward the King's hall.

Erma watched him go, a short, quick, bandy-legged man; she wondered what his name was. He had never even told her his name. Her cheeks were still hot. Her crotch was sore. She gathered the baby into her arms and hugged him.

Behind her, Bertha said, "So you're at it again, Erma."

Erma said nothing. She wasn't at it again. The baby had been hungry. She didn't have enough milk now, he was so big, and no one else would give her anything anymore.

"I should think you'd realize where that's going to get you," Bertha said, louder. "Or what, I should say." She giggled.

Bertha was a gossip, and would tell everybody. Erma got up, swung the baby onto her hip, and went down into the village.

Before the Northmen came, the occasional trip up here to the village on the island had been a wonderful thing, a time of holiday, seeing the churches beautiful with candles and garlands, or walking through a great market day, and then enjoying all the goods and all the people spread out everywhere, the excitement and the stories and the music. All that was enough; she didn't care that she could buy nothing. Now she hated the place. All the people crowding in from the country overflowed it, their camps and hovels packed together, their dogs and goats and cows and children everywhere. Nobody had any work, they all fought and drank and stood around talking. She saw men staring at her and the back of her neck tingled. Everybody thought she was a dirty woman. Probably they were right. She refused to think about that business in the church, the utter stranger banging against her. She clutched the baby against her, the only one who loved her, and went quickly past the wine seller's and the well, into the warren of little huts where her aunt Hilde lived.

As she passed the wine seller's, somebody called her name. She quickened her steps. When she glanced over her shoulder, she saw a couple of the men from the wineshop following her.

"Erma! Come on, let's have a good time!"

One of them was her cousin Ulbert, who had already shown her once or twice what his good time meant. Clutching the baby, she rushed up to her aunt's dooryard.

"There you are, you wretched girl!" Aunt blustered out at her, eyes sharp, and grabbed her by the hair and swatted her across the ear with her hand. "Where have you been? I told you to scour that pot! Throw that brat down and get to work."

She grabbed for the baby. Erma clung to him; he let out a scream of terror. She flung up one arm to ward off her aunt's blows. "Where's the pot, Auntie? I'll do it, I just had to find something to eat—"

"Eat! You had something to eat? And where is mine?" Aunt banged her again across the head. "You selfish slut. Go in and scour that pot so I can cook us up some grass and water for our supper, you selfish pig. Throw that bastard brat in the river! Get to it!"

The pots were stacked by the door. Erma grabbed them by their wire handles and dragged them off outside to clean them. Her heart fluttered. When Bertha told her aunt what she had been doing, back at the church, there would be more beating; they would all join in; sometimes they got her down and all she could do was curl up around the baby to protect him while they went at her with their fists and feet and she was afraid they would never stop, they would kill her, and then him.

She dumped sand into the pot and got a rag and began to scrub. Looking up, she could see Ulbert, off beyond another hut, standing there, watching her. When he caught her eye he grinned at her and stuck his tongue out and wiggled it. She jerked her eyes away. A lump formed in the pit of her stomach. She put her hand on the baby, lying beside her, his thumb in his mouth. Ulbert would do nothing in front of Aunt. She lowered her eyes to the pot and scrubbed furiously at it, to try to make her aunt happy.

8

SEFFRID WAS NOT IN THE CELL where they had slept, nor in the yard. Roderick gave up looking for him. She was hungry; she went back toward the King's hall, where the serving women were sweeping out the rushes and garbage into heaps outside the door. Finding nothing there to eat, she went on back toward the earthworks, where Leovild had been that morning, and there came on him sitting on the ground with three other men, playing dice and eating bread and cheese.

"Roderick." He reached up quickly and got Roderick's arm and pulled on her to make her sit down. "Join us."

Roderick sat down on her heels, her arms on her knees. "God be with us all."

"And you," they sang back to her. She saw in their faces the same shining look they had given her when she met them before; in their regard she felt warmer, larger. One short round-faced boy with a face covered in pockmarks held out a chunk of bread toward her.

"Will you eat, sir?"

She laughed. "Make me no such upward man as that. I am Roderick."

Leovild clapped her on the back. "He is modest as a maid. Where is Seffrid? Have you lost him?"

"Seffrid is a busy man," Roderick said.

She turned and looked around. From here, at the foot of the earthworks, the island narrowed down away from her toward the east; the long mossy wooden wall of the palace bulked on her right hand, with its high tower and swaybacked roof. Beyond was the pear orchard to one side and past that the cloisters and some other halls, and the stable, finally, near the river. Swinging her gaze around, she saw in the middle of the island the broad open common by the bridge, always full of people. Perhaps Seffrid was there. Beyond that rose the squat stone heap of the church, with some other tumbled stones and walls behind it.

She sat down on her heels. The bread was good and she ate it all.

"There is enough to eat?" She swung around now, and looked down the river. "If this siege goes on."

The river swung broad here, to sweep around on either side of the island, and then ran narrower toward a deep southward bend in the distance. The northern shore was a green forest of cattails and rushes, but the southern bank stood higher over the water, and a little way down the river a wooden wharf ran from it out into the river and she could see that some houses stood there, once. Now the Northmen's camp lay on it, the many fires feeding the thick air overhead with their trickles of smoke, the ground littered with garbage and teeming with people, all moving, so that from this distance the whole camp looked to be constantly churning, like cats in a sack. Their boats jammed the river from edge to edge, end-on toward the city, and she saw people running and jumping around on them, too.

"We have a lot of corn," Leovild was saying. "There was a

good harvest last year, in spite of all, and the King is thrifty. We can wait them out the whole summer, if needs be."

The pocky boy said, "I'd like to rip their throats out with my teeth." He was staring stonily down the river at the Northmen.

An older man, behind them, gave him a shove. "You wait until you've been in a fight, Little Hugh. Then talk."

"I've been in fights!"

The other soldiers hooted at him. The boy flushed red as sunburn, and turned his icy gaze on the Northmen. The older man took the stoop of wine from him.

"God willing, we won't have to fight them at all. The King will wiggle us out of it. God save King Charles." He lifted the stoop of wine up in a salute and drank, and handed the cup on.

On Leovild's other side was a bushy-headed man, who said, "Doesn't do any good, either way, they just come back again." He spat. His teeth splayed like a little gateway in the front of his mouth.

Leovild said, "Don't talk like that." He turned to Roderick. "Mind them not, they are good men, good fighters, brave men all. It's just the waiting that's so hard."

Roderick took the stoop of wine. "Why wait, then?"

Leovild blinked at her; she smiled, pleased to have startled him, and the others turned and looked at her. Leovild said, "What do you mean by that?" There was an edge in his voice; she had ruffled him.

She drank deep of the wine, raw and biting in her throat. She gave them all a quick glance, and then fixed her gaze on Leovild. "Why not hit them first? They don't look as if they're even standing guard. Couldn't we steal up on them and surprise them?"

Leovild lifted his head, frowning. The old man said, indignantly, "Well, there are a mightiness of them, and a pitiful littleness of us, for one thing." The bushy-haired man spat again, and nodded.

"Here comes Seffrid," Leovild said. He stood up.

Roderick handed the wine on to Little Hugh. Leovild was hailing Seffrid with bellows and waves. The pocky boy was still flushed, glaring away down the river; his fingers curled around the wine cup, but he did not drink.

Roderick said, low-voiced, "Have you then never been in a battle?"

He went red to the hairline again, and stared down at his feet. She reached out and pounded him once on the shoulder, as Leovild did to her. "The cause is just. God will help you."

He mumbled something. Seffrid came up and Roderick stood to greet him, her man, her responsibility. She said, "I found my horse in the orchard. It must have followed us. Did you get food? There is food here."

"I ate this morning," Seffrid said. He would not quite look her in the eyes, and she wondered what he had been doing. Her man: but not always.

Leovild was hunkering down again. "Have a drink of wine, and listen to what Roderick is trying to tell us to do."

Startled, Seffrid looked her hard in the face. "What is it now, Roderick?"

That ruffled her. She folded her arms over her chest. With her chin she pointed toward the Northmen. "I said only that the Northmen seem very unready to fight anybody; look at them— why not attack them first?"

Seffrid cast his eyes up. The old man said, "Have you ever fought against these Northmen, stripling?"

"Yesterday," Roderick said. "When we came over the bridge."

"But not before," said the bushy-headed man, on Leovild's far hand, and he gave a grunt of contemptuous laughter, and turned away.

"Everybody begins somewhere," she said, becoming angry.

"We are warriors. We are fighting men. We should fight. Men grow dull, who sit around and wait."

Little Hugh and the old man let up a yowl. Seffrid grabbed her arm. "Roderick, we are guests here."

"I think it's a good idea," Leovild said. He glanced at the men behind him, and they stilled abruptly. Smiling, he nodded to Roderick. "I must ask the King, and some others, first, though. Meanwhile, say nothing to anybody else, or we'll have trouble."

Roderick shut her mouth, feeling rebuked. She saw they would speak no more of this idea. Burning, she turned to look over at the Northmen's camp again. If she was a man now, she would be a bold one. Nothing in this seemed subtle. She had hunted all her life, and Markold had taught her how to play chess, in one of his friendlier moods. She wished she knew more about the way the land went, over there; she imagined circling around, taking them from the southern, landward side, all unawares.

She swung her gaze to find Seffrid, and caught him watching her, a long sorrowful look on his face, as if he knew where her thought was going, saw himself dragged along after it, and could not swerve to escape. She said, "Come with me, Seffrid."

She led him away down the riverbank toward the bridge. The path wound like a ribbon through the sparse grass, followed the edge of the riverbank, which rose, as they went along it, until they were going along on a bluff, with a sheer drop down to the water. Up ahead, where the bridge came into the island, was a flat stretch along the shore, and a path up the bank. The river ran thick and brown after all the rain, branches and chunks of wood borne along on its rippling surface. The wind broke its waves over little laps of brown foam. On the far shore a flock of brown and white geese was settling down to a stretch of meadow.

"What are you doing here?" Seffrid said, when they were well away from the others. "You're going to make them chase us off."

"How is it," she said, with a glance around, and then staring into his eyes, "that men are commonly taken to be so forward and brave? All I have seen any of you do is stand around talking about how to avoid anything difficult."

They had come to the edge of the common, near the bridge. There were many people ahead of them, and Seffrid stopped, facing her. "They have no heart, it's true. But Leovild liked your idea. He said so—he'll take it to the King."

"Do you think so?" She turned and started out across the common. Seffrid came after her; the ground near the bridge was muddy and they circled closer to the palace. "But he said to say no more of it. That means if it does come back to me, it will be someone else's idea."

Seffrid laughed, and shook his head; she said, hotly, "What is it now, all these head tossings and eye rollings—"

"Nothing," he said. "Only, sometimes I see a little Markold in you."

"Bah," she said.

Perversely, she enjoyed that: Markold she knew was a great warrior. More a King than this bald Charles.

Most of the people scattered across the common were going nowhere, only sleeping huddled on the ground, or sitting in clumps with their rags pulled around them, here a man trying to make a fire burn, there a woman cooking some watery porridge. A baby was sending up a thready wail. She went along, looking around her, seeing no one who seemed awake enough to talk to. Even the ones with their eyes open looked asleep. Seffrid followed her on her heels.

Presently he said, "Where are we going?"

"I want to find someone who knows that country there. Some of these people must be from the riverside where the Northmen are; there were houses, fields, people lived there; some of them at least must have come here." She stopped, letting her gaze roam over the wide common. "Look how many there are, and all out here with nothing, some of them, not even a blanket. Is no one feeding them? What will happen to them?"

"They'll go back when it's over," he said. "The land is what they have, it'll be there when the Northmen go. Here, I know someone who can help us, maybe."

He led her around toward the church. All along the porch and the foot of the front wall were huts made of sticks and piled brush and scraps of cloth thrown over to hold everything down; the huts were packed so close together they seemed one long brown shaggy thing. At the side of the porch, some women sat, and Seffrid plunged straight over to these ragged people.

He jabbered; the women all stared at him, and one tipped her head back, squinting, and answered him. She pointed away, off to the north part of the island, and nodded, and Seffrid came briskly back up to Roderick.

"Come on. She lives in the city, they say."

"Who?" Roderick went after him, back onto the common, and toward the clustered huts and hovels at its northern edge.

"Her name's Erma. I guess she told me that, but I forgot. I met her today. She said she lived down the river." He tossed this casually enough over his shoulder. Roderick frowned.

They crossed the common to the edge of the village of Paris, stretching away to the northern edge of the island. Some of these houses belonged there, having green growing on their roofs, and a look of being carefully made, but in between were others that had been quickly thrown up, leaning on one another, like something a beast might kick up to nest in. Roderick and Seffrid passed a heap of garbage, larger than any of the huts, swarming with pigs and dogs and crows. At the edge of it stood a nanny goat, eating a scrap of cloth, her belly hanging down from the ridgepole of her back like a great skin barrel. A flock of black crows flapped suddenly upward, screeching, and settled immediately on the midden's other side like a scattering of dirt specks.

Everywhere along the slender lanes of open ground that wound among the huts there were people, some lying down sleeping, some in groups chattering and arguing. Somewhere someone was playing a pipe. A screaming child stood before the closed doorway to a hut, banging on it with one fist while she scrubbed the other into her eye. An old woman came by them hauling a bundle of sticks over her shoulder. Roderick wrinkled up her nose. The air was ripe with stinks.

They were coming up toward a low rambling hall, none so fine as the King's with a green branch hung over its open door. People were going in and out, and crowding around it. They passed two men laughing and holding on to each other as if they would fall down alone. Roderick followed Seffrid as he wound his way in toward the door of the hall. Suddenly he threw his hand out, pointing.

"There she is."

Roderick hung back. The crowd bothered her. Seffrid pushed his way through it straight to a short thin girl, whose heavy brown hair hung in a long braid down her back, and who carried a baby slung comfortably on her hip. She was talking to someone else, but when Seffrid came up she turned toward him, and Roderick saw the quick eager hope in her face, and she asked him something, her hand out.

Seffrid took her by the arm, talking, and turned her and waved his other hand toward Roderick. Erma's face altered, not hopeful anymore, her eyes sharp and hard; she hung back, but Seffrid gripping her by the arm hustled her forcibly along through the crowd to Roderick.

"This is my lord, Roderick the Beardless," Seffrid said. "You should bow, he is of royal blood."

"Seffrid, be still," Roderick said. "Erma, don't do that."

The girl had been sinking to her knees; she bobbed up again, clutching the baby. Her eyes searched Roderick's face. She said, "My lord, I mean no harm, I am only a country girl."

Roderick saw, astonished, that she was afraid of her. She said, "I mean you no harm, either, Erma. I want you to help us. Seffrid says perhaps you might know the land down the river, where the Northmen are camped."

Erma's face softened in confusion; she shifted the baby to her other hip, looked up at Seffrid, and then back to Roderick. "You mean, near the monastery. Saint-Germain. I lived in the Marais—across the river." Now suddenly her expression quickened. "But I know someone who does live there. Shall I fetch him?"

"Good. Yes. Please."

"Here." The girl thrust the baby at them, turned, and went off swiftly through the crowd.

With no effort on his own, Seffrid now had the baby in his arms; he gaped at it as if it were a little monster, and turned toward Roderick. "Take this," he said, gave her the baby, and bounded away after Erma.

Roderick gripped the baby, surprised at its weight. She looked a moment after Seffrid and Erma, and then down at the creature in her arms. It stared up at her sadly. It was filthy, its thin face streaked with mud, its scanty hair caked against its head, and she could feel that it was cold. She shifted it so that its head could lie against her shoulder, and pulled the fullness of her sleeve over it, and it turned at once to rest against her.

She caught her breath, surprised. It trusted her. Her heart opened to it, as if she could gather it warmly into her breast. She shifted her arms tighter around it. Someday she might have a baby like this one.

Not Roderick. She lifted her head, startled, seeing another trap in this.

But Seffrid was coming back, with Erma and a scrawny little old man with white wisps of·hair stuck to his head. She pushed away the worry, to think about later. Seffrid brought the old man up before her. "He lived there—he says that the Northmen are camping in his field."

"Ask him—" Roderick glanced down at the baby, now asleep, and gave him back to Erma, and faced the old man. "What is it like there? Here." She squatted in the dirt, and with her hand smoothed it. "Here is the river. Here is Paris." She made a long squiggle in the dirt with her finger, and a dot near one end of it. "Where is your field?"

The old man knelt down in the dirt and pointed. "Here. No, here."

Roderick frowned down at the lines in the dust. Now that it was drawn in front of her, she could see many obstacles to her first idea. The old man said, "Saint-Germain's well, we call it, there, you see, because the blessed saint made it with his staff." He signed himself quickly. "That's where my field is." He made a dimple with his fingertip in the dirt.

Roderick stared at the map; she could see now how hard it would be to get any force of men over the bridge and down to the camp of the Northmen; but the smudge that meant Paris, the old man's fingerprint, and the squiggle of the river between them put something into her mind that seemed much better. She got up, and went on a little way through the village, to where she could see the river running by.

The current rushed along, bubbling. Down there the Northmen's ships packed the river from edge to edge. She turned and went back to the others.

The old man was saying, "There isn't much left of it, really, now."

She said, "Do you have a boat?"

"A boat!" the old man said, and Seffrid stood up, startled.

"A boat?"

Then from the other side of the island, from the great common, a cry went up.

"Bread!"

The girl Erma jerked around, her face flaming with desire. Swinging the baby onto her hip, she rushed toward that cry; the baby, startled awake, screamed in fear and clutched at her with arms and legs, and all around them, everywhere, all the people turned as Erma did, and ran.

Roderick yelled, "Come on, Seffrid!" She ran up through the crowd, which quickly thickened and packed together into a solid stream of people; they swept through the village onto the common, and she saw, out there, a wagon, and a man on top of it, handing down one loaf of bread after another to the people gathering around him.

It was John, the Irishman. Roderick gave a glad cry. There were some of the King's men by the wagon, keeping order, and she eeled her way through the crowd to them, and fell to helping them. The people surged up against them, crying and reaching out, their hands waving in the air. She held out her arms to fend them off as John filled each hand with a loaf.

Roderick saw Erma seize hold of a brown lump of a loaf, turn, and vanish away among the crowd. The pack begging for bread was swiftly thinning; many were coming back again for more, but John was running out of anything to give them. When the last loaf was gone, he called out, "I will come again after vespers!" He climbed down from the wagon, wiping his hands on the front of his robe. The crowd disappeared like a mist in the sun, back across the common and into the village.

John leapt down from the wagon, and with a few words sent it and the King's men back to the hall. Roderick lingered, and the monk tramped toward her. "God be with you, Roderick. Are you finding your way here?"

"With God's help," Roderick said. She smiled at the monk, who alone of all these people seemed sure of himself. "This was a good work. Tell me what I may do to help you feed these people, and I will do it."

The Irishman lifted his arm, as if to embrace her, and then drew back. His eyes crinkled at the corners. "I will do that. Now here comes Leovild."

She turned to see. The tall man was striding toward them from the direction of the palace. He wore a leather jerkin and his sword belted across it; his face was flushed. He spoke even before he reached them, and reaching them turned at once and started back, so that they had to follow. "You must come. The Northmen are demanding a parley and the King needs you."

"I will go," John said. They walked long-striding back toward the palace. Roderick went along beside Leovild.

"I will go, if I might," she said, eagerly.

Leovild nodded to her. "Come. The King will be well attended, with you and me and John."

"And Seffrid." She turned, looking for him. He was behind them on the common, but already walking after her. Just beyond his back, she could see the girl Erma, with the baby in her arms, watching them.

She shrugged them off. She was Roderick now. She waited until Seffrid had caught up with her, and together strode long after Leovild, back toward the palace.

Charles wore his best cloak, long and full, of blue Byzantine cloth trimmed with black fox fur, and he had his crown on his head. Nonetheless he felt more like a fool than a King.

He had to endure this; there was no way to escape it, or the inevitable consequences. With a few of his men, he rode steadily forward over the bridge and out onto the meadow beyond, where some of the Northmen had come out to parley. The meadow was still high in spring grass, dotted with yellow flowers; birds twittered in it, busily harvesting. He followed the path that years had worn from the foot of the bridge westward, along the riverbank. The wind smelled of stale smoke; he could see the toppled walls of the monastery, off in the distance.

The Northmen were waiting in a clump halfway across the meadow. A little way short of them, the King drew rein, and turned to John and said, "Will you speak for me?"

"I will," John said, and went out across the high grass, his staff in his hand.

There were half a dozen of the Northmen. They stood in a loose open rank, taller than even Leovild, their long fair hair hanging down over their shoulders. On his left hand the King could see young Roderick gaping at them, and remembered that the young man had never seen Vikings before.

"What do you make of them?" the King asked.

The youth turned toward him, his face solemn, but clear and open; it was this, Charles thought, that drew men to him, this clarity, as if he hid nothing. He said, "They are mighty men. Do you know any of them?"

"None of these," Charles said. He frowned; he knew the men who led the Northman colony along the mouth of the Seine River, and he had taken these for that band, when they appeared. Now he thought perhaps these were a different band, and his heart sank. There were so many of them. They were eating his kingdom like wolves on a deer. In the end men would say his name with pity and contempt, the King who lost all Francia. His powerlessness sucked at his heart; he felt hollow as a dried gourd.

Out there, midway between them, John stopped, and called, in Latin, "Charles, King of the Franks, comes here to parley. Who is your King?"

They stirred, murmuring, and one stepped forward. "We have no King, we are free men." He spoke Latin badly. "I speak for all."

The King lifted his reins and they all rode forward. The Viking spokesman walked out toward them, all alone, as if he had nothing to fear from any four men. He wore no helmet and he had no weapons in his hands, but he carried a long-handled axe in his belt. The belt also tucked in the braids of his long red-yellow hair. His moustaches drooping down over his chin were also braided. Around his neck he wore strings of amulets. Gold and silver bands encircled his massive upper arms.

The King drew rein, on John's right hand, and the Viking stopped a few yards away, and held his hands palm up.

"I come in peace, see. My name is Weland. There you see my brothers." He waved one hand behind him. He was talking directly to Charles, and John did not bother to translate. "We want silver. You give us silver, we go away." He smiled again, all made simple.

"I have no silver," Charles said, steadily. "I will pay you nothing. Go, before my army destroys you where you stand."

Weland's smile widened into a grin. His narrow blue eyes glinted. "We will take it if you do not give it to us. We know you have no men."

"God will defend us," Charles said, although he did not believe it; but they would expect him to say this. "You cannot fight against God."

Beside him, suddenly, Roderick stirred. The King started. For an instant, in the corner of his eye, he thought he saw a flash of light, but glancing over he saw only that Roderick was crossing himself, hearing the name of God. The King faced the Viking again.

"I have no silver. Go, save yourselves; this is your only chance."

Weland threw his yellow head back and laughed. He crossed his arms over his chest and looked them over at his leisure, as if he were the master, and they his slaves. He said, "We wait for you a day to think. We want what you have, you give it, or we take it. One day." He turned on his heel and walked away across the meadow, back toward the other Northmen.

The King bit his lips together at this insolence. Leovild called out sharply, "This is the King of the Franks!" Weland paid no heed, but only walked on back toward his friends. Charles bowed his head, humiliated. He saw John looking steadily at him and turned hastily away. Yet he could not look up. He thought, God, ask any price of me, only save my kingdom. He expected no answer and the hollow emptiness in his ears told him no one heard him. With his gaze on the ground, he led his little party back across the bridge and into his doomed city.

Seffrid asked, "Did you take what they were saying?"

Roderick shrugged. Slender and upright as a lance, she rode along beside him after the King. "Enough." She glanced over her shoulder, back at the Vikings. "Seeing was enough," she said.

Seffrid kept his gaze on her. He wanted to leave this place; this King was already beaten. They were fighting, he thought, on the wrong side. He wondered how to say this to Roderick. They rode up onto the stone hump of the bridge. Down the narrow stone throat of it he looked into the crowded dirty common. The city seemed like a trap to him now. He reached out and gripped her arm, ready to tell her.

When he touched her a shock went up his arm. She turned toward him, her eyes round with surprise. Seffrid gulped. He could not let go of her. Some power fastened his hand to her, something he could feel tingling in his arm all the way up to the shoulder. She said nothing, only frowned at him, as if she heard his mind. Abruptly the seething stream of force was gone. He drew his hand back.

She said, "What are you thinking, Seffrid?"

He said, "Nothing. Nothing."

"Good," she said, and turned, and began to stare hard down off the bridge, into the river. Seffrid looked down at his hand, which still throbbed, and fisted it against his chest.

9

CHARLES ATE HIS SUPPER in the women's quarters, with his wife and his daughter, Alpiada, the last of his children, who was his favorite. The quiet and calm of this place made it seem like a different world from the noisy outside. Separate from the rest of the palace, the women's room had its own hearth, its own door, and it own small dooryard; the palace women's looms were here, and their children, and none could go in save them and the King.

He thought without this place to go to, he would have long since been mad. Even the low clatter in the background of the women weaving, constantly weaving, was soothing to him, as if they made the world whole again, warp and weft, on their looms.

He did not believe that. He knew the world was wrecked. He said to his wife, "I should have sent you to Meaune."

She smiled at him, but her face was worn, hollow in the cheeks, her eyes sunken. "We should be with you," she said.

She went to settle the place down for the night. There was the low rustle of women's garments, a sudden giggle suddenly hushed, a murmur of voices. The King sat alone, thinking he should go to the chapel and pray. He saw no use in that; God would not defend him against the Vikings; he had given up on God long ago.

His daughter Alpiada got away from her mother, and came up to him, knelt by him, and leaned on his knees, and said, "Why are you so sad, Father? Will you not speak to me?"

With her curly yellow hair and blue eyes, she seemed like a flower of the field. He reached down and took her in his arms and kissed her forehead. But when he tried to say something to her, thoughts swarmed into his mind like a cloud of black imps; of what would happen to her, if the Vikings took her, and how he should protect her and could not, and he lowered his head, and bade her go and leave him.

There was a knock on the door, and a servant came to him. "It is Leovild," she said.

"Ah, Leovild," the King said, and stared at the wall.

"What shall I tell him, Sire?"

"Tell him to go," the King said.

She went, but in a moment she was back. "He begs you to hear him," she said.

"Ah," said the King. "Tell him to go. Tell him I will speak to him tomorrow." He felt he could not stir himself even enough to see Leovild.

She went; she came back. "He says he must speak with you now, Sire. He begs you to hear him."

The King sighed; there were blistering words in his throat, to rebuke a man who impudently disturbed his weary King. He got up, and went to the door, to tell them to Leovild.

The look on the knight's face stopped him. He went outside the door, and shut it behind him, and said, "What is this, Leovild?"

The knight smiled wide at him. "Sire, Roderick has an idea."

*   *   *

The King said, "No."

Their faces fell. He looked from one to the other, Leovild on his right, and Roderick on his left, amazed that he had to tell this to them. "No. It is too risky. We will draw them down on us. Wait. I will think of some way to get them away again, as I did the last time."

Leovild said, "Sire, we can't just sit here until they choose to jump on us."

"No," Charles said, angry. He was King; why would they not obey him? He began to tremble, a little, as if the ground shook under him, and said, "Leovild, go. Wait until I give you orders!"

"Sire!" Roderick stepped forward. "You have already drawn them down on you. They will attack, when it moves them, however it moves them—"

"Silence," the King roared; he was stooped, as if his back were breaking.

Roderick's grey eyes were keen and wide and fearless. "Every day you are weaker, you have less food, less courage, less hope. You will never be stronger than now. Now is when you must fight them."

Charles gritted his teeth. It flew into his mind to cut this lean young sapling down to the ground—order Leovild to smite him down. His mind whirled, confused. He was staring at Roderick, who was staring back, directly, proudly. The King caught his breath. Roderick gave off an almost visible radiance, a grace, as if he wore his soul on the outside; it flew into Charles' mind that he must be a Prince, of sacred blood. He found himself wanting to draw closer, to warm himself in the glow. He drew another deep, ragged breath.

Abruptly something lifted away from him, and he straightened, surprised, as if he woke from some long dream.

He sighed. He turned to Leovild, and said, startling even himself, "Do you know what you're talking about?"

"We have gone all through it—several of us," said Leovild. He glanced at Roderick, and his face broadened again, smiling. "We have everything we need, I'm sure of it. We'll do it this evening, when the light is bad, and the fog is coming up over the river."

Charles said, "It will draw them. You know that."

"We will be ready," Leovild said. "We can pull them into a trap on the bridge, maybe. Young Roderick is right; we will wilt, if it goes too long; they will walk on top of us."

Roderick was smiling also, his hands behind his back, his grey eyes steady on the King. Charles gave him another long look, wondering how this had happened. The boy said nothing, but only returned his look, smiling.

The King said, "God help you. I will pray for you."

"Thank you, Sire," Leovild said, and bowed, and got Roderick by the arm and they went swiftly away.

They had Seffrid already, and they got Little Hugh and Old Louis and the bushy-haired man with the gappy teeth, Guiso, to help them. They had no boat, and anyhow Leovild said that a boat was so big that the Northmen would see it coming. So they ransacked the palace and the city for barrels, bowls, boxes—anything that would float, and carry fire.

In the evening, when the light was trickiest, they went to the shore of the river, below the earthworks, carrying everything in sacks over their shoulders. The air was still, bitter with woodsmoke, deep and shadowy. From the marshy northern shore came the incessant chaotic croaking of frogs. Rags of mist were gathering on the river. Downstream a little, off on the left bank, the camp of the Northmen gave off a steady riot of noise and firelight, a hot hazy glow in the dark.

Roderick knelt down on the pebbly beach and emptied out her sack. The damp air clung to her face. The river's chuckling and murmuring seemed louder in the mist. The others were working quickly around her, stuffing dry grass and leaves and pieces of wood into the little wooden vessels.

She tingled with a sense of power: she had brought this about.

When that idea came into her mind she shoved it out again. That was part of the lie; they would not do this for a woman.

Leovild was going from one man to the next, looking at the work. He knelt to help Little Hugh finish. Guiso came around with the iron pot full of hot coals. Roderick dipped a straw into it, and brought up a little leaping flame, which she dropped into the first of her fire-boats.

Down by the water's edge, Seffrid hunkered down to set his fleet onto the water. One by one they bobbled away on the current, each crowned in a ball of firelight. Roderick gathered up her fire-boats; Seffrid came up to help her, and they carried them all down the beach and set them adrift.

The water slapped the bank as it passed. Something leapt and splashed once in the middle of it. Up there on the far bank, the Northmen were chanting in a huge chorus. A line of dim red dots, the fire-boats wobbled away along the current of the Seine, down toward the Northmen's fleet. Quickly they were lost to Roderick's sight; standing there, looking into the gloaming, she watched the last faint ruddy moon of light fade away into the dense dark foggy air.

They went back up the earthworks on the ladder Leovild had brought, and he and Little Hugh hauled the ladder up again. Roderick looked for the string of fire-boats but could see nothing. The river stretched away from her, black under the rising mists, into the darkness. She thought, It isn't working. Her spirits plunged. She had made a fool of herself. Failed.

She turned to Leovild. "Have they all gone out?"

Leovild palmed her shoulder in a rough quick shake. "Wait a little. Let the river do it. Remember what we talked about. We have to get ready for whatever they do next." He went walking on along the top of the earthworks, back toward the palace, with Little Hugh and Guiso hard behind.

Beside her, Seffrid said, "Look."

She turned. Down there in the dark and fog, a little red light was moving. She switched her gaze to the Northmen's camp, a fuzzy churning glow on the riverbank; even from here she could hear shouting. Had they seen it? Could they see it from the shore? A great whoop of laughter went up. She shifted her gaze back to the tiny drifting red star.

It vanished. She let out a low cry, disappointed.

Beside her, Seffrid said, "There are a lot of them. Look."

He was right. As the night deepened now, she could see a whole swath of the faint red spots of flame, strewn out in their jiggling courses through the dark. Yet none farther than the first: and as each one came to that point, in the dark and the fog, it went out.

"We should have asked if there was a rapids," she said.

"A rapids. On this river? More likely it ran aground and the water got in."

From the far end of the earthworks, where the wall went down, Leovild turned and hailed them. "Let's go—get your weapons, and gather by the bridge."

"Nothing is happening," she said, and went along toward him. He stood waiting for her, only a tall, angular shape in the dark, with his elbow cocked out; Seffrid came along behind her.

When she was almost to him, Leovild stiffened, and flung his arm out. "There!"

She wheeled. In the darkness down the river, just past where all the little fire-boats had disappeared, a yellow flame was erupting into the air. Its light shone on the packed ships, and as she drew in an excited breath, another flame burst up beside it, and another. In the sudden blaze of light she saw the long beautiful shapes of the ships. The red light of their burning swept out across the ripples of the river and billowed with the smoke into the sky.

With a yell she flung her arms into the air. Seffrid came up beside her and she grabbed him, and they danced around laughing at each other. The other men were yelling, also, and laughing, and pointing down the river. Then, behind her, a sudden, great-throated cheer startled Roderick to her shoes.

She wheeled around. A crowd was gathering along the bank where the earthworks came down. People were running up along the riverbank and from the palace and through the pear orchard. They let up another roar of a cheer, whistled and screamed and laughed and waved their arms.

She drew back from Seffrid's embrace. She had a sudden feeling of things flowing wildly away from her. What had seemed the business of a few men was fast growing larger. Now from the Northmen's camp a general howl went up, and she jerked her head around that way. Even in the dark she could see them all running toward their ships, and already men were scrambling across the ships nearest the bank toward the blazing hulls in the middle of the river.

Leovild came up to her; the fire in the ships was bright enough that she could see his face, and he was smiling. He said, "Whatever happens now, Roderick, you have given me back my heart." His arm went around her shoulders in a quick embrace, and then he was walking off, calling to Little Hugh and Guiso, circling around to avoid the steadily growing crowd of people cheering on the flames.

Seffrid caught her arm. "Leovild's right," he said. "This isn't going to hurt them much, it's just going to make them angry. We have to get ready. Let's go."

She took her sword and helmet, took a shield from a pile of them in the hall, got a bow and eighteen arrows from Leovild. When she and Seffrid reached the bridge, a mob of men was already standing around there, many armed with swords and spears, but most with sticks and hoes and shovels. Leovild was shouting at them, trying to get them into order; he saw Roderick and came to her and said, "Go there, see that wagon, find a place so you can shoot all the length of the bridge."

She went off to the wagon, which was pulled up on the pavement, nearly to the bridge but on the right side of it, so that it gave a good view of the whole arched span. The bridge arched high over the middle of the river. The footings at each bank were big, square-built stonework—Roman work, she realized, fleetingly, as she saw how best to do this. She and Seffrid moved the wagon, getting more angle on the entrance to the bridge on the far bank.

When they had the wagon placed, she climbed onto it, and looked down along the river toward the Northmen's camp.

They had cut the burning boats loose. The hulks were floating away down the Seine, their light dwindling as they went. On the high riverbank, the Northmen's camp was oddly quiet, but even in the dark, because of the many cooking fires, she could see the wild stirring around of the men there. Then she heard a great distant yell, she saw all the stirring gather into a dark mass and blot out the campfires, and she shouted, "Here they come!"

She leapt down from the wagon, her heart beating madly in her chest. Seffrid stood there, a bow in his hand, putting his case of arrows into the wagon so that he could reach it easily. He turned to her, gripped her arm with a steadying hand. He said, low, "Stick together, watch my back and I'll watch yours." She could not speak; her throat seemed jammed shut. She put her arms out and shut her eyes tight and made a quick prayer, giving herself up to God.

When she did this, she felt better, calmer; she opened her eyes again. The horde of the Northmen was running up toward the city on the far bank, almost hidden in the dark, but they let up such a yowling and screaming she could make out easily where they were. The Franks screeched back. Packed thick along the riverbank and on the entry to the bridge, they leapt up and down and waved their arms. Leovild was standing on the bridge, his mouth open and working, but if he was saying words, nobody heard him. He wheeled, cast a long look over at the wagon, and raised his hand to Roderick. She lifted her arm in answer. Then the Northmen were rushing up the road toward the bridge.

She nocked the arrow, raised the bow, and let fly, aiming high to drop in the middle of the dark churning mass of oncoming men. Seffrid beside her was reaching for another arrow. Another bow-man ran up from behind them and flung himself against the wagon and drew his bowstring back. Roderick shot again, and again, the arrows hissing through the dank air. In the dark she could not see what she hit. If she hit anything. The Northmen still came on, they rushed up onto the bridge, and Leovild with his men charged at them from the other side, and the two masses ground together in the middle with a horrible shrieking and grunting and the crunch of blows.

Roderick drew another arrow, her heart thundering in her throat; now the target was nearer, she could see them better. She shot again into the crowd struggling onto the far side of the bridge. Something splashed into the river. Iron clanged on iron. Somebody up there was roaring in a raw cracked voice. Between shots she looked along the bridge for Leovild but could not pick him out. The bowman beside her shouted, "I don't know my aim!" She took his arm, and pointed his arrow toward the far end of the bridge. A man coughing and gasping and clutching his belly stumbled past the wagon and sank to the ground beyond. Seffrid wheeled around to her.

"Look! Down there!"

She leapt up onto the wagon to see where he was pointing: in the dark water at the bridge's footing on the opposite bank, some-thing moved. Crept out into the water. She said, "Push the wagon!" Leaping down, she kicked the chock out from under the front wheel, ran around and got the wagon tree and began to pull. The two men flung themselves against it and together they rolled it to the edge of the riverbank.

From here the bank dropped off sheer down to the little boat landing; kneeling down by the wagon, she could see the enemy massing around the foot of the bridge on the far side. The first few of them were struggling out into the swift-running current of the river. Drawing another arrow, she shot into the middle of the crowd.

The dark pack of men swirled suddenly, and she saw one head go down, but then from the opposite bank came a sudden, rising, screaming hiss, and a blow like a stone fist slammed into the wagon by her shoulder.

She recoiled. A hand's breadth from her shoulder an arrow was jutting from the wood, still quivering. She dropped down behind the wagon like a mouse into its hole. To Seffrid she called, "They have bows too." She had only two arrows left; she nocked one, and looked for a good target.

Then from the bridge a huge shout went up. Suddenly the Northmen were rushing back off the bridge, back onto the far shore. Roderick stretched her neck, and now she could see Leovild, there at the hump of the bridge, in front of all the Franks, waving his sword in the air.

The Franks let out another bellow of a cheer, and lunged forward. Leovild wheeled, his arms out, trying to stop them, but half a dozen slipped by him and raced across the bridge after the fleeing Northmen. At the far end of the bridge, the tailguard of the Northmen suddenly stopped and turned. Roderick let out a yell; she stood, and fired her last two arrows into their midst. The half dozen pursuing Franks skidded to a halt on the bridge. The first two had run almost into the backs of the fleeing enemy before they saw what was happening, and the Northmen pounced on them.

They went down under a wash of men. The last four wheeled and raced back over the humped bridge into Paris again.

In the river, the disorderly mass of bodies along the bridge's footing were scrambling back out of the water and up the bank. The howl and clamor of the crowd on the far side grew dimmer. They were fleeing. They were getting away. Roderick had no more arrows. There was no way now she could fight. She straightened, dazed. In the common, Leovild's men were letting out long rippled screams of triumph and shaking their fists and roaring into each other's faces. She realized she was shaking from head to foot; yet she felt no pain or fear, only the need to do the next thing, to make ready for the next attack. She cast the bow and the empty arrow case into the wagon. "Let's move this back."

Seffrid came to help her. The third bowman was standing staring across the river. This man cried suddenly, "That was easy," and ran down the bank a little, yelling and waving his fist at the Northmen, his voice high and jeering. Roderick turned toward Seffrid, wondering if he too thought that this fight was over.

His face was seamed, fierce; meeting her eyes, he reached out and laid his hand on her arm, and smiled but not well, and she knew there was more to come. Then there was another long oncoming hiss and an arrow thunked hard into the chest of the man dancing and jeering on the bank.

He reeled backward, the shaft sticking out of his body; the arrow was burning toward the feather end, a flickering stream of orange. The man staggered a few steps more. Roderick ran to him; he fell almost at her feet. She stooped and crushed out the little flames on the arrow. He was dead, his eyes staring. She put her hands on him, astonished, and felt the death in him, cold and hard.

"Help me—"

Seffrid came running over. As they lifted the body, she looked up, and saw flights of little fires arching overhead, sailing into the city.

Her fire-boats, coming back to her. She wrestled her end of the body into the wagon and she and Seffrid, heaving and grunting, hauled the wagon up onto the flat ground of the common. The cheering and dancing on the common had died away; she heard people running over there, shouting orders.

While she was throwing the chocks under the wagon wheels again Leovild came running up. "Hurry—they've set the palace on fire."

Roderick said, "The King was right. It's my fault. This is all my doing."

Leovild clapped her shoulder with his hand, and then gave her a little shake. "They would have come on us at their pleasure, without it. We beat them back, just now—we killed many." He swept his arm toward the bridge. "We have hurt them. They know we are men now. Come help me with this fire."

She followed him, unconvinced. She wanted to go off by herself and pray and think, but instead she found a bucket and formed a line with several others to bring water from the river to the palace. The fire was burning up toward the roof, in the middle of the wall facing the river, and half a dozen more patches of flame stuck like fiery moss all along the length of the palace's river-facing wall. As they put those out another volley of arrows rained down. Leovild sent someone for a ladder; a man with a set of blacksmith's tongs was pulling out the burning arrows he could reach from the ground. Three men brought up a swaying ladder and they swung it up against the wall and one scampered up while the rest held the foot. Leaning out, he ripped a tuft of fire from the wall just under the eave of the roof.

Roderick stepped back; Seffrid was drinking deep from one of the pails they had just used on the fire. She turned to him, wondering what he thought would happen next, and beyond him saw a yellow glow, climbing higher and higher into the rusty darkness of the sky.

"Look," she cried. "Something else is on fire."

Seffrid wheeled to look. Roderick spun around, looking to make sure that Leovild had this job in hand. They were putting out the fires as fast as they started; she doubted he needed her. She ran around the front end of the palace, to see what else was happening, and what she had to do.

She ran into a storm of flickering light. The whole broad common streamed with firelight. Flames leapt up from the huts and hovels of the village, just beyond. Wailing people in a tide were fleeing from the village, were spilling out across the open ground, through the watery red light. Roderick ran into their midst, toward the spires of yellow flame spiking into the sky above the heads of the oncoming crowd.

The frightened villagers rushed past her, shrieking. Behind them, the fire crackled and hissed and spat, and like spittle, gouts of flame erupted out of it. A woman fell right in front of Roderick; when she stooped to help her rise she saw, in the glaring baleful light, squeaking tides of mice and rats running by along the ground.

She went in among the first huts. This side of the village was just beginning to burn, and most of the people were gone. The highest, loudest part of the fire was on the far side from the common, near the river. She guessed the Northmen had shot their fire arrows from the far bank. A woman towed her screaming children by; an old man trailed her, three people carrying bundles. The air was stinging and filthy with smoke. Roderick plunged into the middle of the village.

She came on a goat tethered to a midden heap, lunging and bounding at its rope, and she cut it free with her sword. The flames were leaping up the side of the tavern. She heard a child screeching somewhere, but she could not find it. Seffrid was on her heels; he called to her, "Let's get out of here!" An old man wrapped in a blanket staggered along by them. A wisp of smoke went up from a hut directly before Roderick, and before she could draw breath it exploded into roaring, rumbling flames. She shrank back from the blast of heat; the air was full of floating embers. She could no longer hear the screaming child. A cloud of thick smoke suddenly enveloped her and Seffrid and she coughed, her eyes watering and stinging. Then suddenly the smoke blew away, and the girl Erma ran up, her face sleek with sweat, her baby shrieking on her hip.

"Where is—" Looking by Roderick, she saw Seffrid, and leapt toward him. "Help us—help us—"

"Show us."

The girl whirled and ran, and they followed her down a narrow lane among smoking, blazing huts, into the throat of the fire.

The heat made the air ripple; Roderick's face felt scalded. The smoke billowed around her suddenly and she held her breath, her eyes hurting. Ahead the fire blazed up popping and crackling, lashing at the sky, a wall of flame, ahead and all around, spreading in sudden bursts and steady advances, giving up a roar more gigantic than a hundred human throats could make.

"Here!"

Half-blinded from the smoke, Roderick stumbled after Erma's voice, the heat scorching her lungs when she breathed. The girl led her to a burning hut. Even through the roar of the fire Roderick could hear the people inside wailing in terror. She saw that the door was on fire, and she drew her sword and began to break a hole in the hut wall. Seffrid jumped to stand opposite her and between them they hacked through the wood and cast aside great chunks of it. The fire was engulfing the hut faster than they could cut; Roderick cried out, "Jesus, help us!" and aimed her blows heavier and swung the sword higher on the backswing, and from somewhere came a great strength, and between her and Seffrid they split open the hut wall and people gushed out, sobbing and scrambling along on hands and knees, their hair smoking, their clothes on fire. They all shrank back, and the hut blazed like a torch. The heat made Roderick's eyes hurt. She flung her arm up. In the crackling of the flames she thought she heard another screaming, and she started forward.

Seffrid grabbed her arm. "Don't be mad! They're all dead if they're there—dead by now—hurry!"

She turned and followed him away. There was no way. The fire leapt all around them, red, golden, orange as flowers; it bounded over them, to swallow them all. The people they had saved sobbed and huddled down to the ground, pulling their smoldering clothes over their heads. Erma clutched her shrieking baby and turned to Seffrid, her face wild.

Roderick said, "There." She thought she saw the way through. She grabbed the nearest of the terrified people and pushed, and hooked another's arm and dragged him after her. "That way! There!"

Seffrid grabbed Erma. "Follow Roderick!"

"There's no way—!"

Seffrid roared, "Stay close to Roderick!" He lifted a moaning old man in his arms and shoved him, and they all moved at once into the flames.

The howling of the fire muffled all sound. The light blazed blinding into their eyes. Roderick stumbled under the weight on her shoulders. Then suddenly they were out of the fire, they were stumbling toward the common, into a rush of cool air and blessed darkness, and Roderick dropped the people she was carrying and fell to her knees.

Seffrid crouched over her. "Are you all right?"

"Yes. Erma—the baby—"

Seffrid grinned at her. His beard was singed back almost to his face and his eyebrows were burnt off. He said, "Everyone you touched is safe."

She got to her feet again, trembling. She was exhausted; she could barely hold her head up. She looked back at the burning village; she thought of the little fire-boats and how they had come back to her as this great blazing beast, and began to weep. "Seffrid," she said. "It's all my fault." She lifted her arms up to him, and he caught her when she fell.

The fire was still burning; people moved around it, putting out its small scouts of flame, keeping it penned up in the village, where the village had been. Seffrid hitched Roderick up in his arms. She was only tired, he knew. She had suffered no hurt, he had seen that already, he had followed in her wake through that solid sea of fire, he had seen the flames blown back for her, quelled for her sake, making a cool tunnel through which they all could escape. Yet in his arms she seemed light as a child.

He lifted his head. Before him, the baby asleep on her hip, Erma was watching him steadily, a question in her silence, in her not-leaving. He supposed she had no home now. He considered that. Holding Roderick in his arms, he had that power around him; he thought he felt it, watching, all around him.

He nodded to Erma. He said, "Well, come on for now, you can stay with us, for now," and led them off toward the King's palace.

10

JOHN AND THE OTHER MONKS were tending the wounded and burned in the hall of the monastery; John did not sleep until after midnight. At matins he awoke again, and said the office, and said prayers for the King and for the city of Paris in its sufferings, and then he took a candle and went down to the writing room, in its own building behind the dormitory.

There on a tilted desk was his work waiting for him, as he had left it the day before. He had given out bread, dragged dying men into the hall and laid them out and given them water and prayed with them, trying to help them die more easily, and yet, in one corner of his mind at least, he had never stopped thinking about this work. Now sitting down at his stool, he felt a great calm drop over him, as if he entered into another, nobler world.

The book he was copying had rolled itself loosely up again, but the new page was spread across the right side of the desktop, a broad clean sheet of parchment, the lines of script already reaching almost halfway down the creamy page, their black march broken in the second line and the fifth by the dark red ink he used for the first

letters of the names of God. The writing was Greek, loopy and uneven, not the tidy, boxy letters of the Latin alphabet, and he had to
work hard to keep them in line. Tucked under the parchment's
edge was a bit of scrap, where he wrote down ideas that came to
him as he copied, for the commentary he meant to write. When he
got to the end of this page, he would put up another blank, beautiful piece of parchment, and on it he would translate into Latin
what he had just copied in the Greek.

The ancient book smelled of dust and rot. The edges of the
scrolls were feathered and bits fell off when he handled them. It
was very old. Its words had been first written down many generations before, in another empire, halfway across the world. And for
all the frothing passion and ambitions of the men who had lived
since, the men were gone, what they had done was mostly gone,
and the book was still there. Even the burning and the blood of
the night before, so close at hand, had changed nothing, had not
so much as ruffled these pages.

He put the candle on the edge of the desk, where its light fell
on the work. He took his pens out of their case and made sure they
were clean and sharp, and trimmed one nib with his belt knife until it was perfect. He unstoppered the inkhorns and set them in the
wells on the desk; one ink was the dark red called dragon's blood,
the other a deep black made from hawthorn bark, which he had
been saving up for years for this.

He picked up the old book, holding it carefully by the edges,
between his open hands. Finding the place where he had left off,
he hung the roll loosely over the left side of the desk, leaned his left
arm down on the desktop beneath it, stared at the line of text a
moment, and dipped the black pen and wrote the first three letters.
Dipped the pen again, and wrote three letters more.

The big white monastery cat leapt in suddenly through the
window, and bounded up to the shelf on the wall and sat watching
him. The careful work collected him. He knew this was a sacred

rite, to copy books, to pass them on, to read them and unknot their meanings and expand them out into the world. Reading this book, now, he brought it to life again, as God had brought Adam to life, as much a ceremony of creation as the Mass. The smell of smoke faded from his memory and the sounds of people screaming. He took the words up from the roll into his mind, and then with his hand put them down again on the clean page. The words remained in his mind, all the while, and he turned them and played with them, like a cat with a mouse, shaking all the ideas out where he could see them.

Coming to the name of Jesus, he put down the black pen, crossed himself, took up the red pen, and dipped out just enough to make the initial. He left extra space around it, so that the artisan could embellish it, if he ever got back from Rome. Crossed himself again, and laid down the red pen, and picked up the black again.

Presently he realized that the room was growing lighter; daybreak was coming. He sat back, resting his eyes and his hand. A sound behind him brought his head around, and he saw the King, standing just inside the doorway, watching him.

"Sire." He slid off the stool to his feet.

Charles said. "Go on, if you were about to." He came forward now, his face drawn and pale, as if he had not slept all night. His gaze went to the old book. "Is this the Areopagite?"

"Yes, it is. A remarkable book."

"And he was the same man who is our Saint Denis?"

"So they say."

The King drew nearer, looking at the parchment. John laid the black pen down. In through the window now the first rays of the sun were shining, and he went toward that radiance, drawn into its warmth like a butterfly, and opened the shutter wide and let all the light in.

"What does this mean?" the King asked him.

He went back to the page, and read the Greek, with its mouth-filling, jaw-rolling diphthongs, and then translated. "He speaks of angels here. He calls them men flashing like lightning, who heap live coals of fire about the Heavenly Beings—"

The King shuddered, turning away. "He speaks of hell."

"No—it is the celestial fire, the eternal substance, which is the source of all light here, as God is the source of all grace. He says that God's grace comes to us in the sunlight, the light by which we see and work, that makes all things visible." John stood by the window; he put his hands out into the sunshine and felt them instantly warmed. He said, "So near to us is God always."

"An interesting idea," the King said. He moved closer, but he was looking out the window at an angle, not at the sunlight. John turned to see what he saw. Off to the left, out past the ovens and the corner of the stables, some of the burned rubble of the village was just visible, still trickling smoke. "God's grace shines on the ruin of my city, John."

John turned to face the King. Charles' eyes were sunken into pits, and his mouth seemed crooked, like something broken. He stared out the window toward the city.

"When this happened, John—both the burning, and the wonder of it, that they did drive them off—" Charles brought his eyes around to meet the Irish monk's. "I was on my knees, praying. Asking God to tell me what to do."

He dashed his hands violently together. John laid his pen down; the white cat darted away out the door. King Charles stalked across the writing room, his face wrenched awry. He went back into the shadows of the room, away from the window. John stood watching him; he could feel as if it singed his skin how the King burned.

"I prayed for God to save my kingdom. Is this God's answer to me?" Charles swung toward him, intent, pleading. "This little victory—they will come back, we may still lose all—there is so little left—" He twisted his hands together, and his gaze dropped away from John's, sagging toward the floor. "They seem like God's scourge on me, these Northmen."

John slid his hands behind him, into the warmth of the sun coming in the window. "They are certainly the scourge of Paris. Yet, it is true, the city held, with God's blessing. Is there no answer in that?"

"They will come back." Charles swung heavily toward him again, gaunt-cheeked, sunken-eyed, and said, "Why does God do this to me?" His voice rose to a roar; a rage came over him as suddenly as a great wind, and his eyes glared and he shouted, "Why will He not give me an answer?"

John said nothing. The King strode toward him, still in his fury, his fists clenched. "Why does God not come with a flaming sword to rescue Christian folk from these beasts from the North? Tell me, John—where is your God now, when I need Him? Hah?"

The monk felt the sunlight on his hands, and said, into the King's face, "You know the answer, Sire. The trouble is that it doesn't please you, and so you want another. But you know what to do."

The King lifted his fist, as if to strike out at him, but his anger was fading, he had no strength even to keep up his temper. His eyes blinked in the blaze of the sun. He lowered his hand heavily and said, "You dare reproach me."

"I tell you the truth," John said.

"Oh, oh," the King said, with a ragged laugh. "That's a dangerous practice, to a King, John. Even for a Greeking Irishman!" He turned swiftly and walked away, back into the shadows.

John kept his hands behind him, in the warmth of the sun, and waited. He saw how the struggle in the King would not let him rest, but harried him along like a demon, eating up his soul. In the shadows, Charles turned to face him.

"The truth? What has truth got to do with anything? The truth is the Northmen will trample us, not because they are good, but because they are strong. And I am not, and so must fail—must see the whole great kingdom of my fathers fail. Why should I truckle to that?"

At this, the King began to weep. John stayed where he was, waiting still for Charles to steady himself and stand. Then, faint through the sunlit window, came the sound of a horn.

The King lifted his head. Like a drunken man he shuffled forward to the window, leaned on the sill, and looked out. "It's starting again," he said.

John watched his face, the tears drying on his cheeks, the crumpled ridges of his brow. A quick prayer for the King flew through his mind and he crossed himself. "Yes, they are coming back."

"I cannot let it happen again without me," Charles said. "Or I am no more King."

His voice was dull but even, and he came away from the window, heavy-footed and solid. He reached out and gripped John's upper arm. "God bless you, you are a true friend."

"I did nothing," John said, with a laugh. "God bless yourself, then. God's will be done."

The King said, "God's will," and turned and tramped to the door and out, not looking back. John sighed. He could hear the horns sounding all along the bank. He went back to his desk, to put his work away, and make ready for the grim and bloody chores ahead.

Roderick woke, wrapped like a baby in her own blankets; she was lying on the straw tick of the cell in the monastery. Daylight was coming, and in the first murky light she could see the rafters high overhead, hairy with spider webs. Beside her on the cell floor other people slept, shapeless lumps on the dark, dreaming and rumbling out snores. The air smelled deeply of all their breaths and bodies. The straw crunched. She watched a rat creep out across a dusty rafter. She drowsed again, floating; she imagined a light all around her, shining and warm; she dreamt of her mother.

Slowly she woke again. The day was stronger, brighter, and now she saw that it was not Seffrid who lay next to her, but the girl Erma, with her baby. Seffrid was beyond them all, lying against the wall.

He was stirring; he began to whisper and play with the girl. Roderick rolled over, turning her back on them. The baby whimpered. She turned around again; Seffrid and Erma were shuffling together, tangled in their blankets. His thick black hair covered the girl's face. The baby sat up and reached out a hand to its mother and whimpered. Roderick took it in her arms and lay down again. The child stiffened at first, but when she drew it against her it cuddled itself into her arms and went to sleep.

She lay on her side, her back to Seffrid and Erma, and looked down at the baby and touched its hair. A cold despair tugged at her, like a sudden cramp in her heart. The baby made her realize how far she had gotten from where she was supposed to be. Its hair was filthy and its face streaked black with soot. She licked her thumb and wiped at its grimy cheek. It woke and looked up at her and patiently endured her cleaning of it. Behind her she could hear that Seffrid and Erma were finished. She supposed now the baby would want its mother back. But it lay still and looked up at her with its wide dark eyes and without protest let her scrub it clean.

Her eyes felt swollen with tears. Everything she did went wrong. She would never have her crown, her kingdom, her King, her sons and daughters, to be Kings and Queens after her.

Then outside she heard horns blaring, and shouts, and she sat up, the baby in her arms. Seffrid groaned. "They're at it again."

"That's Leovild," she said. She could hear him, outside, shouting.

"They're coming! They're coming! Everybody up! Arm yourselves and get to the bridge!"

Her belly tightened. Now she had to be Roderick again.

There was no way to go but onward. She wheeled and thrust the baby into its mother's arms. Seffrid was scrambling and kicking out of his blankets. She said, "My sword," and he pointed toward the corner. Their arms lay there in a neat pile, and she took her sword and shield and went out the door to find Leovild.

The sun was climbing up the shoulder of the sky, its long rays driving off the last of the fog and cloud. Leovild gathered up his men at the foot of the bridge. There seemed far fewer than the day before. Roderick hung her sword belt over her shoulder; she walked out onto the bridge, where she could get a better view, and looked west down the river.

The Northmen were coming up along the far bank in a long, uneven mass, shouting and waving their swords. She went back down to her side of the bridge; Leovild got her arm and pulled her along, saying, "Go get something to eat. Get some wine."

"They're almost here." On the common, a cheer went up. She turned to see the big grey mule plodding out into the open; John, bringing out his wagon full of bread and wine. The mob on the common was all rushing that way now, streaming across the flat ground, but Leovild's warriors reached the wagon first, and held the crowd off.

"They'll talk first," Leovild said. "Eat."

She went over to the wagon. Over the heads of the soldiers, John saw her at once, threw her a round loaf, and then pointed to a big cask beside him. She wormed her way in through the crowd to get a cup of wine from the cask.

The monk smiled at her, not happily, just the corners of his mouth going up and down. He said, "Take care, Roderick."

"Bless me, John." Tucking the bread under her arm, she put her free hand out to him.

He said, "Rather you should bless me." He gripped her hand briefly, hard, and went back to his work of feeding people. She took the loaf and the wine and went back toward the bridge.

She knew she should pray, but she did not want to. A deep anger burned like a coal in her mind. She ate the bread and finished the wine and took the cup back to John. God would abandon her if she did not pray. Yet she could not, with a mind and heart so full of fury. Still she could not say what it was that angered her.

Seffrid came up beside her. "Are you ready?"

Now she crossed herself. "God have mercy on us," she said, as easily as breathing. He smiled at her, his eyes bright, fearless. Nothing much bothered him; she envied him, how simple things were for him.

The Northmen were massed on the far side of the bridge. They were tall, and taller now for their peaked helmets; some of them carried lances, thrusting up in the air in a little forest. They were shouting and banging their weapons together as they waited, but the crowd of the Franks stood still as stones.

Then at the edge of the crowd there was a murmur, and it rose to a shout. Roderick stood on her toes to see what was happening, and saw the crowd parting to open a way, and down the open way came the King of Francia, Charles Calvus, carrying his sword. Behind him came his page Odo with his shield and helmet.

Leovild's face burned with a sudden joy. Roderick watched him leap forward to meet his King, but she had to fight down the same disappointment she had felt before: he seemed so ordinary, this Charles, like the dull metal of pots and pans, and not the shining gold of crowns.

The King gripped Leovild's hands, and said, "I am come to stand with my champions, Leovild. You have shown me my place."

"My King," Leovild said, "we are ready to follow you."

Charles turned and cast a broad look about him, at the men

waiting to defend Paris, and the crowd beyond them on the common. "God willing, we shall not fail." He crossed himself. On his face, Roderick saw he did not believe what he had said.

Yet he was here, grim and stooped and bald and ordinary as he was. She hitched her sword belt up on her hips. There was no waiting for another, better King than this.

On the far side of the bridge, a harsh deep voice shouted, "You! Franks!"

The King lifted his head. "More jabber?" His voice sounded less steady than the words required.

Leovild said, "Sire, do you want me to—"

"I shall meet this man." Charles turned to the page and took the helmet from him, and he lifted it and fit it over his head. He was watching the bridge.

Leovild said, "Roderick and I will go with you."

The King spoke through the face of the helmet. "He comes alone, I shall meet him so."

"Sire—"

The King was walking out onto the bridge; the big man with the long braids came out again to meet him. Roderick stood a little distance behind them. She remembered that this Northman's name was Weland. The muscles of his arms were shiny, as if they were oiled. He carried no lance. She looked down at the Northmen and saw how all the lancers were standing at the front.

In her mind she saw them coming over the bridge behind their lances; she saw exactly what they meant to do, and what would happen. She gripped the hilt of her sword, her mouth dry.

Weland called out, "King! You think it over? You give up now?"

King Charles stood on the high hump of the bridge; he straightened himself, as if he only then realized how many watched him. His voice sounded thin and sad. "Rather it's you should give

up, Weland. You'll get nothing here. Go away and no more of you
will die here."

Weland showed his teeth. "You make me laugh. We want silver
and gold!"

"We have nothing here," Charles said. "All we have here is
iron, to cut your throats with."

The Northman laughed. "You talk like that. We will see how
your iron talks, then." He glanced back over his shoulder, lifted his
arm, and yelled. The first half dozen of the Vikings charged onto
the bridge, headed for the King, standing there all alone on the
hump of the bridge.

Leovild let out a cry, and dashed up the bridge toward Charles.
Roderick screamed, "Seffrid, let's go!" and bounded after him.
They reached the King three steps before the screeching Northmen. Shoulder to shoulder with Leovild, Seffrid on her left, she
got her shield up and her body set. Before her the bridge was a wall
of helmets and glaring eyes and spears coming straight at her.

Weland had gotten out of the way. Four lancers led the pack,
lowering the long poles in their hands and charging behind them.
Roderick gathered herself. The bridge trembled under her feet. She
heard the Franks crowding onto the span behind her. Before her
were the leveled blades of the lances, flashing in the morning sun.

She watched the tips of the lances, saw the ones aiming at her,
and braced the shield to meet them at an angle. The first lance
struck glancing and slid by her knee and she struck down with her
sword, chopping it in half; the second lance hit the shield more
centered, and flung her backward. The Franks behind her held her
on her feet and she wrenched the shield and sent the lance sliding
upward and then the front of the pack of the Northmen was
jammed up against her.

They came point first, knives and axes. She knew Seffrid was
on her left and Leovild on her right, and King Charles somewhere

to her right also; all she had to do was work in front of her. She caught a blade on her shield and struck straight forward into something that broke and yielded, yanked her arm back and stabbed forward again, leaning all her weight into it. Another blow hammered on her shield. Her blade went deep into something soft. She drew back to free the sword and could not, the body before her was jammed up against her, they were pushing against her all together and her sword was caught and now she had to take a step backward.

She leaned her shoulder into her shield, twisted her body back, and wrenched her sword free. An axe struck her shield so hard a piece of the shield broke off; her arm tingled all the way to her neck. Suddenly she was aware of the people screaming and grunting around her. The stink of blood, and the heat from the close pack of bodies. A ripple of fear went through her. She thought, God, help me. She struck low, under the shield's edge, and the blade bit and met bone and she jerked it back again and slashed again low and the body before her fell.

She roared; she pushed forward into that space. A hot, jubilant rage filled her. She could hurt them, she could deal death. The thought flew into her mind that if she died, she would be out of the trap of Roderick. She flung herself forward and with her sword chewed out another space in the pack of the Northmen. Beside her Leovild was shield to shield with a big man, pushing and shoving, and she lunged in and knocked the Northman's shield aside and slashed at him with the sword, and he quailed back so hard he staggered the Viking behind him, and that man with a wild wheeling of his arms toppled backwards off the bridge and into the river.

Leovild gave a howl of excitement. On his far side from Roderick was King Charles himself, his sword raised, screaming in a fury. She saw him, she realized, because there was a space now before them, between them and the Northmen. The Northmen were backing up, they were yielding, and from all the Franks behind

Roderick there went up a chorus of jeers and screams and hoots and insults.

She swayed. The battle fury in her faded. The Northmen had only gone back down to the far bank; to attack them down the narrow bridge would be stupid. She was panting, and sweat rolled stinging into her eyes, and suddenly she was ferociously hungry. Around her on the stone hump of the bridge lay broken bodies. The air reeked of blood.

The King turned to them, haggard. "We nearly fell. God bless you all, for standing with me." His eyes burned. One by one he clasped their hands, looking deep into their faces. "I shall not fail you again," he said.

She wondered what he meant. Her heart felt like a butterfly trapped under her ribs. With Seffrid and Leovild she helped carry the wounded Franks back down onto the common.

The crowd rushed forward now, roaring happily, a mass of waving arms; ran to the riverbank, and ranged along it yelling insults at the Northmen. Roderick looked down at the man whose feet she was carrying; she thought he was dead. Suddenly, looking into his face, she saw it was Little Hugh.

She gave a shudder. He had been alive. He had been afraid. She had tried to tell him not to be afraid, with silly little words that meant nothing now. Seffrid took his head end and she took his feet end and they laid him down in a row of dead and wounded. A woman came wailing up toward him and Roderick stepped hastily out of her way. His mother, she thought, watching her kneel by him. The woman buried her face in the dead chest. Roderick's stomach heaved.

Leovild said, "They'll come again. This time we should take them at this end of the bridge." He smiled at her. His eyes snapped. "That was well done, Roderick, there at the beginning of it—Weland meant to take us by surprise, and have the King away from us."

"That was wicked," she said. "Wasn't it?"

He gave a harrumphing laugh. "I think Weland is a very wicked fellow, you know." He wrapped his arm around her shoulders. "Well, now, go and get something to eat." He went over to the line of dead and wounded. Roderick hesitated a moment, thinking to help him at whatever he was doing, but her belly growled, and Seffrid said, "Come on—there's bread," and she went after him.

King Charles stood at the foot of the bridge; Odo came running to him, with Charles' cloak over his shoulders, and a cup of wine in his hand. The boy's face was bright red. He held out the cup, and said, "Sire, I want to fight. I can fight. Please let me fight too."

Charles grunted. "You lack a few years yet." He drank deep of the wine. The shouting and cheering of the crowd sounded in his ears like ocean noise, far away and unimportant.

Odo took his shield and sword. "Sire, please."

"No, I have pronounced it, that is all," Charles said. "You are a greenling yet, although your day will come." He slapped the boy's back. He shuddered off the memory of the Northmen charging at him, all alone up there on the bridge. His men had come to him then. He had done battle, as he was supposed to, at the forefront of his men, and he still lived: nothing else mattered. Until the next blow fell, he was the King he was supposed to be.

Odo trailed him, head down. Charles laughed at him. His spirits suddenly lightened. His step felt easier. Perhaps there was a way out of this after all. Ahead of him, he saw his wife waiting, with his daughter. His wife threw her hands up, eager.

"Boy," he said, and turned and got Odo by the arm. "Go fetch me Leovild, but not too quickly."

"Yes, Sire." Odo left. Smiling, the King bent his steps toward his wife and daughter, to warm himself in their praises.

*   *   *

From the edge of the ground on the common, Erma saw the Northmen charge, saw Seffrid and the skinny boy he served leap out ahead of the others and rush up onto the hump of the bridge to shield the King. She screamed; she ran forward, the baby on her hip hanging on to her with both hands. She could not see anything now, save the mass of men fighting on the bridge. Her heart hammered. She ran back toward the palace a little, trying to see better. The noise hurt her ears; the crowd out on the common was shrieking and the men on the bridge howled and shouted like a pack of dogs, and she heard the clang of iron; she saw a man fall off the bridge, and then another, and the river carry them down.

Then suddenly the Northmen were running away. She gave a yell. The baby was clinging to her, sobbing, and she caught him up closer and said, "No, no, it's all right, be good now," and jollied him until he quieted. She kissed him. He was a good baby. She jumped up and down, watching her people spill jubilantly back down off the bridge.

The Northmen hadn't gone away. One look across the river showed her that. She went toward the triumphant men, looking for Seffrid. Everybody was whooping and shrieking and waving their arms, as if this were all over now, but she knew it was not.

She saw the King walking down from the bridge, his page on his heels, and she gave a cheer for him, her breast swelling with her feelings. "Long live King Charles! King Charles!" She thought he could not hear her, in the general uproar; he did not turn his head, but trudged on, as if he bore the weight of all the kingdom on his back.

As the King went on toward the hall, a shaggy grey mule clopped out onto the common, hauling a wagon behind. It was the big monk, the Irishman, with his baskets of bread and barrels of wine. Erma veered toward him; she heard the yell go up, in the crowd, and lengthened her stride. The monk drew his mule to a stop and climbed back over the seat to the bed of the wagon. Erma reached its high plank side just before the great swarm of the crowd rushing across the common.

"Bread!" she shouted. "My men fought—bread for my fighting men!"

The monk tossed her two loaves, saw the baby, threw her another. She bundled the bread into a fold of her skirt and ran off through the loose rush of hungry people, looking for Seffrid.

She had to run all the way back through the mass of people; he was at the back of the crowd, walking along, his lord beside him.

She ran up to him. "You won, you won. Come quickly, I have food for you, you can sit down." Quickly she ran her gaze over him, seeing that he was unhurt; she was beginning to think she could have him, if she wanted him, at least for a while.

He crowed at her. "You think it's over, do you." He seized the bread and began to eat, veering his course now toward the riverbank; she held out the second loaf to the thin boy who was Seffrid's lord, whose name, she remembered now, was Roderick.

"Thank you," he said. He smiled at her, his grey eyes direct; his eyes seemed as deep as wells, as if she could fall into them, and drown. "God bless you."

Seffrid reached into her skirt and plucked out the third loaf. "Well, go fetch us something to drink, don't stand there just staring at us."

Roderick said, "We'll take the baby." He lifted the child up off her hip, and she turned and ran back toward the wagon, light-footed, both arms free.

The big monk gave her a skin full of wine. She carried it back over her shoulder; looking past the men, past the river, she saw that the Northmen were still well away, many sitting down, probably also eating. She walked on up to the men.

As she came near them, she blinked, startled, because it seemed that Seffrid sat beside a mother and her child, and in a leap of mind she saw it was the Virgin Mother and her Child, and she stopped and gaped. But then it was not, it was only the lord Roderick, with Erma's own baby in his arms.

She crossed herself. She went up to them and Seffrid snatched the wineskin away from her, saying, "Why are you so thick today, girl?" He poured wine into his mouth and handed the skin to Roderick.

Erma sank down to sit on the ground with them. She wondered what she had seen, before. The baby was slouched comfortably on Roderick's lap and watched her from there, not moving. Bread crumbs littered his chin. Roderick had fed him. Now Roderick was holding out half a loaf of the bread to her. She said, "Thank you, sir."

His smile widened, as if they had some kind of joke between them. The bones of his face looked as fine as a girl's, his skin baby-smooth. She thought suddenly that he was beautiful, like an angel. He said, "What is your son's name?"

"Hmmm," she said. "I just call him baby. He isn't baptized. Everybody said he wouldn't live." Shouldn't live. Her eyes hurt, remembering that, the spiteful voices saying that, as if a tiny baby were as guilty as his wicked mother. She reached out, and Roderick gave her the child back.

Roderick turned to Seffrid. "We should get John to baptize him." He turned to her again, intent. "John is very holy. Whoever he blesses will surely thrive."

Seffrid barked a laugh. "Tell that to that other monk—that— what's his name—"

"Deodatus," Roderick said. "How are they doing, over there?"

Seffrid turned his head, looking toward the river and the Northmen on the far side. "They are still muddling around."

The baby pulled on Erma's dress and she opened her clothes and nursed him. Roderick was staring at him, a strange sad look on his face. She thought of telling him all her secret names for the baby, Starcatcher, and Bounce, and Little King Bear, of the wild dreams she had that he grew up and went out and conquered Christendom, like great Charles himself, and brought his mother to a fine hall, with women to attend her, and plenty to eat, and good warm clothes.

She lowered her eyes. Roderick was a real lord. She dared not even speak to him. Her arms tightened around the baby.

"I want him to be blessed," she said, not looking at Roderick. "If we can."

"We will," Roderick said.

Up by the bridge, someone yelled. Seffrid got to his feet. "Here they come," he said, drank another gulp of the wine, and turned and gave her a wet kiss on the mouth. "Good girl, Erma. Wait, now." With Roderick he ran off toward the bridge.

11

THE KING SAID, "WILL they surely come this way again? Is there no way they can surprise us?"

Leovild shrugged. "I think they have to come over the bridge, Sire. It's the only way to get a lot of men here all at once." They were standing on the approach to the bridge and Leovild could see down it, like a throat, to the broad trampled meadows on the far side. The Vikings had drawn back almost to their camp; the broad land across the river was deceptively quiet.

He cast a quick look over the city. The common was crowded thick with people, mostly watching and waiting. Under the general rumble of these people he could faintly hear the sound of chanting; some of the monks from the monastery were in the church, asking God's blessing on them all.

"How can they attack elsewhere?" the King said.

Leovild said, "They could bring boats up. We'd see them long before they reached us. I don't know how they could steal on us quietly."

"They shot arrows to burn the village from the far bank," the

King said. He was picking at his cheek with his fingernail, his eyes moving everywhere. "So they have found a way through the marshes."

Leovild said, "I think most of them are still over there." He pointed across the bridge. Over there the Vikings were approaching again; in streams they were walking up from their camp, and now he could hear their voices, shouting and singing. His back tingled. He turned to look at the King again. "What should we do, Sire?"

The King scraped furiously at his face. "We need all our men here, to stop them here, as you said. Yet I mistrust them."

The day had turned hot and bright, with no wind. The river between them glittered in the sun. He turned and looked along the bank, where his own men were scattered, many sitting down and eating. The crowd of people in the common was drifting toward the church, to take refuge there if the Northmen broke through.

It would do them no good, Leovild knew. The Vikings cared nothing for churches.

Roderick was walking toward him, carrying his sword over his shoulder, and a shield and his helmet in the other arm; he had gotten a new shield somewhere, after having the old one chopped to pieces in the morning's fight. The youth was looking down as he walked, his head bent, but now he lifted his head, and his gaze caught Leovild's and he smiled, and Leovild's heart lifted. He thought with Roderick there they had some hope, anyway. He reached out and, as the young man approached him, wrapped his arm around the youth's shoulders.

"Did you get something to eat? Are you ready?"

Roderick faced the King, and made a little stiff bow to him. The King nodded to him, and began to smile.

"Good day to you, young Roderick."

"God be with us, Sire," Roderick said, and looked toward Leovild and back to the King. "What do you want us to do?"

Seffrid was coming up toward them also; Leovild felt a little stab of jealousy that Seffrid was the other part of Roderick's "us."

The King straightened up; he turned to look over the bridge again, and then swung around toward the north side of the island. "Leovild. Send them to patrol the other side of the island, and make sure no one tries to cross over there, and get behind us."

"Yes, Sire." Leovild nodded to Roderick and Seffrid. "Those are your orders."

Roderick saluted him, and turned, but to Leovild's surprise, Seffrid stood his ground and began to argue. "The fighting will be here. They can't cross over that water, with no bridge and no ford. Isn't it all marsh on the far bank?"

The King snapped, "Do as we order you; remember who is master here!"

Roderick said, mildly, "We will do as you bid us, Sire. Come on, Seffrid, let's go."

Seffrid was frowning; he made as if to argue again, but Roderick was starting off. Leovild said, "Go with your master."

Seffrid said, "You know not what you are doing. We should be here, where the fighting is."

The King thrust his head toward him. "Go and obey your orders!"

Seffrid snorted at him, turned, and walked off after Roderick. The King glared after him. "That lout! I'll throw him in chains."

His voice rattled. He faced the bridge again; he seemed to shrink a little, as if the nerve seeped out of him. His finger rose to claw at his cheek again. Leovild tore his gaze from the King. His temper opened like a boil. Charles was weak, full of doubt, full of uncertainty, not a good man to follow, and now he had sent away Leovild's two best warriors.

He went up closer to the bridge. The massive old stone footing here came straight up out of the water and curved around onto the island a little, making a low wall on either side, shaping the end of the bridge into a funnel. When the Northmen came, Leovild meant to keep them penned up in this funnel. He saw Guiso and Louis coming, and threw his arm up, and went toward them to give them orders. The King stood there on the approach, alone.

Leovild came back to him. The King said, "Have we no archers?"

"We have no more arrows," Leovild said. He ran his gaze over his men, standing there with their shields and their swords and clubs. All together, they seemed no more than a little flock of sheep waiting for the wolves.

His heart sank. As he stood there by his doubting, uneasy King, the old exhausted despair crept back like a black tide rising.

Across the river, a horn blew, and the Northmen in a great loose mass started moving toward the bridge. Leovild shouted to his men, running down the riverbank to herd up the stragglers. Standing behind them all, he turned and swept his gaze across the island; the burning of the city had leveled it enough that he could see through to the far side, but he could not make out Roderick and Seffrid.

He went back to the right side of the bridge again, toward the King, who was standing there staring at the ground, his brows knotted. Guiso was standing there, leaning on his big iron-studded club, his bushy hair compacted under a helmet. He spat, his glum look directed toward the oncoming Northmen. He said, "They are going to try the same thing all over again, aren't they?"

Leovild said, "They're stubborn."

He turned again, and looked across the island. He knew the Northmen were stubborn, but they were not stupid. Then Weland was walking out onto the bridge, alone, his helmet in the crook of his arm.

"King! Where is King?"

The King stirred. He turned abruptly to Guiso and said, "Give me your shield and find another."

"Sire," Leovild said. "Be careful."

"Bah," the King said. "I am done with being careful." Guiso gave him the wooden shield, and he walked up a little onto the bridge, holding the shield at his side.

"Weland," he called. "What do you want now?"

Weland cupped his hand to his ear. "What? Come closer, I can't hear you." His yellow beard split into a toothy grin.

The King made no move. He stood a little crooked, as if he were looking at Weland around a corner. Leovild, on the bridge approach behind him, watched the rest of the Northmen. Most were standing on the far side of the bridge, but a clump of them was drifting off along the far riverbank and he saw that they carried bows. He slid his arm through the leather straps on the shield.

Up on the bridge, the King, still standing at the city end of it and not moving, called out, "If it's all the same to you, Weland, after what happened this morning, I think I'll stay here. Why don't you all just go home and forget this? You're only going to get yourselves killed."

Weland said, "Give us silver and gold and we will go."

"I'll give you a grave, Weland."

Weland shrugged. Clearly he was in no hurry to begin this, and Leovild's back tingled in warning. Through the tail of his eye he watched the archers moving up to the brim of the riverbank; they had already trampled the ground there to muck.

The King said, "Weland, there is nothing here you want. You're going to die for nothing."

The big Northman crossed his arms over his chest. "Or you will die for nothing, King. Or maybe I will take you back to—"

Then from behind Leovild, from somewhere distant on the far side of the island, a horn sounded.

Weland jerked around, his arms unfolding. His mouth opened red and wet in his beard, and he wheeled one great paw through the air in a signal. The King was wheeling, spry as a boy, snatching out his sword. Leovild leapt in among his own men, and the Northmen rushed up toward the bridge.

Guiso shrieked. "They're shooting! They're shooting!"

Leovild crouched down behind his shield, like all the men around him, in a great chatter and banging of wood. Arrows pelted down around them, bouncing and shattering on the hard ground of the bridge approach; he felt one thud into the wood just above his face. Behind him Guiso was praying, or maybe swearing, and Leovild wheeled, got him by the shirt, and pulled him down under the cover of his shield.

In the funnel of the bridge approach the other Franks were huddling down, trying to use the walls as cover. The King was screaming. "Leovild! Behind us! Behind us!"

"Watch the front—watch them in front of us!" Leovild roared.

On the far side of the bridge, the Northmen were howling and banging their weapons together in a horrible clash of metal, but they were not charging. Another storm of arrows clattered down around Leovild. Looking down the ragged pack of his little army, he saw men fall. The others were packed together, their shields raised up like the shell of a wooden tortoise. The King was now just one of them, hiding among them under his shield. Leovild thought, quickly, We may get some arrows this way, at least, and then with a yell the Northmen were charging onto the bridge.

Leovild screamed, "Hold! Hold—" In among the massed shields of his men he saw some turn, he saw some few run away, but most of them stayed, hiding under their shields, through another hail of arrows, while the Northmen packed themselves into the narrow space of the bridge and streamed over the hump and down toward the city.

Leovild gripped his sword, watching them come; he knew the archers would stop shooting before their own men came under their arrows. Guiso beside him shivered, his teeth sunk in his lip, and Leovild reached out and tried to steady him. "Wait—wait—"

"Oh God, oh God," said Guiso.

"Now!" Leovild charged forward into the funnel of the bridge.

The Vikings were packed together on the bridge so close that only the front rank could fight. Leovild went at them from the side, shield first. A lance veered toward him and he took a blow dead on, the head sticking into the wooden shield; he pushed hard forward, driving the man holding the lance back into the thick of the Northmen.

"On!" he screamed. "On—" He had no idea if his own men came after him; he could not look away from the Northmen before him. The lancer had flung aside his weapon, and was drawing his sword, but Leovild crowded him hard backward. He stabbed once into the man's middle and when he fell clubbed him over the head. In the space where that man had been, another lance swung down, and Leovild struck awkwardly at it and missed. Through the corner of his eye he saw Guiso's wild red face, the mouth gaping, screaming, while he hacked awkwardly at the long wooden shaft, leaving himself all open from the front. The Northman in front of him dropped the lance and his hand stretched across his body toward his sword, but Leovild killed him before he could draw it.

His feet were trapped. A body against his ankles. He staggered, trying to shove it away, and stepped on something soft that broke under his foot. A huge man with scars all over his face lunged at him, swinging a battle-axe, dealing great crunching blows that numbed Leovild's arm even through the shield. Then the axeman staggered; somebody behind him had pushed him.

When he wobbled off-balance Leovild ran his sword in under the battle-axe and into the scarred man's armpit. The big man's eyes popped. He lurched up even taller, winding the battle-axe back over his shoulder, and the blood fountained out of his mouth and he lurched over and sprawled across the low wall of the bridge footing.

Leovild's men were all around him, battering at the front of the mass of the Northmen. They were holding the Vikings on the bridge. Leovild bent his head to wipe his sweating face on his shield arm. He fought the urge to turn and look around, to see what was creeping up behind him. Up there in the thick of the Northmen he saw Weland, not fighting, waving his arms, driving men on, yelling orders. He wondered where the King was. Then a black-bearded man swung up before him and he was crouching down again under a rain of blows like a cascade of rocks on his shield. The smell of blood in his nose made his stomach heave. The screeching and curses of the men around him boxed him in with sound. He swung the sword low, hit ankles and shins, and the black-bearded man stumbled back.

Leovild looked for Weland again, and saw him up there, on the hump of the bridge, pointing this way and that, cool as a priest at the Mass, sending his men on. If he had a bow, he thought, he could end this all with a single arrow.

He had no bow. No arrows. Nothing but his sword. Another man came at him, his beard dripping blood from a long slash on his face; Leovild slid sideways to dodge the falling blade of his axe, struck backhanded hard and missed, struck again and hit. A horn was blowing somewhere. Not a Frankish horn. His heart quaked. He expected a blow from behind and his back stiffened and he willed himself not to turn. They had crossed the north arm of the river. They had beaten by Roderick and Seffrid, they were coming up behind him. The bloody man reared up before him again, his eyes glaring, but he was suddenly alone; the Northmen behind him were wheeling, were running, were yielding once again.

Leovild gave a cry, and bounded forward, swinging his sword, and the bloody man ducked. Stepped back once, turned his head as if to look behind him, and then wheeled and brought his axe down hard at Leovild's head.

Leovild dodged. The axe struck his shield and split it and hit his shoulder. He felt nothing, but he dropped the shield, he could not move that arm, and now the bloody man was whirling around and running, and the Franks were running, too, after the fleeing Northmen, and Leovild turned, ready to call them back, and the world spun away out from under him and he fell.

Roderick and Seffrid walked around the edge of the island, past the upstream tip, where they could see the low mudbank just upstream from the city island, and then around the long side, past the burned village. Several of the village boys fell in behind them to follow at a distance. Roderick picked her way through the ruins of the burned village where they crowded up against the riverbank, her eyes directed outward, toward the far shore.

Here the island's bank shelved off steeply down to the water; the lower part was bare mud and rock, but grass grew all along the top in tufts and clumps. There was no cover, and she sank down on her heels, Seffrid beside her, and set her shield on end, and looked past it out over the river to the far side. There had been a bridge here once, a little way downstream, and the stone piers still stuck up out of the water like long grey teeth.

Roderick looked across the river. The bank on the far side was lower, a green lake of reeds and cattails. Beyond, the land sloped up, and in the distance there was a low hill. Leovild had told her it was another monastery out there somewhere. Paris, she thought, had a quantity of monks. She heard a sound behind her, and jerked her head around, but it was only the little crowd of village boys, keeping their distance.

The King's page Odo was there among them, watching. She raised her hand to him, and he waved back.

Seffrid said, "We should be back there." He twisted to look over his shoulder.

"The King is our commander," she said. "If nothing happens, we will go back."

"The King's a fool. He doesn't know," Seffrid said roughly.

"Oh, Seffrid," she said. "Nobody knows." Then, over there, across the river, the lake of green cattails was rippling and dividing, and she said, "But he knows about this. Look." She scrambled up onto her feet. A line of men was creeping down through the reeds and the cattails.

"If we had bows, we could finish them all off," Seffrid said.

Roderick said nothing, but stopped, and picked up a rock. One in the thread of men winding in through the swamp pointed up at her and Seffrid. At the front of the line the first of the Northmen had reached the shore of the river, a little upstream from the old bridge piers.

He was carrying a great coil of rope over his shoulder, and she saw him hand the lead of it to the man after him, who waded out into the water, making his way along a mudbank showing yellow through the green water. Three or four other men followed him; quickly they were in the water up to their armpits.

The man on the shore was paying out the rope from his coil. Now he lifted a curved horn from his belt, and blew a blast on it. A signal. Roderick reared her arm back to throw the rock.

As she did, she felt at once that something was wrong. She was doing it wrong. That was the way girls threw rocks. Roderick would not throw like that. She turned her shoulders, got her arm back, and put her back into the action, aiming for the man in front, who was moving steadily toward her, the rope uncoiling behind him.

She made a good throw, but the distance was still too great: the rock splashed into the water, well short of him. She stooped and picked up another.

"Help me!"

Seffrid had been standing there staring at the Northmen. Now he turned, and began to gather up rocks. Roderick turned her body again, using her left arm with the shield as a counterweight, and hurled another rock.

Something was rising in her, some savage pleasure at this, a will to action. Her head went muzzy for a moment, and then cleared, all her body singing with excitement.

Now all the Northmen but one were in the river, struggling against the current. The one left on the shore had dropped his horn and was hanging on to the lead of the rope with both hands, braced against the pull as his companions pushed out into the rushing dark water. They were working their way out along the mudbank, pale under the curling water, but now they reached the end of it, and the frontmost of them, the man with the rope, stepped out, let out a yell, and dropped suddenly under the water.

The others began to swim. The man with the rope surfaced again, his mouth open, the rope floating along behind him. He struck out for the nearest of the old bridge piers. On the shore behind him the horn blew again. Roderick took another rock. The hot joyous singing in her body was like another person leaping into her skin. She flung the rock as hard as she could, and it bounced off one of the heads bobbing on the river's surface, and she yelled.

She wanted to hurt them, to triumph over them, to laugh as they sank down. She ran along the bank, looking for more stones, and found a rocky outcrop and grabbed up a handful of chunks.

The current was carrying her targets away. The rushing water swept up the leader, the man with the rope, and carried him into the middlemost of the bridge piers so hard he went under. She threw another rock, and hit another one of the floating heads; the rock bounced high in the air, and even from here, she heard the man yell.

She gave a whoop of delight. The man with the rope came up beyond the bridge pier, back end first, his hair drifting. The river bore him swiftly away. Seffrid ran past her, to a place where the bank was higher; he flung a rock sidearm, and she saw it hit the water, skip, and sail through the air straight into the face of one of the struggling swimmers.

"Hey! Help! All here—all here—"

Roderick wheeled. That was the King's page, Odo. The boy ran up, with the village boys streaming after him. Behind them came a swarm of people, men and women and children. Rushing down onto the riverbank, they scrabbled in the dirt for stones and let fly volleys of them toward the little fleet of heads now bobbing helplessly along in the river, who were fighting also to keep from being sucked down around the bridge piers.

The rope was floating loose on the river's breast. Two of the Northmen clung desperately to one of the piers, and the rest were struggling back the way they had come. The villagers crowded the riverbank, hooting and cheering and throwing stones at them.

Roderick wheeled, looked for Seffrid, and caught his eye. "Come on!" she cried.

They ran back through the burned ruins of the village. As they crossed the island the howling and clash of battle grew louder ahead of them, and now she could see, across the broad common, the men swarming over the bridge. She remembered the horn blasting. That was the signal for this attack. Her blood leapt. She wrenched out her sword. Seffrid raced up beside her. On the hump of the bridge she could see big Weland, pointing and waving his arms.

She rushed up into the back of the mob of the Franks, looking for Leovild. All the fighting was in the throat of the bridge. A wounded man lay on the ground before her and she bounded over him. The Franks were pushing forward ahead of her. She could not see Leovild. Horns were blasting somewhere, over the bridge somewhere.

A Viking with a skull stuck to his helmet reared up before her and she dodged his wild swinging axe and slashed at him, and he parried her blow and struck back. They stood toe to toe a moment, hacking at each other. The battle rage coursed through her like a fiery tide, a hot delirium of power and lust. She flung herself full behind each blow; she felt enormous, invulnerable, as if she could grind down every enemy before her by sheer will.

Then, behind him, the other Northmen were rushing off, and he leapt backwards and spun and fled away.

With a yell, she started after him, cheated. Someone grabbed her arm and held her back. She cooled. Suddenly she felt her body around her like a cloak falling about her. The Franks sent up a roar of triumph and flung their arms into the air, whistled and stamped and screamed insults after the fleeing Northmen. All around her men laughed and beat each other on the back. None of them was Leovild. She went toward the side of the bridge, where there was a low stone wall. He was nowhere. She looked down over the wall, and saw him floating in the water, in the lee of the boat landing, facedown, his hair around him like a lily.

She screamed his name. The great footing of the bridge made an eddy here, so the river had not carried him off. Flinging down her sword and shield, she scrambled over the wall and jumped down into the water. She went in over her head, came up again beside Leovild. His helmet was gone. She gripped his long floating hair and pulled his face up out of the river.

Water gushed from his nose and mouth. She wrapped her arm around him, trying to pull him upright, as he flopped against her like a half-full sack. "Seffrid," she screamed. "Seffrid!"

"Here," he shouted; he was scrambling down the path to the boat landing, first of half a dozen men. She kicked, trying to carry Leovild through the water to the shore. Seffrid reached the water's edge, and she struggled toward him, her arms full of Leovild's body, and her legs thrashing at the cold river.

"Leovild!" she shouted into his ear; his head flopped back against hers. "Leovild! Help me!"

He stirred. She shouted at him again; the river was catching at them, would carry them away, and Seffrid's outstretched arm was almost within reach. She lunged forward, and Leovild, feebly, stretched out his right arm toward Seffrid. Seffrid gripped his wrist and drew Leovild along behind him. Leovild, scrabbling weakly with his feet against the wall, climbed up out of Roderick's arms, and one of his kicking feet struck her in the chest and knocked her down under the water.

She went deep into the cold and dark. The river caught her. Her mouth and nose were full of water. She struggled upward, flailing with her hands. She could feel the river dragging her away. Then her outflung hand struck another hand, reaching down below the waterline. Someone else was there. Someone had come into the river to rescue her. The warm strong hand gripped her tight, and drew her up, and in one long smooth effortless boost heaved her upward into the air, and Seffrid caught her by the arm and swung her up onto the boat landing.

Her legs gave way and she sat heavily down with her back to the wall, coughing up river water. She was shaking all over. Her chest hurt where Leovild had kicked her. Her eyes were bleary.

She whispered, "Somebody—somebody down there—" And coughed and coughed. "Save him—"

Seffrid knelt beside her, pulled her forward over his arm, and whacked her on the back. Water trickled from her mouth. Her chest heaved. Her throat felt raw and her nose burnt. She lay along Seffrid's arm, grateful for him. "Did you get him?"

"Leovild's alive. Bad hurt but alive. They're taking him to the monks."

"The other one," she said. "There's another one down there—somebody saved me—" She lurched up onto her feet and turned and looked down over the side of the boat landing into the river.

The water swirled by, its surface blistered in the eddy; there was no one there. Seffrid was smiling at her. "You saved him. Are you all right?"

She leaned on the riverbank, exhausted. Her face had stopped hurting. It must have been Seffrid who saved her. She reached out and clutched his arm, grateful. Turning, she looked over at the Northmen's side of the river.

"Are they gone?"

"They went back to their camp," Seffrid said. "I think the fight's over for a while."

"Thank God for it. God help us," she said. The hot delirium was gone. She felt shrunken down like a starveling, weak and sick, and her legs caved in and she sat down hard and shut her eyes.

Roderick was streaming wet; Seffrid sent Erma off to find them bread and wine, and got Roderick into the sun to dry off. Some of the Franks were going through the bodies of the Northmen who had died on the bridge, taking whatever they could and then pitching the corpses into the river. Roderick looked exhausted. Where she sat, a puddle of water was forming, rolling down off her soaked clothes, but in the afternoon heat her hair stuck up like milkweed fluff, already dry, white and fine.

The King came up to them, trailing soldiers. "What are you two doing here, anyway? I sent you to the far side." He turned and waved his soldiers off. "It happened, what I said, didn't it?"

Seffrid gave him a little bow. "You were right, Sire."

At those words, the King expanded a moment, but then he began to fret again, twitching with his fingers at his face. "Leovild's gone now. I wonder if they will attack again. Without Leovild—"

"Sire—" Roderick gripped Seffrid's arm and dragged herself to her feet, her eyes fierce. "Leovild is dead?"

"No, no, he has a broken shoulder, but he is no use now." The

King struck his hands together again. "You are well? You saved him, they said. For that, all honor, young Roderick."

Roderick said, "Where is he?" She turned intently to Seffrid. "I want to go see him."

Seffrid said, "We will. Here comes Erma with something to eat."

"I want to see him now."

"We will," Seffrid said, patiently. Erma came up with a basket. The King was watching them, his eyes nervous; it came to Seffrid that he wanted more compliments. Seffrid said, "Will you have some bread, Sire?" He took a round loaf from Erma's basket. Roderick had already taken over the baby, in whom she showed an unsettling interest.

The King said, "No—no. I must go—I must attend to my many duties. Thank you. You have my leave." He went bustling off into the common. One or two of the other men followed him. He was beginning to take command, but Seffrid thought the battle would be over before he succeeded.

He reached into the basket for the wine. A sudden high-pitched gurgle brought his head around. Erma crowed. Roderick had gotten the baby to laugh. His mother scooped him up out of Roderick's arms and jiggled him, beaming into his face; the baby kicked out, and gave a long loud shrill aimless cry.

Roderick pulled at her clothes, stiff from the river water. "What a mess," she said. "I'm still all wet underneath."

Seffrid dug out another loaf of the bread and thrust it into her hand. "Eat," he said. "We'll be fighting again before you know it. Eat." He tipped up the wine bottle and took a long drink. They had won another fight, and if there was no booty, yet the King admired them. Of course he was a slipshod little King, but nonetheless. He poured another good gulp of wine into his mouth, pleased.

12

THE MONKS HAD HAULED the wounded and dying off to the hall of the cloister beyond the pear orchard. Roderick went along with the King and some others to see Leovild there. On the way, the King made much of her again, full of wind like an old nag, and she felt herself flushing under the unwelcome attention.

Young Odo had come in among them again, unobtrusive. She turned to the King, and said, "This boy fought also—all uncalled, praise him, sir."

Odo turned dark red under the soft edge of his cap. The King gave him a startled look, and cuffed him. "Well done, boy. Even if I did tell you to wait. What did you do?" Odo mumbled something, his gaze lowered, unable to bite off his smile.

"Well, then," the King said, "later, you must regale us with your battle stories." He gave the boy another jovial whack.

Roderick was trying to stop thinking about the fighting, about that deep hot fury that had come over her, the delight in seeing other men down before her. That was not her, not really her. Yet her heart still sang with that hot, holy rage. She felt Roderick growing in her, bigger and stronger with each blow, each spurt of another man's blood. She felt her real self sinking into the dark beneath, disappearing into nothing.

She thought that Roderick might kill them both, in the course of this. And now, as they walked through the pear orchard toward the monastery, as the King again told all the others how she had saved Leovild, she knew that Roderick thought very little of this haunted King, hollowed out with doubts and uncertainties.

She wondered if she herself were haunted. She remembered the hand reaching down into the water for her. She did not think now it had been Seffrid. She wondered if she had imagined it.

Of all things that had happened in the past few days, the swirling of the flames and the clash of weapons and the screams of men dying, Roderick's wild lust to overcome other men, what seemed most real and true to her was the feel of that hand, reaching down under the dark water to save her.

In the hall, they stood among the wounded in rows lying on the floor, their groaning like prayers in the long shadowy room with its roof beams draped in cobwebs and swallows flaying in and out the open windows. Leovild lay against the far wall. Following the King, Roderick drew closer, and saw the wounded man's left arm wrapped around with dirty bandages and all bound to his chest, and her belly clenched. She lifted her gaze to his face, drawn with pain, his eyes swimming. A broken shoulder, they had said. She wanted to fling herself down beside him and weep.

Roderick could not do that. Roderick, even now, itched for the battle to start again, for the heat and blood of that other life. She stood behind the King and Seffrid while they roused Leovild and poured the honey of their compliments over him.

Leovild said, "Roderick. I see you there—Roderick, come here."

Then, red-faced and stammering, she was drawn forward into their midst again, and was being told again how brave, how strong, how noble, all the while hanging her head and unable even to look at Leovild, lying bandaged in his sickbed, for fear someone would see what she felt. She crossed herself. Abruptly, even while the other men still talked, she knelt down by the bedside and took Leovild's left hand and looked him in the face.

"Does it hurt, much? Is that all—the shoulder?"

Leovild's long face warped into a smile. "That's enough, youngster. I may not wield a sword again." His hand tightened on hers. "You—" His voice shook a little. "You—"

"No, no, say nothing," she said, afraid of the feeling quivering in his eyes. She gripped his hand. "I will pray for you."

"Thank you," he said.

A monk was coming toward them, fussing, trying to draw them away from Leovild's side. The King held one hand up to stay him, and turned to Leovild and said, "I have a plan. I shall put it to this Weland soon—it may draw them off."

Leovild's eyes switched from Roderick's face to the King's. "You mean to buy them off again." His fingers were cold in Roderick's grip. She let go of him, and he slid his hand back under the blanket. The pain had sucked his face thin. He looked much older.

"If I can," said the King. "What they want is silver—we have none here, but there is silver in other places and maybe I can send them there."

Hollow-eyed, Leovild studied him a moment, and then turned his gaze to Roderick. "Kill Weland," he said.

In her belly the hot lust coiled, eager. A wild panic fluttered through her veins. She said, "If I can, Leovild."

"Kill Weland," he said, again, as if to himself. His eyelids shuttered down. The monk slipped in past the King and knelt by the wounded man and tucked his blanket closer, laid a hand against his cheek, touched his throat where the pulse beat. The King turned, and led them all out of the sick house.

Outside, at the edge of the pear orchard, in the sunlight,

Charles turned to face them. "I shall go to the Northmen's camp in the afternoon, and put my offer to them. You must go with me."

"I will," Roderick said. Beside her, young Odo straightened. "And I, my King."

"This afternoon," the King said. "I will send for you all. Now let us all go rest and gather ourselves for the next matter." He went away toward the hall. The boy Odo hung back a moment, his eyes on Roderick.

She thought he meant to say something, but then Seffrid called her; he was already tramping away toward their cell in the dormitory. She started after him, and Odo went at a run after the King.

The women were singing, in the back of the room, as they worked their looms. Odo drew back near the wall. Usually he liked to be here, waiting for the King to send him on an errand, filling his cup of wine or announcing someone come to see him, but now he wished with all his heart to be gone.

He remembered the riverbank, the hot sunlight, and throwing the stones. Then he had fought, like a man. Then he had been at the center of things, not just a little page, standing behind the King, waiting.

The Queen called to Alpiada, and the girl answered in her light, high voice. Charles was sunk down in his chair, dozing. His head tipped forward. The nape of his neck showed through the last wisps of his hair. Odo slid his hands behind his back.

Charles was not the true King, he thought. As soon as the idea leapt into his mind he was ashamed of it: disloyal. He was a bad knight. He fastened his gaze on the back of the King's head, sternly reminding himself where his duty lay. And his whole life: Charles could have slain him, when his father rebelled. He owed Charles everything. Yet, he thought, again, he is not the true King.

The true King would be the greatest knight, like Roderick. His heart thundered a wild music in his chest. Or like himself, some-day. He fixed his gaze on the King's drowsing head. Someday. He shut his eyes, dreaming.

Deodatus was hiding in the church, and intended to remain there until the battle was over; he thought not even Vikings would find him there. In the middle of the night, he crept out of his hiding place, and went first to the front of the church, where he knew there was wine. He found the jar under the altar, and drank it all up.

He went to the door of the church, and looked out. It was deep in the night, and a dank mist hung over everything; but even from the church porch he could see lights moving, over in the vil-lage, and he heard people's voices. He drifted that way, thinking of the tavern there, but as he drew nearer he saw that it was all ruined; the lights were torches that the people carried as they picked through the wreckage, and the voices were their wails, and they found bodies, and bones.

The place stank. He went back across the common, pocked with little knots of people sleeping around dead fires, and made his way to the palace.

A sleepy sentry called to him, and he waved his cassock and made the sign of the cross at him, and the sentry subsided again into his drowse. Deodatus went into the palace.

He crept around from corner to corner, past the snoring ser-vants lying like broken branches on the floor. As he went he looked for food, on the table, by the hearth, in people's wallets as they slept. He found a bit of bread, and some cheese, and at last, near the little door out to the storehouses, came on what he really sought: a full skin of wine, still stoppered. He slung this over his shoulder, and went back. Crossed the common to Our Lady Church, and burrowed down again into the dark.

*   *   *

The King had sent beforehand to the camp of the Northmen that he would meet with Weland, and with Roderick and Seffrid and young Odo, he rode over the bridge and down along the empty, trampled meadows toward the Viking camp.

Some of this ground had been plowed once, but now it was ruined. Seffrid, riding beside Roderick, saw the burned hulls of a couple of huts, and then, farther off, another building, much bigger and loftier, only charred beams now. The stink of something dead inside reached his nose even at this distance. Over all the country as they passed there seemed a dull silence and greyness, as if it had stopped living when the Vikings came.

Roderick, beside him, rode straight as a pike, her face still, except for her eyes. The black horse was gamesome and kicked up and curvetted and she let him out a little, galloped away in a wide circle to stretch him, and then came back beside Seffrid, and to the sedate pace they were taking. The King went first of them all, wearing a fine blue cloak trimmed in white and black fur and embroidered with very curious designs, and his crown on his head shining in the sunlight. Beside him the boy Odo in a green jerkin turned to watch Roderick running her horse.

As they went on west along the riverbank, the Northmen's camp spread out before them, along both sides of a little stream where it met the Seine. The ships jammed the Seine and a lot of them were drawn up on the river's sloping bar. The narrow water of the inflowing stream had vanished into a lake of muck. On either side of it thin smokes went up from dozens of campfires. All around the dusty ground was littered with clothes and gear. Black crows swarmed and fluttered boldly everywhere. Near the edge of the camp, there was a great clump of them, that flew off as the Franks rode up, uncovering a lance thrust straight into the ground.

A lump of half-eaten meat and bone was stuck on top. Most of it was eaten off, but Seffrid could see some teeth, a swatch of hair on the side of the skull.

He pulled his eyes forward. The Northmen had seen them approach, and they came up out of the middle of the camp to stand along the edge of it, waiting. In their midst was big Weland with his long braided hair flowing down.

The King drew rein; he called, "Weland, I am here to offer you what you want."

From the packed ranks of the Vikings went up a little general rumble of greed. Weland came forward several steps, his hands on his iron-studded belt. Behind him stood the man Ulf, who had been at their first meeting also, his eyes narrow.

Weland said, "We want silver and gold! You said before you have none—now you admit you are rich?"

"I am not rich," the King said. "My city is jammed with poor and hungry people, and none of us have anything. I'm not offering you silver of mine, but silver that used to be mine. There is a big camp of Northmen near the mouth of the Somme River, west of here. They have been looting and ranging wide for years, and they have wrung tribute from me, last year and this. Defeat them, take their treasure. And I will pay you tribute, next year, as much as I would have given them."

The Northmen rumbled again, stirring, murmuring to one another. Ulf, behind Weland, uncrossed his arms and then crossed them again. His gaze was steady on his chieftain. Weland's mouth worked, as if he chewed over this, and then he turned his head suddenly and spat.

"Thorulf's men," he said. He squared his shoulders back again. "You lie. We take the city, we take all."

The King's first tightened on the reins; he leaned forward a little in his saddle. "Don't be a fool. Many of you will die, and for nothing; we have nothing. Even if you do win here, you are wasting yourselves, especially when you could get what you want just going downstream a day."

Now Ulf suddenly went up toward Weland, and spoke to him. Weland turned, frowning, unwilling to listen, and yet listening, as Ulf murmured low-voiced but fiercely to him, his hands jerking up and down in hard gestures. Weland held his head high, looking down at the other man, and replied, almost spitting the words. Ulf said something more, and then Weland raised his hands between them, palms out, and jerked them up and apart, and said something loud in their speech, and turned and walked a step toward the King. Ulf did not follow, but shook his head, and stood sideways staring after Weland, his arms folded over his chest.

The Northman tramped up toward the King, set his big hands on his belt, stood with his feet widespread and his shoulders back, and shouted, "I will take your city, King! Go back and get it ready for me—I will have it. That's all! I make no trades, no deals." He waved his hands back and forth, palms down. "No trades, no deals."

There was a little silence. Then Roderick said, "Will you take a challenge? I would fight you—man to man—here and now."

Seffrid drew in his breath, alarmed. He wondered what she was doing. Beside him, the King moved suddenly, and then was still again. Weland's head jerked. His slitted eyes opened wide, glittering, and he stared at Roderick, sitting on her horse beside Seffrid. "You?" His wet mouth pursed. "I fight no babies. Go home, crawl under your bed and wait for me."

Seffrid murmured, "Roderick, be careful."

She never even looked at him, all her attention focused on Weland, but she tossed her reins to him, and slinging her leg forward over the horse's withers, slid to the ground. She walked out into the open space between the King and Weland, where everyone could see her. A shiver went down Seffrid's spine. There was no woman left in her; she stood tall and straight as a young pine tree, all grace and pride and strut. The long edges of her white hair hung like feathers over the neck of her tunic. He wondered if he actually saw the glow of her power around her, or only knew it was there. The Northmen were hushed, watching her. In the silence Seffrid could hear the distant calls of the crows.

Weland stood alone before Roderick. Something warned him; off-balance, edgy, he had lost a little of his swagger. Maybe it was all mostly show anyway. He said, too loud, "Why should I fight you, little boy? Go find your father!"

Her cheeks went red. Seffrid, knowing her, saw the anger draw her tighter, like a bow. Her voice rang harsh and keen, pushing Weland. "I have an arm, and a sword in it. Will you fight, or no?"

Among the Northmen, some voices went up, urging Weland on. He stared at her again, and then turned to the King. "I win, you give me the city."

Before the King could speak, Roderick spoke. She moved, at the same time, shifting around to the side, so that Weland had to face her, and not the King.

She said, "I thought you made no deals, Weland. No trades. This is for my honor and yours. Will you fight, or no?"

The center of everybody's gaze, Weland could not now refuse. He stepped away, back toward his own men, and bellowed an order in his own tongue. Beside Seffrid, the page Odo stirred, a sudden, eager jump of excitement.

Roderick stood where she was, her hands clasped before her; she bent her head quickly, and Seffrid knew she prayed. Around her, the voices boiled up, the Northmen surging up closer, swinging around to watch. The King turned also to Odo and spoke, and then to Seffrid, saying, low-voiced, "I shall permit this, but we must be ready to flee." His face was white. His eyes blazed. He drew them back a little, to the edge of the circle that had now formed around Roderick and Weland.

Seffrid's heart was pounding. He thought of things he should tell her. He was clutching the pommel of his saddle with both hands, his body rigid. She stood so straight, but she was so slight, out there, and now the Northman turned around and faced her, in his hands a blade as long as his arm. Someone behind him was handing him a shield.

Seffrid broke out of the grip of his fears; he leapt down from the saddle, unhooked the shield from behind her saddle, and took it to her. As he did, all manner of advice flooded through his mind, but when he reached her, and gave her the shield, their eyes met, and he said, only, "Do it." Her eyes were pale as water, seeing through him like water, and she said nothing. She took the shield on her left arm, and drew her sword. Seffrid went back to their horses, and watched.

With a roar Weland came straight at her, lashing and stamping. She moved quickly, got out of his way, and struck behind him, so close he had to leap to escape it. His eyes popped; from the watching Northmen there went up a yell.

Again the big Viking charged at her, as if he could trample her down under his weight, and again she got him out of step and this time neatly clipped him across the arm. Seffrid had fought beside her, the last few days, not watching her, and now he saw, amazed, that she had learned the unteachable art of counterstroke. She used Weland's blows against him, going in behind and under them, slipping past, catching him on the wrong foot, and then slashing hard at his knees.

Yet the Northman was bigger, and he was shrewd, also. Stumbling away from her third stroke, he saw he would not bull her over, and quickly he settled to another kind of fighting, driving her before him, forcing her to keep moving backward, giving her nothing to strike at, leaning his weight and height against her, wearing her down.

Seffrid licked his lips. He saw things Weland did badly, that way of dropping his shield when he struck, and he did not keep his feet under him. Backing up as she was, she could not take advantage of that. She was trading him blow for blow, but he saw how Weland's blows paid on her. Then, unaccountably, she flinched and stepped out sideways, and Weland lunged straight at her.

She flung herself backward, dodging the blow, and the tip of his sword sliced the front of her jerkin. Seffrid yelled. She was a fool; she had given him that. What was she doing? He beat his fists on his thighs. She had gotten her balance, was holding Weland off again, gamely, steadily backing up in a slow curve toward the King, and then, horribly, she flinched again, and stepped out again, giving Weland that same opening.

Seffrid shrieked. Weland sprang forward, eager, his sword thrusting, but Roderick was not there. She had spun lightly out of his way, so that he lunged past her, wide open to the counterstroke. With the screams of the Northmen echoing around her, she set her feet and struck hard at Weland, over the shield arm he had let drop again, catching him extended and exposed and moving into her blade.

Weland grunted. Blood gushed up from his side. Roderick leapt back, jerking the sword free, and Weland stood a moment, his mouth open, his eyes wide. Then blood dribbled from his lips, and he pitched forward onto his face in the dirt.

The King let out a cheer and shook his fist in the air. All around, the Northmen were sending up such a howl that Seffrid could hear nothing else. He opened his fists, and let himself breathe again. In the middle of them all, Roderick, slim and straight, went up to Weland's body and touched it with her foot.

A cold shiver went down Seffrid's back. The way she stood, the set of her head, reminded him of someone. In a cold clear leap he recognized him: Markold.

Then she lifted her head, and faced him, and he saw the girl she had been in the sudden softness of her eyes. She crossed herself. Her shoulders slumped. He went down to help her, lifted the shield from her arm, and put his arm around her. She looked haggard; he knew not to speak to her, only led her back to her horse.

Behind them, from the Northmen a yell went up. "Ulf! Ulf!"

"Yes, yes." The warrior lifted his hands and went up past Weland's body. He stopped there and looked down at the dead man. Seffrid mounted up, gathering his reins; Roderick swung into her saddle.

Ulf lifted his head and stared at Roderick a moment. Then he faced the King.

He spoke very good Frankish. He said, "Yes, we will go down and push off Thorulf. They are not so many as we are, and I think you are right, they have been fat too long. Then I will come back and you will give me seven-thousand pounds of silver, every fall and every spring, forever."

King Charles said, "That is my bargain. But then you must hold the mouth of the Somme and not let others of your friends sail upstream."

Ulf smiled. "I am no King. I make no promises except to take Thorulf's treasure. I only want silver." He turned and walked back toward his fellows, shouting, and the whole pack of them abruptly turned and walked away, back toward their camp. The crows were circling around now, watching the corpse, which they had abandoned behind them in the dust.

Charles said, under his breath, "Heathen pigs." He crossed himself. But when he turned to Roderick, beside Seffrid on her horse, his face was sunlit with his smile. He said, "You have saved Paris, Roderick. I shall find a suitable reward for one so brave and strong of arm."

She said, "I did only what Leovild told me to do, my lord." She licked her lips, looking back toward the body. Through the great swarm of men leaving, a few women had made their way up; they hung back, wary of the Franks, but when the King swung his horse around and started off, they rushed forward to Weland's body. Their wailing voices rose. The crows fluttered away again, braying.

The King said, "You are a mighty warrior, I have never seen such a skill. I shall make you a count in my kingdom, Roderick."

Roderick was twisted around in her saddle, looking back. "They have women with them."

"There are always women," King Charles said. "Where there are men and beds and booty, there are always women."

Seffrid laughed at that, nervous; he glanced at Roderick again, who was still slewed in her saddle to look behind at the women and the dead man. Abruptly she straightened and faced forward again. Her face was pale. She lifted her hands up before her and stared at them. "I must go pray," she said, and spun the black horse and galloped off.

Little Odo cried, "I'll go—" and started after her, but the King caught him by the arm.

"No, no, you are attending me." Charles turned to Seffrid. "What is wrong with him? It was a great victory, he has saved the city. I shall have honors and rewards for him. I shall make him my knight. Where has he gone?"

Seffrid said, "It was a good fight." He was watching Roderick fly away down through the meadows, the black horse moving like a ghost through the yellow of the meadow flowers. "I never taught him that counterstroke."

"Ah, well." The King smacked him heartily on the shoulder. "He'll come back. I shall make you a count, too, Seffrid, for teaching him. Now let us go back to the city, and tell them they are saved."

13

E RMA HELPED JOHN AND the King's cooks make and
bake the bread for the poor, and got some loaves for her
work. John had given her an apron, and she hid the loaves in
the big pockets, took her baby on her hip, and went to the village.

It was the heat of the day. The whole broad field of charred
wreckage was bobbing up and down with people, going through
the mess, looking for things to save. A steady train of them struggled up and down between the village and the river, hauling baskets and armloads of garbage down to dump into the water. Where
the alehouse had stood, a few men were dragging charred balks of
wood up to build another. Around it some of the huts had not
been much burned and the people were mending them, with
cloth, with poor thatch of weeds, with reeds and driftwood off the
riverbank. Most of the place was burned down to the ground, a
great barren of ashes and soot.

Yet people stayed where their homes had been, as if the walls
were still there. Erma went by families squatting inside rings of
trash. One woman had spread her dress out on poles to shade her

children; in her ragged shift, she squatted by a fire, stirring a pot, her broad freckled shoulders peeling from the sun.

Someone called, "Erma!" and waved. She put her arm up to him, unafraid now; everyone knew now she had Seffrid. Even when her cousin Ulbert fell into step beside her, she felt no fear.

Ulbert said, "You are living in the palace now, are you." He reached out to finger her sleeve. "But still raggedy, though."

She slapped at his hand. "I've been busy. I've been helping in the war. And taking care of Seffrid." She gave him a sideways look, calculating him. "Did you fight?"

"Me." He gave her a shocked look, his eyes white. "I have no weapons." He walked along beside her, looking her up and down. "You look good, Erma," he said.

She tossed her head at him. Ahead, where the old hut had been, she saw her aunt Hilde and her uncle, sitting in their own trash. Their hut had burned down utterly and they had raked out the ashes from the middle into a little knee-high wall around it. Over it on poles they had strung up a mat of woven reeds to shade themselves. Erma went in where the door had been and took the bread from her apron.

"Here, Aunt."

Her aunt seized the loaf. "You're a good girl, Erma."

Old Jean woke, and thrashed on his bed of grass. "What about me? Where's mine?"

"There's one for everybody," Erma said. "Just keep quiet or we'll have everybody in Paris here." She took the second loaf to Jean, and gave the third to Ulbert. The bread vanished into them like water into the dry soil. She sat down and watched them, pleased, the baby on her lap.

The baby huddled against her, wary, his eyes on them. Aunt licked the last crumbs from her fingers.

"That's a good girl, Erma." The old woman poked at the baby. "How's your little boy doing now? He looks better."

"We're going to baptize him," Erma said, unable to hold that back. "John is going to baptize him, the Irishman, the monk."

Ulbert hunched closer. "I want more."

"Later," she said. "There isn't much." Ulbert squatted, watching her, his eyes vague.

He said, suddenly, "You look pretty, Erma."

She flirted her head at him. "Leave me alone, Ulbert."

Her aunt was looking her over. "He doesn't beat you, I see. That's good. You must bring him here, and let me look him over."

Erma laughed. "Seffrid is too busy to come here. He is defending the city."

Old Jean lay down on his side again, crooking his arm under his head. "Goddamn the Northmen," he said, feeble. In his hand the rump of his loaf went uneaten and Ulbert sidled over and plucked it deftly away.

Aunt was still trying to get the baby to play with her; when she poked at him he shrank back against his mother and turned his head in to her breast. "What are you going to name him?"

Erma said, "I don't know. Maybe I will name him for Roderick."

At that, even old Jean looked up, his face bright. "Roderick!"

Ulbert said, "You see him much?"

"He is my man's lord," she said, proudly. "And my lord, too, I suppose. He is tender as an angel with the baby." She juggled the baby in her arms; he was trying to creep away from Aunt entirely, and hide behind his mother.

Aunt said, "He saved us, praise him to God. God keep him."

Ulbert leaned forward, intense, the last bit of bread still clutched in his fist. "Where did he come from? Who was his father?"

"He is Spanish. He is a Prince in his country."

Aunt was crossing herself. "God sent him to us to save us from the Northmen."

Ulbert said, "You are not good enough, Erma, for a Prince's man."

"Bah," she said. "I'm good enough for Seffrid. I take right enough care of him." Out there, in the village, there was a yell, suddenly, and she turned her head toward the sound. Seeing nothing that way, she swung back to the argument with Ulbert. "I have a room in a house to live in now, Ulbert, I have a man now, you can't—" Abruptly she realized that, all through the village, the people were standing up, dropping what they were doing, and running off toward the west. They were shouting and cheering as they went, leaping, shaking their arms in the air. She stood up.

"What's going on?"

Ulbert leapt to his feet, looking all around. A fat woman carrying a baby waddled past them, and Ulbert yelled, "Irgen! Where to?"

"The Northmen!" She turned the pink moon of her face toward them. "They're leaving! They're leaving—"

Erma let out a shriek. She bundled the baby onto her hip and ran, not bothering to go out by the door but rushing straight through the little ridge of piled trash that marked the wall. Ulbert followed her, and Aunt. They ran across the burned village, among a flood of other people, cheering and laughing, ran in through the pear orchard and by the horse stables, to the earthworks at the end of the island.

The great wall of dirt was already swarming with people. Erma scaled rapidly up the side, clutching the baby with one hand and using the other to help her climb. She went up into the heat of the sun and stood in a long crowd of people on the broad top, looking down the river.

The Vikings' ships still packed it. She lowered her arm, disappointed. But around here the others were still cheering, and now she saw, beyond the jam of ships, that other ships were rowing away down the Seine. Her chest swelled with relief. She felt light enough to float off her feet and fly. They were going, one by one; she saw another now detach itself from the back of the fleet and drift away into the current, and then the feathery lift of the oars.

She yelled. The baby on her hip suddenly let out a yell also, looked into her face, and laughed. She clutched him, dancing. She loved to see him laugh. All around them people leapt and laughed and danced. Ulbert came up to her.

"It was this Roderick," he said. "He fought the Viking chief, and killed him."

"God sent him to us," Erma said. She flung her free arm around Ulbert; he hugged her back, smiling wolfishly down into her face, but keeping his hands off her. He let her go as soon as she pulled away. "I must go find Seffrid," she said. "He'll need me." She boosted the baby up in her arms and waved to Ulbert and went away quickly down the earthworks.

The King proclaimed a procession with all the city's relics, to celebrate the victory over the Northmen and thank God for the salvation of Paris. Deodatus made sure he walked very near the head of it, where God and the King could see him well. He chanted loudly and crossed himself with every other step. Surely, he thought, God paid more heed at times like these than in ordinary moments. He saw the King watching him and bowed his head down and wiped at his eyes as if he wept.

The procession went all around the city, gathering people, and then to the church of Our Lady, where they all sang and prayed. After all the walking, Deodatus was exhausted, and he went back to his cell in the monastery and went to sleep.

*   *   *

After the Northmen had gone, the King opened his hall up, and let in the whole city for a banquet. There was not enough room, and not enough food, anyway, but with the Vikings leaving, some of the men went out and killed deer, and there was a pig left and a couple of sheep, and John ordered the last of the flour baked into bread. There was a little wine, which they watered to make enough. The people who could not crowd into the hall sat around outside it, and passed the thin wine from hand to hand. Every so often someone or another of them let out a cheer, and all around, everybody answered with a roar.

When John came out among them, giving out bread, they whooped and called his name and screamed blessings at him until he stopped and stood, his head a little down, his face smiling and red. They tugged on his cassock and swatted his backside and grabbed at his arms, shouting happiness into his face. He fed them all, glad there was enough, and went back to the hall.

All the King's men packed it, his soldiers and his servants and his priests, and when John squeezed in the door they were already booming and shouting out cheer after cheer. At the door Erma was standing, pressed against the wall, her baby in her arms and her face shining. John moved off through the crowd; he saw Deodatus, up near the King's long table, and realized he had not seen him in a while, and gave a shake of his head. He wormed his way steadily toward the front table, where the bench was empty.

Then the crowd was stirring, and a sudden great shout went up. John wheeled, bracing himself against the surge of bodies all around him. The King was coming in, with the Queen and Princess Alpiada. His people cheered his name all the way from the door to the front table. He took his place in the high seat, and raised his hands and called something. John could not make out the words, but the crowd howled approval. The King sat down.

John went closer, and then he could hear the people outside

beginning to whistle and scream, and he stopped again, and watched Leovild come into the hall.

His left shoulder was wrapped in linen, and also half his arm, which was strapped to his chest. At the sight of him the crowd shrieked his name and clapped their hands together, making room for him to walk up to the high table, and held their children up to see him, and reached out their hands to touch him. He waved to them with his good hand. As he drew nearer John saw his face was grey with pain, and he walked kinked, favoring his whole left side. He reached the table, and went around it to a place on the King's left hand.

The crowd subsided. John moved up to the high table, and Charles saw him and beckoned to him. Odo stood just behind the King, his hands behind him, and at a word from Charles the boy went around to fetch the wine forward. Leovild bent himself down slowly, carefully, onto the bench.

Then outside there was a roar like a sudden storm. John, looking down the hall, saw the whole mass of people there abruptly leap toward the door. It opened, and Roderick and Seffrid came in.

They stopped, as if the wall of sound that met them there held them back. John put his hands over his ears. The people stamped their feet on the ground, shook their arms in the air, and from every throat came a bellow that shook the roof. Seffrid stepped back a little, leaving Roderick there alone, and the people cheered her until the walls resounded and their voices gave out.

"God has delivered us," Roderick said, and went forward, through the crowd, through a waving line of arms stretched out to touch her, up to the high table. Her face was pale as bone. She did not smile. When she came to the high table, with Seffrid just behind her, the King got up and with his own hand brought her around to the place beside him, and sat her down in the place of honor, with Seffrid on her other side.

John drew back. He could have sat down at the high table, but he stood by the wall instead. His gaze fell on Roderick, what he could see of her, since he was now behind her. She took no part in this rejoicing. He thought she wore all this honor and glory like a cloak of nettles. A murky foreboding brushed him. He folded his hands into the sleeves of his robe and stood back to watch what went on.

The King's hall resounded with shouts and whoops and greetings, the buoyant upward voices of all the gathered people loud enough that even the King had to shout, just to talk to Roderick, on his right hand, and Leovild, on his left. The King was a little drunk, and very pleased with everything. He raised his cup to everyone who would meet his eyes, and cut bits of meat from his own cuts, and had Odo take them around the table.

He sat between Leovild and Roderick, and the crowd cheered them all, the three who had saved them, heroes. He smiled and waved back to the crowd, every time they cheered.

On his left side Leovild was hurt, and hardly talking. Clearly it cost him all his will just to sit there. The King turned to Roderick.

The youth grew more pleasing to him with every meeting. Even now with the hall ringing with his name he took no pride in it, but kept his eyes down modestly, and spoke only when the King asked a question of him. He was grave and quiet and graceful of speech as a poet, and yet he had the sword arm of an archangel. Charles thought over the battle with Weland again. It had seemed the boy must lose. He himself had grabbed up his reins to flee, when Roderick flinched that second time; he had thought the Spanish knight had failed, but then suddenly Weland was on the ground, and Paris was saved, and now, looking back, he saw it all sure and clear: he should have realized.

He saw something sure and clear ahead of him, too, growing more definite with every cup of wine.

The room seemed to be getting hotter. Down the table in front, where his warriors sat, men were roaring out songs and shoving each other and laughing, thoroughly drunk, the whole room a wild whirl of deep color and sound. Beside him sat the youth Roderick, quiet, solemn, upright as a rooftree. Charles turned to him.

"In Spain," he said, "there are some mighty Kings, I am told."

"None so mighty as you, my lord." The young man lifted his gaze to the King's, his grey eyes clear as ice. "Coming here, we rode over your kingdom for many days. My father was no such King as that."

"But nonetheless," Charles said. Odo had brought the ewer and was filling his cup again, the ivywood cup he had inherited from his grandfather, a cup for making pledges. He raised it to Roderick, and drank deep. "But nonetheless, a King. You are a Prince, then."

Roderick looked away across the room. "I may never go back, my lord. I know not what I am." His voice had a sudden, leaden note.

"Well, then," Charles cried. "Stay here. Stay where you have made a name for yourself. Be my paladin, chief of my court. Be a Prince of Francia!" He straightened, talking to the whole room now, and seeing he spoke some great words, people around him hushed and turned. The attention spread out across the whole room. In the sudden silence, with all eyes upon him, Charles stood up, almost spilling his wine.

"I proclaim this! I, Charles, King of Francia, will bind this noble knight Roderick to me forevermore! Let him be the champion of Francia! And let him be as high in Francia as my own son!"

A roar went up, a hundred arms waving in the air. He beamed out at them, seeing he had done the right thing. He turned now to his left, where down the table a little his wife and daughter sat, smiling at him.

"You know all I am a man of true speaking. I mean Roderick

to be as my own son. Therefore, I give him now—for his wife—my daughter, my Princess, my Alpiada."

The applause and cheers thundered up all around him. His head buzzed. Suddenly before him like a parade of unborn Kings he saw his dynasty made new again, his throne secure, his empire real again. A heat of exaltation filled him, of triumph. Drinking deep, he gave the cup to Odo to be filled, and sat down, smiling.

He turned now to his new Prince of Francia, expecting to find a smile there too, but Roderick was white as lamb's wool.

He said, "Sire, I am chaste."

All around them was still the tumult of congratulation. Charles' high mood receded a little. He felt flushed; he knew he was drunk. He knew also that Roderick would not refuse him this, not in front of all these people. He wiped his mouth, seeking a way against the boy's will. "Have you committed yourself then to God, Roderick? Are you a monk?"

The young man's face fell a little. His mouth was curled down; Charles, surprised, saw he was much unhappy. He straightened, puzzled, wondering what he had not seen in this, which seemed so excellent to him.

Roderick said, "No, Sire, I am no monk. I mean one day to marry, but—"

"Then you will marry Alpiada," Charles said. He struck the young man a fatherly clap on the shoulder. Whatever the objection, he would get him over it. "I will hear nothing else, Roderick. I have seen God's purpose here. You are meant to be a Prince of Francia, and I have made you one." He lifted his cup. "To your marriage. May it be soon, may it be fruitful."

Roderick's face was clouded over; he looked away. All around them the hall leapt with excited, drunken people. The King poked the cup at him. "Drink."

Slowly the young man reached for his wine.

*   *   *

John, in the corner, clenched his fist. A white fury rose in him against Charles, who would force this all to some bad end, just to save himself. He watched Roderick struggle, and then subside. He knew she dared not argue here. He gathered himself. He would help her find a way out. There had to be a way out. He crossed himself, uncertain.

Roderick sat rigid in her place, staring blindly into the air. This was her fault, she knew, the consequence of her sin. Like Erma she had brought forth her own punishment. The shrieks and cheers of the crowd scraped on her like a rasp. They shouted her name, over and over. Not her name. Her name they would never know, would never cheer. They trapped her; she could not escape, and should not: her sin. Her punishment. She poured the wine down her throat, trying to drown the awful feeling in her gut.

Erma heard them coming across the pear orchard, knew the banquet was over, and ran out to meet them, laughing and clapping her hands. "The Princess! You're to marry the Princess!" A single look at Roderick's face showed her that he was none so happy about all this as she was, and she stopped; they went by her, into their chamber, Seffrid close on the young lord's heels. Erma followed, confused.

Seffrid was saying, "You might as well make the best of it. Or we could go, you know, just leave."

Erma's heart bounded; she crossed the space between them like a blown leaf, and said, "Why must you go? What's wrong?"

Roderick gave her a single glancing look. "Where's the baby?"

"Asleep," she said, shyly, and drew back; she felt he had dismissed her, sent her back to the child. Seffrid got Roderick's arm and drew him away, talking in his ear.

"Make the best of it! The girl is young, she may stay with her mother awhile yet. Just agree, and give and get a ring, and in a few years—"

"You're mad," Roderick said, and turned and walked away.

Erma said, helplessly, "What's wrong?"

Seffrid turned toward her. "Never mind. Did you eat?"

"Yes. I—" She glanced at Roderick, who had gone to the back of the room, where the baby slept. Seffrid had come up to her, and she put her hand on his chest. Suddenly the thought that he might go was like a stab in her belly. She looked up into his face.

"Don't go. Please don't go."

He slid his arms around her, smiling down at her, amused. "What a goose, Erma. We're not going anywhere, not for a while." He bent down and kissed her. His hand slid down over her hip, and she leaned against him, worried.

Roderick went out, into the dark drizzle of the night, and walked back past the King's stables and the bake ovens to the end of the earthworks. A blustery cold wind was coming up the river and she climbed the earthworks into its rough buffeting, and sat down on the top, her back to the city.

She could hear the rush of the river pouring down past the ruined stone bridge piers on the north; the wind seethed through the brush on the marshy bank. The drizzle soaked her. She began to make out shapes in the dark: the paler sandy shore below her, and over there, to her left, the river's bank rising up above the current. The wind beat at her.

It was all alive, and wild, out here, she thought, not like the city behind her with its dead confining walls and its hard angles, all those people wanting something from her, tricking her, breaking her into pieces. Suddenly she hated it back there. She wanted to flee out into the dark and the wind and the wild, drop to all fours, and run like a wolf.

She shut her eyes, heartsore. The rain dripped down her face. "Roderick!"

She turned her head. The voice was faint, still far-off, but she knew it. She slid down the inside of the earthworks into a mass of dense brush.

"Roderick!" Closer.

"I am here, Leovild!" She picked herself out of the clinging, stabbing grip of the brush and went toward the sound of his voice, and saw him, walking stiffly, misshapen in his bandages. Another monster, she thought, and went gratefully to him.

"What are you doing out here in the rain?" he said. "The King sent me to you. I am to make you one with this marriage he wants."

She grunted at him. In the dark, she could not see him well, but she knew him, she knew how he turned to her now, smiling, knew that he would reach out and wrap his arm around her even before he did it, awkward in his bandages.

He said, "In truth, why you don't want it, I can't say, but if you don't, I am no man to argue with you."

"Leovild," she said, and suddenly it was there, on her lips, to tell him everything; her eyes filled with tears; she longed to tell him.

He said, "No, say nothing, you need not, you have your reasons, and I know enough of you to have faith that they are worthy. Only, don't do anything too quickly; I hear the girl is not happy with it, either; this marriage will not happen, believe me."

Her soul soared. She said, "She isn't?" in a half squeak.

Leovild, beside her, laughed, and nudged her. "Apparently you are not so winsome to everybody. Though, faith, if I were a maid, I would be first to ask."

She laughed at that, light suddenly and easy as a feather in the breeze. They were walking back toward the monastery. The wind gusted up suddenly and blew hard through the pear trees, scattering wet leaves and old blossoms and big loose drops of rain. An unlatched door banged somewhere. They went along together, not speaking, side by side. She held her breath for the pleasure of it. She thought she would endure anything, forever, to be with Leovild this way. They reached the monastery wall, at the door into the hall. A few candles burned in the wide dim space; only a few wounded men remained there, besides Leovild, the rest all dead or mended.

Ahead of them, there stood Erma with the baby. Leovild turned, his eyes merry, and said, "You seem to have a little family here already. I'll leave you to them. Good night," and went in the door into the hall, and away from her; she watched him go through the gloomy shadowy room.

Her heart tumbled. She wondered what he would do—if he knew. If she had told him. She felt steadily lower. Nothing was solved, nothing was over. Wearily she trudged away down toward Erma and the baby and her own cell.

Erma aired out the whole room, took the straw ticks out and shook them in the sun to chase the fleas out, and spread all their clothes on branches of the pear orchard. The sun was bright and strong. A little wind blew. It came on her, as she worked, that she should have a coif, to cover her hair, now that she had a man, and she went up to the hall and found a length of linen and went back to their room and bound up her hair in it.

The baby was off with Roderick somewhere. Her breasts were sore; she knew he was hungry, and she went looking for him. She waggled her head as she walked, liking the feel of the coif over her hair. She was a good woman now. She walked carefully, neatly, her hands on her skirts. Once or twice she skipped. She went around the corner of the cloister, where here was a little patch of grass, and found Roderick and the baby sitting in the sun.

She stopped, enjoying the look of them. In the warmth of the sun Roderick had taken off his jerkin; the thin shirtsleeve fluttered in the slight breeze. He sat running blades of grass through his fingers, obviously half-lost in daydreams, while the little boy played beside him. The child reached out and took hold of Roderick's shirt and pulled himself up onto his feet. Erma went forward a little, smiling; he had been doing this with her, too, trying to stand. She saw Roderick turn toward him, reach out to help him, and as he turned, the child sat down hard and pulled on the shirt again, and Erma gulped.

Her legs went a little weak. She stood there a moment, watching. Roderick picked the baby up and shook him giggling in the air. Erma's head spun a little, as if the world were moving under her. She went forward and sat down next to them.

"Roderick," she said, looking full into the beautiful grey eyes, "are you a woman?"

The grey eyes widened. Roderick said nothing. That was an answer. Erma reached out and took the baby, and Roderick drew away from her.

"You are," Erma said.

Roderick turned her face away. "Erma. Be quiet."

"I will." She sat still, the baby in her arms. Roderick was still staring away from her.

"How did you know?" Roderick said, presently.

"The baby pulled your shirt—I saw your breast."

Roderick shut her eyes. She said, in a dull voice, "I never meant to lie." Reaching for the jerkin, she pulled it on over her head.

Erma clutched the baby against her, afraid. "Never mind that I saw. I'll keep the secret. You can just go on the way you want. Never mind."

Roderick looked away. "That's exactly what I can't do," she said, and got up and walked away.

Erma picked up the baby and held him, and watched Roderick go, her heart hammering. Even now, knowing, Erma would have taken her for a man, walking with a man's long stride, a man's set of head and shoulder.

A wild mirth boiled up in her; they all thought Roderick was a hero, they thought Roderick was the greatest knight in Paris, and Roderick was a woman, like Erma, just a lowly woman.

She would never tell.

The wind blew up in a big gust. A sudden wild fear shook her. Her head whirled. She held the baby tight. She watched Roderick walk away, a man. Surely a man. It was witchcraft, she thought, with horror. This was witchcraft, or worse.

She went around the monastery, her knees quaking, to the cell. Seffrid was there. She went in, staring at him, wondering wildly what he really was, and he lifted his head, saw the look on her face, and reached out behind her and shut the door.

"What is it?"

She babbled something. She was thinking of all that Roderick had done; could she do that without power—without some wicked power? Seffrid got her by the arm.

"Erma." He shook her. "What is it?"

"Roderick is a witch," she said.

At once, blurting it out, she cringed, clutching the baby tight, knowing he would hit her. He did not. He let her go, glanced at the door, and turned to face her again.

"You found out."

She began to cry. "It's true, then." The baby began to howl and she clung to him. "My poor baby. My poor baby."

"Erma." He grabbed her by the shoulders and held her still.

"Listen to me. She is not a witch. God strike me as I stand, she is not a witch. She is as good and true as a beam of sunlight, Erma."

Erma stared at him through the blinders of her tears. He shook her a little by the shoulders. "I don't know how you found out, but it was bound to happen. She's running away from her father, that's all. The rest just came on us."

The baby was screeching. Erma lowered herself onto the ground. Slowly the panic was fading. She opened her dress and gave her breast absently to the baby, thinking over what he had told her. He was watching her, sharp-eyed, but now he turned and went back to what he had been doing: sharpening his sword with a whetstone. She saw it was not so much to him. She felt herself flatten out to ordinary.

The door opened, and Roderick came in.

She stiffened. Roderick stared at her a moment, and then turned away. Erma blinked, seeing her as a woman. She was unhappy. Her shoulders slumped. She seemed all inward, tucked inside herself, untouchable. But the baby crowed, and held his arms out to her.

Erma tightened her grip; she could not give him to a witch. But he was crawling eagerly out of her arms already as if he could launch himself across the empty air, and Roderick reached out and took him.

Erma clenched her teeth, her heart banging in her throat. Her arms itched to seize her son back. Roderick turned her eyes down at the baby, which laughed up into her face. The baby loved her. Erma stood watching them, frozen in her doubts. She thought suddenly of a sure test.

"You said—you said—he would be baptized."

Roderick lifted her head and faced her. "Yes. Soon."

"Will you hold him at the font?"

The clear grey eyes warmed. "Yes. Yes, I will. Thank you, Erma."

Erma's load of worry slid away from her. No witch would stand so close to holy water, would hold a baby being blessed.

Whatever she was, she could not be a witch. She watched the strange girl before her turn back to the baby and murmur to it. She was beautiful, she saw suddenly, beautiful as a white flower. Erma said, "When?"

"I'll talk to John," Roderick said. The baby was pulling on her clothes; he reached out one hand and patted her cheek.

"Dada."

Roderick laughed. "No, silly one. Here. Go to your mother." She held the baby out to Erma. "I'll talk to John," she said. Her voice shook slightly. "Thank you, Erma."

She went into the back of the cell. Erma took the baby off to nurse him, feeling better.

John caught up with the King after morning Mass, and fell in step with him. The King was on his way to the women's quarters; they walked along the outer wall of the palace, looking out toward the river. The page Odo trailed after them. King Charles said, "I'm glad to see you, I want you to do something for me."

"Sire," John said, "I came to tell you you must not force this marriage on young Roderick."

The King stopped abruptly. "Why is everybody in my way about this? I won't hear it! He'll do it—he must do it." He glared at John. "What's your objection to it?"

John was looking out across the river, where the meadow beyond was thronged with people going home, now that the Northmen were gone. He had thought already how to talk of this without lying and without betraying Roderick, and he said, "It is against his will, and God's too, I warrant."

"God sent him here to save my dynasty!" Charles said, tramping along.

John turned toward him. "God sent him here, perhaps, to save the kingdom. Will you bend God's will below your own?"

"Ah, you argue like a Jew." The King stretched his legs, trying to walk away from John. The big Irishman kept up with him effortlessly. They went along a little in silence, John looking out over the river again at the streams of people going back to their fields. There had already come into the city a caravan with wheat and some wine and beer. On the road now he saw more wagons rolling toward Paris.

They had reached the end of the palace, where around the corner the door into the women's quarters opened. The King turned to go that way, and John stopped, remembering something the King had just said. "Who else is objecting to the marriage?"

The page Odo had gone by the King, and opened the door. Out through it came the answer, a high girl's voice shouting, "I won't! I won't, Mama—that's all!"

The King lifted his head, listening, and sighed; not angry anymore, his gaze came to John's.

"Well, as you hear. Enter in, I need your help in this."

John followed him down the wall and through the door there into the front of the room. The morning sun was reaching through the narrow windows. Against the back wall the looms were working, the women sitting with their backs to him, sliding the shuttles back and forth, with a rattle of wood and the clicking and ticking of the weights. The Queen stood near the hearth, wringing her hands, while before her, on her knees, was Alpiada, sobbing and screaming.

"Mama! I won't do it!"

The King went to his chair and sat heavily down, and the girl came across the room in a rush and flung herself down on her knees beside her father.

"Papa, please, you can't make me do it." She lifted her face toward John; her eyes were red and sore. "Father John, they cannot make me marry against my will, can they?"

John smiled at her. "No, they can't."

Charles struck at him, stirring in his chair. "I will. You're a foolish girl, Alpiada! He is handsome, young, mannerly, and the greatest knight in my kingdom—why do you reject him?"

The girl's face was dead white under the slicks of tears. Her eyes were sunken hollow. It came to John suddenly that she was afraid. Her mouth worked. She said, "Papa, don't make me," and laid her head on his knees. The Queen had come, and stood in the shadows just behind her child, watching.

Charles stroked the girl's shoulder. John knew he loved her best, maybe alone, of all his children; she would win him over. The King bent suddenly and kissed the girl's hair, and then faced John.

"Go find Roderick and ask him if he will speak to her. If they come face-to-face, a man and a maid, surely they will win to one another." He lifted his child up gently by the arms, smiling into her face. "You are so pretty and good, and he is so good, it will match. You'll see."

"I won't," she said.

John said, "Sire, she's distraught."

"Do as I bid you," the King said, still doting on her, smiling into her face, although she groaned and scowled at him. "Go talk to Roderick. They may have each other's company for a little while, and talk it out, and see how they like each other—then we shall go from that."

John nodded. That made much sense from all sides of it. At least it gave some room for a way out of this. "I'll talk to Roderick," he said.

14

YOU'RE BEING A STUPID LITTLE goose," her mother
said. "Now, listen to me." The older woman took Alpiada
by the arm and pulled her over to the corner. The girl
shivered at the tone of her mother's voice, and her eyes as sharp as
needles. She shook Alpiada a little, as if she were wakening her.
"You will marry, my girl, someday, whatever your ideas to the otherwise. You are a Princess of Francia and you will marry as your father needs you to, for the good of our house and our kingdom.
This young man is an excellent match, and you'd be a stupid silly
goose to decline him. Do you hear me?"

Alpiada wrenched at her arm; her mother did not speak so
roughly to her much. She gulped. If not her mother, who would
help her? "Mama, how can you do this to me?"

"Do this to you!" The Queen shook her again until her shoulder joint hurt. "What a goose. What will be done to you has been
done to every woman since Eve, and we're the better for it. A
woman must have a man, as the vine needs the elm tree. Now, listen to me. He doesn't want you either. Do you understand that? I

don't care how you feel about it, but your father needs him bound to us, and you are the rope. Go in and win him, Alpiada." She let go of Alpiada's arm with a little shove.

Alpiada backed away a step. Her mouth was dry and her arm hurt where her mother had gripped her. Her mother's hard relentless look chilled her more even than the ache in her arm. Her father was angry and now her mother too. Her mind flinched at what they wanted her to do. On stiff legs she went to the door into the little room where she was to meet Roderick.

He was already there. He stood by the window, taller than she was, slender as a wand, with the sun behind him. She went a few steps toward him, and stopped, her throat clogged with fear; with the sun shining in behind him, she could not see him. He came toward her through a blaze of light.

She flinched back. At once he went down on his knee before her.

"Alpiada." The low, musical voice was startled. "Are you afraid of me?"

Her lips were too stiff to speak. She thought of crying instead. What her mother had said spilled into her mind again; they would make her marry someone, it would happen somehow, with someone, this stranger in front of her, or someone else. "I can't bear it." She pressed her hands to her eyes against the tears. "To be given to someone. I know—what men do to women—I saw it once—" She sobbed.

He was moving, not standing up to do it, just sidling over, so that to face him she turned away from the glare of the light. With the sunlight falling in from the side, she could see him clearly. She looked down, startled.

She had never looked at him before. His face was open and soft. She had heard him called Roderick the Beardless and his cheeks were smooth as her own. The grey eyes were like water in a deep spring. She raised her arms; she had the sudden impulse to reach out her hands to him, as if toward a warm fire.

Roderick said, "I will not hurt you, Alpiada. I promise it."

"I know you will not," she said. In an instant, all her fear had fled. She felt calm, and brave, as if she could do great deeds, like a man.

"I cannot marry you," Roderick was saying. "We must agree on that, and how to convince your father not to force us."

She swallowed, vaguely disappointed. She said, "Sir, why do you not want to marry me?"

"I cannot marry anybody," Roderick said, with force. "That is the whole of it."

"My father will make me marry someone," she said. She put her hand on his arm. "You are kind." When she touched him, she felt him jump, a little, like a startled horse. "I like you, I think."

His eyes widened. He said, in a higher, sharper voice, "We cannot marry. You must believe me."

"Am I not pretty enough?" Everyone told her she was pretty; had they lied? She took hold of his hand, liking the touch of his skin.

"This has nothing to do with you," he said. "It's only—it's simply—"

She watched his face turn red, and his eyes shift around, looking for some way out. Holding his hand between them, she lowered her voice. "Tell me why. If it is a secret, I promise I will keep it."

Roderick lifted his clear, tormented eyes to hers. In the little silence Alpiada could hear the monastery bell begin to ring, off in the distance, and the big brazen bell of Our Lady Church. Then the handsome boy before her said, "Because I am a woman also."

Alpiada's mouth dropped open. Her fingers loosened, and Roderick reached up to the front of his jerkin and drew it down, enough to show one small white breast.

"Oh," Alpiada said. Astonished, she reached out again and took Roderick's hand in both of hers. "Oh, but how brave you are."

The girl before her lowered her eyes again. "Not so brave. I was only—I had to escape. From my father." Swiftly she looked up again, and their eyes met. "It was—you and I have that much in common, I would not marry against my will. But now—you see— everything's gotten so tangled up, I can't get it straight again."

Alpiada laughed. For a moment, she was confused, not certain what to think of this, a woman passing herself off as a man, but then, suddenly, it all burst upon her, how perfect this was, how this made everything work.

"But you can now—don't you see?" She laughed, clutching Roderick's hand. "This will solve everything for both of us, if we marry. Don't you see?"

"What are you saying?" Roderick asked, her hand limp in Alpi- ada's, and her eyes wide.

"You must marry me," Alpiada said. "It's the only way."

"Alpiada! That's mad!"

"It's the only way." Alpiada was clinging to Roderick's hand with both hands. "I will love you, and wait on you like a wife, and make you happy, I promise, Roderick. You must marry me now. Now that I know."

Roderick stared at her a moment, turned, and looked over her shoulder at the door, where the Queen would be waiting. Her mouth trembled, but she said nothing. Alpiada said, "I'll protect you, Roderick. I'll make you happy. Wait—I'll call my mother. Just wait. All will be well. Don't you see?" She leaned forward and kissed Roderick on the lips, and got up to call the Queen.

Deodatus served at the Mass at dawn, in the church of Our Lady, holding the book and taking the cup to the priest; he knew this rite so well he could sleep through most of it, waking only enough to move when he had to. Yet it was hard to sleep. The church smelled horrible. Even now that the Vikings were gone and the troubles over, people were living here, in the back corners, in the dark, and once in the middle of the pleasant drone of the Mass there was a shriek from one side that brought him up on his toes, all his hair on end and his eyes popping.

No one saw. He settled down again, thinking they should run the people out of the church, after the Mass was over. They could live in the village. They pissed and shit in the dark at the back of the church and built fires and now there was this screaming in the middle of the holiest of ceremonies.

The priest's voice dragged along through the offertory. Deodatus fell asleep again.

After the Mass, he went off quickly to avoid his abbot, who would have something for him to do, and went around behind Our Lady Church. There, beyond a little strip of green grass, was the ruin of another church, Saint Stephen, which had been burnt down in a Viking raid a couple of years before.

Deodatus kept a cloak hidden behind one of the columns of the broken porch, so that he could take a nap here. The columns were round, and ridged, and they had fallen apart into sections like drums, which were tumbled in the overgrowing grass before the church porch. When the church had been whole, the open spaces between the columns had been filled in with smaller stones to make a solid wall, and those too lay scattered around, although people had taken away anything they could carry. The roof had burned away completely, and the top courses of the walls had fallen down, so that the walls stretched away like ribs to the sagging choir wall. Grass and brush grew up along the walls and in the space between, and made soft places where a man could hide away and sleep his fill.

But when Deodatus went up to the porch of the church, he saw people from the village picking through the ruins and carrying off stones and pieces of wood.

He drew back, furious. They were stealing the body of the

church, just to rebuild their houses. He gathered himself. He should run out there and drive them off. His heart began to race. He knew if he did that, rushed out like a fool, he would get some of those stones flung at him. He forced his temper calm. He could tell the abbot. But then would the old man not know that Deodatus had come out here to avoid work? And probably they already found his hidden cloak, and stolen it. He pronounced a soft curse against the wretch who had stolen his cloak. Turning, he went back toward the great common in front of Our Lady Church.

Most of the crowd that had poured into the city when the Northmen came were gone now. On the common some people with wagons were offering nuts and chickens and braids of onions to the scattering of passersby. Deodatus walked across the hard-packed ground, considering where else he would find the solitude necessary for his nap, and there coming across from the village he saw the girl he had seen earlier with Seffrid.

What Seffrid did with her, that was sin, he thought, with satisfaction. And the baby in her arms, sin. His belly tightened pleasantly. He went on a course to intercept her.

She saw him coming; she slowed down, wary, and he smiled and bowed his head to her. "Good day, sister. God's blessing on you."

She shifted the baby to her other hip. "Thank you, Father." And when he stood there, smiling at her, she said, "Is there anything you wish of me, sir?"

"Only that you give me good tidings of my dear young Roderick," Deodatus said. "I see so little of him now, but we were so close, when we traveled here. Is he well?

Something in that amused her, he saw, with surprise; she smiled broadly at him, her eyes narrow with mirth. "Roderick is very well. You know he will marry the Princess."

Deodatus' breath slid out his nose. "No. I had heard that was not to be—neither wanted it, I heard." He rolled a smile up onto his face. "What good fortune for him—he had nothing, when he came here."

This amused Erma even more, he saw, startled, and she beamed at him. She said, "So it is. Thank you, Father. God be with you." With a little dip of her head she went off, swinging her hips, the baby riding along like an imp of Satan attached to her.

He itched to know what made her laugh so, in what he said. He thought it over; he saw nothing strange in it. He rubbed his palms down the front of his robe. He hated secrets. He hated Roderick, also, he realized, again; now he had somehow won the Princess to him, he would be here forever. Deodatus ground his teeth. Such a weight of sin everywhere bore him down like heavy shoes. He dragged himself off around the monastery dormitory, toward the stables, where he could nap in the hay.

John had finished the last Greek page of the Areopagite. He cleaned his pens and sharpened them and began to turn it into Latin.

The languages were different, not only in their surfaces, but in their understandings. The Greek with its coils and complex rhythms spoke the ideas differently than the solid Latin laid brick by brick in its rigorous order. He was laying one course of this wall across his page when a stir in the doorway brought him around; he looked, and saw Roderick there.

"Well." He laid his pen down and put the inkwell carefully on the top edge of the page, to keep the parchment from curling. "Come on, I am glad to see you."

"You are busy," Roderick said, hovering on the threshold.

"You are very welcome here. Come sit down."

Still she loitered in the doorway. Her face was lean, hollow-eyed, her lips curled down at the corners. She said, "Did I not tell you of the child Seffrid has now—that he is not christened?"

John nodded. "You told me. Shall we do it?"

"Yes. Please."

"We can use the King's chapel, by the palace; there is a font there."

"Thank you," Roderick said.

Her face was pale. John studied her, seeing the care in her; she seemed much older than when he had first met her.

He said, "Is there something wrong, Roderick?"

She gave him a wild stare. "No!"

John pressed his lips together, not wanting to smile; if she could not speak of it, he could not either.

"He is a boy child, this new son of Seffrid's? Who will hold him at the font?"

"I will." Roderick was composed again, taut, almost grim.

"Then tomorrow, I think," John said. "Has she—have they named him?"

Roderick said, "I don't think so."

John waited, watching her. She wore the outward look of manhood as easily as a birthright. Her hair was growing down toward her shoulders, curling at the end. He knew the ordinary folk said it was her sanctity that made her beardless. She said nothing, but she did not go.

Finally he said, "How went your council with the Princess?"

She jerked her head up, her wide eyes aimed at him. "They want me to marry her."

"But you will not. Then do not."

"Father—" She came in, went past him, and sat down on the stool before the window, facing him. "Does God hear liars' prayers?"

John put his hands together. "God hears everything."

"But—then—" Her head rose. "What is the use of telling the truth? If God will hear you anyway? I don't believe it."

He shrugged one shoulder. A quick little sermon popped into

his mind, all adorned with quotes and sallies, to the point that liars lost their own trust as well as the world's, and so wrought their own doom, and he put that hastily away. He said, "You must trust God to love you, Roderick."

She looked away, toward the far wall. The sunlight fell onto her face, and in the bright light he saw along her cheek a fine down. A shiver went through him. She noticed nothing, she was staring out the window.

She said, "When I was in the river, after Leovild, that time, I went under, and someone pulled me up. I don't know who. All I remember is the feel of the hand, catching hold of me, and drawing me out." Her shoulders hunched. "I am looking for that hand to draw me out again, but I can't find it."

John said, "Trust in God, Roderick."

She got violently up, so that the stool clattered over. "I have no right to God anymore," she said, and went out the door.

John braced his hands on his desk. Her words shocked him. He should have followed her, he thought, and tried to console her. He knew she would not heed him. He crossed himself. Kneeling down, he prayed to God for her, there in the sunlight coming through the window.

John said, "What will you name him, Erma?"

She smoothed her hair back, her eyes on the baby in Roderick's arms. Then she turned quickly to Seffrid, standing beside her.

"Shall I name him after you? Seffrid?"

The stocky little Frank shook his black head. "Not my son."

"Then—" She faced the child again. "I want to call him Roderick."

Roderick lifted her head, her eyes bright. The child twisted in her arms, trying to sit up, and she turned her face down to him and spoke to him, and he quieted. John dipped his hand into the holy water and came to him, and began to speak church words. Seffrid, beside her, was restless, kept looking around. In fact the little chapel had some pretty pictures, Erma thought, as the incomprehensible words flowed on: there was Jesus above the altar, and hangings on the walls. The one she could see without turning her head was of Mary and Joseph with Baby Jesus on their knees. She twisted a little, looking more behind her, to the other wall.

That hanging was all eaten up with rot; all she could see was a tree, with a snake hanging out of it.

She turned straight again, alarmed. She knew what that meant, that was Adam and Eve. Or should have been, under the rot. They ought not to leave things like that here, she thought. Where people can see them. She kept her back to it. They were blessing little Roderick now, and he laughed at the touch of the monk's hand, just as if he knew that now he was a real person, with a soul.

Afterward they went out to the warmth of the summer morning. Big Roderick gave the baby to his mother. John kissed the baby and kissed Erma's forehead and went quickly back to his work. Big Roderick stood watching him go, and then turned to Seffrid.

"Have you told her?"

Seffrid fussed with his moustache. "No."

"Then tell her," said Roderick. "Remember, the stables, when the nones bell rings." She strode off without even a glance at the baby.

Erma said, "What does he mean? What are you to tell me?"

Seffrid got her arm and towed her along toward the monastery. Erma gripped the baby, who was trying to squirm down and get to the ground; they went in through the pear orchard, the ground all littered with fallen blossoms.

"What is this?" Erma cried, and stopped. There was no one anywhere around them. She glared at him. "Tell me now."

He faced her. "You know about the Princess, that they are trying to make them marry."

Erma bobbed her head. "Yes."

He said, "So we have to leave."

"What?" she said, startled. "You mean—all of us? Leave Paris?"

"Do you want to go?"

"I—" The baby struggling in her arms became an impossible weight, and she let him slide down to the ground. "I have never been anywhere else, save here, and the Marais."

"We have to go," Seffrid said.

"Where?" she cried.

"Bah." With a jerk of his hand at the sky he turned and strode away from her.

She stood staring after him, her throat locked, her lungs frozen; she turned her head suddenly and looked all around her, at these sights she had seen all her life, and thought of leaving, to go nowhere, he could not even tell her where, he did not know himself where they would go. At her feet, the baby—Roderick—was sitting up, his fists stuffed with dirt and twigs and his face smeared with mud. He had his name now. She could stay here. She stooped and picked him up, against his squawks of protest, and carried him away after Seffrid.

Seffrid got two good mules from the pen behind the stable, and brought them out to the stable yard; his gut fluttered. He hoped nobody asked him what he was doing with these horses. Three boys were chasing a colt around a nearby pen, but they paid no heed to him, beyond a wave—everybody knew him now.

It was sore, then, to leave, when everybody knew him and waved, and he had a good dinner every night and a warm bed and a lively girl to share it with him. He knew he would not find another girl like Erma, not soon.

He thought he might not find another like her ever.

He knew she would not go. He had nothing to use to entice

her into going, no promises of anything. He rubbed down the grey mule's hind legs, hoping she decided to follow him anyway. If she came, he would put her on this mule, which was kinder than the other; she probably had never ridden.

She would not come; he knew that already.

Maybe he would take this grey mule anyway. It as a fine, strapping mule, and calmer than most.

Then Roderick was walking up to him. "Good," she said. "Where is Erma?" She slapped the grey mule's neck. "Give her my saddle, I can ride bareback."

"I don't know if she is coming," Seffrid said. "There's nones." The bells began to ring, first the big clanger in Our Lady Church, and then the sweet singing bell in the King's chapel, and, much closer, the monastery bell.

"She'll be here." Roderick climbed though the fence. "I'll get my horse."

"Roderick!"

She straightened; she gave Seffrid a wild look. Leovild strode toward them, his bandaged arm in a sling across his chest.

"I'm glad I found you, I've been looking for you. The King wants to see you—you should come now, and dine with him." Leovild was smiling at them, his eyes narrow; he had taken good notice of the mules, Seffrid guessed, and knew what was up. He said, in a light voice, "Are you going somewhere?"

Roderick leaned her folded arms against the top rail of the fence. Seffrid stepped back a little, startled at the way she looked. She saw nothing but Leovild; her whole body had turned, hips and shoulders and knees, everything in her drawn toward him. She said, "My horse needs some running." Her face flushed suddenly, under the sunburn. Her eyes never left Leovild's face.

She said, "Are you dining with the King, Leovild?"

"I am. Come with me; someone brought in a deer; they have been turning it over the fire all morning."

Roderick turned toward Seffrid. "Then take my horse out, and run him well, get him into a good sweat."

Seffrid grunted at her. "As you wish, Roderick."

She reached out and shoved him in the chest, but he saw her flush again, all over her face, he saw she could deny Leovild nothing. He wondered when this had happened, why he had not noticed it, that she had come to love this yellow-headed Frankish knight. She climbed away from him, through the fence rails, and she and Leovild went side by side away around the bulk of the monastery, toward the palace.

Seffrid turned back to the mule. Women were unsteady, that was the whole of it, falling in love with other men, leaving people behind. The nones bells had long ago stopped ringing. The King would dine on his fat roasted deer all afternoon. There would be no leaving Paris this day.

His mood rose. That meant he would have Erma again tonight, at least. He went back to get Roderick's horse out, and take it for a gallop.

Roderick said, "You have a school, you told me—where are your students?"

She was sitting by the window in the monastery writing room. The white cat had come up and jumped into her lap and she stroked it. John dipped the red pen into the carnelian and made the first letter of the name of God, a *D,* now that he was writing in Latin.

"They are all scattered, because I was gone so long, bringing back these books," he said. He stood back and cleaned the pen and laid it down again. The red always pleased him, the color deep and strong against the mottled cream of the parchment. There was another monk who wove gold and blue around these red letters, making them beautiful as small prayers. "Now that the Vikings have gone, they will come back."

He turned toward her, seeing how she sat, twisting on the stool, her head at an angle. She was angry, he saw, not in a temper but a long slow burning, her body skewed around that hot core.

He said, "I hear you are going to marry Alpiada."

"I can do nothing else." She lifted one hand and let it drop. "Even she, now—" She bit her lips, looking off. "I'm trapped, there is no way out."

John lifted the black pen. He said, "It is a mistake, Roderick."

"I know, but there's nothing else I can do. The King is insisting we marry soon, too. I had hoped—"

She broke off. Her face was taut. John dipped the black pen into the ink, gathered up three letters worth, and leaned over the parchment. He said, "What will you do, then?"

He expected her to say, or not to say, that she would run away. She shrugged. There was a long stillness. Then she burst out, "Once we are married, I can take out some of the men. We can ride down the river and see what the Vikings are doing." She chopped her fist down on her knee. "God, God, I wish I were out there now, in the wild, and not here, where everything gets so complicated."

John said, "You mean you will go through with it?"

"What choice do I have?" She let out a long deep sigh. She faced him, her mouth crooked, her eyes narrow. Abruptly, imperiously, she was changing the subject.

"What good are these books, hah? Tell me. Puny little human makings, when there is God's work all around to wonder about."

John straightened. He saw, unnerved, that she wanted to fight. He spoke slowly; this was his writing room, a place of calm and quiet. "The books are words, and God's work began with words. God spoke, and His words made this world. So when men write words, they too can make little worlds."

"Bah," she said. "That's blasphemy, or so I promise you Deodatus would say. Only God makes real things."

That spurred him; he straightened, and fired his words at her like arrows.

"God gave us words to make ideas with, which are real things: they have effect, they have purpose. This is a true magic, this matter of words and books, and if you cannot see it, Roderick, you are the worse for it. Books knit time together—without books, the past would be gone, utterly gone, and how else can we even begin to think about the time to come?"

She raised her head. "I think about the time to come, but it doesn't do any good." She slid off the stool; she was going.

"It's just words, John," she said, her back to him. "It's all words, and it doesn't help."

He said, "I mean no harm, Roderick."

"There is no harm in you," she said, and went out the door and was gone.

15

RODERICK AND ALPIADA WERE MARRIED in the old church of Our Lady, across the common from the palace. The clustered fluttering candles on the altar made the only light, a bright little room where the new bride and bridegroom stood before the priest, with all their followers packed close around them. Under the tang of the incense, the church stank deeply of rot and garbage. Overhead was only darkness, loud with the twitterings of birds and nameless banging scraping things and the wind.

Seffrid stood behind Roderick, his hands clasped before him, wishing this would get over with. Erma, beside him, was watching it all intently, a dim smile on her face. Seffrid looked down at the stone floor at his feet—he could feel through his shoes how the rock was rippled from endless walking on it, all the edges worn round as bones. The whole church was half falling down, the back wall sunken, with great tree trunks bracing up the stones. He gave a shudder, wanting to be out of here before it all gave way and landed on him.

At the marriage feast Roderick sat at the King's right hand, Alpiada beside her. They hardly spoke, although Alpiada laughed and leaned on Roderick's shoulder. Roderick was drinking hard. Seffrid sat far away from her, down below the table with the ordinary folk.

Her mood nettled him. Even from a distance he saw she was getting drunk. She had a way of throwing her head back, of looking down her nose at people, that he had seen before, on someone else, and he knew what it was: Markold coming out in her.

She was boisterous; he watched her exchange a toast with someone, standing to drain her cup, and shouting some reply; suddenly she flung the cup wildly away, and a roar of laughter broke out, and a burst of clapping.

Seffrid had his fist clenched. He opened it carefully. He wondered if Markold in his youth had been so great as Roderick, and in a leap guessed why Queen Ingunn had chosen him, for that other, earlier wedding. But it had been a crooked choosing, as this was a crooked choosing, and he could not see that two crooked things ever made a straight.

He reminded himself this was not his matter. He would follow Roderick, whatever happened.

Up there at the table, Roderick was booming out another toast. Everybody was watching her. A yell went in answer to her. The girl Alpiada looked on her with shining eyes, her hands gripped together. Seffrid turned away suddenly, his belly like a stone.

The King had caused a bower to be built, just beside the palace for the wedding chamber. All the men wanted to escort Roderick to it, a great crowd of drunkards traveling around her, pulling on her and shouting. Roderick kept her arms down; her head was reeling with drink, and her throat was raw from making loud stupid boasts, but she had enough mind left not to let them undress her, although they kept trying. Leovild was beside her, bundling her along, yelling raucous and startling advice in her ear. She laughed at him, their faces inches apart; suddenly she wanted to kiss him. She jerked back, cold beneath the gloss of the wine.

They came to the bower and she went in, and in the doorway stood and held them out until she could get the door closed. With the door closed, the sound faded. She let her muscles go slack. A nauseous rumble edged up into her throat from her belly. She wondered why she had drunk so much.

Alpiada had already come, and had sent away her maids. In her nightdress, with her hair all down over her shoulders in long golden ripples, she sat up in the big bed with its piles of coverlets, watching Roderick approach her. Roderick came up to the side of the bed, feeling groggy and sick, and the girl said, "Come to bed now. Shall I help you?"

"I'm all right," Roderick said, although she wasn't. Her head was spinning. There was a cup on the table by the bed and she reached for it. Alpiada crawled across the bed to her, sat there next to her, and began opening the front of her jerkin.

The cup was full of wine. Roderick dropped it. "I want some water," she said. Her head felt huge and she couldn't see very well.

Alpiada leapt off the bed and went to the side of the room. Roderick braced her arms on the bed. It came to her through the haze of drink that this was all wrong, that Alpiada should go, and Leovild come back. Alpiada brought her a cup of water, and while Roderick drank it down in great gulps the girl undid her belt and pulled her boots off.

"Alpiada," Roderick said. "I just want to go to sleep."

"You have to take your clothes off." Alpiada lifted her jerkin up over her head. Roderick lay down gratefully on the bed. She felt the girl's hands drawing off her leggings. She was naked; she had not been naked for a long while. Alpiada lay down beside her, and propped herself up on one elbow, brushing her long curly yellow hair back.

"Tell me why you have hidden yourself." She stroked Roderick's shoulder. "My Lord."

Roderick laughed unhappily. "It's all so mixed up."

"Don't you like being a man? You are wonderful, everyone says so. I think so. And men have everything, and women have nothing."

"It's all a lie," Roderick said. "It isn't hard to be a man. You only have to give up everything sweet and good in life, and do murder, and trample other men under your feet, and then to die, be trampled under another man's feet, another man's murder. They give men everything, as you say, to make up for that they really have nothing, no babies, no love, no sweetness in life, save what they can steal or beg from women. They tell you men are the noble, the good, and the pure, but if I had known—"

She stopped, all her body aching, as if she could force herself back to that moment, in the mountains, back in the cave of songs. Her eyes burned.

"Tell me." Alpiada slid closer to her, touching her all over, and her skin answered, yearning, as if it wakened everywhere the other girl stroked. "Tell me why you did it, then."

"My father wanted me to . . ." She shut her eyes. Alpiada kissed her. She stirred toward the other girl, longing for the comfort of her touch.

"Tell me."

"He wanted me to—to marry him. I had to escape. I disguised myself as a man, because he would not be looking for a man." Roderick kept her eyes shut. Alpiada was touching her breasts. Her nipples tingled. "Now I'm trapped in Roderick."

Alpiada kissed her again. "I'll make you happy. You'll see." She lay against Roderick, breast against breast, and Roderick put her arms around her, pulling the warm body close. Shyly she moved her hand down to Alpiada's breast, the warm womanly curve in the palm of her hand. An ache began in her chest. She pressed her face against Alpiada's throat, trying to disappear. The other girl's arms tightened around her. She murmured gentle words. Roderick lay still in the warm embrace, her hand on Alpiada's breast, and fought a tide of tears.

The soft sweet slow love ended. Alpiada fell asleep; Roderick heard her breathing change, felt the tension in her body drift away. When she could she moved softly away from the other girl, and crept out of the bed.

She was drunk no more. Now her head was thick and sore and her throat was dry. She knelt down by the bed. Alpiada lay stretched out naked on the bed like an altar before her, her woman's body like an unattainable goal. Roderick crossed herself. Tears slipped down her cheeks. "O God," she said. "Please." She laid her hands palm to palm and pressed them to her face. "Please, God. Make me a woman again. Please. Please."

With Roderick gone to the marriage bower, Seffrid and Erma and the baby had the monk's cell to themselves. Erma cleaned everything out of it onto the grass just outside the door and swept the room and knocked down all the cobwebs she could reach. The baby Roderick woke up and she put him on the grass beside the bedticks and the stool and the chamber pot. He had learned a new game, pushing himself up onto all fours like a little dog, and swaying back and forth, and she called out to him, as she swept, "Horsey, horsey! Giddap!"

She had gone to the river in the morning, and cut armloads of sweet rushes. Now she shook them out of their bundles onto the clean floor and kicked them around. By the back door of the palace was a tremendous rosemary bush and she had snipped some of that too and she scattered the rosemary into the rushes.

Then, outside, the baby wailed suddenly. She went straight to the door and looked out.

He was sitting there, staring off toward the pear trees, his face all wrung up, and where he was staring was the monk Deodatus.

She went quickly out the door and picked the baby up. The monk stood watching her, his head slumped down over his breast like an old woman's. She quieted the howling baby and patted his back. The monk raised his hand suddenly and made a cross at her.

"God be with you, sister!"

"And you," she said. She had told Seffrid about seeing him, the other time, and Seffrid had said he was no friend of any of theirs and she should have nothing to do with him. If he were not a monk, she would have thrown a stone at him. She said, "What do you want of me, Father?"

The monk made a sort of grin at her. "Only to make inquiry of my dear Roderick. I see him so little, now that he is married."

She laughed, thinking how little he really knew. "Well, none of us sees much of Roderick. Now that he is married." The baby squirmed in her arms and she let him down onto the grass again. The monk watched her mournfully. She could not help smirking at him, who made a fool of himself with every word. "I shall tell him that you spoke of him. When I see him again."

The monk's fingers opened and shut into fists. He said, "And your lord, the noble Seffrid, he does well?"

"Well enough." She could not resist taunting him a little; she said, "You came north with them to Paris? All that way?"

"Oh, yes, it was a wonderful journey, hallowed by God."

She folded her arms over her chest. A devil of mischief quickened in her. "All that way, you came with them, and never realized! Well, well."

She wondered how Roderick had done that; she wondered again if some special power hovered over her, and she thrust it off.

She thought of Roderick standing at the baptismal font, she thought of the new-blessed baby smiling up at her, and knew it was not witchcraft.

God made wonders too, she thought.

Deodatus was watching her like a cat stalking a mouse. His eyes glittered. He bared his teeth at her. "What are you saying, girl?"

She gave a little skip, out of lightness of heart, that she was clever and he wasn't. "Nothing, nothing."

He came creeping toward her, his hands together, as if he were praying to her. "Sister, is there something of my Roderick?"

She laughed again, and went around gathering up the bedticks to put back into her room. He followed her. "Sister, you may tell me, I am his dearest friend. He saved my life, there by the ford, when Leovild betrayed us to the bandits—young Roderick! I taught him how to pray!"

She shook her head, smiling, took the bedticks into the room, and laid them down neatly on either side. The room smelled wonderfully of the rushes and the rosemary. The sun coming through warmed her. She went back to get the stool and the chamber pot.

Deodatus was still there. The baby sat scowling at him. Erma said, "Now, go away, I have my work, I'm too busy taking care of my family to gossip."

"You'll give greeting from me to Seffrid," the monk said, backing up a little. "When you see him."

She laughed. "I will," she said, thinking how Seffrid would take this: Seffrid might go after the monk, and she thought how she could fire him to it, with some hints. She tossed her head at Deodatus, watching him out of the corner of her eye.

"And to my dear Roderick."

She gave a chuckle. She could not resist one more jab at him. "How dear can she be to you, Deodatus, if—"

She clapped her hand over her mouth. The monk was staring at her, and his jaw dropped. She grabbed up the baby. The monk's eyes burned, hot.

"She," he said.

"I said nothing. You misunderstood me." Erma bundled the startled baby up against her. Over his tousled head, she said, "You are a fool, Deodatus. They hate you. Leave us alone." She flung her chin up in the air and stalked back inside the cell and shut the door.

Behind her, Deodatus suddenly began to laugh.

The King went hunting with Roderick and some of the other men, and coursed the deer all along the river with hounds. Alpiada stayed the morning with her mother, in the women's quarter of the palace, leaving the marriage bower empty. Deodatus spent a little time there, making ready, and then went to loiter around the dooryard of the women's quarters until the men came back.

He nursed what Erma had said to him, coaxing it gently rounder and sweeter. It seemed to him that he had always known about Roderick.

He saw, from a distance, the hunters returning, the men leading their horses over to the stables, walking under the pear trees with their growing bulbous fruit green among the branches. He heard Roderick's harsh laugh, and the hair on the back of his neck prickled up.

Alpiada came rushing out of the women's quarters to meet them, her long white gown bright in the dappled sunlight under the pear trees, and she ran to Roderick and made a deep curtsy to him and then laughing threw herself into his arms.

Not his arms. Deodatus startled. Not a man. What was she, then? She seemed a man, in shape and ways. He struggled with his eyes to pierce the spell that hid her. Not a Christian soul. Some spirit, or witch, or demon, surely. The thought swelled in him, growing large up into his throat, until he thought it would burst out of him.

The King was walking toward him. Odo came at his heels, carrying Charles' bow and a floppy hat and a horsewhip; Deodatus frowned a little, considering how to divorce the boy from this meeting. He stepped forward toward the King, as he reached the dooryard, and said, "Sire, I must talk with you."

The King stopped. His face was smeared with dirt and he smelled like sweat and blood and dogs. He said, "What is it, Deodatus—John again?" His eyes glittered. "By the by, I did not see you, in the fighting, Deodatus—where were you?"

The little monk bowed his head. "Praying, Sire. And you mark, God heard my prayers, because we are saved." He saw his opening, and went smoothly into it. "Or so it seems, for now."

The glimmer in the King's eyes darkened. "What is it?"

"That which I shiver even to think of, which I quake to tell Your Grace, and yet must, for all our sakes, for only you can save us."

Charles stared at Deodatus a moment and then went on into the women's quarters. His voice boomed back out the door. "Come, then! Odo, go fetch me some wine, and see where Leovild is."

The little page set down the things he was carrying and went away at a run. Deodatus went after the King into the quiet and shade of the women's quarters. He smelled flowers, and his nose wrinkled; weak and idle, the women had brought in wildflowers and strewn them. He felt raw suddenly, as if they itched him.

He went after Charles, forming his next speech in his mind, but the Queen had come forward to chatter awhile to her lord. Deodatus drew away, uneasy, to a place near the wall. He could not speak with her there. They stood beside the King's chair; the Queen was merry, and laughed, and took her husband's hand. Charles kissed her. Deodatus looked away, remembering to be a monk.

Charles was settling into his chair; a girl brought him bread

and an onion and a bit of cheese. He had the Queen slide a cush-
ion in behind him against the carved wood of the chair. Deodatus
glanced at the door, afraid that Odo would come back. He rubbed
his palms together. The Queen hung on the King's shoulder, whispering in his ear. Deodatus glanced at the door again.

"Deodatus, now, what is it?" The King leaned on the arm of
his chair. The Queen was going off.

Deodatus went closer to the high seat; he licked his lips, thinking again how to speak of this, and he leaned on the side of the
chair and stared at the King.

"Sire, if someone did you great good, but then did you greater
evil—"

"What is this?" the King said sharply. He turned, glancing
toward the back of the room, and the women, and then faced Deodatus, his brows curled down over his nose. His eyes were hard.
"Speak quietly. They hear everything. What is this? You are circling
and circling like a vulture here. Show me the corpse."

Deodatus knelt by the high seat. His voice sank into his chair.
"Sire, what I say will shock you—"

"Say it."

"There is one who betrays you. One very close."

"Speak it! Who?"

Deodatus pressed his lips together, and the King thrust his face
closer. "What proof do you have? Who is it? Speak!"

"Sire, it is Roderick."

"Roderick!" The King sank back, his eyes wide, and his mouth
dropping open. He rubbed a hand over his face, and then snarled
at Deodatus, "How? And what proof? Ah, you meaching little
rat—"

"Sire." Deodatus leaned closer, his voice softer still. "I dare
not hold my tongue, for all that may come about because of
Roderick—whatever he is, or she, or it—"

The King recoiled, "What do you say?"

"Roderick is not a man. Not always."

"Ah! What do you say?" With an effort Charles kept his voice to a whisper. "You filthy-tongued—"

"Sssshh!" Deodatus put a finger to his lips. The King glanced at the back of the room.

"It cannot be!"

"It is, sir."

"I shall flay you, you wretch, you fox." The King clawed at his face with his fingers. "What proof? Prove this! If you are lying—"

"Sire, only go to the bower. There is a place by the back wall, a little chink in the wall, where you may see in. And look." Deodatus smiled. "See what you see."

The King lurched to his feet. "Stay here until I come back." He skewered Deodatus with a look. The monk bowed, smiling, but his heart hammered. He should have stayed, should have peered in himself, made sure what the King would see. His skin felt rough. He remembered the harsh heat of Roderick's presence. Surely by now they would be naked in the bower, taking filthy pleasure of one another. He started after the King, but Charles saw him and glared at him and Deodatus went back to the chair to wait.

Alpiada had sent for wine and bread, and then ordered the servants away. She shut the door and put the latch to, and went to Roderick, sitting on the bed, and began to take her jerkin off.

"You'll get dirty," Roderick said, "it's dirty, the deer bled all over me," but Alpiada laughed, and pushed her hands away, and set to undressing her.

"No, you must let me, I am your wife now."

She took off Roderick's jerkin, which was soaked with thick blood, and then pulled off her boots. Roderick sighed, leaning back. "Ah, that feels good." Alpiada rubbed her feet.

"You killed, then."

"We had to ride out for leagues to do it. The hunting's bad, all down the river; the Vikings chased everything away." She lay down along the bed, stretching her arms up over her head, her eyes closed.

"Where did you start the deer?" Alpiada rose, and poured the wine, and brought it to her. Roderick sat up, taking the cup.

"A place well east of here—a crossroads, and then a rising hill with some trees, and broad meadows below. The deer went up, and we got two clear shots."

She sipped from the cup, and then held it out to Alpiada, who sipped. It was a game that Alpiada had made, that first night in the bower, and she was glad to see that Roderick remembered it. She took the cup.

"Who shot the deer? You?"

"I and the King." Roderick's eyes shone. "But neither of us hit him well enough to bring him down. With the arrows in him the deer went straight up the hill, as you know they do, and the dogs hard after it, and we had a long hard chase; I thought to go down once or twice."

Alpiada sipped of the wine, and then held the cup for Roderick. "Thank God you did not. You could be killed. Are you not afraid?"

Roderick sipped the wine and wiped her mouth on her hand. She said, "That horse is handy as a cat. And what if I did fall? I'd get up again." She took the cup and put it down on the table.

Alpiada leaned on her and stroked her face. "You sound like a man. Can you not be a woman here, with me?" She kissed her cheek.

Roderick twitched, startled, and turned to look at her. "I can never stop," she said, and her eyes brimmed.

"You can stop here, with me," Alpiada said. She opened the front of Roderick's shirt and drew it off her shoulders, her skin white and soft, her breasts like little white plums. "You are a woman, you must be one here, with me." She thought of something suddenly that surprised her, and she laughed. "Tell me your name! I don't know your real name!"

Roderick moved against her, sliding an arm around her, and smiled down into her face. "Ragny," she said. Her eyes were still flooded with tears. "My name is Ragny." She leaned forward and kissed Alpiada on the mouth.

The King went wide around behind the bower, afraid of being seen. It came to him what people might think, if anyone noticed him sneaking around his daughter's wedding chamber, and his neck went hot. Deodatus was a fool. He had been dreaming, wherever he had been, hiding out the war.

Yet now Charles was behind the bower, and he could see, already, the hole in the wall there.

He stood, his mouth dry, thinking of this. What was it Deodatus thought was going on here? It was madness, folly. He had no reason to doubt Roderick. Why was he even listening to the wretched little monk?

He saw something move, beyond the hole, just a shadow, as if something walked across the light.

He cast a look around him. No one could see him; it was the end of the day, anyway, when people were going home. He went up to the wall of the bower and stooped, and put his eye to the hole.

In there he saw, clearly, the far end of the bower, with the bed, and sitting on it, Alpiada, his own daughter, with only a robe thrown around her. Her face was laughing; she spoke spiritedly to someone not visible to the King. Roderick. He could not hear the words.

He should not be watching this. He looked away from his daughter, trying to see Roderick. Then, slender as a deer, the young man walked straight in front of him, utterly naked.

Tall and thin and white-skinned—

His eye blurred suddenly, as if something just inside the room swept down across the hole. He drew back and rubbed his eye; it felt hot.

His heart pounded; he should not be doing this. He stooped again to the hole, and put his eye to it.

They were sitting on the bed now, side by side, kissing and laughing at each other. Yet before he could make them out clearly, his eyes blurred again, he could see nothing.

He drew back. He should see nothing. His daughter, her new lord, cavorting as such newly wedded people did, he should not see that. A wild rage heated him against Deodatus. Leading him to sin, the damned monk. Leading him to spy on his daughter, to wickedness and sin. He turned and marched away toward his palace, his teeth clenched.

Roderick said, "What will happen when we have no children?" They lay sprawled together on the coverlets. The wine was all gone.

Alpiada brushed back her hair. She had been thinking about this already. "We shall find some way to have children."

"You cannot do it like this, Alpiada. We are both virgins and we will stay so, this way."

"Ssssh. I will think of something." She took the wine cup and put it on the table by the bed. Lying down, she reached out one hand and stroked Roderick's arm.

"Why are you unhappy? You have me now. Isn't that good enough?"

At that, Roderick stirred, restless, looking elsewhere. Alpiada took hold of her arm. "What are you thinking about that makes you so sad?"

"My children," Roderick said. She sat up suddenly.

Alpiada's heart churned. "Stay."

"I am going nowhere, I am just putting on my shirt."

Yet her voice was curt, harsher, a man's voice. She stood, and the shirt went on over her head like a piece of armor.

"You are turning into Roderick," Alpiada said.

"I am condemned to Roderick." She picked up her hose. "We should dress. They will have that deer up on a spit now, and I want some of the backstrap."

"Then wear something fresh, at least," Alpiada said, and went to find her some other clothes.

16

THE KING WAS ALREADY in the hall, sitting in his high seat, Odo behind him. Roderick led Alpiada up before him, and they made their greetings to him, hand in hand. As Roderick bowed, she squeezed Alpiada's hand, and the other girl squeezed back. Then Roderick led her to her place beside the King, and sat her down.

Odo was watching them steadily, solemnly, from behind the king. He bowed to Roderick. "God be with us, sir."

"And you," Roderick said. "What is it, Odo?"

"I shall bring you of the meat, sir, if you will. And my lady Princess."

"Bring my lady the best of it," Roderick said. She had seen Leovild, out in the room, talking to John.

Alpiada caught her hand. "Where are you going?"

"Just to see my friends." Roderick lifted her hand up and kissed it and went down around the end of the table into the middle of the hall.

The servants were bringing in another table; John and Leovild stood in the middle of the bustling, paying no heed to the grunting workers. Leovild was smiling, but John looked angry. As Roderick went up to them, she heard John say, "It will make trouble with Hincmar, you can be sure of it." He turned to face Roderick. "Hello, my Prince, I understand you outrode everybody today."

Roderick flushed. "Who told you that? I barely kept up with the King."

Leovild said, "Odo thinks you are another Roland."

"Odo," she said. "He was a mile behind, most of the way." She looked from one to the other. "But that was not what will make trouble with Hincmar, is it?"

John grunted. "Ah, well. Tell him, Leovild."

Leovild said, "The King has Deodatus under arrest and in chains."

Roderick started. "I have not seen him since we came to Paris. What has he done?"

"The King will not say."

"The King cannot judge him," John said sharply. "He is a priest, he belongs to God, and only a court of God can judge him. Hincmar will not let it go, I tell you."

Roderick gave a shake of her head. None of this mattered to her. She wondered what Deodatus had done. She swiveled her head to look at the hearth, where the deer turned, glistening.

"They are cutting my meat," she said. "I shall go. Are you two not dining with us?"

John said, "In a little while, hotfoot."

"I'll be there," Leovild said.

Roderick went back up to the table, and sat by Alpiada. Odo brought her at once a fat piece of the deer, and she feasted on it, cutting off bits for Alpiada also. Odo hovered over them, filling their cups and bringing them bread. Roderick remembered what John had said. It galled her that Odo told stories of her. She was half-drunk already, the red wine warm in her belly. Odo hurried over to fill her cup again and the sharp urge rose in her to thrash him, for telling stories.

She gripped herself. She knew this was all Roderick, this feeling; she felt Roderick enveloping her; soon she would be only a little spark at the center of him. She reached for the cup, and Alpiada laid a hand on her arm.

"Slow, slow, my lord." Her voice was light and she smiled, but she gave a quick, rigid shake of her head, a warning.

Roderick grunted at her. There seemed no other way to get through this than to go headlong.

Then, up through the hall, past the servants gathered along the sides waiting their turn to eat, past the table where Leovild and John sat, and up before the king at the high table, came two guards, leading Deodatus.

The little monk was staggering in their grip. His face was bruised. His arms were bound behind him. As folk saw him they sent up cries, and wails, and they crossed themselves, so the whole room was arustle when he came at last before the King, and the King had to shout to be heard.

"Silence! I want silence!" The King stood up, his arms raised over his head.

The chatter quieted to a low hum; all the people were crowded forward to watch, packing the center of the hall. The King pointed down at Deodatus, standing alone just across the table from him.

"Some say I may not judge this man, because he is of God's men. Yet this false priest, this coward, this sniveling rat, came to me with dirty lies. Tell me then that I may not judge him, and find him guilty, who brought false charges against the most noble of my men!"

Roderick lifted her head; a tingle went down her spine. Alpiada was leaning on her. The room was utterly silent now. The King's voice rang through it like steel on a stone.

"He dared come to whisper in my ear against Roderick, my beloved son, prince of Francia."

All the eyes in the hall now moved toward Roderick. She felt the attention like a blow. Without willing it she stood up. Deodatus was cringing before her, his face working.

She said, "What did he say about me?"

The King gave a broad smile. "He said you are a woman."

There was a sudden hush. Then, all around the room, people began to laugh.

Roderick felt herself go hot all the way down to her heels. The laughter seemed to her like stones cast at her. Deodatus sank to his knees, his head hanging. There were bruises on his neck. They had beaten him. She wondered how he had found out. From one side Alpiada's hand crept into her hand.

The King said, "Roderick. You judge him. You condemn him—you, whom he has wronged, judge him as you will."

A thrill ran through her. She looked quickly around the hall, at the people laughing at Deodatus and smiling at her, and to her amazement she saw she was safe. No one believed him. She lowered her gaze to Deodatus. She could have him torn slowly to pieces, or starved in a cage, where she could see him suffer. His cringing and whining and wringing of his hands stoked her temper; she wanted to grind him into the dirt with her heel, like a worm.

A wave of nausea broke over her. The air trembled all around her, like an unfolding of wings. She saw what she had been about to do. Her blood cooled. She lifted her eyes to look around the hall again at the other men. They were all watching her, expectant, grinning, while Deodatus whimpered at her feet.

She squeezed Alpiada's hand, and let her go. Her heart was hammering.

"Deodatus is a liar," she said. Her voice rang through the hall. All eyes watched her, all in a dead silence now.

She said, "Yet he must not suffer for telling the truth. It is the truth. I am a woman. I am Ragny, the rightful Queen of Spain."

There was no sound. Alpiada was hanging on her arm, trying to pull her down into her place. She looked around at them again, and one by one, each saw her, and knew. Their faces fell open, their jaws hanging. A low murmur of talk sprang up, and built, like a new-laid fire crackling higher. Leovild lurched up and bolted out of the hall. The King leapt to his feet.

His face was purple. His body was contorted like a gnome's, his arm pointing, his finger jabbing at her.

"Seize h— Seize her! Get h—her out of my sight—throw her into a prison cell." His eyes bulged. He spoke in such a rush the words ran together over his tongue. "She is a witch! She must have cast a spell on us—get her away from me—she has bewitched me—get her gone!"

All around the room the men started up; Roderick was staring at the King, red-faced and panting, but she thrust one hand out against the knives coming toward her.

"Stay back!"

They all stopped. She lifted herself. A calm fell over her. She dropped the King with her gaze and swept the rest of them another, final look, and paced to the door. Half a dozen men fell in around her; no one touched her. No one spoke. Some of them followed her. She didn't bother looking around to see which men they were. She went to the monastery, to the dormitory, to the last cell there, which she knew to be the penitential, and went inside, and shut the door, and behind her they turned the key and locked her in.

Seffrid, eating down at the bottom table with the lesser men, heard what the King had said, and saw Deodatus brought out, and lost his appetite. It was all up now, he thought. He wondered how Deodatus had found out and turned his head and looked for Erma, over in the doorway with the other skulkers. She had gone, or was hiding. He clenched his fist; he would pound her for this. His gut was wrapped in a knot like an oak gall.

Then Roderick stood up to judge Deodatus, and a wild premonition went over him like a rough hand, and he slid away from the table and made for the door. Her voice carried clear and high and strong through the hall. He turned at the door, packed with onlookers, and saw her declare herself.

She shone, as she spoke, like a star. In the stunned silence after her words he turned and slid out the door and ran.

He caught Erma at the cell they shared, in the monastery; she had a basket in her arms and was stuffing cloth into it. He pounced on her, grabbing her by the neck of her dress with his left hand. "Running away? You did it, didn't you? You told Deodatus." He balled his right fist up. The baby, sitting on the floor over by the window, let out a yell. Erma clutched at Seffrid's arm.

"I did, I did, I'm sorry, I didn't mean to, it just came out, Seffrid, I'm sorry—" She was crying, her eyes huge, her nose slick. "I'm sorry—"

He lowered his fist. He should hit her, he even wanted to, but something stopped him; he thought of Roderick, who would not have hit her, and the will went out of him. He pushed her instead. "Pick up the baby and let's get out of here. We aren't going to be much help to her if they lock us away too."

She looked down at the basket. "She'll need clothes." He realized she had been packing, not to flee, but to give to Roderick.

He shook her. "She won't wear your rags. Let's go, we have to hide somewhere, while I figure out what to do next." He could hear shouting, nearby, and getting nearer. "Hurry," he said.

The key clinked in the lock. Alone in the cell, Roderick stretched her arms out into a cross, shut her eyes, and thanked God for delivering her.

She thought if she had yielded to that last sin, if she had condemned Deodatus, she would have been lost. She remembered the pulsing of the air, all around her, a rustle of wings, like something making ready to leave. If she had destroyed Deodatus, she thought, that would have been the end of Ragny.

She shut her eyes, lost in gratitude, that God had not abandoned her, even though she sinned. No matter what happened now, she could endure it, now that she was whole again. She put out her arms and prayed once more in thanks.

A little while later, the door opened again, but no one came in, only a bundle was stuffed in through the opening. She took the bundle across the cell to the bed and opened it, and found women's clothes.

She recognized them right away for Alpiada's. The feel of the soft stuff on her hands was delicious. She shucked off her men's clothes and kicked them aside and put on a long white dress she had seen the other girl wear, with deep sleeves and a belt of braided stuff. She wished there were a glass, to see herself in; she shut her eyes, luxuriating in the freedom at last of being who she really was.

She brushed her hair back; it was growing longer, from Seffrid's hacking of it, back at the cave of songs. She smoothed her hair with her hands, thinking how the trail lay from there to here.

She had run away from Markold to this, a bare little cell and borrowed clothes and probably a bad end to come. Yet she was light as a breath. She had shed her man's life like a husk. She felt her body new again, her mind and soul whole again, she felt herself springing upward, as if all this long time she had stooped beneath some terrible burden. Now it was gone. She went around the cell, enjoying the feel of the dress on her body, dancing her feet over the floor. Every few steps, she stopped, put out her arms, and prayed to God in thanks for making her a woman again.

She thought fleetingly of Leovild, bolting from the hall, and pushed that aside. She would think about Leovild later. They all hated her now. Yet God did not hate her. She remembered the hand reaching out to her, under the river, and drawing her forth.

There was a little timid tapping on the window ledge, and she went there, stood on the bed to look out, and saw Erma, down below.

The window had a lattice of ironwork fitted over it. Roderick stretched her hand out through an opening, and Erma reached up and clutched it.

"I'm sorry, Roderick." Erma kissed her fingers.

"It's in God's hands now," Roderick said. "Don't be afraid. God will take care of me. Where is Seffrid?"

From beneath her vision over the sill, the baby called out, and Erma lifted him up into sight. He crowed to see Roderick, and his face lit like a lamp with his smile. Stretching his arms out, he aimed a long babble of words at her, and she gave him one of her hands.

"See? He always knew who I was," she said. "I wish I could hold him, I have missed him sore. Where is Seffrid?"

"He will find a way to free you," Erma said. "He says keep heart, he will do it, and I will help—"

"Leave it to God," Roderick said. "Tell him that."

"Do you want for anything?" Erma was crying. The baby held Roderick's hand but turned to his mother, his face fretted.

"God will take care of me," Roderick said. "Go tell Seffrid, do nothing."

"Roderick, Roderick," Erma sobbed.

"No, go. Don't let them catch you here, go, Erma. Tell him."

Erma went away. Roderick watched them go until she could not see them anymore. A pang of loneliness went through her. There was nothing to do now, save wait, and think. She had done everything already, everything she had to do. She went to sort through the rest of the bundle of clothes.

*   *   *

At the morning's Mass the royal chapel was full of people, the dusty darkness murmurous with prayers and gossip, all the heads leaning toward one another behind their hands raised, their eyes on the King. Charles felt like a naked man among them, like a white bird in a black flock. He pinned his gaze on the altar. It had to have been witchcraft, to have fooled him so. To have made such a fool of him. Marrying his daughter to another woman. What a fool.

When he thought of Roderick everything in his body clenched, furious. He should have killed her himself, before them all, the night before, when she confessed. Thou shall not suffer a witch to live. Right then he should have struck, to keep his honor. Regret tormented him, that he had let the moment slip. God was watching him, to see how he did this, to see if he weakened, if he cleaved to unholiness, if he was truly Christ's man, and already he was seeming dubious. He ground his teeth together, thinking how she had stood up there so calmly before them and spoken.

He had to prove she had no power over him; he had to destroy her.

The message sent, he got up from his knees, and went out, and John at once came at him.

"Sire, you must hear me, as I am your friend."

The King hunched his shoulders. He went on out the door of the chapel and turned to go back to the women's quarters. It was midmorning; the pear trees were still heavy with dew, although the sun shone. John pursued him, and the King whirled.

"Yes, I think you are my friend, John, and yet I believe you knew of this—this blasphemy!" He marched up to the big Irish monk, thrusting his face into John's. "Tell me you did not know she was a woman!"

"I knew," John said.

"She seduced you too—I thought you at least impermeable—"

Charles ran out of breath suddenly, out of words; he stared around, and saw, some way off, a clot of people watching. Everybody was watching him. He waved angrily at them. Odo was standing by the wall, and the King snarled, "Get them out of here!" The boy ran off toward the onlookers. Charles wheeled and walked down along the palace wall, toward the door into his wife's quarters.

John clung to his heels. "I know also that anything you do against this pure and noble girl will come back a hundredfold against your crown."

Charles wheeled around toward him again. "How did you know?"

"I looked at her, Sire."

The King took this for a reproach, and bridled up. "I am going to burn her for the witch she is, John!"

"Pagh." The Irishman's face darkened with a surge of temper. "She saved you. Will you do her death, then?"

Charles could not hold the monk's gaze. Suddenly after all his brave words he felt his resolve melting. What John said opened up another window on this. It was a test from God, surely, but what kind of test? He raised his hand to his cheek. Maybe he was about to be wrong again.

"What if she is come to destroy us all? To pervert and corrupt us. Such things have been done! The Devil can make himself look beautiful, and women are a breeding ground of sin."

John said, "You look for subtlety where there is none. She has done you no ill. She asked for none of what you lavished on her."

"It could be the perfect subtlety, to seem innocent," the King said, not looking at John, keeping his voice low. "If she is not a witch, the flames will not burn her, God will save her, and then we will know."

John growled. His eyes narrowed, his jaw jutting out. "You fool! Think on that. What righteous blast may save her—what horror come on us all for this deed—"

The King shouted, "I am not a fool. I am lord here! She—

she—" He shook his fist. "She made me look— I will burn her, John, and God may pluck her from the flames if she's so fair to Him—" He wheeled and ran away, down the wall to the door, and in.

John stood, not watching the King flee, but staring blindly at the wall of the palace, and wondered what he might do next. The morning's dank grey was lifting; the wind blew suddenly through the orchard and scattered dew over him. The page Odo came up to him. He had shooed most of the curious away toward the common. Down past the far end of the pear orchard, past the edge of the stables, a few smokes rose from the half-built village.

He turned to Odo, remembering how the boy had followed Roderick around when he could, and said, "What do you make of this, boy? This of Roderick?"

The boy gave a shiver. "I will never believe anyone again," he said, in a dull voice. "Nothing, ever again."

"She saved Paris," John said. "Was that not God's work?"

"King Charles saved Paris," Odo said. He kicked at the dirt with his shoe. He had his cap stuffed in his belt and his brown hair stuck up in tufts. He refused to look up at John.

John grunted. "You saw more of that work than I, perhaps. Nonetheless I think he would have had a much harder time of it without Roderick." He yearned to go back to the monastery, where a clean new parchment awaited him; he was almost done with his translation of the Areopagite. He lingered, watching Odo. "Yet you saw what I saw of Roderick, surely. Why can you not believe?"

Odo lifted his head, looking elsewhere. He pulled his cap out of his belt, shook it, and crammed it onto his head. "I should go to the King," he said. He sighed. John waited, watching him, and the boy raised his eyes finally to his.

"That could all be false."

John grunted. "All could be false. The world itself, some say, is false. Believe that, and what can be done? You have to start somewhere. What's wrong with believing what you see?"

"What does it matter if I believe, anyway? What can I do?"

John gave up. "If you have no more heart than that, nothing." He nodded to the boy. "Go to your master." He turned on his heel and walked long-striding toward the monastery.

The King went in the door to his wife's quarters, and started toward his chair. He had not gone half the way to it when some-one leapt toward him.

Charles shrank back; his hand went to the dagger in his belt; he thought swiftly of murderers. But the creature flopped down at his feet, harmless. It was only a girl with a dirty face, dressed in rags. "Who is this?" he cried.

The other women were watching, his wife tall and silent among them, and Alpiada beside her. They had set her on him then, this peasant wretch. He fumed at their disloyalty.

"Sire—" The girl huddled at his feet, not even lifting her eyes to his face, but staring at his knees. "I beg you, Sire. Let Rod-erick go."

"How did she get in here?" Charles wheeled toward the watching women. "You did this!"

Alpiada walked toward him, her head back. "Listen to her, my lord Father!"

"Bah!" The King put his foot on the girl's shoulder and pushed her away. "Get her out of here. As for you—" He went up to his daughter, poking his finger in her face.

She stood her ground, her head back and her wide eyes un-blinking. She said, "Roderick is innocent, sir. What you do is a foul offense to honor and to God and to our House."

"What you have done is the foul offense, my girl! You knew—you let me go on believing—" Behind his eyes a burning rage welled up, as he remembered them laughing and naked together on the bed, and he shouted at her. "You betrayed me! Go, then, see if the sweet and sinless nuns at Sainte-Geneviève will take you! Go now, before I strangle you. Go before I have to look at your face another day!"

Behind them, there was a stir among the women. The King swelled, feeding on that; he could make them obey him, at least. Alpiada's face settled, but she did not flinch.

She said, "As you will, my lord. That is my whole wish now, anyway, and I shall happily go. Only, if you deal any hurt to Roderick, I hope most heartily that you suffer for it." She turned and went back toward her mother. The Queen held out her arms to her, but her dark angry eyes fixed still on Charles.

The King turned his back on her. He had to make them obey him. He was master nowhere if he was not master here. "Odo! Where is my page? Send for Leovild—he will escort her out at once. Immediately! Odo! Damn him, where is he?" He stamped back and forth before the door a moment, until Odo came breathlessly in, and sent him off for Leovild. The women were silent, behind him, but he could feel their eyes on him. He ignored them. He went to his chair and sank down into it and shut his eyes.

Leovild swung up onto his horse, keeping his gaze away from Alpiada; he thought if he looked at her, he would strike her down. His temper roiled like an evil brew. He could not bring himself even to think about Roderick. He started off toward the bridge, and Alpiada fell in beside him, silent. They had given her a woman to wait on her, even in the convent, who came after on a mule, with a hamper of her goods.

It was all over, anyway, Leovild thought, for him, at least. Paris was saved, for this year, but in the next the Northmen would be back. He would not fight them, then, or if he did, with no hope of valor. He shifted his left arm a little under the heavy stinking bandage. It hurt steadily, in there somewhere, and although he was not sickening from it, he knew he was no good anymore. He imagined himself a poor hungry cripple telling old stories at the tavern door and whining for his bread.

Some part of him had gone, had been struck away, and he dared not even put a name to it, or think of it. Below the throb of his shoulder was another ache, soul-deep, that he suffered now even in his dreams.

They rode over the bridge and out across the broad meadows there. The country people were working in the fields, trying to get in some crops, now that the Northmen were gone. Under the pale summer sky the broad rolling land spread away in a haze of green. As they went away from the river the sunlight grew stronger, turning everything bright and beautiful. He remembered something John had told him, gleaned out of his books, of the sunlit hands of God.

He shut his eyes. He had forgotten how to pray. The sun warmed his face; he wished it would touch his soul, lost out of sight like a little rock down out of reach in the dirt.

On the far side of the river, they turned east, and rode up the winding path to the monastery, on top of its hill; there were goats grazing on the bleached grass sprouting between the trees, and a little brown kid dashed up and capered along beside Alpiada's horse for a way, until the monk-goatherd came panting up to shoo him back. Alpaida laughed to see the kid caper, and Leovild tightened his fist.

That she should laugh, when—when—

He could not bring himself to think the rest.

Then they came to the gate of the monastery, where he would

go no farther; he rang the bell for them, and turned his horse. They were side by side, then, their horses head to tail, and Alpaida stretched out her arm to him.

"Help her," she said. "Leovild, you must help her."

He reared his head back. "You speak," he said, angry, "you dare—" But then the gate opened, a stranger's voice said something, and she was riding by him into the monastery, her woman trailing after her, and he was alone.

He rode back down the path. His shoulder was throbbing. He could go, he thought. Turn the other way, at the foot of the hill, and ride away from Paris, away from everything, into the wilderness, and be free. He had obeyed orders all his life. Now he could fly away, free.

He saw himself scattering away like chaff, blown on the wind, weightless. At the foot of the hill, he went on, back to Paris, where his orders were.

17

THE KING COMMANDED THAT DEODATUS was to go free, but he got no apology. In the morning, still sore all over from the beating, he went to the tavern, to find solace there.

The tavern had been rebuilt first of all the burned village, with wood from the country, on a foundation of stones out of the ruined churches. Three or four men were thatching the roof; they had only covered part of the frame up, and the sun poured through the opening into most of the room. Deodatus went away from the heat of the sun, into the shade under the finished section of the roof. There several other men were standing around, already half-drunk, talking about the witch Roderick.

Deodatus promised the alewife a paternoster, and got a cannikin of beer, and went over where he could listen to them. They were young, loose men, he saw, and they had no good thoughts for Roderick.

"Have to wonder 'bout the King," one said.

Another snickered, a tall thin man Deodatus had seen before, although he could not remember his name. "Amoon over that Roderick, he was. I saw that. Serves him right, the thankless clot. You know, I fought the Northmen too."

There was a general rumble over that, as they all claimed to have fought in the vanguard against the Northmen, slaying many.

"Never gave me his daughter."

"You're not a witch."

"Was witchcraft, certain. How else could a woman overcome a man in battle? They say she struck them all dumb, when they rose to seize her. Flew right out the window and escaped!"

Deodatus saw his opening, and leapt in. "Oh, she is seized. She is in the monastery, in the penitential cell."

They swung toward him. He smiled, slid in a little closer, to make himself one of them. He said, "She enspells the King yet, surely—why else would he not slay her right now, for the foul thing she is?"

The greybeard on the bench said, "I knew a witch once, she could fly. Why didn't this one fly away, then? If she is a witch."

The tall man swung around toward him. "Now, now, Chram, this is a priest here, says she is a witch—she is therefore, with no doubt!"

The old man grunted. "You, Ulbert, you haven't been this close to a priest since you were blessed."

The others cackled out a windy gust of laughter, even Ulbert. Deodatus laughed also, to be one of them. He lifted his can to them.

"I have known all the while something was wrong." The words tumbled from him as if he had suddenly broken open. "It was my doing, you know. Exposing her. I knew. I watched—waited—until finally I got her to reveal herself! I tricked her!"

The more he thought of this, the cleverer he realized he had been.

"Well done it was, too," Ulbert said, the tall lean man. He

whacked Deodatus on the back so hard the little monk almost fell. "No mere woman could have done what she did, that's for certain."

"The King will deal with her," said Chram, the greybeard, stubbornly.

"Ah," Deodatus said, moving a little away from Ulbert, "the King is bewitched, though! You saw how he treated Roderick, when we all were fighting against the Vikings, how the King acted as if only Roderick fought, only Roderick deserved honor and reward"—their heads were nodding, their eyes fixed on him, greedy for his words—"when it was you, and you, who really won the battles! She stole your glory! We have to save the King from her spell, before all Paris—all Francia—is ruined."

They growled at him. He stood up, lifting his arms. "Who will save the King from this witch?"

"I! I! I!" They leapt to their feet in a crowd, jumping, their arms round each other, as if they were being given money. The bench overturned. Even old Chram was cheering. Deodatus waved his arms.

"Come with me, then! Let's kill the witch!"

He started off, his new army behind them. "Kill the witch! Kill the witch!" They walked out through the village, chanting, and waving their arms, and marched down around between the stable and the pear orchard, toward the monastery.

Away from the village, their shouts seemed less thunderous. Deodatus turned, under the trees, and looked over his band. He was disappointed. He had hoped to pull the whole village along, but instead he had only those he had won to him in the tavern, and a few others.

"Where is she?" said a yellow-haired boy.

Deodatus pointed toward the penitential cell, on the end of the dormitory. "In there."

The boy bent down to the ground. Deodatus was looking

around for a way to attack the cell; the door, he knew, was locked, and bound with iron, and the barred window very small. He looked back at the other men, wishing there were more of them. Then the boy straightened, and flung a handful of stones at the cell.

The others yelled. They scrambled around, stooping and gathering stones, and then flung them in wild volleys, laughing and hooting. "Kill the witch!" The stones clattered against the cell wall and bounced off. Deodatus thought this no use, and he ran forward, his arms out, to stop them.

"No—let's burn it!" If they set fire to the monastery, he realized, they might also burn up John's books, and this gave him a sudden keen delight. He grabbed the arm of the yellow-haired boy. "No—let's burn—"

Then suddenly a shower of stones fell on him. He cried out, letting go of the boy's arm, and flung his arms over his head. "Not at me—" Stones rattled all around him, bouncing painfully off his shoulder and his arm. He ran to and fro, trying to avoid them.

Ulbert screamed now, ducking, his arm raised to fend off the storm of stones. Chram was running. All Deodatus' little army was dodging and flinching back. Someone else was throwing stones at them, their own stones. Now they all turned tail and ran off, away, back toward the village. Deodatus crouched behind a tree and yet another blast of stones clattered down on him. He gave a wail. He would get them for this—throwing stones at him. His arms over his head, he ran away through the trees.

Odo stood under a pear tree, watching Deodatus' little mob rush away; he laughed. He was unsure what he had seen. He had come up from the women's quarters on an errand, and seen the mob steal through the edge of the orchard, toward the monastery. Realizing what they meant to do, he rushed forward, angry, to stop them, but before he could, the stones had come back at them. He watched Deodatus go bounding off, his monk's skirts hitched up in his hands.

He looked at the little cell at the end of the monastery building. She was in there. Roderick. He saw no one else; there was no sign of whoever had thrown the stones.

His doubts slid away from him. John was right, he thought. It was not so much that the Devil could be fair, more fair perhaps than Roderick, but that God could not be so mean and low as Deodatus. He felt his mind fold together again, made whole. He ran to do his errand for the King, and then went looking for John.

The monk was in his writing room, leaning on his desk, his quill in his hand, but not writing. Leovild paced up and down before him.

"The King wants her burned, he is giving me orders to have her put in chains now, to keep her from escaping." He glanced at Odo as the boy came in. "What is it, boy? The King wants me again?"

Odo said, "No, sir. I came—" He looked past Leovild to John. "Shall I come back, Brother John?"

John said, "No, no, what brings you, Odo? Is it about Roderick?"

"Ah," Leovild said. "Say that name no more to me." He walked off across the room.

Odo went up to the monk; he looked at the broad creamy page on his desk, on which the words ran like mice. He wished he could read. He lifted his gaze to the monk.

"I think you are right, Father. I was just in the orchard—you know Deodatus, the King's confessor, who accused her—"

He told them of the mob, making merry of it, as it seemed to him. Leovild came back toward him, his eyes sharp. John began to smile, hearing it, and glanced at Leovild through the corner of his eye.

Leovild said, "Who threw back the stones?"

"I did not see," Odo said. "Seffrid, very like." There had been great handfuls of stones, thrown very hard. He remembered Seffrid's woman, who must have helped him. To John he said, "I believe."

The monk nodded at him. He set his quill down carefully. "Well done, Odo. Now, go back to the King, seek a hearing of him for us. We must change his heart."

Odo said, "Can we save her, Father?"

"I hope so. Go and ask the King for a hearing."

Odo went out with a leap.

When the boy had left, Leovild said, "This is witchcraft, John. This of the stones."

"Bah," John said. "So a little boy can see true, but not you. I think the blow struck your head on the way down."

Leovild growled at him. "You're a big Irish fool sometimes. The King is right. For a man who thinks so much, you are sometimes very stupid." His chest ached. He felt himself being cloven in two. "This is all witchcraft," he said. "How otherwise could she have fought as she did? Women can't fight."

John said, "Why? Because you have never seen it?"

Leovild thudded his fist on the desk. "Women are not warriors. I fought beside her, I believed . . ." His breath ran out. He had touched her, hugged her. Loved her. "Some power attends her. It cannot be otherwise."

"Perhaps," John said, all serene. "But why must it be a wicked one?"

Leovild wheeled away, back toward the middle of the room. "You talk tricks, John."

"No!" John strode around and got in front of him. "I talk no tricks. You it is who sees tricks, everywhere—you and the King."

The monk's face was flushed, and his eyes glittered. "Will you come with me to talk to the King for Roderick?"

Leovild licked his lips. Low-voiced, he said, "How dare you ask me this. The King is my lord, I do his will, not yours, John."

John stared steadily at him, almost nose to nose with him. "Not God's?"

"Ah, you have no proof of that—no conviction—"

"She saved your life."

Leovild twitched. He twisted, trying to favor his aching shoulder. "I would not have my life back at such a price—if it means my soul—"

He bit his lips. He felt hollow, an unreal man. She had already stolen away his soul.

John said, "Battling hand to hand, you have no such doubts. Then you know your enemies and friends, full well."

"This is a greater battle."

"And a greater prize."

"Ah, it's all words with you."

John leaned heavily on his desk, one big ink-stained hand braced on the edge of it. "God gave us words, and reason, too, that we could read the world, and find Him everywhere in it. But you won't take up the work. Is that not true sin—to be afraid to see and do good? Think, Leovild. For her life, and for yours, too, God willing, think hard." The Irishman turned his shoulder to Leovild, and picked up his quill again. Bending over the page, he studied it a moment, and then laid down letters on it.

Leovild watched his hand move along the scraped hide. Could that not also be called witchcraft too, he thought, that sent dreams and thoughts sailing through the air from one head to another? His mind reeled. He felt unsteady on his feet, as if the world were dissolving away beneath him.

John ignored him. John like a great rock doubted nothing. For all his talk of reason, it was faith that anchored him. Leovild ached to be so sure. He went toward the door. Into his mind leapt the idea that he would go to see Roderick.

His belly tightened. He dreaded facing her again. She could not enchant him anymore, now that he knew, and he would see her as she really was. What that might be made his hair crawl.

He had loved Roderick, and Roderick was gone. Had never really existed. Had been a lie.

He shook himself. There was still the matter of what to do about her. He had to see her. That would settle everything. He would know what to do, when he saw her.

He went to the refectory, to get the key, and walked back along the side of the monastery. His gut churned. What John said clung to his mind. It came to him that he wanted to believe but he dared not. It was a joke, then, faith—that let you believe only in wickedness. Then, coming around the corner of the building, he saw people skulking around under the trees.

Deodatus was among them. He saw at once that Deodatus had brought back his mob. A steely rage went through him like a shock. He clamped his bad arm tight to his side and ran out into their midst.

"What do you here—get your rotten bunghole carcasses out of here—" He kicked and swatted at the nearest of them; startled, they recoiled from him, clustering together, and he saw they meant to hold their ground and stooped and picked up a branch at his feet.

"You think you can stand against me—hah!" He charged them, swinging the branch. They scattered. One fell and Leovild smashed the branch over his head and whirled, empty-handed, looking for another weapon. From behind him someone jumped on him, jarring a surge of agony through his shoulder. He bellowed. He reached up one-handed and tore the body on his back away and flung it down. The rest were turning, running away. One was Deodatus. Leovild ran after him, caught him like a flapping bat by the back of his cassock, and spun him.

"Think you can fight a man, Deodatus?" He swung his good arm full hard around and slapped the monk across the face.

The little monk fell on his back with a cry. He scrabbled away a little distance across the grass on his back, pushing himself along crabwise with his hands and feet, and then stood up again. From this safer distance he shouted, "I'll get you, Leovild—I hate you!" His face narrowed down behind his pointed nose, his eyes gleaming. "I hate you all!" He spat at Leovild and raced away.

Leovild stood watching him go. A sound behind him turned him around. The man he had thrown to the ground was getting unsteadily up onto his feet. Leovild wheeled, looking for a stick to hit him with, and the man—a boy, really, yellow-haired—gave a screech and darted off under the trees.

They were all gone. Leovild clutched his shoulder, throbbing with pain; he worked his left hand, thinking if his fingers still moved, he would be all right. He turned back toward the monastery.

The penitential cell was right before him. There should be a guard, he thought, wondering why none had been set. He stood before the door gathering himself. He was not thinking about Roderick; he refused to think of all those days on the road, the fighting on the bridge, any of it, because that was all lies, it had never really happened. He was thinking about what he would find on the other side of this door, now that the enchantment was over, what was real and true and ugly. For a moment he could not bring himself to put the key in the lock.

He had to warn her he was coming. He knocked heavily on the door, put the key in, and turned it, and the door swung open. He went into the little cell.

In the dim light, he stood blinking, making out the room. She was standing at the far end, by the bed. She had just gotten up, he thought, when she heard him come in. The light came through the door behind him and fell on her. She said, "Leovild." Her clear bright voice went through him like a ray. She came a couple of steps toward him into the sun from the windows, and then stopped, uncertain, her eyes on his, and her whole face sunlit.

His heart was pounding. He looked at her from head to toe. She wore only a long white gown. She stood slim and straight in it, her head high. She had not changed. She was still Roderick. He stammered something. A rush of gratitude swept over him. She was exactly as he had always seen her, save her clothes—the slim straight body, the ragged silvery hair, the clear eyes. He could say nothing; his throat was clogged. Instead he went forward toward her, his good hand out, and she came into his arms.

He held her, warm and sweet, carefully fitting his arm in the sling around her. He laid his cheek against her short pale hair.

"Leovild," she whispered. "I'm sorry."

He tightened his arms. "Hush." He remembered, once, she had started to tell him something; now he realized what it must have been, and knew that he himself had told her not to speak.

He had thought she was lost forever, and now here she was in his arms.

He said, "Roderick."

"No." She stepped back a little, her hands on him. "Call me Ragny." She was as fierce as before, he saw; that had not been false. Her eyes still so direct he could not look away. "I shall never deceive anybody again, I swear it."

He smiled at her. "Ragny." He took hold of her left hand in his right one. "You could have told me."

She said, "I thought you would all hate me."

He said, "Never," and put his arm out to her again, and this time when she came to him, he kissed her.

Her mouth was like the rose, and he the bee. She shivered in his embrace. Her arms went around his neck, and she pressed her-self against him, said his name in a low voice.

He looked down at her, wondering how he had believed her to be a man. He had wanted her always, always.

A thread of cold fear went down his spine. "We have to get you out of here," he said.

She said, "What does the King judge of me?"

"He says—" He could not force the words out; he said, instead, "We will deal with the King, John and I."

"As bad as that, then." She leaned her head against him. Her hair was feathery along her shoulder above the loose collar of her dress. He laid his good hand on her hair. She said, "Whatever happens, Leovild, it doesn't matter. When you came in—"

"Ah, well," he said. "I should have come sooner."

"I love you, Leovild," she said.

He held her against him, who at his command had slain Weland. "I am no knight anymore."

"You are the best knight," she said.

"I have no King's blood."

"You have a King's heart." She moved, warm, in his arms, her breath against his throat. "Do you deny me?"

"God, God." He tightened his grip on her. "I do not think I can ever bear to let you go."

"Then you are mine, and I am yours, forever."

He kissed her again. "Forever." He lifted his head, cold again, thinking of what was to come. "Which I must now go and try to make happen."

She stepped back from him, her hand on his arm. "I'm so glad you came. Whatever happens."

"You have many helping you," he said. "And we will win you out, I promise you." The coil of alarm twisted in his gut. He wished he was so sure as that. He backed up to the door. She stayed where she was, in the middle of the room, her arms at her sides; for an instant, in the dusty air, he thought he saw a shape of light around her, like great wings folded.

She smiled at him. He went out the door. Locked it, more for her protection than to keep her in. And went with a pounding heart and a fresh fierce urgency to find John.

Deodatus said, "Sire, I go about in the village. I hear what people are saying. Everybody is wondering if you are not under her spell. If you don't act against her soon—"

The King twisted away from him. In the back of the room, the women were utterly quiet, which meant they were listening. He had not slept, all the night, he had lain in the dark struggling to find a way out of this, and he was worn down to the bone, and yet the problem stood before him. He hated Roderick, who had brought this on him.

Deodatus had moved around to the other side of the King's chair, between him and the women. His voice went on singsong in Charles' ear. "You must burn her. It is the only penance that will atone for having believed her before."

Charles snarled at him, "Leave me alone, Deodatus."

"I am duty-bound to save your soul, my lord, and will not shirk that task." The monk leaned toward him, lowering his voice, his nose sharp and his eyes like beads and the words spilling from him slick as an anointment. "Why do you abhor your duty, sir? She is surely guilty." He leaned forward, and the King slumped down, trying to avoid him. "Proof enough she is a woman—they are all guilty, since Eve. You know how evil enters in through women's holes, through their mouths, with their wicked gossip, and the other, that sucks men in to their dooms."

"Sire."

The fresh more distant voice cut through Deodatus' monotonous oil. The King stirred, seeing himself rescued: that was Odo, coming from the doorway.

"She threatens all of us, and you must save us, Sire," Deodatus hissed in his ear. "You are the King."

Charles straightened, glaring at him. "Get back, you kite—you just want flesh, don't you?" He nodded to Odo, standing there before him; now that someone else was there, Deodatus relented, stilled his tongue, slipped back and away. The King smiled at the boy. "What is it?"

"Leovild and John will see you now, my lord."

Deodatus whispered, loudly, "Sire! Do not heed them!"

Charles plucked at his chin. He had no wish to face them, either, but he wanted less still to be alone again with Deodatus, and he nodded to Odo. "Tell them to come in." Behind him there was a surly grunt. The King leaned on his chair, relieved.

Then John and Leovild came in, with Odo just behind them, and the whole thing got worse.

John said, without any cordial welcome, "Sire, you must come to some judgment of Roderick."

"Bah," the King said. The skin prickled up on the backs of his hands. "The very name is a lie. I shall do as I please with this wretched girl; you make too much of it; leave off." He turned to Leovild. "What is this, now? I thought you were my man."

Leovild said, "Let her go, Sire."

Hearing this, Deodatus began to croak again, "Burn her, Sire. Burn—"

The King twisted in his chair, to shut him up with a wide gesture. Now Leovild, who never argued, whom he had depended on completely, trusted totally, stepped forward, crooked with his bandaged arm and shoulder, and his voice grated. "You listen to this magpie, sir, who just today I saw whipping up a mob of people to attack the monastery."

The King jerked around, startled. Deodatus scurried up behind him. "He struck me, sire! He laid hands on an anointed priest of Jesus Christ—"

John knelt by the King's chair. "You see how this tears apart what you just wove together, Sire, fighting off the Vikings—You must act, now."

The King sank down in his chair. Deodatus and Leovild were ranting at each other, the monk carefully keeping the King between them, so that their voices jarred back and forth over his shoulder. Charles twisted his head and saw, behind him in the shadows, all the women watching. God was watching. He dragged in a breath, and struggled for resolve like a man in a fog. Suddenly, as if the sun rose in his mind, he had an idea that would stop them all.

He said, "Heed me! Silence!" He was on his feet, even without knowing it, and his arms out, and they were suddenly still, all watching him. He said, "I shall end this, as John has said, and you, too, Deodatus." He licked his lips, making sure he went through this properly. "First, I judge this Ragny, whom we called Roderick, to be a witch!"

Leovild cried, "No!" The King gritted his teeth; he had never imagined that Leovild had any will of his own. Behind him, the women let out a yowl like a string of cats under the moon. Deodatus burst into a broad smile, and the King turned to shut him up with the next part of this.

"Second, I say that to prove herself innocent she must suffer the ordeal. Let her be bound to the stake, and let one who will champion her come forward, to take all challenges against her, and God will make clear who is right."

Deodatus' mouth sagged. He stepped back, glancing at the others, uncertain. His little bony hands rose like paws before him. He looked up at the King again. "Who will be her champion?"

The King's head swiveled around, to Leovild. "You. Since you favor her so much, Leovild, you be her champion.

John roared. "He's still injured. You can't—"

"I will," Leovild said. He swung out his good arm and drew John back out of the way. "As you wish, my lord." His voice trembled with anger. His eyes were level with the King's and not respectful. "I shall defend her against whoever comes, wherever you care to do it."

The King settled himself. So it was managed, he thought, and very tidily, he told himself, and yet he stirred, uneasy. "Well said, then. We shall put this to the test, three days hence, on the common here. Now, get you all away, and let me be." He went back to his chair, to sit and think through what he had done.

18

D EODATUS WALKED ACROSS THE COMMON to the village. After everything that had happened, he was very thirsty, and he went to the new tavern, where he had so many friends now, and they gave him drink for nothing.

His mind seethed. Just when he thought he had the King pinned, somehow Charles had eeled free.

But he saw chances in this of the ordeal. For a promise of prayers, he got a jar of fresh beer in the tavern, and went out to the yard, and stood in the shade of the front door looking around.

The Parisians were rebuilding the village, little by little. Just at the edge of the tavern yard stood three new huts, well made of stone and wood, with tolerable thatching on their roofs. Beyond them the ground was still smeared black with old soot, crusted like snow; a little flock of hens pecked and scratched through it, casting soot and dirt around them with their clawed feet. Farther away there stood another row of houses, and some green stuff growing already in the yards. There were far fewer people, of course, than during the siege.

Two women came into the tavern yard with baskets, sat down, and spread out goods to sell: some eggs, mushrooms from the woods, nuts and fruit. Immediately folk began to gather. Deodatus got up and went among them, looking for something to eat.

For a quick blessing, he got a handful of nuts. He went off munching them, ignoring the foul look of the nut seller.

Other people came in to trade and offer, and a market began. Somebody tied a squealing pig to a stone and began shouting for a price. A big old woman had a basket full of bread. Deodatus squinted, recognizing her: she lived across the bridge. Hilde was her name, and it was her wayward girl who had gone with the witch's man, Seffrid.

He debated saying that, and stirring people up against her. The crowd was swiftly grabbing up her fat little loaves; they gave her turnips and eggs and nuts which she stowed away in a basket beside her. He wandered nearer.

"Old woman," he said, "where is your wicked girl Erma?"

"Ah." She swatted at him with her hand, not looking up; she was haggling over the last of her bread with a man carrying a fat clay honey jar. "Wherever she is gone."

"Is she a witch too, then?" A few of the people around were beginning to listen. The attention heated him; he pitched his voice to reach more ears. "You know the King is still bewitched. Nothing but trouble may come of this. I pray for us all." He crossed himself.

The old woman harrumphed a laugh, but she raised her eyes to him. "I know nothing of the King, for certain. If Erma is bewitched, it happened long before this Roderick came here."

But someone else now pulled at his sleeve. "What will he do with—with Roderick?"

At that name, more people turned, and all at once gathered round him, and a chorus of voices babbled up questions. Deodatus raised his hand.

"Peace! I must not reveal the King's mind, although, of course, as I am his confessor, he confides all in me." He bowed his head, to show how humbly he received that honor. The people were jostling noisily around him, and he had to take a step back.

"What will happen to her? She saved us!" someone called.

"Bah!" went up another roar. "A witch! The Devil take her!"

"No wonder the Northmen came—she brought them!"

"Yes—yes—she it was who burned our village down around our heads with her spells!"

"That's a lie!"

The crowd surged, they were shoving and pushing at one another, and voices rose now, people shouting at once.

"Kill the witch—"

"Let her go!"

Deodatus scrambled away from the noise and fighting. He found himself among people watching with pursed lips and cocked eyebrows. Someone said, "It takes no witches' work to get those ones brewing."

Right beside Deodatus, an old man cleared his throat. "Better to let her go, even so—what power she has, who knows? Who would have all the wild people angry with us?"

Deodatus started at that; but he held his tongue, a little afraid, surrounded by sinners. Then suddenly right in front of him, face-to-face, was the long narrow man Deodatus had met earlier, who had gone with him to storm the monastery. Erma's cousin, he remembered. Ulbert. He had fought against the Vikings, or claimed so, anyhow.

"Deodatus!" the long man said, his breath ripe with wine. He flopped his arm around Deodatus' shoulder. The monk, much smaller, staggered to keep from falling. The long man spoke hot moist words into his ear.

"They gonna burn the witch?"

"Maybe," Deodatus said. "If a good man will save Paris."

The long man made a rumbling sound in his belly, like a fire burning in a kettle. He was very drunk. He seemed not to be holding much in his mind. He turned his head to watch the fighting, which had drifted off down to the far side of the tavern. Through the fading uproar came the hoarse voice of the man with the pig. Then suddenly long Ulbert swung back to Deodatus and said, clearly, "I know where Erma is."

"Ho," Deodatus said, startled. "Do you."

"Do you want me to take you there?"

Deodatus thought of Seffrid. Yet the girl Erma, surely, was another witch, and needed burning. He licked his lips. Seffrid might be there. "Can you get help?"

The long man grinned. "I'll get some friends," he said. He slouched away toward the tavern. Deodatus finished his wine and hurried the jar back into the tavern.

"She said to do nothing," Erma said.

"You stay out of this." Seffrid actually could think of nothing to do to help Roderick. He was lying on his belly in the grass on the high bank above the river, watching the water flow by twenty feet below. The sun was warm on his back. In the ruined church just behind him some people were still hunting for building stone and wood, but in the past few days they had carried off everything small enough to lift and now the place was mostly empty.

Erma was fussing around their little camp, which lay between the riverbank and the back of the ruined church. Seffrid rolled onto his side and watched her. When she bent over, her gown flattened against her rounded backside; he imagined cupping his hands over those pretty cheeks.

He had to think about Roderick, about how to rescue Roderick. He took his gaze off Erma's round behind. He thought of the power that attended Roderick; surely that would save her. He licked his lips, wondering if he had only imagined it all along.

He wondered what he was supposed to do here. It worried him to have no one to give him orders.

The choir wall of the church loomed up over them, made of big blocks of grey stone all patched and seamed with moss. Some of the lower stones had crumbled away from the fires and dropped the whole top half down in a great sag, the upper courses still holding to one another. The rest of the church—Saint Stephen's church, Erma had called it—was all tumbledown. Between the long ribs of its disintegrating walls were stretches of green grass, like this one; brush and little trees grew along the edges. When they first came here to hide, Seffrid had raked up broken bits of stone and grass and brush to make a kind of wall around this space, and within it, now, Erma was gathering up the baskets. She turned toward the baby, asleep on the grass.

Seffrid recognized signs that she was about to leave. He stood up. "Where are you going?"

"I have to find us something to eat, you know." She shook her head at him, as if he were trying to stop her. He saw she was angry with him and went up to her, throwing his chest out.

"What's this? Keep yourself sweet with me, girl, or I'll beat you."

"She said you should do nothing," Erma said, grimly. "You can hit me all you wish, Seffrid, it doesn't make me afraid of you, and I will not keep still."

"What—" He spread his hands apart, palms up. "Am I doing anything? What do you see me doing here, anything at all?"

"I know you," she said. She went by him, to the baby, and scooped him up. Seffrid blocked her way.

"Be careful. And find out anything you can."

She gave him a dark look. "Me! I'll do as I do. You're the one who will get us all in trouble." She brushed by him, the basket on one arm, the baby on her other hip, and started away down the path around the flank of the ruined church.

Seffrid turned slowly back toward the river. The idleness gnawed at him. He had to get Roderick out of the cell. It would take a slick bit of work, maybe, but he could do it, get their horses, send Erma over the bridge earlier to wait for them. Once they escaped from here, they could go to Germany, or to Rome. He saw the way ahead of them a long brown road winding away over the horizon toward the sun. Then suddenly, a little away, Erma let out a yell.

He wheeled. The baby screamed; down there someone was scuffling on the rocks, and Erma shrieked again. Seffrid bounded across the scrappy wall he had made and ran toward the noise.

On the stretch of green grass there, between the lines of tumbled stones, Erma was thrashing in the grip of a tall man, who stood braced on wide-spread feet to hold her. The little rat-monk Deodatus was trying to pick the baby up off the ground, while four other men ran toward them from the shadows behind the great church of Our Lady.

Seffrid bellowed. He should have brought his sword. He plunged down the loose sliding slope of broken rock, reached the little grassy stretch running, and crashed shoulder first into the man holding Erma.

They all went sprawling. Erma screamed again; the four other men reached them, and Seffrid, rolling to his feet, saw them circle around him. He shouted, "Erma! Run!" Lowering his shoulders, he charged at the nearest of the men facing him.

This was a hollow-chested yellow-haired boy; he saw Seffrid coming and scrambled backwards, and the others closed in, bawling, getting in each other's way. Seffrid pulled his head down and stiffened his shoulders and rammed the boy backward. Dumped him down, leapt over him, and wheeled to face the rest.

Two were on the ground; three of them rushed him. Beyond

them, Deodatus was lifting the baby awkwardly by the arms. Erma charged him, her fists milling. The three men closed on Seffrid, who set himself. As the first man reached him he stooped suddenly and caught the oncoming body just below the waist, and straightening up hard, flipped it up and over. Something struck him hard on the left shoulder, but he reached out in front of him and got a handful of a shirt, and wrenched, and the body in the shirt came lurching after him and he swung it hard into whatever was to his left, and they all went down in a tangle.

Now Deodatus shrieked. "Brat! Hell's spawn!"

Seffrid leapt up, panting; Erma was clutching the baby by the legs, but Deodatus still held his arms, and the baby had twisted around to bite at Deodatus' hand. The monk let go and Erma wrenched the baby to her and raced away.

Deodatus turned to chase her. Seffrid ran three steps to him and knocked him flat.

"Leave her alone!"

The other men were getting to their feet. Lying on his back, Deodatus turned his popping eyes on Seffrid and thrust his arm out, pointing.

"He's the witch's man—he is evil, too—get him! Help! Get him—murder—"

The other four men stood in a loose half circle around Seffrid, their heads lowered, and their eyes baleful. The tall man called, "Come on—everybody together—" He was glaring at Seffrid. He started slowly forward, and now he reached to his belt and drew a knife. Under his breath, he said, "You are meat, you bastard." Seffrid whirled and ran.

He headed toward the tumbled wreckage of Saint Stephen's Church, thinking he could get his sword, but the other men knew the place; two of them bounded nimbly up a half-standing wall, and saw he was cut off. The other three pursued him across the rocks to the high bank of the river, a hundred feet down from where he had just been musing of Rome and Germany, and he had to climb up a heap of collapsed stones toward the high choir wall.

The three on his tracks followed him. He wondered if the other two had given up, or gotten lost, and guessed they were circling around to come at him from the back. The stones as he climbed were tilted and uneven and one rocked violently under his feet; under him something gave way just after he passed and crashed down in a slither of stone.

From the top of this slide, where the last few courses of the choir wall still stood one on top of the other like a great broken highway, he looked down, over the other ruined walls stretching away like rock roots growing down into the grass, toward the great wall of Our Lady Church, itself half-fallen down into rubble. He saw no sign of Erma. A stone whizzed past him and he crouched.

The tall man was climbing toward him up the crumbled bank of rocks below the choir wall. The three men coming along his tracks were panting and cursing at the steep slippery slope, and stopped a moment. Deodatus was nowhere. With his eyes, Seffrid picked out a way out across the top of the choir wall, stretching away like a river of stone, that would take him to one of the side walls. He scrambled off from stone to stone, on all fours most of the way.

Another rock sailed by him, and something hard and sharp hit him on the thigh. He slid down over the edge of the choir wall, down toward the ruined side wall, and got a foothold in the broken rock. As he let go with his hands, his feet slipped. He fell off the wall. For an instant he was dropping free through the rushing air. Then he crashed down into deep brush, and hung there a moment, caught in a young tree, his chest and arms across a bouncing branch, his heart thundering.

Up there, shouting. He heard someone screech, "No! Go back—go around—" He flailed at the tree, and kicked, and the branches cracked and dumped him hard. Brush lashed his face. He swallowed something soft and hairy. He was to his armpits in brambles, the young trees hanging over him, dark and full of insects. He wrestled and lunged and clawed through the brush, the thorns ripping his hands and face. They were coming; he could hear them coming toward him. If he were with Roderick, they could not kill him. He thought a prayer to Roderick for help, and laughed in his heart, struggling through the brambles, to think he could pray, and that Roderick could heed him.

"Where is he?"

"Here! Here—"

He slid between two huge grey stones covered with green moss like fur; his feet sank deep into wet and muck, and then he was suddenly out of the brambles, in a dark lane along the foot of the wall. He started to run. He broke out of the dark into the sunlight, onto one of the long narrow green meadows between the rock ribs of the old Church. If he could get around Our Lady Church, he could reach the common; from there he could go anywhere. He climbed over a broken wall, and somebody shouted.

"There he is!"

He ran, headed for the side of Our Lady Church, where part of the wall had come down in a long talus of broken stone. Then from his right suddenly the tall man burst into sight, carrying a big stick.

"Get him! Get Him!"

Seffrid shied away from the tall man and his stick. He climbed up the high talus behind Our Lady Church, scrambling on the loose rock, which stirred and slithered under his feet; once he nearly slid back down into their arms. He could hear Deodatus yelping orders. His breath hurt. The talus gave up white dust that choked him. Like a dog on all fours he climbed higher, and turned and saw them below him, all now with sticks and knives.

Deodatus trotted up behind them, his head tipped up toward Seffrid on his little mountain of broken church-rock. "Come down! You are a witch! Confess!"

Seffrid got his feet under him. He stepped backwards, looking for another way down the slide; with one hand he groped over the sun-warmed rock behind him, feeling for a weapon. They would have to come at him one at a time here. A rock flew by him. He crouched. Then his groping hand slipped into a crack in the wall behind him.

Rocks and pebbles showered down on him, banging painfully off his legs, his shoulder, and his forehead. He turned around, and saw the narrow seam in the wall, where a stone had fallen, but those around it had not. More rocks pelted him, and he crept into the seam.

It went on, narrow, pressing against his back and belly. He crawled deeper, into darkness, going down.

He heard, suddenly, ahead of him, the drone of many voices. The stones ahead of him shimmered in a vague flickering glow. He crawled down past a huge timber bracing up the wall behind him, and came to his feet.

He was in Our Lady church, at the back, in the dark. The air stank and he could hear the scurry of rats. Up there, beyond the columns of the church like an old stone forest, was a fuzzy yellow light, and from it came the sound of prayers.

He was safe here, he realized, with a shudder of relief. He went forward toward the first row of columns. Out there, surrounded by the deep gold of candles, John the Irishman stood before the altar, and raised his arms.

"Dominus vobiscum."

"And with your spirit," Seffrid murmured, and crossed himself, and went to go find Erma.

Seffrid seemed to sink down, he seemed to fall under the weight of the stones they cast, but when one of Deodatus' mob climbed cautiously up to see, he was gone. There was no body, nor even any blood that the yellow-haired boy could find, and he came down shrugging, and wiping his hands on his sides.

"Somehow he got away. I don't see how, he did it anyway." The boy shrugged. "You said he was a witch. Maybe he turned into a bird."

"I saw a bird," one of the men said, and they fell to arguing about whether it could have been Seffrid. The long man swore and kicked at the ground. Deodatus pressed his hands together, not liking evil language, and wandered away. It bothered him that Seffrid has escaped, but they had nearly caught him. Had nearly caught them all, Erma, too, and the witch-brat. Now all his henchmen were wandering off, cursing under their breath, and Deodatus himself needed some wine, and soon would want his dinner. He went off toward the monastery.

He would find them again. They would not escape him again; let them make themselves birds, mice, rats, or fish, he would root them out.

He went across the common. Evening was falling. The market had shut down and most of the people were gone back to the village or over the bridge. Up in the western sky the great star Hesperus burned in the dark violet of the sky. A little boy struggled up from the river with pails of water in each hand. Three women, walking still-bodied and straight under the bundles of linen on their heads, paced toward the village from the riverbank.

Under the little bustle of the end of the day Deodatus thought he heard a baby cry.

He turned toward the river. His ears sharpened. It seemed to come from down there, by the water. Dark was falling, the long blue twilight of the summer; he could see the shape of the bridge like a long tongue across the river. He did, he heard a baby crying.

He went up the bank a little, but heard it no more. Went down again, past the last few workmen coming in over the bridge from the fields, and after their footsteps had died, he heard it again, low and soft and sad, a baby's cry.

He went out onto the bridge. It grew louder. The cool night wind touched him. He heard the rushing of the water, rollicking past the piers of the bridge. The baby was crying steadily now. Had she abandoned it? The wretched girl had left it under the bridge. He bent over the edge of the bridge, looking down after the cry.

His feet slipped; he fell through the air, and plunged into the cold water. For a moment he struggled, afraid, his cassock entangling his arms and legs. He got his head up above the surface, and gulped for air. There was no one around, no one to call to. The current swept him under the bridge, and then into the deep eddy by the pier and down.

The river rushed over the place where he had been. Under the bridge, the wind keened along the edge of stone, crying.

In the morning she would be taken out to be burned.

She ate some bread and cheese for her supper; she had a good appetite, which seemed to her strange, that someone near to dying could want so much to eat.

Her full animal belly rolled. She wondered how it would feel, the burning.

Dark fell. She had only a little stub of a candle and she lit it, and sat on her bed, thinking she would not sleep, but would live awake until the last.

She knew they believed that no one would come. Leovild had not said so, but John, when he came to explain it all to her, had it in his face, in his voice: she was saved, because the ordeal was only a game, a trick to let the King free her.

She did not think a trick could save her. They could not play a trick on God.

In spite of her resolve, she began to drowse, as if the weight of death crept into her limbs even now.

She stood up, stretched her arms out, and prayed. She asked God to forgive her, and to love her anyway. She asked God to help Leovild, who was offering up his body for her, as Jesus did for the world. When she thought of Leovild a new guilt wrung her, at what he might suffer for her sake.

She did not ask God for her life. Yet she trembled, thinking of dying, and her mouth dried, and her heart began to hammer. Before Leovild came in, and kissed her, she had been willing to die. But now she could not bear it, to be so close to that happiness, and lose all.

The candle flame trembled. She sat down on the bed again, and leaned her head against the wall, and struggled to keep her eyes open.

The door opened, and Leovild appeared. She leapt up, glad, and he was gone. She had dreamt him. She sat down again. Drew the blanket up over her feet, against the chill of the night.

The candle flickered out. Yet there was light, a faint glimmer of light. She sat up, smelling smoke. Up the side of the door a flame was crawling. She gasped, horrified, and the flames sprang up onto the wall.

She bit her lip to keep from screaming. There was no way out. Scrambling back on the bed, she pressed herself against the cold wall. The flames bounded up the door and onto the rafters and she felt the heat blister her face. She thrust her hands out before her and saw the skin of her arms crackle up.

A blind devouring terror took her; she screamed, she huddled down, her arms over her head, and wept.

Then from nowhere he came; he was big, and strong, and gathered her into his arms, as he had before. He had found her and saved her again. Triumphantly he carried her away beyond the flames, into the cool of the night, and she flung her arms around his neck and raised her face to his, and he was Markold.

She bolted upright. Around her the cell was quiet and dark. The night lay deep around her. She drew a ragged breath, the dream whispering still around the edges of her mind.

She gave a violent shiver. It had seemed so real, the dream. She remembered the strength and safety of his arms. She wiped her hand over her face. The longing still clung to her, for the strength and safety of his arms.

She pulled the blanket around her, and leaned against the wall. If she had stayed with Markold, none of this would have happened. In the cold pit of the night she began to despair. Nothing she did came to good. It would be better to die. She leaned against the wall, struggling against sleep, waiting for the daylight to come.

She remembered the hand that had reached down to her, when she was drowning in the river, and drawn her up.

Her spirits rose. She felt warmer and easier. That had been real, that hand. That had been true. She thought of her mother, how her mother had promised that she would not be alone. Her mother had been greater than Markold. It seemed to her that she felt the grip of that hand, even now, holding her fast. Her fear shrank away. Whatever happened, she would bear it. She crossed herself. Leaned against the wall, and waited for the first light.

Odo carried the King's blue Byzantine cloak over his arm, although the sun was rising bright, and the day would be hot. He went after Charles toward the common. The King had ordered his horse brought to him, and was riding the little distance to the common, but Odo walked.

Ahead he saw the great crowd already gathered; people were steaming in over the bridge, country people, the women with baskets over their arms, and their children trailing after, and the men slouching along. As the King approached, a cheer went up. The crowd hurried out of the way and the King rode to the middle of the common, where his chair waited, and dismounted.

The chair stood on a great table from the hall, so that even sitting down, Charles was above all the rest. Odo spread out the cloak on the chair and the King climbed up to it and sat. Odo took up his place just behind the King's right shoulder.

From this height he looked out over the whole common. On his left hand, the collapsing front porch of Our Lady Church, braced up on columns and tree trunks, was swarming with people, and on all the common before the church they laid blankets on the ground, and set their baskets around, and then sat there and shouted at each other and waved and drank.

Directly in front of the King, beyond the crowd, was the bridge, still busy with people coming into the city. On his right, more people, children running wild, someone dancing, everywhere people moving and sitting and talking and lifting cups and filling them, and yelling. It was like a festival day, he saw, amazed.

In the middle, in the open, was the stake, with the bundled firewood. If Leovild fell, the King had already decreed, Ragny would burn before the blood dried.

Odo glanced down at the King, slumped before him in his big chair, with the fine Byzantine cloak rucked up under him. Charles wore his crown. His bald head was spotted on the top, like big freckles. Odo could see the red mark where the crown was pressing into his skin.

He looked away. He owed the King his life, and could not think ill of him.

Then the crowd to the right began to shout and roar, and the screaming spread across the common and Odo looked, and saw them bringing Ragny to the stake.

The hair on the nape of his neck prickled up. He had not seen her since that night when she stood up before them all and told them who she really was. His throat thickened. Her face was pale, and still, her eyes shadowy. She wore a long white gown, the only ornament a braided belt. Her white-blonde hair hung down past her shoulders. Guards surrounded her, but no one touched her. Behind her, holding his horse to a clipped walk, came Leovild, with his sword and shield.

She came through the shrieking mob of people toward the King. In the crowd, Odo heard some screaming to burn her, and others calling out to her to take heart, and shouting to Leovild to defend her; in the crowd people began to fight.

"Stop that," Charles called, feebly. He sounded like an old man. In the uproar nobody heard him.

The guards led Ragny up before the King, and there she advanced through them, her head up, and her voice rang out.

"God's blessing on you, Charles, King of Francia!"

The King straightened. He said, "I need no blessing from you! You come before us condemned as a witch. Will you confess, and let us be lenient?"

"I am innocent," she said. "As Jesus Christ is listening and knows the truth, I am no witch. I have done no harm to you or to your kingdom or your people—far from it. You it is who must be just. Let me go!"

Charles stood up, his face red. "This is rash defiance. Tie her to the stake! John, read my proclamation."

The Irishman climbed up onto the table. Ragny turned her back on the King and walked across to the stake, and stood with her back against it, looking out over the common toward the bridge. One of the guards looped the ropes around her and knotted them, and the rest piled up the wood around her, burying her to the knees.

John's voice stretched across the common. "'God be with all here, and God be the judge of this woman Ragny, who called herself Roderick to us. For her crimes, she stands at the stake, and let any man who will come forward. Let him for the greater glory of God contend with her champion, and overthrow him, and set the flame to the stake. In Jesus' name, let there be justice. Amen.'"

The guards drew away, and the crowd hushed, eager, expectant. Leovild circled the stake once on his horse. Odo swept his gaze around the common, and saw no one coming forward.

He let his breath out, relaxing. Nothing was happening. Now the crowd, disappointed, was settling down, turning to their baskets of food and their children and their gossip. A pieman went by the King's table and Odo's stomach growled. He gripped his hands together behind him. The sun was only a little up the sky. It would be a long day.

Erma hovered at the edge of the crowd, the baby on her hip. No one seemed to pay any heed to her, and, bolder, she went closer, trying to get near Roderick. Then suddenly her cousin Bertha came up to her.

She gripped Erma by the hand. "You should hear what Ulbert is saying. Come along."

"What is it? I have to go to Roderick."

"Pagh, there is the whole day, and this is about your Roderick." Bertha towed her along through the crowd. Erma looked out toward the stake, and the girl bound to it; Roderick's white sleeves fluttered in the wind.

She looked small there, and frail. Yet she stood straight, her head high. The wind blew her pale hair across her face. Only her eyes moved, watching Leovild as he rode in slow circles before her.

Bertha towed Erma up to a little knot of men, of whom Erma's cousin Ulbert was the center. Ulbert had a mug of wine in one hand and was talking furiously, as if to convince someone.

"I could go out there and take on Leovild. He has only one

arm, how can he fight? I could burn the witch." He nodded at them all, solemn. "Then who would be the great man of Paris, hah? I'll do it." He threw down his mug, reached around to his hip, and took out a long knife. "Where's Deodatus?" He looked around. "Deodatus would say aye to me."

"Probably drunk somewhere," an old man called. "Do it yourself, Ulbert!" There was a low general rumble from the men round him.

Someone behind Erma shouted, "Yes, do it, then! Go to it, Ulbert! Let's have some fun here!" Erma clutched the baby; she should be Roderick's champion, she knew, but she was afraid; there were so many of them. Other people were calling out to Ulbert, to go and challenge Leovild.

"Where's Deodatus?" Ulbert swung his head around. "I need him to bless my sword!"

"I'll bless it!" A big bald man stepped forward and poured wine over Ulbert's knife, and a roar went up all around.

"Go get him, Ulbert!"

In the middle of the whooping and jostling of the crowd, Erma licked her lips, wondering what to do. Then, suddenly, she saw Seffrid plowing forward through the mass of people opposite her.

"Ulbert! Fight me!" Seffrid with his arms flailing pushed his way up past the bald man, who staggered back, startled. Ulbert wheeled, the knife dripping wine in his hand.

A shriek went up from the onlookers. All around the people pressed closer, shouting, straining to see. Somebody screamed, "Kill him! Kill him!" Erma held the baby close against her; someone banged into her and she nearly fell.

She cried, "Seffrid! Watch out!"

He could not have heard her. He circled around Ulbert once, his hands out; Ulbert turned to keep face-to-face with him and held the knife between them, the tip up. Seffrid made no move to get a weapon. He bounded forward and seized Ulbert's wrist above the knife. They struggled together; Ulbert swung his free fist at Seffrid, who caught hold of his shirtfront, ducked the swinging wild blow, and kicked Ulbert's legs out from under him.

The crowd shrieked. The knife sailed into the dirt. Seffrid and Ulbert leapt up to their feet, nose to nose. Ulbert was much taller and had long arms like tree branches, but Seffrid took no heed of it. He leapt forward again and grappled with Ulbert, their arms entwined, and then with a jerk and a twist he threw Ulbert down again.

"Seffrid!" Erma cried, joyous. The baby was clapping and crowing. The crowd around her roared out cheers and advice. Ulbert scrambled up, but before he could gain his feet Seffrid pounced on him and slammed him down again.

"Not so good on your own, hah, Ulbert?"

Seffrid danced before Ulbert, his fists raised. Ulbert came up on one knee, breathing hard. There was dust in his hair. His eyes were glazed. Seffrid bounced up and down before him like a demon bird, jabbing the air with his fists, and finally Ulbert lifted his hands.

"Enough. Enough."

"Good. Mark it, then," Seffrid said. "You could not stand against Leovild either." Now suddenly all the people around them were cheering Seffrid; men reached out to clap him on the arm. He brushed them all off. Pulling his jerkin straight, he came over to Erma and got her by the hand and led her away.

Ragny scratched her back against the stake. The hot sun blazed on her and she was sweating under the long dress. She was thirsty. She wondered again what it felt like, to burn, and cast the thought aside. All around her the crowd seethed and rushed, people selling cakes and nuts and pies and drink, children chasing one another in their games, and bursts of laughter and sudden thrashing fights. Yet no one came forward to challenge Leovild.

He rode back and forth around the common; once Odo came down from the King's dais, and brought him a cup of wine, and another time a girl ran out of the crowd and cast an armful of flowers over him. He carried himself stiffly, Ragny saw. She guessed his shoulder hurt him.

He rode up to her, in the early afternoon, and sat his horse there beside her. He said, "How are you faring? It is almost done, you see."

"God let it be over soon," she said. "Perhaps John is right. Who would fight you?"

"I think it is not me that holds them back," he said, with a laugh.

"I wish I had not made this happen so, that you find yourself in such a place."

He twisted in his saddle, and looked straight at her, not smiling. "I asked you to slay Weland. I owe you this."

She looked sharply into his face. "Is that all?"

He nudged his horse nearer to her. "You are all to me now. When this is over—" He clipped off his words, looking around, looking for a challenger.

She said, "This is a sort of wedding, is it not? We are joined together here, our lives, our deaths—whatever happens. Yet I would not be tied to this stake for the ceremony, but rather riding by your side."

"So it shall be, when the sun sets." Leovild lifted his head, looking toward the sky, where the sun was sinking down into the west.

John walked around through the crowd; it struck him odd that Deodatus was not there, and he asked for him, but no one had seen him. No challenger was coming forth to take on Leovild. John thought, reasonably, no one would. He began to see an end to this for all of them.

He went up before the King, who was sitting slumped in his chair, staring into nothing, with no one paying much attention to him; even Odo had drifted off to the edge of the dais, was sitting down, his shoe in his hand, poking at a hole in the toe of his hose. All around the people laughed and danced and ate and waited for a fight that wouldn't come, while the King sat brooding in their midst.

John thought that God had saved Francia, but not the King of Francia. Now soon the sun would sink, and the ordeal would be over for Ragny and for Leovild, but the ordeal would never end for Charles. John moved away, got himself a drink of watered wine, and went back to his restless walking.

At the end of the day, with the sun sinking, the challenger came.

He was a big, black-bearded man; he rode a black horse and his shield was black. His vestment was green and he wore a helmet set above the ears with deer antlers like tree branches; his face looked green in the late light.

He rode across the bridge and up before the King, and all around the common, people stopped and grew still and watched.

Before the King, he turned and cast a long look at the girl tied to the stake, and a smile spread across his face. He turned his eyes back to Charles again, and said, "I have come to take what is mine."

Charles lifted his head. He was sore from waiting. He said, "In this kingdom, all is mine. Who are you?"

"I am Markold," said the dark rider. "King of Spain. And this girl Ragny is my daughter. Since she ran away from me I have been searching for her. When I heard of your matter, I knew that this was she."

From all those watching there went up a murmur of surprise. The King turned toward the stake, and said, "Is this so?"

Ragny's face was pale as ice. She stood stiff as an icicle against the stake. She said, "It is."

The King swung his gaze back to Markold. The crowd was pressing close toward him on his table, and the boiling noise of their voices overrode him for a moment, but then they stilled, watching him.

He saw at once what to do, what would make him blameless. He said, "King Markold, as this is your daughter, I will yield her to you."

"No!"

The King jerked his head up, startled. At the stake, the girl cast one long hard look at Markold and then faced Charles. "I will not go with him. I will die here first."

The crowd let out a howl, and surged forward. Charles flinched down from the noise and the sweaty meat rush of people. He picked at his cheek with his fingers, wondering what to do. Markold bounded his horse up almost against the edge of the table, face-to-face with him.

"Yes! I accept her from you, King."

The girl shouted, again, "No!" The crowd rumbled. Charles bit his lips, his mind frozen.

"You'll have to take her from me, Markold!"

With a sudden twitch, Charles jerked backward, looking past Markold. Leovild was riding up between them and Ragny, alone at the stake. His voice rose, harsh.

"Ragny is mine to defend. The King has set this ordeal; let him hold to it! What is your charge against her?"

King Markold stared at him, his face rigid; but then his face settled, and a little smile came to his lips. He had seen that Leovild was hurt. He wheeled his horse, and moved around onto the center of the common.

"She ran away from me," he said. His words boomed distorted off the stone front of the church. "I am come to take her back where she belongs."

He reached behind him on his saddle and drew out an axe; as he lifted it the slanting light flashed around the arc of the curved blade.

King Charles sat back, his heart pounding. It was no business of his anymore, he thought, and licked his lips. No one could blame him for whatever happened, He gripped the side of the chair and leaned on it, helpless.

The crowd was shrieking all around, but at a distance, so that the noise seemed somewhere else. Leovild rode around toward Ragny's stake in the center of the open ground where they would fight. Her face was taut, her eyes narrow, watching Markold steadily. She said, "I will die before I go with him, Leovild."

He said, "I will die before I let him take you." His horse spun on its hocks, and he galloped out across the common.

Slowly they came together, before the King, with the whole people of the city packed like a wall around the fighting ground. Leovild had his reins caught in the fingers of his bad arm. Markold was bigger than he was, massive across the chest and arms; Leovild watched how he moved, looking for weaknesses. They circled a little, each one studying the other, and then abruptly Markold heeled his horse around and charged.

Leovild reined hard to the left, and when Markold's horse followed, swung to meet him at an angle, and cut hard, but Markold caught the edge of his sword on his shield; for a moment they were locked together, Leovild with all his strength forcing his sword down across the top of the shield, and the bigger man on the far side set stiff against him. Across the shield rim their eyes met, and Markold smiled.

At that Leovild went cold down to his heels, as if he looked at the face of death. He shrank back just as the axe struck, and the blade sliced past his ear and glanced off his bad shoulder, and he sagged down, all the world spinning and dark.

Through the fog he heard Ragny calling to him. He felt his

horse surge up onto its hind legs, and he let go of his reins and swung sideways out of the saddle to the ground. His vision swept clear. He landed on his feet beside his rearing horse, while Markold flogged the air with his axe, and the crowd howled. Leovild lunged forward, his sword cocked, and chopped the blade around hard across the back legs of Markold's horse.

His left shoulder throbbed, shooting arrows of pain through his body; he staggered backward, watching Markold's horse collapse. The crowd was a vague blur all around him, a fence of noise. Markold leapt lightly down and turned to face him.

And smiled again. Leovild gritted his teeth. He would not think of Ragny in this man's grip. In the Spanish King's shining dark eyes, he saw the hard scheming, and, already, a gloating triumph. Markold threw his shield aside with a contemptuous snort. Lifting the axe in both hands, he came at Leovild, his shoulders bulled forward, and his teeth showing.

Leovild backed up. He feinted to one side and when Markold followed cut behind him, but Markold was ready for him, struck his blade aside, and lunged at him with the axe high, aiming to crush his bad shoulder again. Leovild dodged, circled, watching for an opening, and the King charged him.

They stood toe to toe for a moment, hacking at each other; each blow Leovild struck was an agony, jarring his shoulder into a swelling, searing heat. With all his strength he knocked aside Markold's axe and struck hard, and the King staggered back, and the smile disappeared.

"Had I both arms," Leovild said, panting, "You would not see sundown, King." Yet he himself could hardly keep his feet,

Markold's face twisted, darkening, and his lips curled in a red snarl. He set himself, and battered steadily at Leovild. Under the rain of blows the Frank could not hold his ground. He stepped backward, parrying off the axe, looking for any chance to strike back, his breath short, his legs turning to stones.

He heard Ragny's voice, behind him, very close, saying his name. He was almost at the foot of the stake. He gathered himself, realizing what Markold intended: to drive him here, to slay him at her feet. He raised his head, and lifted the sword for a last blow. Markold caught it easily on the haft of his axe, and thrust at him, and knocked him to the ground.

The sword slid away out of Leovild's hand; Markold stepped down hard on his wrist. Above him the axe rose, its notched edge silver as the moon. Markold was grinning. But he held the blow a moment. Arrogant, he turned his head, looking up toward Ragny at the stake, to relish what he saw. Leovild gathered the last of his strength.

Then Markold's face as he looked at Ragny went white as a skull, and his jaw dropped, his eyes starting from his head. "In-gunn," he said.

Leovild lifted his legs and drove them hard into the King's body, knocked him back, and sent him sprawling. Rolling over, he grabbed his sword off the ground. Markold still lay on his back, his stunned gaze fixed on the woman at the stake, and his mouth working. Leovild looked nowhere else; he sprang forward and drove the sword down hard across Markold's head, until the blood gushed.

He straightened, astonished. The sword dropped from his hand. His shoulder hurt unbearably, but he was alive. His shoulder pounded and burned, but he was still alive, he had endured it, and he had freed her. He turned and went up to the stake; she was standing there with sunken eyes so wide they seemed like pools, her mouth trembling. He kicked away the clumped firewood to get to her.

"Leovild," she said, "I thought—I thought—"

"It's all right," he said. He took his belt knife and cut the ropes. "It's all right now, see." She shook off the bonds and came to him, her arms around him; her face shone with her sudden smile. The crowd was screaming, he realized now, people flooding over the common, a crowd around Markold's body, a swelling mob in a laughing, giddy ring all around him and Ragny, and in front of them all, he turned his head, and kissed her.

EPILOGUE

S O THEY WERE MARRIED, and Seffrid and Erma were married, at the same altar where Roderick had married Alpiada. Most of the people from the country came in to witness, and then they would not let Ragny and Leovild go, but had to drink to them, and dance around them in the common, as if they were at a maying, and they the new King and Queen of the world. The king gave a speech, which nobody much listened to, and John blessed them.

He remembered all his life after, how they looked when he blessed them.

Then they were leaving, Ragny on her black horse, and Leovild on a grey horse that the King gave him, and Erma and Seffrid and the baby. John gripped their hands, and kissed them, and then stepped back to let other people say good-by to them, but his heart was sore, and he could not stand and watch. He went on by himself away, off to the palace, thinking he would read the Are-opagite with his flights of words. His feet took him instead to the earthworks, and he climbed up the edge, past the dozing sentry who did not know who and what were leaving Paris.

He knew that he could never see them again. The thought of that pierced him like a thorn.

He climbed up the side of the earthworks into the tumbling air; the wind lifted his clothes away from his body. On the flat height of the earthworks he turned. From here he could see the bridge, and the crowd still gathered by this island end of it, but already the little party of horsemen were riding away over the span to the other side. He clenched his fists. He had loved other people, but he thought his heart would burst his chest to see these two go.

He saw the angel go.

His eyes sore from watching, he saw the white dazzle of the light around them. The little train of horsemen went on into the broad distance, while the light grew upward, and upward, stretching out across the sky, sheer as sunlight, until it filled up the sky. The light-filled wings spread, reaching from horizon to horizon over Francia. He saw the great golden head raised up toward Heaven. He saw that great head turn, casting one last look into the mortal world. Then the fiery creature stretched its arms upward toward Heaven, and rose, carrying John's gaze after it into the peak of the sky, and faded, and faded, until only the sunlight was left.

He crossed himself. The radiance of the sun shone all around him. The world, he thought, was a glorious place. He started down the earthworks and met the page Odo coming up.

"Well, little Odo," John said.

"The King says you are to come dine with him, Father," Odo said. His eyes were red. He had been weeping. He fell into step beside John, going down the bank. "He says he's going to make me count of Paris," he said.

"A wise choice," John said. They went on through the pear orchard to the palace, to join King Charles at his dinner.

*   *   *

In 885 the Vikings did come back to Paris, and laid siege to it; the King then was Charles the Fat, who was off in Rome chasing the Imperial Crown, and did not come to defend his city. It was Odo, Count of Paris, who drove the Vikings off, and in time Odo's grandson, Hugh Capet, became King of Francia, first of a line of Kings that would rule there for fifty generations.

In the twelfth century, under one of these Capetian Kings, the Abbot of Saint Denis, Suger, read the work called the Pseudo-Dionysius, which John Scot Erigena had translated from the Greek three hundred years before. From it he drew the principles on which he raised the first of the great Gothic cathedrals, the glory of the Middle Ages, through whose stained-glass windows and vast interior spaces the sunlight streams unbroken, bearing with it the unfailing grace of God.